WHAT OTHERS ARE SAYING

Forgiveness for Yesterday is truly a book that should be read by a wide variety of people of all ages. The message is woven together in a way that walks one through the tests, trials, joys, and victories in life. Marley presents the story so well that the characters come alive on every page. Building on the values that the author cherishes, she brings a powerful message of redemption and hope.

—Pastor J. Ronald Hester, Mount Vernon
Baptist Church, Bladenboro, NC

Tracey Marley provides great insight and in-depth knowledge of the struggles in the modern-day love life. She confronts the real issues head on, dealing with religion, morals, and values in today's society. She also proves that losing sight of one's faith ultimately leads one down an unfulfilling and complicated path. Marley keeps the reader intrigued by her ever-evolving characters and leaving the reader wanting more with unexpected twists and turns. *Forgiveness for Yesterday* is a story full of hope and learning what it means to forgive.

—Kim Yselonia, Licensed Clinical Social Worker, St. Augustine, FL

To Brenda –
el pray the Lord blesses
you with a fresh look at His
mercy and grace as you read!

Tracey Marley

Forgiveness *for* Yesterday

Yesterday

a novel

Tracey Marley

HERITAGE HOUSE
SERIES
II

Forgiveness *for* Yesterday

a novel

Tracey Marley

TATE PUBLISHING
AND ENTERPRISES, LLC

Published by Tate Publishing & Enterprises, LLC
127 E. Trade Center Terrace | Mustang, Oklahoma 73064 USA
1.888.361.9473 | www.tatepublishing.com

Tate Publishing is committed to excellence in the publishing industry. The company reflects the philosophy established by the founders, based on Psalm 68:11,
"The Lord gave the word and great was the company of those who published it."

Book design copyright © 2016 by Tate Publishing, LLC. All rights reserved.
Cover design by Joshua Rafols
Interior design by Richell Balansag

Published in the United States of America

ISBN: 978-1-68187-468-5
1. Fiction / Christian / Romance
72. Fiction / Romance / General
15.12.02

To Jesus Christ, my true Redeemer!
And to all the "whoevers" I know. This is your story retold.

Acknowledgment

Thank you to everyone who has patiently asked and waited for this story. God wrung it from my heart, and I praise him for his patience with me because it went deeper than I ever expected. I hope this is a story you'll remember.

For God so loved the world that he gave his one and only Son, that whoever believes in him shall not perish but have eternal life.

—John 3:16 (NIV)

Prologue
November of 2001

Laurie Callahan bit her bottom lip as she watched the numbers overhead light up. One after another, they signaled the elevator's climb up the interior shaft of the building. Feeling the slow ascent to the top, she blew out through her mouth, willing the seconds to tick off a little faster. Ever since the September 11 attacks being in confided spaces made her uneasy. Not that she was anywhere near the Twin Towers that tragic Tuesday morning nearly a month past, but today marked a more private but nonetheless tragic event.

She pressed her shoulders down and closed her eyes as she willed the images of her sister Elizabeth from her mind. She was in Greensboro, North Carolina, on a beautiful fall morning, weeks away from marrying the man of her dreams, not in the cold waters of the Chicago River. She shivered despite the warmth of the space.

A glance to her right revealed that the woman beside her was welding a yellow highlighter and was lost in a file folder. The man to her left was staring straight ahead, admiring his reflection in the wall that doubled as a mirror. Both of them were oblivious to her anxiety.

Thankfully she heard the slow drone of the elevator's brakes. The doors slid open, and the man stepped off. Now it was just her and the woman.

Laurie took a step forward, knowing her floor would be next—floor number 10. She tried not to repeat the man's narcissistic behavior, so she closed her eyes. The bell chimed, and once again her lungs filled with air.

"Good morning," she exhaled to the trim blond manning the phones of The Carlson Group, the city's most lucrative architectural firm. Laurie had worked here for over a year, and not once had she shown up when Janet wasn't on duty.

"Good morning, Laurie. There's a call for you on line 1. It sounds important."

Laurie looked down and checked her watch, her heels clicking a little faster on the porcelain tile. It wasn't even eight yet. Taking in the nervous expression on Janet's face and how she chewed the end of a pen, she had to ask, "Mr. Lanning?"

"Yes. He sounds angry. Something about the plans for the medical park project you're working on."

Laurie smiled. "Put him through."

She pushed open the heavy glass door of her office and tossed her designer purse on the gray chair across from her desk. The room all but echoed at the disturbance. "One day I'm going to get some photos on the walls of this place," she said, hitting the hands-free option on the phone.

"Good morning," she practically sang. "This is Laurie. How can I help you?"

"Ms. Callahan," an overly deep voice sounded through the room. "These plans you've drawn up for Premier Medical—I can't read a thing on here! Everything is backward! You'd think by hiring the best architectural firm around I'd at least be able to read something as simple as a blueprint! This is scribble-scrabble!" Laurie pressed a hand to her mouth and fought the urge to snicker. It was Chris. And he was almost yelling.

"I do apologize, Mr. Lanning, but have you tried turning them around?"

Stunned silence followed. "Turning them around?"

"Yes. It sounds like they might be upside down." This whole phone call was a prank. He was teasing her in reference to a drawing she had done of him during a meeting one day soon after they'd met. She had been doodling on a notepad rather than taking notes and opted to see if she could render his face. Chris was none the wiser of it because she had done the drawing upside down. The fact that she had done an excellent job completely intrigued him—so much so that he ended up asking her out.

"Ms. Callahan, are you insinuating that a man of my vast experience in commercial construction can't figure out which way is up? Why, I ought to come over there and…and…"

A smile spread under her fingers as she heard the sound of rustling paper. "And *what?*" she challenged.

There was a long pause and then a voice she actually recognized. "And kiss that beautiful face of yours. Do you realize you're the only person who can leave me speechless?"

"You're not speechless. You've just run out of things that are appropriate to say."

"True," he chuckled.

"You've got to stop doing this, you know. You were about to give Janet a heart attack."

"Hey, I'm not the one who wants to keep our engagement on the down-low. They're going to find out one way or another."

"Yes, but there's something totally nerve-racking about telling your boss you've decided to marry his biggest client. Especially when it all happened so fast."

"Well, two more weeks, and you won't have to say a word. You can just show up wearing my ring. He'll figure it out. Did you miss me last night?"

Laurie had worked late, and they'd not spent their usual evening together. "More than you know." She took a seat in her chair and picked up the receiver. Something about having Chris's voice pressed to her ear made her smile deepen.

Once again images of Elizabeth tried to surface, and she pressed them back down. Halfway reading her phone messages, she hit the button to start her computer and waited for it to boot up. "I think I've had about three hours of sleep. The bags under my eyes match my shoes. These deadlines are killing me."

"I know. Things are crazy right now…this project…our house. Our trip to the Caymans. If we're lucky, it should all come together just before we leave."

Laurie chuckled. "You know I don't believe in luck. They haven't even hung the sheet rock upstairs. There's no way the house will be ready. Speaking of which, are you sure you don't want to push the wedding out a few weeks until things settle down? We are eloping, so no one would know."

"If there's anything I've learned from being in construction, it's that there is never a good time to take off. If you want downtime, you have to take it." There was a long pause. "You aren't second guessing, are you?"

"No. Of course not. There's something about being whisked away that is terribly romantic."

"That's not what I meant."

Laurie looked out the window, and images of Elizabeth flashed before her eyes. She still hadn't told him. "No…it's just that…" She took a deep breath. This wasn't the way she pictured telling Chris about her past, about her failures. He had no idea who he was getting for a wife. "Never mind. It's just the stress. I'll be fine."

Chris was quick with an answer. "Think of it as a break. After the headache the last few weeks have been, seven days in Grand Cayman sounds like heaven."

Laurie laughed. "What about you? Are we eloping because you need to get away, or because you want to get married?"

"I'm going because I'm in love with you and I'm in love with you because you are beautiful, spontaneous…and one of the best architects I've ever worked with—"

"Hmm…flattery this early in the morning?"

"I'm serious. You're everything I've been searching for my entire life. I understand why you don't want to tell your boss about us, but I love you, Laurie, and I have no doubts. I want to spend the rest of my life waking up beside you, loving you."

Laurie stilled, treasuring Chris's words and his confidence. Everything would work out just fine. Today's date had just brought back some old anxieties. That was all. "Promise me when things settle down, we'll get some time to talk—and not about work."

"Promise. We'd do it today but…"

Laurie let herself get comfortable with the change of subject. She listened intently, hearing the man she loved more than life go on about what his plans were for the morning.

Although Chris was complaining about some meeting he didn't want to go to, she knew that his blue eyes were sparkling the way they did when he was excited. She could hear it in his voice. She also knew that even though he was meeting with the mayor in less than an hour, his tie was crooked and he had his feet propped up on his desk.

She longingly reached over and traced the photo in front of her with her finger. It was a picture of Chris and her two children, Shelby and Kyle, who she called her pride and joy. It was taken at a baseball game in War Memorial Stadium back during the spring. It was also a token from the first day Chris kissed her.

Laurie smiled thinking how Chris had changed since she'd met him. Sure their lives were stressful right now, but he had come so far from being the nothing-but-serious CEO of Greeson Developing that she met nearly seven months ago. The difference had been finding each other, which had changed everything. If Chris didn't have a dime to his name, she would've fallen for him anyway.

Her smile deepened as she thought of what it would feel like to wake up every morning for the next fifty-some years in his arms.

There was a pause in Chris's rambling, and she took her turn. "All this trouble just to tell me your agenda, or is there really something wrong with the prints?"

"There are a few changes we need to make. Minor stuff."

Laurie groaned but transferred his call to speaker again so she could examine her copy. Within a few minutes, they had everything worked out.

"Other than those few changes, things look great. As soon as I can get the inspector to sign off on the revisions, then we're good to go."

That's easier said than done. "You know what they say. It's easier to ask for forgiveness than it is for permission."

"I think you might be misquoting that, but let's hope we don't have to ask for either. Where're we meeting for lunch?"

Laurie giggled. "I haven't had breakfast yet!"

"I could bring something over."

"Thanks, but from what I'm hearing, you have a company to run. It's well past eight. You have a meeting in"—she checked her watch—"less than thirty minutes."

She could hear the sound of his leather chair squeaking and imagined he was putting his hands behind his head and tipping back in his chair. He was gorgeous.

"I'm thinking about food because next to you, it's my number one passion. What'll it be? Green Valley Grill? Lucky 32?"

Laurie paused. Chris was holding out on her. There was a million things he needed to do, and he wasn't ready to get off the phone. That meant there was something he wanted. "Why do I still get the feeling I'm being buttered up for something?"

"Who me?"

"Yes, you."

"There's no hidden agenda here. I'm simply a man who's in love."

"With who? Me or your stomach?" Laurie didn't wait for an answer but went with her hunch. "What about Giovanie's?"

"Giovanie's? We were just there on Saturday."

"I know, but I can't say our last visit was the best experience."

"You're never going to let me live that one down, are you?"

She tried not to laugh in the phone. They'd gone on a double date with Bret, Chris's best friend and coworker, and some girl Chris was trying to set him up with. Everything had gone according to plan until her ex-boyfriend showed up looking for a fight. "Is Bret still mad?"

"Mad? Why should he be mad? The swelling has gone down significantly. You can hardly see it."

"Chris…."

"Okay, so it wasn't like I *knew* she had some deranged ex who was stalking her. I thought she and Bret would make a cute couple. Besides, that guy was huge. Bret should be glad he walked away with just one black eye."

"And a busted lip. I take it he's still not speaking to you."

"Of course he's speaking, but guys don't sit around talk about that sort of stuff."

"What sort of stuff?"

"Feelings. You know, all that mushy stuff girls get all sappy over. It's uncalled for, and we know it."

"Uh-huh, and all that *stuff* you were purring in my ear a couple of nights ago was…?"

A long pause of silence followed by a heavy sigh flowed into her ear. "How do you do that? How do you *always* call my bluff? It drives me crazy."

"I know," he sighed into the phone again. "I need to apologize. I was hoping you could help me out. You know? Give him a call, put in a good word of reason…or two?"

So that was it. He wanted her to make excuses for him. "Chris, this is Bret we're talking about. The two of you go way back, and you're right. *You* owe him an apology. Not me. Just say you're sorry. Why is that so hard?"

"I know. I will. But don't tell anyone I'm this big softy. It'll ruin the whole image thing I've got going."

Laurie wanted to tell him that it would be their little secret. Before she could lace her words into something he wouldn't object to, Janet stepped to the door.

Line 2, she mouthed in silence. Laurie nodded.

"Listen, someone is on the other line. I'm going to have to take it. I'll call you back sometime before lunch, and we can decide where to meet." She paused and then added, "By then you should be able to tell me all about Bret's reaction to what it is you know you have to say."

"I guess…but remember, in two weeks it's you and me, Grand Cayman, and forever. No worries. Okay?"

"Okay."

The line went dead but only until she pressed the button for line 2. "Hello, this is Laurie," she said as she stood and started to shrug out of her sweater.

"Laurie…sweetheart," another man's voice filled the room. "Long time no see. For a while there, I was starting to think you weren't going to take my call."

The sinister laugh that followed turned her blood to ice. The peace Laurie had found at the end of Chris's call was sucked from the room, and her sweater dropped to the floor. She snatched the receiver up and pressed it against her cheek, afraid that someone else might hear.

"I told you to never call me again," she whispered through clenched teeth.

"Calm down," Jim said. "Did you really think I wouldn't call to give my congratulations? That would be rather inconsiderate of me. After all, it's not every day my ex-wife gets engaged to one of the area's most eligible bachelors. I knew you had potential but this…this is *big*!"

"How do you know anything?"

"Do you think I'm a fool? It pays to keep tabs on you and who your friends are."

Laurie's breath caught in her throat. Jim was right. He knew everything. "Why are you doing this?"

"Doing what, darling?" he drawled like they were two long-lost friends catching up over afternoon tea. "Are you insinuating that I mean to hurt you? After all these years I've been keeping you up, that's the way you treat me? And here I thought you enjoyed being taken care of. The clothes, the cars…keeping tabs on you is how I see where my money is going. Just how much is Chris worth these days? I'm sure it's more than enough to repay me for all those luxuries you've enjoyed since we parted ways."

"I get exactly what the courts say I have coming to me."

"Oh, you're going to get what's coming to you. That's for sure."

Laurie felt her face pale. "What's that supposed to mean?"

"Exactly what you think it does, but I didn't call to discuss alimony. Let's call it something more like…retribution. Here's what you're going to do…"

Laurie listened in disbelief while Jim gave her specific instructions on how once she and Chris were married she was to start wiring money from Chris's private accounts into ones that would eventually make Jim a very wealthy man. Evidently his plan was to see her bleed Chris dry. When he finished, she was speechless.

"Hello?" Jim finally asked.

"Have you lost your mind? Jim…this is…absurd! What on earth makes you think I'd ever agree to this?"

"I think we both know there are a few family secrets in your closet you'd go to great lengths to keep from getting out. How is Shelby these days?"

"Leave her out of this!"

"I've been holding this card for a long time," Jim cooed. "As long as I'm the only one who knows the truth about her and what it is you did to betray your dear sister, you will do exactly what I say. Write this down."

He rattled off an absurd amount of money, the date he wanted it along with the name of a bank and an account number.

Laurie scrambled for a piece of paper. "Jim, this is crazy. I can't transfer that kind of cash. Not right after we're married." *Not ever*, she thought. "I need time."

"You need time?" Jim laughed. "To what? Build up a trust? Let me guess, seven months and you still haven't told Lover Boy all the gory details about where it is you came from and what it is you've done? But then wait. You didn't have the decency to tell me either. At least not until I beat it out of you!" There was a long pause. "I guess today does mark a special date on your calendar, now doesn't it?"

Laurie didn't speak. Having Elizabeth repeatedly brought up was more than she could argue against.

"Exactly. Chris doesn't know anything because you know the moment he finds out he'll be long gone," Jim sneered. "In two weeks, the money had better be in my account or else one little girl is going to be getting a visit from her daddy-dearest and a little lesson on her family history."

Laurie was scared, but she wasn't going down without a fight. "Aren't you forgetting I'm not the only one with secrets? You have a few of your own I wouldn't mind exploiting!"

Jim was unperturbed. "Darling, you played your hand when I gave you the divorce you wanted. That threat doesn't work anymore. You might have cost me through the years, but as far as I can tell, that too is getting ready to work toward my advantage."

"My father's name was ruined because of your lies!"

"Hearsay."

Laurie seethed in her anger. Fat tears pooled in her eyes thinking of how she had once thought Jim was her knight in shining armor.

"Now don't start crying on me. You know what a mess you are when you get emotional. You need to keep your head on your shoulders and do the right thing. This first transaction will do…for now, but unless you want me to make you a widow I'd start making a plan that will cover your tracks."

"You wouldn't!"

Jim's voice didn't falter. "If it means getting what I want, I most certainly will. If I don't end up with everything Chris Lanning owns"—Jim's voice dropped off and leveled out with calculated malice—"you'll have insufficient funds to bargain yourself out of the trouble I'm willing to make for you!"

The line went dead, and Laurie sat in her chair, too stunned to move. Moments passed, and slowly she eased the phone back into its cradle with unsteady hands. *This can't be happening. Not now. I was so close to being free of him.*

Chills crept up her arms, and her eyes scanned the windows of the adjacent buildings. The familiar feeling of being watched seemed to radiate to her bones, and it caused the tears she'd been holding at bay to break loose and run down her face in streams.

It was true. She had taken Jim's controlling demands for five years before she played the only hand she had against him when she'd bargained for her divorce. A computer file containing evidence he'd been embezzling money from her father's company handed over in exchange for what she had thought was freedom.

He'd nearly killed her the night he found she'd been compiling it against him. In the end, Jim had given her the divorce she wanted and left her life completely as part of the deal. Her victory, however, had felt shallow and short-lived when Jim publicly ruined her father's good name by convincing a woman to come forward and give a confession that she was Seth's mistress.

Laurie buried her head on her desk and cried. She might as well be dead for all the misery she had allowed Jim Callahan to put her through.

The images she tried to suppress earlier came rushing in all around: Elizabeth, the sounds of her car hitting the water, extreme cold. Death. And then there was her parents' divorce. They might have stood a chance if Laurie had had the guts to confront her father's supposed mistress. But she hadn't.

It was by sheer force that Laurie sat up, opened her eyes, and tried to focus on her surroundings. It seemed Jim was determined to ruin her life one way or another, and she was sick of living under the illusion that she was free of him. By whatever means possible, he would get what he wanted. If he had to make her a widow, one way or another, Jim would take everything.

"Oh God, what have I dragged Chris into?"

I should've told him the truth about who I am…and what I've done… but now…now I don't know how. And Jim is right. Chris could never love me if he knew.

Laurie succumbed to another wave of tears. With one phone call, everything was ruined. Slowly she studied the numbers Jim had given her. Jim was always one step ahead, and she had no doubt he'd make good on his word.

"Help me, God! I need an answer!" She was desperate in her plea for something tangible she could do to remedy her problems with her ex once and for all. The only words she found were "Be still and know that I am God." It was scripture from the Psalms.

Be still? I can't be still! The words were a mockery in light of her situation. Being still was what had gotten her into this mess. She should've shared Jim Callahan's secrets long ago when she had the chance. Now she had others to think about. The years had proven that silence was for cowards, but if she was ever going to change, today was that day. She stood up to pace out her worry on the carpet in defiance.

"I am not a coward, Jim Callahan! Just you wait and see." She wiped away a stray tear, thinking it was cruel how after all these years Jim could still force her hand. She flopped in her chair at her drafting table. She needed a plan. Her fingers traced the numbers she'd scrawled at Jim's command. They were written on her copy of the medical facility blueprints.

Forgiveness for Yesterday

She could always refuse to marry Chris, pack up her life, and walk away, but she knew Jim well enough to know that he'd always be there lurking in the shadows waiting for her to resume some kind of life again. She should've known this was coming. Again, Elizabeth came to mind, and she wondered if God were telling her there would always be a record of what she had done. That the scales would always hang in her debt.

"A record of all my wrongs," she said out loud as her vision focused on the papers under her hand.

Blueprints were a record—a record of a detailed plan. *But all of this is so…unexpected. Or is it? If only I had the courage to do something no one expected…*

Suddenly Laurie knew her way out of the situation. Her only option was to do the unexpected. She would tell the truth. The truth she should've told long ago—only it wasn't just a truth about her and her past, but about Jim and what it was he had done.

Jim saw her as weak and dependent—a coward he could control. Jim was wrong. He would never expect her to sacrifice the things she loved in order to make him pay. *But can I really do that? Leave my children? Leave Chris? All in the name of justice?*

Laurie sat there trying to figure out a way to make it all happen. The information Jim had given her over the phone was indeed quite valuable. It probably wasn't a personal account number that he'd given her, but it might lead to something that was. She would have to do some homework. What she found combined with what she already knew might just be enough to send him away permanently.

"But how? How do I disappear without hurting everyone I love and make it believable at the same time?" She briefly considered faking her death but quickly concluded she didn't have the means, nor the time. Jim wouldn't believe it anyhow, not without a body. That, and she planned to return. She couldn't stand the thoughts of her kids grieving her at a fake funeral.

She started writing a carefully worded, but vague message to Chris. It was written on the edge of the blueprints so that maybe, just maybe, Chris could read between the lines and understand this wasn't something she had planned or even thought about. As a bonus, he would also unknowingly have the account number Jim had given her—just in case. He may never put the pieces together, but if things went like she planned, he wouldn't have to.

When she got to the end, she simply told him to tell the kids she loved them. No instructions, no contact numbers, and no date that she would return. He couldn't know what she was about to do because at this point, it wouldn't take much for him to talk her out of it. She had to separate herself from Chris completely if this was going to work. Otherwise it would be too dangerous.

When she finished the note, she rolled up the prints and slipped them in a mailing tube marked for Chris's attention. From there she moved to her computer, made a few calls and e-mails, then with a shaking hand she cleaned up her makeup.

Staring at her reflection, she could hear something inside of her screaming that she should stop and think this through. That she should just come clean with those she loved and let the cards fall where they may. But she was tired of being a coward.

Laurie snapped her compact shut. If she paused to consider other options, it would rob her of the courage she'd unexpectedly found in the desperation Jim's call had caused. It was time she do what she should've done from the start.

She collected her belongings and headed for the door.

"Janet," she said, handing the woman the mailing tube, "there were some more revisions to the project I'm working on for Mr. Lanning. Please see that a courier hand delivers them this afternoon."

"Sure." The woman nodded.

"Oh, one more thing." Laurie stopped and tried to act normal. "Something personal has come up. I'll be out of the office for the rest of the week. Clear my calendar and take messages for all my calls." Laurie met her eyes to make sure she had Janet's full attention. "I *will* be back…sometime next week. Do you understand?"

"Yes, ma'am." The woman eyed her suspiciously but took the tube and placed it by a mail cart.

Forgiveness for Yesterday

Laurie reached out to press the call button for the elevator but opted for the stairs instead. She took the first nine flights faster than was safe, glad to relieve some of the anxiety trapped in her body.

When the last landing came into sight, and she was sure no one was watching, she stopped and pressed her back into the rough bricks behind her. Her hand came to her chest, and unconsciously, her thumb brushed the bare spot on her left ring finger. Although she had never publicly worn Chris's ring, she had accepted it and in doing so given him the impression that they really were going to get married. Now she wondered if her actions and reluctance were her way of subconsciously playing out what she already knew. A happily ever after wasn't going to happen for her.

That's why just before sealing the mailing tube now in Janet's care, she had carefully taken the ring from her purse and placed it with the blueprints. The note she had written complete with her engagement ring would ensure Chris and everyone else that she had changed her mind. She hated hurting him, but this was the only way she knew to get Jim off her back once and for all. *I know they won't understand. Just a few weeks, Lord, that's all I'm asking. I promise I'll face it all when I get back.*

A tear slid down her cheek and was quickly followed by another. Who was she kidding? It would only take moments and the damage would be done. Still, she couldn't stand the thoughts of telling Shelby or Chris the horrible thing she had done. Not like this. First she had to at least try to right her wrongs starting at the beginning.

Laurie reached into her purse and drew out the last thing she grabbed before leaving her office. It was a photo from her desk—the picture of Chris and her kids. Whether for good or evil, the visual was a reminder that she would go to great lengths to protect what she loved. And what she loved was her family.

The slightest smile lifted the corner of Laurie's mouth. *God, I know this won't bring Elizabeth back, but if I'm to ever have the things you've promised…true joy, peace…forgiveness, I can't let Jim keep calling the shots. I can't let this continue to haunt me.*

In the end, she would tell Chris the truth—the whole truth. Not just about her desperate marriage to Jim Callahan and his abuse but about her parents and how they were impossible to please, about her beloved sister and how she had died. She would even tell Chris about Shelby. Anything less wouldn't be fair. If Chris changed his mind and wrote her off completely, at least he would do it with her having a clean heart.

One more shaky breath and she straightened her spine. "You are a complete fool, Laurie Callahan, a complete fool," she said to herself. *Oh, that Chris Lanning would find it in his heart to forgive such a fool as I.*

It was then that Laurie knew she couldn't go back to her desk and pretend the phone call from Jim never happened. She had to go back much further than that. She had to go back far enough to face the truth of how one misplaced summer and a bad decision had changed her life forever.

Part One

"Come now, let us settle the matter," says the
Lord. "Though your sins are like scarlet,
they shall be as white as snow; though they are
red as crimson, they shall be like wool."

—Isaiah 1:18 (NIV)

1

January 1, 2004
A little more than two years later

It was a new year. Chris Lanning sat in his living room and unbuttoned the collar of his tuxedo shirt, hoping it would be the year he forgot her. He had wanted nothing more for the last two and knew this year wouldn't be any different.

"Laurie," he said, letting go of a deep sigh that radiated from somewhere around his feet. Chris leaned back into his recliner, having released the weight of the word into the air. At thirty-four, he should have his act together.

Car lights moved across the ceiling, signaling that Bret and Karen were turning down his driveway and were heading home. Tonight the three of them had gone to his company's annual New Year's Eve party. The limo they'd gone to the party in had dropped them back at his house so Bret could retrieve his car and take Karen home.

Bret Sears was his best friend and coworker, and although a couple of years younger, he was the one who had life all figured out. His recent relationship with his near-perfect girlfriend was testimony to the fact.

Chris recalled Karen's parting words and the sincerity he felt behind them. She had thanked him for how he'd gone out of his way to make her feel comfortable in a crowd that would put anyone on edge. Although it had been no big deal to him, the expression in her eyes said his kindness meant the world to her.

Karen was one of the sweetest women he knew, but she was also one of the most naïve. She was a widow who lost her husband to a car accident some time back and had recently started to date again. Her finding Bret probably made her think all men were honorable. If she had any idea about the type of man Chris was, she would have saved her admiration for someone who deserved it. Without effort, his mind went back to a certain blond who was able to see straight through his pretense.

Chelsey Greenich, a former employee who just so happened to be one of Bret's old girlfriends, had shown up at tonight's party unannounced. As a way to keep her from turning Bret into a public display of humiliation, Chris had come to the rescue. He did it by slipping a glass of champagne into Chelsey's hand and acting completely enthralled by her beauty. The charade only lasted until he was able to whisk her away to some place private.

"What are you doing here?" he said. "Don't you have someone else to stalk on a night like this? I hear there's a full moon." The words were harsh, but Chris had learned early on that Chelsey didn't take no for an answer.

She reached up to finger the lapel of his jacket, obviously not put off by the comment. "Now, Chris, is that anyway to talk to an old friend? I bought this dress with you in mind."

"Yeah, well, something must have been on your mind. It looks like you left the other half of it back at the store. I have no idea how you made it past security!"

"Oh, come on," she cooed, as her hands dipped to his waist. "Don't you want to have a little fun?"

He quickly removed her hands from him and darted around a corner to put some space between them. "No, I don't. You and I are not old friends. The only reason you're here is to get some kind of revenge for being dumped—or fired—I'm not sure which, but I'm not going to let you ruin this evening. There's too much at stake. Leave Bret alone. He's finally found someone worth having."

Chelsey leveled him with a gaze and pursed her perfect set of red-stained lips. "Tell me, how is it that one woman has single-handedly managed to wrap two of the finest bachelors around her little finger and not even know it?"

"What're you talking about?"

"The girl you and Bret are sitting with. I saw the way you were *looking* at her." Chelsey smiled, and Chris felt as though he were about to be devoured. "You've got it *bad*."

All thought had escaped him knowing she'd caught him looking at Karen. For a moment, he'd been completely wrapped up in her presence, mostly because of the way she was taken with Bret. His emotions were so confused, there was no telling what Chelsey had seen cross his face.

"I don't know what it is you think you saw, but I'm not in love with Karen. Bret is."

A soft and confident chuckle came up from his opponent as she stepped in for the kill. "Who said anything about love? I'm no fool, Lanning, but you need to be careful. Jealousy doesn't suit you. You're much too impatient to sit back and wait for Bret to blow it so you can take your shot. I know from personal experience Bret does not give second chances."

Chris shook his head. Bret was one of the most tolerant people he knew. He knew because he was always testing the fact. Just within the last few weeks, Chris had tested their friendship with angry words due to Bret meddling in his love life. If that weren't enough, he had purposefully ignored Bret's advice regarding a major business deal with Clay Heritage. Despite the strain caused by their disagreements, Bret was always the one who chose to turn the other cheek.

"Bret's just smart enough not to give second chances where they're not due. And you, my dear," Chris said, turning on some of his own manipulative charm, "have exhausted more than one man's patience. Good night."

He turned to leave, but somehow Chelsey snagged him by the arm. All the sweetness from her earlier expressions was gone. "Who are you kidding? We both know Bret takes a lot of your *junk* because he has to! If he didn't, his job would be at stake. Trust me, if Bret finds out you've got a thing for his girl, you'll be losing a lot more than a best friend. You'll be losing your top accountant, and what's left of your reputation!"

Chris was speechless, but it hadn't mattered. Mr. Carlisle, Chelsey's date, stepped around the corner. "Chelsey, doll," the man said, eyeing the two of them in suspicion. "What are you doing over there hiding in the corner? The party's out here."

Chelsey loosened her hold on Chris's arm and checked her features. A smug smile replaced her scowl. She discretely gave Chris a wink before sauntering off toward the ballroom on the arm of a man who was old enough to be her grandfather.

Even now, hours later, Chris closed his eyes and ran a hand down his face, staggering at the woman's gall. He wasn't in love with Karen, and even if he were, it wouldn't change a thing. Karen was in love with Bret. Fate had brought the two of them together, and he wasn't going to mess with that.

Something big was at work always drawing things together for his smart, successful, and morally sound friend. It was just a matter of time before Bret got the future Chris knew him to be chasing. The idea that Chris would step in to ruin it on some jealous whim like Chelsey suggested was ridiculous.

The ticking of the clock on the mantel sounded off slow seconds as the memory faded and the excitement of the evening wore down. Chris's gaze fell across the dim room, and he found himself like he often did these days—alone.

Just for the sake of entertainment, he pondered the insanity of Chelsey's bold and unmerited assumptions. If anything, he was in love with the *idea* of Karen, and how at one point in life it had been him looking at a future that was nothing but bright. Sadly, it had all fallen apart before his very eyes, leaving him with only his memories.

Without Bret and Karen around as a distraction, Chris was sure they'd come: memories of Laurie, his one true love, and the perfect life he'd almost had. Chris stood and poured himself a drink, just so he'd be ready when they did come flooding in.

More than two years had passed since Laurie Callahan had walked out of his life leaving him with two children, a million unanswered questions, and an ache in his chest that would not go away. Immediately he lifted the amber liquid to his mouth in an attempt to dull the pain.

He lowered the half empty glass in his hand, knowing he had tried everything he knew of to rid himself of her memory, yet somehow she was as fresh in his mind as the events from earlier in the day. And memories of Laurie didn't just include the presence of her in his life, but the little things.

Why, he questioned himself, could he still remember her rich southern accent and the way her voice reverberated off his soul when she sang? How certain shades of green would set her hazel eyes on fire, and when she was upset, how she would wind a lock of hair around her right index finger? These were things that should've disappeared from his memory by now, but were as fresh and alive as the fire that blazed just a few feet away.

Chris took the glass and moved closer to the warmth filling his house. As he did, he realized that even it was a reminder of what might've been. He'd built the massive fireplace and the southern Victorian-style home it stood in with the dream that one day Laurie would become his wife and that together they would raise a family.

As he was standing close to the fire, his gaze became lost in the constantly changing but never resting flame. The patterns changed and danced before his eyes with only one purpose—to consume. He swirled the remaining brandy in his glass, thinking his emotions were much the same. They were relentless.

When Laurie left, disappointment and grief threatened to overtake him but then came the anger. He would give anything to find her and ask her why—why she walked out on him, her life, her job, *and* her kids. How she had the nerve to pretend just long enough to give him hope and then destroy it completely without so much as a good-bye.

Her leaving had tainted everything he knew about love, faith, and family with the mark of disappointment and question. For a while he searched for her along with a reason as to what had happened to make her change her mind. After coming up empty handed time and time again, it became apparent she didn't want to be to found. Whatever it was that made Laurie decide to walk away would forever remain a mystery. Or at least that would be the case until she showed up and gave him answers he was helpless to find on his own.

Chris's anger simmered as he envisioned what he would do if somehow their paths did manage to cross again. He didn't consider himself a violent man, but he imagined the urge to throttle her would be stronger than he could resist. He would call her a liar and a fake who was completely self-centered, and his questions wouldn't just be asked; they would be shouted in her face and an answer demanded.

Just the thought of confronting her drew him close to throwing his glass into the flames. But Chris knew better. Losing his temper wouldn't solve a thing—not when his anger went this deep. One quick and uncontrolled display would never quench the hatred he felt in his heart. The cup of wrath he wanted to unleash on Laurie was so full it had a way of sloshing out and spilling over onto everyone, whether he wanted it to or not.

He should have known better. He should have seen it coming. There had to have been some hint, some clue…some something that said things didn't add up—something that would've stopped him from becoming totally vulnerable and then completely rejected. No, there wasn't a person in the world he wanted to hate more than Laurie Callahan and hate her he did. He had every right.

Chris blew out a tired sigh and closed his eyes. *If that's true, then why is my hating her making me miserable?* If anything, it should be fulfilling.

Chris thought about the way he'd spent the last two years of his life, moving on to something or someone new the moment things got dull. Success and wealth kept his calendar and his bed full, but in the end, it always left his life more complicated and the depth of his disappointments a little more defined.

Amanda, his last girlfriend, came to mind along with the disillusionment and manipulation their relationship involved. In all his sorrows, the way he'd played and used her was the worst. But Amanda was no innocent bystander. She knew what she was getting with him— or at least she should have.

Somewhere during their time together, she made the grave mistake of falling for him. What he felt for her wasn't love. Honestly, Chris wasn't sure he even knew the meaning of the word.

He set the now empty glass on the mantel and braced his hands against it to support his weight. Amanda's was simply one more heart he had squandered in the name of redemption. It was shameful that he still felt empty and wanton inside.

The only thing he found any kind of fulfillment in these days were his children, but that too was subject to change without notice. Shelby was eleven and Kyle was ten. After Laurie's leaving, Shelby and Kyle had clung to him. Their situation of complete abandonment by both parents resonated deeply with him. Having never known his biological father and losing his mother at an early age made Chris quick to claim Shelby and Kyle through adoption.

The framed photo beside the clock caught his attention, and Chris lifted his eyes to marvel at a resemblance. Every day Shelby looked more and more like her mother: long mahogany hair, hazel eyes set above high cheek bones smoothed over by a porcelain complexion. The stunning features were anchored in a heart-shaped face that twisted the knife in his back every time he looked at it.

In a few short years he would be fighting the boys off with a stick. Shelby was that beautiful. Unfortunately, something told him those days were probably closer than he realized. Something was going on with her, and he was at a loss as to how to coach her through it. She needed a mother. She needed a woman, a woman like Karen.

Leaving the fire completely, Chris made a sound of disgust as he wandered aimlessly around the room. No matter how many times he ran the details back through his mind, they just didn't make sense. One day he and Laurie were making plans for the future and the next he was staggering over a note she'd written, telling him it was over—that he should move on and forget. Chris filled another glass with liquor, wondering if and when that day would ever come.

His thoughts raced back to Karen. Even if Chelsey were stupid enough to betray him and mention what she'd witnessed to Bret, he would deny the accusation to his death. Bret and Karen weren't just the best friends he had. They were the only friends he had. Even though the burden of loss he'd picked up with Laurie's leaving was still sitting firmly on his shoulders, as long as he had a rational thought in his head, he would do anything to protect that friendship.

Chris started on his second glass of brandy, thinking there had to be some way to shake the feeling of having been weighed and found wanting. He swallowed and squinted his eyes against the pain. It wasn't the trail of fire burning down his throat that hurt. It was the ache in his chest. It was a feeling so intense that it told him Laurie Callahan had walked out of their lives and left everything—everything except his heart.

2

Monday morning things were busy at Greeson Developing. It was Chris's first day in the office since the New Year holiday, and he was glad to have something to put his mind to other than the dark thoughts that had haunted him a few nights ago.

Last week's party was the talk of the town, and by Saturday night rumor had it that Richard Velmore and Edward Klein, two investors looking to construct a new shopping complex, were in Greeson's back pocket. The structures they were looking to build would secure a huge sum of money and push the company even deeper into the black.

Chris shuffled through the paperwork on his desk and knew they were going to need the extra income. The number of active contracts they held had slowly been declining, and he had less than a few weeks to pull together the preliminary work for one of Greeson's projects that was much more of a financial gamble.

Last fall he and Bret had gone to Asheville, North Carolina, to research a property they were now calling the Heritage House. Their plans were to renovate and lease what was a ten-thousand-square-foot plantation house, dating back to the 1820s, as a modern-day bed-and-breakfast complete with horse stables. Being within twenty minutes driving time of Asheville and far enough out in the country to attract tourists looking for a quiet getaway, it was in a prime location. The stables would give tourists an outdoor adventure option that was popular in the area.

Chris flipped through the latest inspection reports, no longer sure if the property was the deal he had originally thought. A termite infestation, contaminated well, and busted septic lines weren't things that would be cheap to fix. Chris read further down the list, finding it longer than he anticipated.

In addition to the main structure, the property included nearly fifty acres of land on which there was a pond, barn, and a few smaller buildings he was sure served some purpose regarding life in the early 1900s. There was also a small cabin located along the back of the property. It was a one-room structure that was rustic, almost like a fisherman's or hunter's retreat.

Just half a mile up the road was an old farmhouse. He originally thought it to be part of the Heritage Estate, but once an official survey was taken, he discovered that it wasn't. It was just as well. The place was condemned and sitting on less than half an acre of land.

Chris closed his eyes and let his imagination take over. Tall and majestic, the house alone had a real presence to it. The main part of the structure dated back to 1823 and had been built by a local doctor, Vincent Heritage, for his wife, Sandra. The house had been added onto through the years and then passed down through the Heritage family until the early nineties when it fell into disrepair due to its owner suffering a stroke and moving to an assisted living facility. With the passing of Owen Heritage, the property fell into the hands of his grandson, Clay Heritage, the man whom Chris had bought the property from.

At twenty-five, Clay had come off as being ingenuous, which translated to Chris as opportunity. "I've got a lot more to spend my money on than some old piece of dilapidated real estate. A new set of wheels to start with," Clay had said during their initial talk. "I'll tell you what. You come out here and see if you think it's worth 20 percent less than tax value, and you've got yourself a deal."

After Chris made a trip to Asheville and had gotten excited about the project, Clay had come back with a price tag that was a half a million dollars more than tax value.

Dollar signs danced in front of his closed eyes, and Chris opened them. What Clay had originally called a dilapidated piece of property in his eyes had the potential to be a one-of-a-kind national treasure. That was why Chris had forked out the extra money even though everyone thought he was crazy. *Oh well*, Chris thought. *We've come this far, I can't back out now.*

Chris started back to work, marveling at how a kid like Clay had managed to get his full asking price out of him. Under normal circumstances, he would've told Clay what he could do with his new offer. Even though Greeson Developing had come to be his through the untimely death of his adoptive parents, Robert and Victoria Lanning, some twelve years prior, Chris worked hard to maintain his authority, and that meant he couldn't afford to take junk off anyone.

While his father had been the man to turn the small residential construction company onto the path of success during the housing boom of the eighties, unfortunately Chris found he was much more adept at swinging a hammer. Combine that with the fact that people who unquestioningly trusted his dad somehow expected him to earn their respect, and he had his battles already picked.

That was why he asked his father's long-time friend and financial advisor, Darrell Flenning, to come on board and steer the company toward the success his father had known was possible. Chris eventually gave Darrell the position of chief of operations to appease employees' minds, but that didn't mean he didn't work hard learning the ins and outs of the trade.

It was that kind of thinking that led Chris to act the role of a senior project manager instead of the CEO he truly was. He allowed it because he liked being out in the field and working with all types of people. Something about sitting behind a desk doing paperwork made him feel claustrophobic and trapped. The title of CEO was still attached to his name because Greeson was still his company. It always would be. If it eased stockholders' minds to think Darrell was the man in charge, that was fine with him. After all, when it came down to it, the right people knew who really pulled the strings. The new Heritage Project was proof of the fact.

Chris poised his fingers on the keyboard, trying to decide the best plan of action to redeem his most recent decision. For a project like this, he should start with the structure itself making any necessary repairs to the foundation, roof, and walls before moving inside to the

Forgiveness for Yesterday

smaller details. But this was January, and with several more months of bad weather ahead, he wasn't willing to wait till spring to get started.

Dates rolled through his head, and eventually Chris decided he could get more accomplished if he simply moved in. Living in the estate house held no appeal for him, but the cabin was every man's dream. All it would take was a couple of updates, and it would be ready for occupancy.

A tap on the door brought his head around to see his assistant standing in the door. "Here are those history books you asked for," Adam said.

Adam handed him at least a dozen books that weighed several pounds each. The titles piled high on his desk: *Historical Accounts of Western North Carolina*, *The Civil War—An Uncivil Time*, and so forth. "Tell me again what you're doing," Adam insisted.

"Research," Chris replied. "If we're going to renovate this old house, we're going to do it right. That means appreciating the part it played in history."

"Whatever." Adam started back toward the door and stopped. "Nathan called. He said the shipment of block that was supposed to arrive this morning didn't show. That means the masons won't get to start until end of the week, and they're calling for rain."

"Thanks," Chris mumbled, shoving the heavy books to a corner of his desk where a few slid off and onto the floor with a crash. He didn't reach to pick them up but turned back to his computer and pulled up the details on the Center Point Plaza project. Checking the dates against what he'd promised meant somebody was working the weekend. They were already two weeks behind, and if rain was in the forecast, that meant even more downtime.

Chris picked up the phone and punched in a number. Within five minutes, he had the assurance a shipment of cinderblock would be across town by the end of the day along with an apology from one very disgruntled supervisor.

Another tap on the door, and this time it was Bret. "What is it now? Don't tell me. We're being audited."

Bret smiled and lazily walked into the room. "Actually I was coming to see if you wanted to do lunch."

"Can't. Too much to do."

"I see that," Bret said, taking a seat and observing the mess that surrounded the room. "I guess all this paperwork means you had to cancel your golf lessons too, huh?"

Chris chuckled. "Yep. For three weeks now all I've done is put out fires. For some reason this job keeps sucking me back into exactly what it is I hate to do. What about you? Haven't seen you putting in any overtime since Thanksgiving."

"Karen doesn't like it when I work late. Says it makes the evenings long."

"How nice," Chris teased. "Three months, and she already has you on a leash."

"You're jealous."

Chris ignored the comment. "Here, take a look at this," he said, holding out the inspection report on the Heritage House.

Bret studied the paper and let out a low whistle. "Has Darrell seen this?"

"No, and he's not going to."

Chris watched the way Bret's eyebrows rose in surprise. Just to be sure they were on the same page, Chris clarified. "Do you want to know *why* Darrell isn't going to see it?"

"Why?"

"Because you're going to keep him busy wining and dining our newest clients."

"The VK account? They signed? When?"

Chris didn't see the need to mention no signature had actually been placed. A verbal in this case was sufficient enough. "I got the call first thing this morning."

Bret's facial expression changed. "Great, but if Richard and Edward signed, this report isn't such a big deal. You promised their project would be top priority."

"Correction. *Darrell* promised their project would be top priority."

"You mean you're still leaving for Asheville?"

41   Forgiveness for Yesterday

"And here I thought it was just your suit that's sharp. Of course I'm still leaving!"

"But you're the best we've got. How can you…leave? Theirs is a multimillion-dollar job! It's guaranteed profit! This Heritage thing… it's all a gamble!"

Chris looked around at the sea of paperwork surrounding him and opted for total honesty. The bed-and-breakfast might seem like a lot to tackle, but an out like that didn't come every day. "I need a break. I need something more to do than sit behind a desk and manage other people's problems. The bigger this company gets, the more I end up playing referee. I can't wait to get my hands on something that's actually going to make me break a sweat—something I'm going to enjoy."

"Enjoy? You own a successful company that nets you a seven-figure income annually. How do you expect Darrell and I to explain to Richard and Edward that our senior project manager slash CEO is ditching them so he can skip town and play construction worker instead? We had these guys on the hook a couple of years back, but they never took the bait. It doesn't make sense to do anything that would cause them to question Greeson's stability."

Chris collected an open file folder that was lying on his desk. He tapped the papers that were inside. He wasn't sure he liked the tone of Bret's voice, nor what he was implying. "VK revenues were over 7.3 million for the last quarter alone. You'll get creative." He put away the file and reached for the inspection report Bret handed back.

"Is there something else other than lunch you came in here to ask me about or are you through?"

Bret smiled as he changed the subject. "I need a favor," he said, easily shifting their conversation to the personal. "I need you to meet me at Karen's Saturday morning. I'm going to ask her to marry me."

Chris stopped what he was doing. "Already?"

"Hey, when you know, you know. I've already got the ring and everything."

"Wow. That was fast. What do you want me there for? Moral support in case she says no? Because she is going to say no. She's not a woman who likes change."

Bret chuckled and stood, still confident. "She'll say yes, trust me. I'm taking her to the park, and I want you and your kids to stay with Holly and Scott. She doesn't know I'm coming. That way she'll have no reason to say she can't go."

Ah, the element of surprise. That should be interesting. Women said they loved it, but that was a lie. "Sure. I'll be there. Just give me a time."

"Seven o'clock. I want to be at the park by sunrise and don't be late."

"Seven o'clock? On a Saturday? You're kidding, right?"

Bret walked to the door and didn't look back.

"What?" Chris said. "You're not going to give me the details? I'm sure you've got some mushy plan all laid out being the ladies man and all."

Bret cast a wry smile over his shoulder as he crossed through the door and walked down the hall. "I wasn't sure a man who's given up on women would be interested. You've not had a date in what? Six weeks?"

Chris shook his head but laughed out loud. Bret's words were said louder than necessary just to get the company grapevine going. He hadn't given up on women; although, the thoughts of spending time with one beyond a few hours in the sack did sound like torture.

He turned to his computer but sat for a moment before lifting his fingers to the keyboard. Bret was going to ask Karen to marry him. Bret was confident that she'd say yes, and he was probably right. *I knew this was coming, but why is it so hard to hear? How long have they dated? Three months if that?* He'd been with Amanda for at least four and hadn't even been able to tell her he loved her. "Hey, when you know, you know, and I know better," he said to himself.

A deep breath left his lungs as he started back to work. Amanda wasn't the type of woman a man asked to marry, and if he did, he was stupid enough to deserve her. Karen on the other hand was another story. At the moment, he couldn't say he knew anyone who was more the marrying type, anyone except for the dark-haired beauty who was never far from his thoughts.

A scowl deepened the lines around his mouth as Chris realized the reason why he hadn't congratulated Bret on finding that special someone. Chelsey was right. Jealousy didn't suit him.

3

Saturday morning Chris did as he'd been asked. Karen returned to her apartment with a dozen red roses and a diamond the size of a gumball while wearing a glow that was indescribable. He shared in their happiness, but at the same time it was stifling.

Karen's kids were thrilled at the news, and Chris was sure they would come to love Bret as much as Shelby and Kyle did. He could still remember the excitement in Scott's voice as he'd wrapped his arms around Bret's neck, overcome with excitement, "You *are* going to be my new daddy! I knew it! You're gonna be the bestest dad ever!"

Chris took off his coat and watched the way Shelby went straight to her room without saying a word. Kyle collapsed on the couch, anxious to go back to sleep. He shook his head at the sight.

Bret was going to make a good husband and a good father. He couldn't begrudge him that. He just hoped parenting someone else's kids turned out to be easier for Bret than it was for him. He loved Shelby and Kyle, but for some reason, he had a hard time connecting with them. Kyle wasn't so bad, but Shelby was a complete mystery. Half the time she didn't speak to him, and when she did, it was usually to ask some off-the-wall question he didn't have the answer for.

Chris sank down in his recliner and reached for the TV remote. One pass through the channels determined there was nothing on worth watching. Just as he closed his eyes, thinking Kyle had the right idea, he heard the knob on the back door turn.

"Hey, Marie," he whispered, seeing his housekeeper come in. She was wearing a big smile, and her gray hair was perfectly in place from a morning spent at the beauty shop, no doubt. Chris smiled as she entered. Marie was often the only sounding board he had when it came to the kids.

"I thought I'd come by and check on you. Is there anything you need this weekend? They're calling for bad weather." The woman shrugged out of her long wool coat and hung it by the door. She kept her voice low, seeing how Kyle was starting to snore.

Chris sat up. He was glad to have some company. "No, the house looks great, as always. I have your check," he said, walking into the kitchen and opening a drawer. "Here you go."

He handed her the slip of paper, and she neatly folded it before sticking it in her purse. Rather than turn toward the door, she went over and reached for the teapot sitting on the stove. "You don't mind, do you? It's awful cold out for an old woman. A cup of tea sure would be nice."

Chris smiled. "You're not old, and of course I don't mind. Actually, I'm glad for the company. Shelby and Kyle seem to live in a world that's all their own."

Marie got down two cups from the cabinet, and he waited for her to join him at the table. "So what really brings you by today? I know you have better things to do than check on us."

Marie filled the teapot with water and pulled out a spoon from the drawer by the stove. She placed it on the table with the sugar. "Now that you've asked," she paused to smile, "something has been on my mind."

"Go on," Chris instructed, half-expecting her to ask for a raise. Marie hesitated as she fingered a china cup he'd never seen before. It had delicate gold etching along its rim and a fancy scroll-like handle.

"It's Shelby," she finally said as she set the cup down and raised her eyes to his. She really did look older than her sixty-some years this morning. "She needs a mother, Chris."

Chris looked down at the table stretched between them. Marie knew all his secrets, and like Bret, the two of them went far enough back that she felt free to shoot it straight with him.

"I've tried. There's not much left that I can do about that."

Forgiveness for Yesterday

Marie's voice became determined, almost angry. "Maybe so, but you can do something about her father! You might think she lives in a world where you don't fit in, but she needs you. Specifically…she needs to know you love her and that she has value in your eyes."

Chris groaned and leaned back in his seat. "I do love her. I just don't understand her. She's always so emotional. One minute she's up and the next she's biting my head off over something I said. The other day she burst into tears when I asked her if the mail came. What am I supposed to do with that? I can't even count the lies I catch that girl in, and she's always asking questions I don't have answers for."

Marie's gaze never wavered. "What kind of questions?"

"Last week she asked me about the deity of Christ. She's been going to church with Holly, Karen's daughter, and I must say it's sparked some interesting discussions. I've done the whole church thing, but don't ask me to explain eternal security or what the Holy Trinity is. I have enough questions of my own, let alone trying to deal with hers."

"What did you tell her?"

"I sent her right back to the source."

"And this Karen…is she pretty sound?"

"The soundest. She even has me questioning things I wrote off a long time ago."

"What's so bad about that?" Marie asked. "Everyone is entitled to a change of mind. So what if it takes a little digging to get some answers?"

Chris shrugged. "I know, but just because Karen has me questioning faith and Christianity doesn't mean I'm ready to partake in it." Chris thought about it some more, weighing his decisions against Shelby's curiosity. "For all the bad experiences I've had with Laurie and her version of Christianity, it doesn't seem right to keep Shelby from developing her own beliefs. If Shelby wants to believe and have faith, then fine, but don't come asking me for the definite because I just don't have it."

Marie smiled and stood to lift the boiling water from the stove. "Maybe you should start dating this Karen. She sounds like she's got a good head on her shoulders."

Chris laughed out loud. "You make it sound like all I'd have to do is ask! Besides, Karen is Bret's girl. As of this morning, they're engaged."

"Really?" Marie beamed. "How sweet. Bret's such a good man. You're both tall, with dark hair, and an athletic build. The two of you could've been brothers. But you're right. Marriage and love are complicated things. That doesn't mean that just because they didn't work out for you the first go around, they can never happen. You're going to have to open yourself up to someone or one day your life is going to be gone, and you'll be all alone with nothing to show for it. The last time I checked, we don't get a do-over."

Chris took the steaming cup she offered him and added a couple teaspoons of sugar. He took a tentative sip and paused. The liquid wasn't coffee, but it would do. "Can I ask you something?"

Marie's eyes lit up. "I was hoping you would."

"Am I really that bad of a guy? Bad enough to make Laurie leave without looking back?"

A sympathetic hand touched his. The movement was a balm for his soul. "Chris, no one truly knows what goes on in a relationship except for those who are in it. You've not been yourself since the day she left, and even still, knowing you like I do, it's hard for me to imagine why she would do such a thing. If you were that bad of a man, she never would've agreed to marry you in the first place. I still think there's something missing—something we don't understand—but I'm also smart enough to know that whatever drove her away probably had more do to with her than it did with you. You shouldn't be so hard on yourself."

Chris frowned at the idea. It was simple in logic, but one he had never considered in depth. He propped his elbows on the table. "Do you think there was another man?"

Marie rolled her eyes. "Stop viewing this through a microscope! I don't know what it was that made her leave, but as for Amanda, she wasn't the one. You should feel guilty for the way you used her and all those girls before her. Any relationship based on sex doesn't have a leg to stand on. You should at least know that much. It's almost like you don't want them to stay. Hurting everyone around you is not the way to get back at Laurie."

Chris squirmed in his seat at the confrontation. Marie was being a little too honest for comfort, but it would do no good to get mad at her. She was only speaking the truth. "I thought you said you came by to discuss Shelby. Did she say something to you?"

"Nothing in particular, but I can tell. She's at that age where she's starting to change. She's trying to find out who she is and where she belongs in the world. That's hard for her to do without her mom to look to as an example. She needs someone who's not afraid to stand up to her and tell her how things are."

"How what things are?" Chris asked, not fully understanding Marie's advice.

"I told you. She needs to know someone loves her, that you are her father and that she is of value in your eyes regardless of what she does or who she turns out to be. Both of Shelby and Kyle's parents abandoned them. They have a history no child would want. Now they're a part of your life, and you can't keep ignoring them. The only reason I'm willing to move in and take care of them for the next few months is because I hope that by being away from them, you'll come to understand just how much they mean to you.

"You have a good heart, Chris, I know it. I just wish you'd figure it out and then find someone to share it with, namely your kids. Letting go of your pride and getting past the hurt is the only way you're going to be able to give Shelby and Kyle the love they need."

Chris was silent. He couldn't help but wonder where all of Marie's wisdom came from. "I wish I understood women. You're all so... complicated. It's exhausting."

The left corner of Marie's lips went up. "We're not complicated." She tsked. "We're mysterious, and mystery is a lot more fun than complicated."

Chris shook his head, amazed. "If you were twenty years younger, I think I'd marry you. At least you're not afraid to give it to me straight."

Marie smiled and waved him off. "Don't be silly. You couldn't keep up with a woman like me. I know all your tricks, and where's the fun in that?"

Chris laughed. Marie was spry despite her age, and she was probably right. He would have a hard time staying on top of his game with her as a companion. "Just give me time. I'll get it together... sooner or later."

Chris watched her finish off her tea and then helped her into her coat. "Thanks for coming by. For a while there, I was scared you were going to hit me up for a raise."

She chuckled, then lifted her arms up to give him a hug. The gesture surprised him, but he welcomed it anyway. "That's not a bad idea, but I mean what I said. It's time to heal and move on. You deserve it. So do the kids."

Marie left, and once again the house was filled with silence. Chris thought about her words and the moving on she mentioned. He wasn't sure if Marie knew the depths to which his feelings for Laurie ran, only that the attempts he'd been making at putting his hurts aside were failing and fast.

He sank back into his recliner and wondered if Shelby really did feel as insecure as Marie led him to believe. He'd always let her and Kyle both have whatever it was they wanted. Didn't that say something as to how he felt about them?

Marie had even suggested that his hatred for Laurie was what limited the depths to which he was able to connect with her kids. The idea pricked his conscience, and Chris pondered the idea a little further. It wasn't like he was totally neglectful in the areas Marie mentioned. He purposefully made an effort to keep Karen involved in their lives. If anyone was solid enough to handle the issue of Shelby's budding faith and womanhood, it was her.

Who cared if having her in the picture had him second-guessing long ago decisions regarding faith? Just because there was more to Karen's and Bret's faith than he wanted to admit, it didn't mean *he* was at the point where he thought Jesus was the answer. It only had him

Forgiveness for Yesterday

thinking. It was worth it if it gave Shelby some sort of stability that he himself couldn't offer.

Faith strong enough to see Karen through the loss of her husband wouldn't be based on shallow illusions and wishful thinking so similar to what he saw in a lot of believers. Her faith would be based on experience. That alone should be evidence enough for him to give God a try.

More questions and doubts rolled through Chris's mind. What if he tried to know and experience God like Bret and Karen did, and it didn't happen for him? Opening himself up to the hope of faith threatened great disappointment, and he was already disappointed enough.

Maybe Marie was right. Maybe Laurie had personal issues or mental issues even, and one day she came to the point where she couldn't handle it anymore. Surely having a clearly defined reason would make her leaving easier to handle. Wouldn't it? Chris didn't know that either.

All he knew was that whatever Karen and Bret had went beyond the Sunday morning ritual of attending church. He knew them better than anyone. If there were any flaws, he would be able to see them.

Chris remembered the way Bret and Karen were entangled in each other's arms the night of the New Year's Eve party. He'd walked in and found them in an intimate kiss in front of his fireplace. It was the first time he'd seen them do more than hold hands. Chris sighed.

Bret's level of sexual integrity might not be what it was three months ago, but who could blame him? Women were a weakness he knew well. That was why he told Marie it didn't feel right to restrict Shelby's interest in religion simply for the fact her mother hadn't turned out to be very genuine in hers. Maybe if Shelby figured this stuff out, she could explain it to him in simpler terms.

Chris toyed with the idea and decided he should at least tell Shelby that much. He ascended the stairs but was only halfway up when the phone started to ring. It stopped after the second time, and he knew Shelby had picked up.

"Shelby," he said, tapping on her closed door once he got to the top of the stairs. "Can I come in?"

"I'm on the phone!"

Chris didn't like the tone of her voice but decided to let it slide. He was trying to bridge the gap between them, not widen it. "Shelby," he said, tapping louder this time. "I want to come in."

Chris heard the muffled sounds of whispering and then a long pause of silence before she jerked opened the door. "What is it? Is something wrong?" she asked again, holding her hand over the mouthpiece.

Chris ignored her irritated look and walked into the room and looked for a place to sit down. He found a seat atop the bed's flowered comforter. He felt strangely out of place among all the frill.

With an exasperated sigh and a roll of her eyes, Shelby pressed the phone to her head when she saw he wasn't going to leave. "Brittney, I'm going to have to call you back." She clicked the phone off and tossed it on the bed beside him.

Chris looked around unsure of what to say. "Where are all those stuffed animals that used to be up here? There were hundreds of them."

"I got rid of all that stuff last year. Stuffed animals are for babies!"

"Oh," Chris said, feeling completely out of the loop. Shelby continued to stand and stare. He narrowed his eyes at her, studying his daughter. "Are you wearing makeup?"

"Just some lip gloss and a little eye shadow. It's nothing." She shrugged like it was no big deal.

Chris nodded. "I don't like it."

"Is that what you came up here to tell me?"

Pick your battles… "Actually, Marie stopped by. She suggested you and I have a little talk. She says you're…you know…changing and that we should talk about it. So…is there anything you want to talk about? Is there anything you *need*?" Chris pushed.

A look of embarrassment flooded her face. "It's okay. They showed us the video at school."

Now Chris was totally lost. "Video?"

"Yes…" Shelby hesitated. "*The* video. The one about how our bodies change?"

Chris was still drawing a blank.

On a huff she clarified. "What happens to a girl's body when she starts her period! *That* video."

"Oh!" Chris went red all over. *You idiot! Of course this is what Marie was talking about!* "Uh…yeah. I…was…um…just following up. Making sure…you didn't have any questions." *Please say that you don't.*

"I'm good," Shelby said, crossing her arms over her chest as an awkward silence descended on the room. "So…is that it?"

Chris let go of the breath he'd been holding. "Yes!" He was way in over his head here. He shot off the bed and actually reached the door before his conscience got the best of him. "Wait," he said, turning around. "Are you sure there's nothing you want to talk about? You know, other than…well…the video?"

Shelby studied him long and hard. "There is this one other thing."

Chris gulped. "Go on."

There was another sigh of exasperation, and she started pacing like a caged animal. "This is so embarrassing! I can't believe I'm asking your advice on this."

Chris could only imagine what was coming.

"You know Brittney Kennedy. Her and her cousin Sierra Foster, who is a total backstabber, told the entire sixth grade that I have a thing for Howard Crestmire! Can you believe that? Howard Crestmire! They wrote him a note pretending that it was from me asking him to go to the spring formal, which I wouldn't go with him if he were the last boy on earth, scratch that, the last *person* on earth and—"

Chris was getting lost again. "Wait a minute. Who is Howard Crestmire?"

"Howard Crestmire is the ugliest kid in school. He picks his nose and wears suspenders. They wrote him a letter asking him to go with me to the spring formal, which he loudly answered by coming up in the middle of the cafeteria and sitting down beside me! Brittney and Sierra thought it was hilarious, and now the whole sixth grade thinks we're a couple. He actually mailed a love letter to our house saying he wanted to marry me! Brittney's only doing this because she has a crush on Sierra's older brother, Josh, and Sierra doesn't like me."

"Why doesn't Sierra like you?"

"How should I know? The same reason Kara and Michelle don't like me anymore either."

Chris made every effort not to roll his eyes at how childish this was. Shelby was acting like a crazy person all because some kid who wore suspenders had a crush on her. In a few short years, she wouldn't even remember this kid's name.

"I'm sure come Monday it will all blow over."

"Are you kidding? This has been the talk of the school all week!"

The phone started ringing again, and Shelby stopped pacing in order to tap her foot in impatience.

"Whatever," Chris said as he tried to wrap up their "talk." "I just wanted you to know that I'm here if you need me. And…if it makes you feel any better, you can tell this Howard guy you're too young to get married and will be for the next twenty-some years."

"Gee, thanks," she said, preparing to shut the door. "Hey, can I have twenty bucks?"

Chris noted her extended hand. "What for?"

"The deposit for cheerleading tryouts was due Friday. I forgot to ask."

Chris lowered his brow as Shelby's eyes darted to the phone that continued to ring. He slowly fished out his wallet and handed her the twenty. He didn't know about Shelby's sudden interest in being on the cheerleading squad. Usually those girls turned out to be very clique-ish, and from what he was getting, Shelby was having a hard time fitting in. At least it would give her something to do instead of talk on the phone.

"I'd better not get a letter from the school next week asking for the money. Understand?"

"Yes, sir."

"And go wash your face."

She closed the door, and right away the ringing stopped.

"The phone rings all the time. Someone has to like her!" He descended the steps, unsure how the conversation he'd meant to have with Shelby had gotten so derailed. At least he'd told her he was there if she needed him *and* he'd given her the twenty to back it up. What else could he do?

4

Later that evening, Shelby sat at her dresser doing her nails when Kyle came into her room and plopped on the bed.

"What is it with you two? You and Dad never come in here, and now it's both of you in one day!"

Kyle kicked all her flower-shaped pillows off the bed and onto the floor, then threw one at her head.

"Knock it off! If I spill this on the carpet, Dad will kill us both."

Kyle settled on the fuschia-colored spread. "Dad was in here? What did he want?"

"None of your bee's wax."

There was a long silence. Something important was on Kyle's mind. "What do you think about Karen and Bret getting engaged?"

Shelby dipped the brush back into the pretty pink polish, trying not to think of Howard, and started the next nail. "That's what people do. They fall in love and then get married. Why?"

"Not Dad. I can't even count all the women who've shown up here, and he's not asked a single one of them to marry him. Just as soon as we get to know them, they disappear." There was another long pause, and then he added, "Just like Mom."

Shelby put the brush into the tiny jar of paint and screwed the lid on tight. When Kyle was worried, there was only one way to fix it. She got up and walked over to sit down on the bed by her brother, careful not to mush her nails. "Dad's different. I don't know why, but when he's with those women, he never stays happy. You have to be happy with someone for more than a few weeks if you're going to marry them."

"He was happy with Amanda. I liked her," Kyle argued.

"I liked her too, but not anymore." Shelby could remember their weekend away in the mountains last fall when she confided in Amanda about the truth of Chris not being their real dad.

"Wait a minute," Amanda had said in complete surprise. "You mean to tell me you and Kyle are not Chris's real kids, that he was never married to your mom?"

The reference to not being "real kids" had hurt, but Amanda had gotten really mad after that and started asking all kinds of questions. Shelby regretted telling her anything because things immediately changed. Amanda and her dad started fighting, and then Amanda didn't come around anymore. She felt like their breakup was her fault.

"If Amanda was the one who was meant for Dad, then you and I wouldn't have been a problem. It was obvious she couldn't handle the fact that he adopted us."

"What's the big deal with being adopted? Chris is the only Dad I can remember having."

Shelby blew on her polish and debated on what to say. Chris *did* have a problem with raising the two of them. Kyle just couldn't see it. The words of reality were on her tongue, but today Kyle seemed extra insecure. Reminding him of Chris's true parental status was the same as pointing out the fact that they had already been abandoned—twice. For that reason alone, she let it go unsaid.

Kyle eventually grew restless, waiting on her answer and started tossing a fuzzy pillow into the air. "I just wish Mom would come back. That way she and Chris could get back together and this whole mess would be over and we could all get on with life. It's obvious he misses her."

A twinge of pain shot through Shelby's heart. *Not as much as I do.* But that type of thinking seemed futile at this point. "Mom's not coming back, Kyle. Get over it."

"What do you mean 'get over it'? She's our mom. I should want her to come back."

"I used to feel the same way, but who's to say that if she did show up, she would stay? There has to be some reason she flaked out on us. And you can't honestly expect Dad to take her back. Besides, I don't know if I could trust her again. If she loved us, she never would've left in the first place. We deserve someone who loves us enough to never leave us. Chris deserves the same thing."

"Mom loved us. Don't you remember what she used to say? She always told us that we were her pride and joy. That wherever she went, whatever she did, we would always be the best things that ever happened to her."

Shelby remembered the words her mother had spoken nearly every night of her life as she'd tucked her in bed. What had happened to the times when she felt her mom was the greatest thing on earth?

"I stopped believing her when we spent that first Christmas in Chris's apartment not knowing where she was or if she'd ever come home. People change. Feelings change. Get over it."

Shelby said the words in anger but immediately realized her mistake. Kyle sat up, looking as though he was on the verge of tears.

"What if Chris changes? What if he changes his mind and doesn't want us anymore either? Then what will we do?"

"Calm down and stop calling him Chris. I shouldn't have said that. He's Dad. People do change, but not him. And even if he did, all change isn't bad."

"How so?"

Shelby thought for a moment. "Take Holly for instance. She was less than thrilled to see her mom start dating again, but now…now she's all for her mom and Bret getting married. She's accepted the fact her real parents will never be together again."

"Holly's dad died. Of course he's not coming back. But Mom…we don't know what happened to her. There's always a chance, isn't there?"

Shelby huffed. "She left us. Face it. Jim never came back, and Mom's not coming back either. They're both as good as dead in my book. I know that and Chris…Dad…knows it too. He's going through a hard time right now. Give him a break. We should try to stick by him like he did for us."

"I don't know," Kyle said in question. "Now that you mention it, I'm sick of him being so mad all the time. Last week he yelled at me for forgetting to let the dog out. And the week before that—when I aced that math test—he didn't even seem to care. I'm starting to think *he's* the reason everyone leaves."

"Kyle, you're not being fair! I told you. He's struggling with something, and we should stick by him until he gets through it. Lay low and don't get on his nerves. He's leaving in a few weeks on some kind of project for work, and Marie is moving in. She's been around forever, and you know we can get away with murder when it's just her." She slung an arm around his shoulder. "Dad will be back on the weekends, and after spending all that time away from us, he'll probably feel guilty and let us do whatever it is we want. I bet he'll even get you that four-wheeler you've been begging for."

"Hum. What makes you so sure *he'll* come back?"

Despite Kyle's words, she could see that her plan was working. "I told you. He needs us."

"If you say so. I'm going out to shoot some hoops. Wanna come?"

"And mess up my nails? No way."

Kyle stopped at the door and grabbed the flower pillow from the floor. "You're such a priss pot. And don't tell anyone I came up here to this sissy room."

Shelby caught the pillow midair and placed it back on the bed where it belonged. It wasn't until she heard the consistent sound of Kyle's dribbling on the driveway that she chanced a look out the window.

They might argue and fight a lot, but Kyle would always be her little brother and therefore her responsibility. Unfortunately there would probably come a time when it would be harder to convince him of their security. Shelby wrestled with the thought. Chris had already done some changing, and it wasn't in ways she wanted to point out to Kyle.

Chris couldn't possibly still have feelings for their mom after he'd dated all those other women. Was that what love was? Something that lasted only a few months before you moved onto something new, something better? Shelby gave herself a hug, scared of the thought.

If love were something that came and went like the girls in her dad's bedroom, she and Kyle had less security than she hoped. At least

Kyle and Chris had everything in common: basketball, smarts, guy stuff...you name it.

She was the one who caused Chris to look as though he were seeing a ghost. What if *she* was the source of his problem? What if one day Chris realized he hated her as much as he hated her mom? The best thing she could do was strive to be someone he loved. Someone everybody loved.

5

Bret slung a towel around his neck as he heard Chris and the guys they were playing basketball with exit the gym. They'd just finished a game, and he stopped for water before pushing through the locker room door.

His plans were to grab a quick shower before heading over to Karen's apartment. They were supposed to take the kids out for pizza and rent a movie. He promised Scott he could pick, and although that meant they'd end up watching something juvenile, Bret was still looking forward to the evening. Karen's kids were great.

Bret jumped in the shower and soaped up his hair.

"So, Lanning, got a hot date tonight?" Bret heard Preston, the guy in the stall beside him, ask Chris.

"Nope. Too much going on with my job for me to think about women."

"Ah, it's the weekend! There's never too much going on to have a little fun!"

Chris's laughter echoed off the tile. "There is this redhead who works at my favorite steakhouse. She doesn't mind serving up more than a meal, if you know what I mean. I guess I could always look her up."

"Now you're talking," the other guy named Kurt answered.

Bret looked over the top of the shower stall in disbelief. He knew the woman Chris was talking about. "You didn't! The ugly one?"

Chris's smile never faltered. Bret cut the faucet off and shook his head. "There is something seriously wrong with you. She's barely legal."

Preston and Kurt suddenly became very interested, and Chris started to explain. "Hey, once you've had everything, it becomes an

Forgiveness for Yesterday

adventure to branch out…broaden your horizons. And she's not ugly. At least not from the neck down."

They all laughed, everyone but Bret. "Whatever," he said, not only disappointed in Chris but also thinking those were horizons he never hoped to see.

"What happened to that Amanda girl you were dating?" Preston wanted to know. "I thought you two were hot and heavy."

"We were, only the heavy started to outweigh the hot. She wasn't worth the headache." Chris cut off the water behind him and stepped out to dry off.

Bret glanced across the steamy room as Preston exchanged a look with Kurt. "Care if I ask her out?" Preston tested.

"I'm not sure she's your type."

"Sounds like there might be some feelings there. You two weren't getting serious, were you?"

"Me? Feelings? Yeah right. What do I care if you ask her out? Go for it. I was only trying to save you some trouble."

Preston smiled. "Thanks. She's a looker. What about you, Sears? How's…what's her name?"

"Her name is Karen, and she's fine." Bret hated how his words sounded so touchy, but these guys were real pigs.

"Just fine? I guess that means you still haven't closed the deal."

"Shut up, Preston. There's some stuff that's none of your business!"

The guy climbed from the shower and didn't bother to grab a towel. Bret pulled on a clean T-shirt and raked a comb through his hair; his gazed honed in on his reflection in the mirror.

"What are you two waiting on? Christmas? Oops, that already came. What's next, Easter? The girl's nothing but a tease, Sears. Cut her loose."

Chris chimed in now that he was dressed and wrapped a teasing arm around Bret's neck. "Preston, some guys are cut from a different cloth than you and me. Bret here is one of them. Honor and respect mean more than having a good time." Chris paused to show his disgust at Preston's undressed state. "You're embarrassing yourself. Go put some clothes on!"

Preston laughed, catching the towel Chris threw at him. "Honor and respect? What kind of cloth is that? Something with pansies on it?"

Bret rolled his eyes and grabbed his gym bag as the others got a good laugh at his expense.

"What? I'm just joking! Come back!" Preston called over Chris's and Kurt's laughter. Bret didn't stop to hear whatever else Preston wanted to rag on him about. He'd heard it all before.

A few seconds later, Chris burst through the locker room door behind him in a slow jog. He caught up just as Bret was entering the parking lot.

"Don't let them get to you. Guys like Preston and Kurt are too shallow to know girls like Karen even exist," Chris said.

"Yeah, well just because you *pretend* to be just like them doesn't mean I need you to come to my rescue. I can handle guys like Preston." Bret slammed the trunk of his BMW after tossing in his duffle. *Great!* He'd left his coat in the bag, and it was freezing.

"Take it easy. I was just trying to do you a favor."

"Well don't. Last I heard, you were laughing just as loud as they were."

"Lighten up! It was funny. It's not like you did *me* any favors in there."

Bret popped the trunk again and yanked his coat from his bag. He put it on with short jerky motions. "Did you really sleep with that redhead?"

Chris's head fell back in tired frustration. "What does it matter? As long as those guys think I did, that's all that counts."

"Unbelievable. Un-bee-lievable!" Bret walked around to the driver's side door but stopped before getting in. "Are you still good with Karen and me coming over Monday evening because if you're not, we can let it slide. I'm sure you have tons to do." Bret held his breath, hoping Chris would read between the lines.

Chris climbed in his oversized Chevy and cranked the engine. "I wouldn't miss it," he said, his smile plainly visible. "Karen has promised her cooking is the best. Call me tomorrow, and we'll hit the weights as a countermeasure. No sense wasting my weekend by lying around and getting fat."

"No sense spending the weekend where you belong—at home… with your kids," Bret mumbled as Chris drove off and left him standing in the cold. Chris had obviously missed his signals.

Bret opened the door to his car and sat down behind the wheel. He was reluctant to leave. He turned the key in the ignition to cut on the heat, and gospel music filled the air. He reached up and turned down the volume. Finally, he was content to be alone.

God help me here. This is harder than I thought it'd be. He prayed a few more sentences and then looked up at the white birch trees lining the perimeter of the lot. They were standing tall and proud despite the fact that their beautiful golden fall colors had been stripped bare during the bitter trial of winter. Their trunks were peeling, and they looked barren. The wind picked up, and Bret wondered how harsh the enduring season would be.

Something in the corner of his eye caught his attention. It was Preston and Kurt coming out of the gym. They were laughing and carrying on, probably about their plans for the weekend—or over more jokes about him and his celibate state. *Disgusting.*

On the way over, he'd had the same carefree look, but all that changed with Chris's and Preston's comments. Why was it so hard being the odd man out? Didn't anyone understand he wasn't holding back with Karen because it was easy? With every day that passed it became a little less what he wanted to do.

There was silence in the car, and Bret felt some of his temper fade. A woman like Karen was worth waiting for. She was strong, faithful, had a successful career, and she was beautiful and not just in ways that ran skin deep. Sex was a small part of the equation. He'd gone without for years. A few more wouldn't kill him. The thought of waiting years to be with Karen was overwhelming. He was so thankful she'd said yes to his proposal. Now all he wanted was a date.

He turned the radio up as a distraction, and an announcer came on. "Today's verse is Matthew 5:11 and 12: 'Blessed are you when people insult you, persecute you and falsely say all kinds of evil against you because of me. Rejoice and be glad, because great is your reward in heaven, for in the same way they persecuted the prophets who were before you.'"

Bret looked down at the radio in the dash. There wasn't a more fitting verse for what he was experiencing. A little locker room persecution was nothing compared to what the disciples had gone through. He should be stronger in his faith.

"Sears, you need to get it together," he coached himself. "What's wrong with you?" A few short months ago, his spiritual state was the best it had ever been. Why did he suddenly feel like he was facing a wilderness?

He pulled the car from the lot and waited at the stoplight while trying to figure it out. If he were as strong in the Lord as he should be, he wouldn't feel so insecure. Fitting in wouldn't be such a big deal to him. But it was, and for the first time ever, he wished he had some stories of his own to share with the guys. Not that he would give specifics, just something he could say so the others would know. He wasn't a reject.

Events from the past few weeks rolled through his head. He thought about the private time he'd had with Karen and the things that went on between them. Whispered endearments and tender embraces were not what any of his guy friends wanted to hear about. He would have to stretch the truth way out of proportion to make it something even remotely close to the kind of things he had overheard.

What does it matter what they think? he asked himself. Karen was the one who saw eye to eye with him on where the boundary lines were drawn. They had agreed to honor God in their relationship, and that meant saving the sex until after the wedding. A lot of the time they were careful enough to not even put themselves in tempting situations. Waiting was important to Karen, and it was to him too.

Bret paused in his rambling thoughts to ask himself if he really believed that. Did he really believe in waiting until marriage to become sexually involved with someone? He didn't even have to make it to the basement of his heart to find out that he did. He believed in sexual purity and had thus far practiced it; only the longer he and Karen were together, the less rational of a decision it seemed. They were in love. They were getting married. Knowing what was to come and waiting on it only seemed to make the temptation more unbearable.

A memory from last week came to mind, and Bret felt the hairs on the back of his neck stand up. For some reason, the pump at the gas station had refused his debit card. He'd gone inside to see why, and while he'd been standing in line at the check out counter, he looked over at the magazine rack. It was something he'd done a thousand times before, but that day there were all kinds of vulgar things on display. Porn was nothing new to any male who'd lived long enough to see his teenage years, and most of the time he didn't have trouble turning the other way. But last week what he saw totally captured his attention. He found himself not only reading the titles but angling his head and wondering about the parts that had been censored out on the covers.

Luckily he didn't have to wait in line long because if he had, an uncanny suspicion told him he would've come home with at least one purchase. Even with the incident a week old, the images were fresh in his mind.

The memory faded, leaving a sense of guilt behind. Defeat washed over him as he shook his head in disappointment. If he were secure in his faith, he wouldn't be getting aroused by what was on a magazine rack while his fiancée, who was a godly woman, sat waiting at home. Where was his backbone? His values? For some reason, he couldn't imagine Jesus struggling in the locker room with guys like Preston or ogling porn while waiting in line to pay for gas.

A deep sigh left him as he pulled into Karen's apartment complex and parked beside her beige Camry. He bounded up the stairs to her apartment. After one knock, she opened the door and he entered.

"Hey," he said, kissing her cheek and burying his face in the brown hair that fell just to her shoulders. She smelt like strawberries. It was her shampoo, and he loved it. "How was your day?"

"Good. Yours?" She slipped her arms around his neck.

"Hmm, let's just say I'm glad to be here with you."

She studied him a moment before cocking her head to the side. It made her look adorable, but it was also a sign that she was thinking. "Are you okay? You look a little stressed."

"I just got back from the gym where Chris and I got spanked in a game of basketball." He let her go and moved further into the apartment. "Where're the kids?"

Karen shrugged a shoulder and smoothed her hands down her jeans. She was the most modest woman he knew, but she was wearing the ones that were just tight enough to hint at her amazing figure.

"Holly had a sleepover, and then a friend from school called at the last minute to ask if Scott could stay. It's just us."

Under any other circumstance, Bret would've cheered at hearing the news. He had an entire evening to himself with the woman he loved.

"Let's go out," he said before he could change his mind. "We can still do the pizza, but we'll see what's on at the theater instead of renting."

Karen agreed and then turned to grab her purse. They settled on Elizabeth's, an authentic and family-owned Italian restaurant and pizzeria. By the time they ordered their drinks, there was hardly a trace of the anxiety that had plagued Bret so terribly on leaving the gym.

He smiled at his date and slipped his hands across the table to join hers. God would forgive his moments of weakness and help him through the upcoming months. That was what was written in his Word, and everything in the Bible was true. Karen had a way of reminding him of that, even without words.

"I love you, you know that?" he said, hoping to hear Karen say the words in return.

"I do know that, and I love you too. So when are you going to tell me what's really on your mind?"

Bret shook his head, surprised that she could read him so easily. "What makes you think there's something on my mind?"

Karen poked her straw through its paper and placed it in her soda. She pursed her lips and started to drink. "Whenever you're stressed out over something, you get this little crease"—she paused to touch the spot right between his eyes—"right there between your eyebrows. It's almost like a little wrinkle."

"So you're telling me I've got wrinkles?"

"No," she giggled. "I'm asking what's going on. Everything okay at work?"

Bret took the out. "For the most part. I ran into a guy I used to work with when I was in Statesville. He's a realtor now and is looking to do some investing of his own. I think he's interested in building a small business park over on the north end of town. He called the office today asking some questions."

"Good. Maybe landing a new client will help soften the blow of what Chris is doing in Asheville."

Bret chuckled. "Only if my friend decides to put up a shopping mall in addition to the business park! Chris is in way over his head with this old house."

"That's a shame. That place is gorgeous. I can easily see how restoring it would make a lovely bed-and-breakfast."

"True, but it's not going to come cheap. In case you haven't noticed, Chris tends to overdo. The price we paid for it on top of what it's going to cost to renovate it and make it operational will run into the millions. There's no way Chris can get even half of that back off some tourists. Not with the current economic trends."

"Wow. That does sound like a lot of money to pour into something the company's never done before. I mean you guys mostly take on contracted work or invest in things you can lease out long term, like warehouses and strip malls, right?"

"Mostly, but like always, Chris wants to try something new. Says it's good for diversification or whatever that means. Enough about work. How was your day?"

Karen pushed the soda aside. "I heard from Mom today. She's seeing someone."

"Really?" Bret felt his expression open with the news. Karen lost her dad to cancer years ago, and it seemed as though her mom was content to be alone. "Is this the first guy she's dated since your dad?"

"No. She's dated a few men through the years, but then we lost Eric, and she just never seemed to find anyone after that. I think she was too busy trying to take care of me. Anyway, now that I'm on my feet, I think she feels the freedom to explore her own options."

Bret nodded. "That makes sense. So this is good news?"

"It is. She's very excited about our engagement. In fact, she's already throwing out ideas for the wedding. She thinks we should get married there, in Asheboro."

Bret nearly choked on his drink. "What on earth…I mean…why?" he said as he reached for a napkin and schooled his features.

"I tried to tell her my life is here now. Then she started talking about roots and not forgetting where it is you're from, extended family, and so forth. In a way I'm hoping this whole dating thing will be a good distraction for her. She also asked if you got the sweater she sent for your birthday."

Bret drew his brows together and frowned. His birthday had been Wednesday, and to his surprise, Karen's mom sent him a gold sweater to celebrate the occasion. It was one of the ugliest things he'd ever seen, but out of respect, he played it down. "About that…"

A touch of a smile played on Karen's mouth. "I told her you loved it, but that you haven't had the perfect opportunity to show it off just yet. She said something about my dad having one just like it back in the day, only his was blue."

"Lucky me," Bret said, not realizing the words had actually slipped out with so much sarcasm.

"It is rather ugly." Karen giggled.

"Actually…" Bret paused. This was Karen. He could be honest with her. "Yes, it is. It's the ugliest thing I own to be exact."

"I knew it!" She cackled. "But I'm warning you. Now that I've told her you like it, she's going to ask you about it herself. She and her new boyfriend are coming up next weekend. Mom wants to make a trip to Sam's Club."

"Maybe I should just wear the sweater and get it over with." Bret shook his head. "It looks like it's from the seventies!"

"If Dad owned one, it probably *is* from the seventies!!" Together they laughed, and Karen smiled. "Don't worry. They won't be staying long, just an afternoon. I was thinking we could invite Amanda over."

"Still no sign of her?"

"Nope. She's still pouting over Chris and their breakup. I was hoping for something to draw her out. It still feels weird that they're not together anymore. It was through the two of them that we met. Now I find myself watching every word I say so that I don't set her off. Has Chris said anything to you?"

"Nothing worth repeating. Invite her if you think she'll come."

Karen smiled and slipped her hands into his again. "You know I love that about you, the fact that you're willing to wear an ugly sweater to make my mother happy, the way you try to help me help Amanda. It says you're sweet...caring...self-sacrificing."

Bret let one more chuckle slip out. "I think it says I'm whooped, but I like you're version better, so we'll go with it."

"One large white cheese and spinach pizza," the waitress said, placing an oversized tray on the table between them. Bret smiled over the sizzling pie, and his improved mood followed them to the theater where they decided to see a romantic comedy.

It wasn't until over halfway through the movie that his thoughts started to wander. For the most part, the movie was completely predictable with the leading male, who was playing the part of a declared bachelor, breaking the heart of every woman he meets until he finally meets his match. Although the woman was playing hard to get, Bret expected them to fall in love before the credits started to roll.

He looked over to Karen now that the couple on screen had finally admitted their feelings and were starting to kiss. Her eyes never left the screen, and she didn't seem embarrassed by the display of affection. Bret turned back to see the couple's kiss become intimate and involved as they stumbled into a bedroom scene. The whole picture was larger than life. Clothes started to come off, and although there was no full nudity, lots of skin was being shown.

"Do you think we should go?"

Bret looked over at Karen who was now staring at him in the semidarkness. *Go? I've been sitting here bored to death for almost an hour. This is just getting good.* "Um…I don't know. Let's give it another minute and see what happens."

He looked back to see the movie cut to the next scene. *I missed it!* He shifted uncomfortably in his seat, wishing there had been more to see. Immediately guilt whispered over his heart, and he felt the defeat from earlier wash over him.

I'm a horrible man, he chided himself. Images from his struggle in the line at the gas station came to mind, and this time, he could actually feel the wrinkle between his eyes deepening like a canyon. His anxieties became hard to tame.

By the time he was walking Karen to the door, he was all over the fence about what was right and what was wrong, where he wanted to take their relationship and where he didn't. Time ran out, and he was forced to decide as Karen slipped her key into the lock.

"So…can I come in?" he asked, hopeful.

Karen slowly turned to face him. "It's late and the kids aren't here. Remember? We agreed that whenever—"

"Yeah, but we both know nothing's going to happen. Please?"

"Believe me"—she smiled—"I want you to come in, but it's really not a good idea."

Bret bit the inside of his cheek and nodded his understanding. He wanted to beg. "See you at church tomorrow?"

"Definitely." She slid her arms up around his neck. Standing there gazing into her eyes, he realized she was giving him an unspoken opportunity to change her mind. He brushed his thumb over her cheek, admiring her beauty. Slowly he brought their mouths together and made every move that would ensure the passion between them started to build.

After a few heated minutes slipped away, Bret felt her withdraw. "Tomorrow, okay?"

Bret didn't say anything. He couldn't. Slowly he turned away and descended the stairs.

Instead of getting in his car, he paced along the sidewalk just out of sight. *Doesn't this woman understand what she does to me? How can she tie my insides up in knots and then tell me she'll see me tomorrow? Like we're just two people ending a date. Because we're not. We're engaged. We're supposed to be crazy about each other. We're supposed to be like that couple in the movie!*

He stood there a moment, sucking in the cold night air while nursing his wounded pride. He paused only long enough to shush his guilty conscience. He knew better than to flirt with temptation, but at the moment, he couldn't say he cared. It cut to see how Karen didn't even struggle with it. She was still firmly anchored in her convictions after all these weeks—and after that passionate kiss they'd just shared. He, on the other hand, had continued to grow more and more miserable by the hour, and it left him feeling disappointed and rejected.

Acknowledging his feelings allowed the images he'd been pushing to the recesses of his mind all week to surface and play before his eyes like the movie they'd just finished watching.

A few more minutes passed, and Bret sucked in another deep breath of cold air. He climbed in his car and slammed the door. He had taken stock of the situation, and in the process, he'd come to a conclusion. He loved Karen and would wait for their wedding day to show her just how much—but he was only a man and every man had limits. Karen didn't have to know everything, including the stop he intended to make at a certain gas station on his way home.

6

Chris turned the knob on the back door of his house and found that it was already unlocked. He pushed the door ajar, and immediately, something that smelled divine filled his senses. It was Monday—the day Karen was coming over to cook for him and the kids. He checked his watch as he finished pushing the door open with his foot. Bret should be right behind him.

He hung up his coat and stepped into the living room to kick off his shoes. "Hey there," he said to Karen while taking a deep breath of whatever it was that promised to taste incredible. "It smells good in here. What's cooking?"

Karen lifted her head from what she was working on to look at him. "Lasagna, Bret's favorite!"

Chris chuckled. Bret was getting rather spoiled. "I should've known. You're ruining him, you know? All this catering to his every whim and he's going to start expecting it on a regular basis. Aren't you sick of Italian yet?"

Karen looked at him and flashed the rock on her left finger. "Deathly, but you're not telling me anything I don't already know. Love does that to you. How was work? Make any headlines?" she teased.

"Ha, ha," he said, shuffling into the kitchen in his socked feet. "Other than firing one of our foremen, it was actually a slow day."

He walked over and washed his hands before stealing cheese out of the bowl on the counter. Chris leaned back beside the stove to watch her work. A thousand things were spread across the counter, and he couldn't help but think she looked right at home in his kitchen.

"I hate to hear that. Firing someone is hard."

"Not when a guy tries to operate a crane while he's intoxicated. He knocked down half the building and put another worker in the hospital. How much longer till all this is ready?"

Karen's eyes got large, and she ignored his question about the food. "Is he going to be okay?"

"He has minor cuts and bruises along with a broken leg. The biggest problem is now I'm out two employees on a project that was already behind schedule. At this rate, I'm never going to get out of town."

Her brows drew together in concern. "If that was a slow day, then maybe you should hang around. Things might fall apart completely when you leave."

"They'll manage," Chris said, this time stealing a cherry tomato.

"If Bret likes Italian, what's your favorite food?" Karen pulled open a drawer to withdraw a large knife and started to shred a head of lettuce for the salad.

"Me?"

"Yeah, I was thinking we should do this again before you head out only with your favorites. Last time I checked, there's not much out there in the middle of the woods."

Flattered by her thoughtfulness, he considered his choices. "Hmm, a nice juicy steak is always a favorite, but I guess if I had my pick, it'd be home-style food. It's hard to beat fried chicken, mashed potatoes and gravy, home-made biscuits…"

Karen put down the knife. "You are such a country boy!"

"Country boy?" Chris grinned, liking the idea.

"Yeah, where I come from, that's what we call guys like you." She shrugged a shoulder as if her explanation made perfect sense. "You've got the big truck, you like to play in the mud…I'll even bet the idea of getting up at the crack of dawn to go hunt something down sounds like a hobby."

Chris felt his smile deepen. Searching for his best country accent, he questioned, "You tryin' ta say I'm sum sorta redneck?"

Karen giggled. "Not exactly, Mr. CEO"—she paused to look at his socked feet—"but if the shoe fits…"

Chris got a good laugh and grabbed another handful of cheese. "I might like beer, bikinis, and going barefooted, but I like living in luxury too much to go trading in all this for a trailer." Another chuckle slipped out. "This neighborhood would seriously frown on me owning a yard car." He tried to reach for the bowl of sliced cucumbers, but she stopped him.

"Get out of that!" she snapped, popping his hand. "You're eating all the ingredients before I can put them together. There won't be anything left for the salad!"

"I'm hungry," he whined, trying to look completely pitiful. All he got was a pointed look from her. "Oh, all right," he said, giving up in defeat, "but I could get used to this. A beautiful woman cooking in my kitchen…It's something worth coming home to."

She laughed at him. "What do you mean 'could get used to,' you already are. Marie has *you* spoiled rotten! I pity the woman who marries you."

"Okay, it's true. I am rather spoiled, but surely I have some kind of redeeming quality that would make up for it." He stole one last handful of cheese when she turned in the opposite direction. "I am rich."

"So hire good help."

"Good point. I'm sure it's cheaper in the long run," he said through a smile before sorting through the day's mail and tossing most of it in the trash.

Seeing a letter from Shelby's teacher, he tore into it. Words were written explaining that she wanted to meet with him to discuss Shelby's attitude and grades because they were failing. *Great*, he thought. *Just what I need. Another person who probably has the same questions I do.*

"What's wrong?" Karen asked, seeing his face.

"Nothing. It's just a note from Shelby's teacher. At least it's not the cheerleading coach asking for the deposit I gave Shelby to turn in last week at tryouts."

Karen stopped chopping. "Chris, they don't ask for money until you make the squad."

Forgiveness for Yesterday

"You mean she was lying to me? So what was the twenty for?" Chris shook his head. "That girl! Sometimes I swear I could strangle her." He tossed the letter on the bar to deal with later.

"Hey, thanks for coming over right after work and keeping an eye on the kids. I hope it wasn't too much trouble."

"Nah, you know how they are. They can never wait to get together. Besides, as soon as we got here, they all disappeared either upstairs or outside."

Chris debated on asking what Karen's advice was regarding Shelby but reasoned that trying to figure out the opposite sex was too much to handle on an empty stomach.

Karen continued to put the meal together. At one point, she moved to get something out of the cabinet over the stove beside him. When she did, her shirt lifted to reveal a flat stomach. His eyes naturally moved to the exposed area, and immediately, Chris felt himself warm.

He rubbed a hand down the back of his neck, pretending to work out some muscle tension. Just a second ago, he was thinking about how good a friend Karen was, and now he was checking her out. What was wrong with him? Karen was pretty in a natural sort of way, so he chalked up his looking to the fact that he'd picked up some really bad habits over the years. It still didn't make ogling his best friend's girl okay, but there was no harm done since she hadn't noticed.

"What are you going to do with the kids when you leave town?"

Chris breathed a sigh of relief. "I've asked Marie to move in and become a live-in nanny for the next few months. I'm scheduled to leave a week from today, but I'll be back here every weekend until the project gets going full time in early spring. I'm hoping to move the kids there over the summer."

"That sounds pretty permanent. You are coming back, aren't you?"

"Who knows? With this job, anything is possible."

Karen turned her back toward him but not before he could see she was upset. A few seconds later, he heard her sniffle and knew she was crying. The sound sparked some kind of reaction in him, and he felt the urgency to fix whatever was wrong.

"Karen, why are you crying?" He asked the question as he moved around the kitchen island to stand beside her.

She put the knife down and hesitated as if she were considering her words. Her face was scrunched up, and he knew she was fighting for control. It was best to let her have it, so he backed off. "I don't know. It's just that Holly and Shelby are so close. I can't imagine what it'll do to Holly if she loses that friendship on top of all the other changes she's going through. I have such a hard time with her already! Some days I don't even recognize her. She's moody, unpredictable…and the sass. I don't know where she learns to talk like that. Some days I think she hates me!"

Chris stared at her in disbelief. She could easily be describing Shelby. "I know what you mean. It's like I don't know whether to speak or stay silent, and whatever I do, it's never the right thing."

Karen smiled and wiped a tear away with the back of her hand. "I guess we do have a few things in common, huh? It would be hard to see you go too. We've all grown so close. I feel like you and I are finally friends."

Her words touched his heart, and when the tears picked up again, it was the most natural thing to open his arms for comfort. Karen slipped into them and rested her head on his shoulder.

"Sh, don't cry," he said. "Nothing's definite about moving. I was just speculating." Chris felt her chest shudder against his and knew she was crying in earnest. "Karen, it'll be okay." He chuckled, stroking a hand down her back. "You've got to be the sweetest woman I've ever met along with one of the most emotional. I think I see where Holly gets it."

She groaned and squeezed him one more time before she pulled back. When she did, her cheek brushed against his, but he continued to hold her loosely. Her head was bowed between them, so he buried his face in her hair. She smelt fresh and faintly of summer despite the evening hour.

Holding her in his arms, Chris suddenly became aware of how much Karen reminded him of Laurie and the unspoken qualities about her that drew him. His thumbs brushed her waist, and he appreciated the way her high heels and his bare feet positioned their bodies.

It had been months since he'd held anyone this close and thinking of Laurie brought a tidal wave of emotions to the surface of his heart—only the emotions washing over him weren't the intense hatred he'd come to expect but a powerful longing for something he couldn't have. For the first time ever, he wondered what Karen would do if he kissed her.

Rather than stepping away, her face lifted, and he stared down into her eyes. Was she saying yes? Deviling in the moment, he tried to imagine how she would respond if he did make the move. Would she wrap her arms around his neck and kiss him back? Would she tell him that she loved him?

What he was considering must've been evident on his face. Her tender expression changed, and Chris felt her hands press hard against his chest. The action snapped him back to reality, and he dropped his hands as if she'd scalded his flesh.

There was question and alarm written on her face as she backed away in surprise. "Chris…what? That's not what I meant. That's not why I…" Her eyes were clouded by confusion and then anger. She shot past him and around the counter. It was obvious she planned to leave.

Chris moaned seeing what he'd done. "Karen, wait! I'm sorry!" he said, chasing after her, but she was too fast. He managed to grab her wrist when she reached for her purse lying on the couch. "Please, you don't understand!"

With surprising strength, she jerked away from his grasp, stopping only when she was out of reach. There was fear in her eyes. "What don't I understand, Chris! That you were about to do something we would both regret? I care about you, but not like that. I am engaged to marry your best friend for crying out loud! Show some respect!"

Okay, so she wasn't as naïve as he thought, but in that moment, he had never hated himself more. With several feet separating them, it gave him the space he needed to think clearly. "I'm sorry. I don't care about you. I mean I do, but not like that—I promise. I just lost my head. That's it. I swear." His last comments bounced off her back. The only way he knew to stop her from walking out of his life and telling Bret what a lousy friend he had was to tell her the truth—the brutal and honest truth.

Her shoes clicked on the hardwood as she headed for the stairs to get Holly.

"Karen, please! I'm sorry," he said, forcing the next words from his mouth. "It's Laurie, my ex. In a lot of ways…you remind me of her. Something about the way you carry yourself—your confidence and the fact that you're not afraid to stand up to me. You're one of few who'll call my bluff. No one else does that."

His eyes fell when Karen stopped dead in her tracks. Slowly and out of the corner of his eye, he watched her turn around to face him. He braced himself for the verbal attack he deserved only it didn't come. Her voice was soft and hesitant, all the anger from before was gone. "Laurie? As in…your ex-wife?" Karen asked in uncertainty.

Evidently the source of his heartache was more private than he thought. Chris sunk onto the nearest barstool and hung his head in his hands. For the first time in a decade, he thought he could cry. Karen and Bret had been dating for months, and Bret still hadn't told her about Laurie. Bret was that loyal of a friend.

"Amanda didn't tell you?"

"No."

Chris took a deep breath. "Laurie is Shelby and Kyle's mom, not my ex-wife. We were never married. She walked out on me two weeks before our wedding. I hate to talk about it, and I've asked Bret not to say anything because…well…" His voice trailed off from the embarrassment of what he was saying.

Nonetheless, he made himself finish if for no other reason than Karen deserved to know why he'd wrecked their friendship and demolished any kind of trust she had in him. "Even though I hate her for ruining my life…there are times I miss her so much I don't know what to do."

The only sound in the room was the water boiling on the stove. He closed his eyes in hopes that she believed him because both his heart and soul were completely exposed at the moment.

"I'm sorry," she eventually said, somewhat confused. "I didn't know. But if the two of you were never married, then how did you end up with Shelby and Kyle?"

"Their father has never been a part of the picture, so I adopted them when Laurie never returned. She didn't just walk out on me, she walked out on all of us. They had no one." A half-cry, half-laugh slipped out. "Seven months and all I got was a lousy note saying she couldn't do it anymore, that she didn't love me. She didn't even say good-bye." Chris shook his head at the memory and the fact that he was actually making this confession to someone. "And now look at what I've done. I'm a complete loser."

"Chris…I'm sorry. I…I…don't know what to say." There was a long pause. "You're not a loser. What she did…that's horrible." The tenderness in Karen's voice gave him the courage to look up. What he saw staring back at him launched him into another apology just to remind her of who he was and what he'd done. He didn't deserve her compassion.

"I'm sorry too, but that doesn't give me the right to do what I was about to do. You are completely right, and I am *really* sorry. I'm a dog, and I know it, but it'll never happen again, I swear. But you can't tell Bret. You two are the only friends I've got left. He would hate me, and although he has every right, I don't think I can bear that right now."

The sound of a car pulling up outside turned their heads toward the back door. Chris knew his time for pleading was running out. When their eyes met again, he knew he was going to have to beg. "Please, Karen. I swear. It will never happen again. I promise you. You've got to believe me. I'm just really…screwed up. I lost my head, that's all. Please!"

She hesitated, but with the slightest nod, she tossed her purse back on the sofa and slipped past him into the kitchen to finish preparing the meal. In that instance, Chris knew she had not only believed him but also accepted his apology. A ragged sigh left his chest, and he let his shoulders sag in relief.

He couldn't bring himself to look at her for the fear of breaking down and having his own crying spell. "Thank you," he said, head still hung in shame. He stood and moved for the back door, thinking any words of gratitude he could ever manage to find would somehow fall short in this situation.

Karen's forgiveness and cooperation were absolutely priceless to him. But Bret…when it came to Karen, Bret wouldn't be so easy to convince. Words he had heard weeks ago rang true. Bret didn't give second chances, and he had just messed up one time too many.

Karen watched Chris slip out the door and into the backyard with a sigh of relief. She turned the stove burner down, and a shaky hand came to her face. He was gone.

"What was I thinking?" She'd been so tied up in her thoughts about what Chris's leaving would do to Holly that she failed to keep her guard up.

In the months she'd known Chris, he had never once made a move on her. That didn't mean she hadn't always had the sense that it could happen at any given moment—despite his affections for Amanda. His track record with the opposite sex was anything but flawless, and the man had a way of oozing sex appeal. *This is crazy. Me and Chris?*

Frantically she searched her mind looking for any signal she may have given him to make him think the kiss he'd been debating on was welcome. She stood there remembering the last few minutes. They'd been talking about the kids, she started to cry, and then he opened his arms to comfort her like any decent friend would. And that's how she defined their relationship—friends.

Karen shook her head. She had been clear about that. From there she'd started to bawl all over the place, and the next thing she knew she was staring into those piercing blue eyes of his. But still…was there something she'd done somewhere along the way that made

Chris think she would be interested in his advances? They picked on each other a lot, but that couldn't be considered flirting…could it?

Karen felt a little queasy at the idea. Okay, so maybe somewhere during the last few months she'd flirted with Chris once or twice, but none of it was intentional. Chris was just a guy who was easy to flirt with. She certainly hadn't meant anything by her jokes and fun.

She unconsciously tapped a finger to her chin. Maybe he had. A few minutes ago, she'd been able to read his mind completely. He was going to kiss her, and it wouldn't have been just any kiss. It would've been one of those here's-my-heart-and-soul-for-the-taking kind of kisses. He had explained himself and apologized. *But what if he tries again?*

Although she hadn't verbally given her word, she had given Chris the impression that she'd not mention the incident to Bret. "This is bad," she continued to worry out loud. "I know better."

Karen moved across the kitchen to wipe down the counter and remembered the hurt in Chris's eyes when he spoke of Shelby and Kyle's mom—Laurie, he called her. It was the first time she had ever known him to mention Laurie by name. To this point, she thought Shelby and Kyle were Chris's kids and that he had full custody. So who was their real dad? Karen wondered. And where was their mom, Laurie? If that weren't disturbing enough, something about her reminded Chris of his one true love. Another wave of warning washed over Karen.

"How sad," she muttered to the empty room. The infamous bachelor Chris Lanning had been rejected, his heart broken all because he'd fallen for the wrong woman. With her and Bret getting engaged, Chris probably felt alone again, the same way she suspected Amanda felt. And Chris had said something about insisting Bret keep Laurie a secret. She knew from her friendship with Amanda how dominating Chris could be, so she didn't blame Bret for not saying anything. It really wasn't any of her business.

Karen was surprised, however, that Amanda had not told her all the facts regarding Chris's fake marriage the moment they'd been discovered. That was the part that didn't make sense. Even still, deep down under all his problems, Chris had a good heart.

Her body went through the motions of preparing their meal. Karen dropped the lasagna noodles in the boiling pot of water, salted them, and started pulling down the plates from the cabinet. If anyone knew what it was like to suffer the pain of disappointment and loss, it was her. She had spent years battling depression, not knowing how to move on in life when she missed her husband beyond description. That reason alone gave her a certain depth of understanding to Chris's pain—probably more so than he'd ever know.

Mercifully, the Lord had stepped in and showed her the valuable lesson of letting go and trusting that he still had something good in store for her. The only problem was Chris didn't believe like she did. In fact, she didn't know if he believed at all. There had to be a way to show him. So intent on finding the words she knew she needed to share with him, she didn't hear the back door open.

"Bret!" she said, jumping back in surprise, nearly dropping the last plate. "How long have you been standing there?"

He walked around the counter, not taking his eyes from hers. "Not long. Why?"

Karen's eyes narrowed, hearing the suspicion in his tone and how his words were clipped. He hadn't even bothered to take off his coat.

"I didn't hear you come in. You startled me."

"Yeah? It's pretty obvious you were lost in thought. What were you thinking about? Or should I say *who*?"

Karen's mind raced. Surely Chris hadn't been the one to say something. Not after all the pleading he'd done. "What's that supposed to mean?"

Bret continued to walk around the counter and raised his arm to point toward the backyard where Chris was outside with Kyle and Scott. "Karen, your lipstick is all over his shirt collar! Mind telling me why?"

Karen felt her eyes grow big. "What? Oh…" She let out a nervous laugh, and the plates rattled to the counter. "Chris was telling me how he was thinking of moving Shelby and Kyle to Asheville over the summer. We both know what that'll do to Holly. I got upset. I started crying. He told me nothing was for sure yet, and we hugged. It must've happened then. Yes. I'm sure it happened then. You know what a good friend he is and how close those girls are. Holly would be devastated if Shelby moved away. I have enough trouble with her already."

She could see he wasn't entirely convinced, and it hurt that he didn't trust her. She was telling the truth—just not to its fullest extent, but she was babbling on like a flooded brook. She needed to cut to the chase.

"Come on. It was just a hug. You know when I kiss a man, I don't leave lipstick on his collar. I'm much more precise." She slipped around the counter, intent on reenacting their first kiss as a reminder and as a distraction.

She wrapped her arms around his neck and drew his lips to hers. At first he resisted her advances so she combined them with words. "I'm in love with you," she whispered into his ear. "Chris might be every other woman's dream, but he's not mine. The whole time we were talking, it was like you were right there in the room with us. You can't possibly think there would be anything about him that would turn my heart. I can see past all his pretense. *You're* all I can think about." Her hands went up to search out his face. "This chin, these lips, those eyes…I dream of *you* every night."

Eventually she felt him relax against her in the kiss she sought. Afterward his head slid down onto her shoulder, and she felt him let go of a deep breath. "I'm sorry. I trust you, really I do. Chris is the one I can't figure out. He's never gone this long without showing up with some woman dangling on his arm, and I can't help but to wonder if it's because he's got his sights set on you."

Karen's spine stiffened, and she wondered if Bret had felt some of the unspoken warnings she'd recently come to acknowledge. Probably so, but as unlikely as it sounded, something told her that what Chris had done wasn't anything he had planned. If it were, she couldn't see him bearing his heart or begging like he had just because it didn't pan out the way he hoped. Chris wasn't a man who groveled easily, if ever, and for a second, she'd been sure he was going to cry.

"I still think he's searching. Besides, even if he did make a move on me, you can take my word for it, I'd not follow through."

Bret tightened his hold on her, and she felt his head move closer to her neck. "I know, and I'm sorry for questioning you. As much as I care about him, it'd all be over if he made a pass at you. And I don't just mean our friendship. I mean my job...my career...you name it. Gone."

Karen battled a mix of emotions. "You'd do that for me?"

Bret leaned back and looked into her eyes. "Absolutely. You mean more to me than anything else in the world."

She smiled and slowly let her lungs expand as she pulled him close again. She was making the right decision by not saying anything about the intended kiss. The last thing in the world she wanted to do was give Bret a reason to sever ties with someone who held so much power over them. "I love you, Bret Sears, in every way imaginable."

"Yeah? Wanna show me?" he asked, the intimacy of his voice telling her he wanted in on the details.

"Nope!"

His head popped up, and he began searching her eyes for an explanation. "No? How come?"

"Scott is watching us from the living room window." She laughed when Bret spun their joined bodies so he could see for himself. Someone had cut on the outside lights, and Bret groaned seeing Scott's nose pressed to the clean living room window twenty-some feet away. He was smiling and waving at them from the backyard. He motioned for Bret to come outside and join him.

Bret's chest expanded and deflated in a heavy sigh before he kissed Karen's forehead in surrender. "I love you too" he said, slipping back to the door, this time without the tie. "I'm sorry about how I came in here expecting the worst. Forgive me?"

"Always," she murmured as she tried to ignore the heaviness that settled where she had planned to put her supper. "Always."

7

"Oh Bret! You're wearing the sweater I sent! It's so…you." Karen's mom, Lillian, smiled as she held out Bret's arms and examined him like a doll. "It looks fantastic, don't you think?" She was speaking to Brad, the new boyfriend, only Brad hadn't made it into the apartment yet.

"Bradley?" The woman turned, having not heard an answer.

"I'm still out here trying to fix this confounded umbrella!"

An attractive man in his early forties stepped to the door and was shaking an oversized umbrella. His motions sent a spray of water arching out in front of him and onto the living room floor before he finally got it closed and tossed it in the corner.

"Now," he said, wiping his hands off on his pants, and planting a kiss on Lillian's cheek. "What did you want, sweetcakes?"

Lillian blushed. "The sweater. It's the one I got him for his birthday. Isn't it perfect? It brings out the color of his eyes!"

Bradley eagerly shrugged out of his coat revealing that he too was wearing the same sweater only in a shade of powder blue. "We look like twins!" the man said.

Bret blinked trying to recover from a state of shock. He caught Karen's expression and hoped he covered his own surprise better than she had. Where Bradley was in his forties, Lillian was in her sixties. There were maybe ten years between Karen's and Bradley's ages when they had been expecting somewhere close to thirty.

The knowledge had obviously left Karen speechless; therefore, Bret felt the need to intervene. "It's nice to meet you, Bradley. This is Karen, Lillian's daughter, my fiancée."

"Br-Bradley," Karen stammered, extending her hand when Bret elbowed her gently in the side. "Mom has told me…so…little about you."

Bret was handed a dripping rain coat to hang up and missed whatever Bradley had to say in defense of himself. All he heard was Karen's mother telling her to mind her manners.

When he returned, he discovered the ladies had retreated to the back of the apartment where he was sure Karen was grilling Lillian, leaving him to question their subject directly.

Bret plastered on a smile, wanting to come right out and ask the man his age. "So…Bradley, is it?"

"My friends call me Brad. Only Lillian calls me Bradley. It's sort of like a pet name. You know, like sweetie pie or honey? What does Karen call you?"

"Bret. She calls me Bret." There was a long awkward pause. "So, Brad…how are things?"

"Great for weather like this. It's raining cats and dogs out there! They say it's going to turn to ice later on this evening. I hate it when the weather gets bad. I don't mind driving in the snow, but the ice," he explained, "you can't keep a truck out of the ditch in that stuff. Last year I got hit head on. Nearly totaled Marge."

"Marge? I'm sorry, Marge is your…?"

"Truck."

Bret leaned back in disbelief as he listened to Brad describe Marge in detail. "She's a '69 Ford pickup. Got three hundred horses under the hood, headers with three-inch straight pipes. Yes, siree, you can hear her a comin' from half a mile out. Had to change the jets in the carburetor last week. Still think she's running a little rich. I'm only getting ten miles to the gallon, but hey, what do I know?"

Bret smiled. *Obviously, not much.* "I take it you like to tinker on old cars."

"Marge isn't old. She's a classic. Besides, there's no sense burying a fortune in one of those imports. Not when you can have a good 'ol American-made machine sitting in your garage. What kind of truck do you drive? You do drive a truck, don't you? It's the American way."

Bret nodded, trying to get past the fact they were discussing Brad's truck like it was an ailing relative. Luckily, before he could answer anything, Brad went on to relate some long story about icy roads and a car with no headlights and how Marge ended up in the shop where she got her latest paint job: two-tone, no doubt.

Bret blew out through his mouth. It was going to be a long afternoon. Some ten to fifteen minutes later, he missed his chance to launch into a debate about the ingenuity of British transportation when Scott and Holly came in from next door.

"Grandma!" they squealed in unison as they rushed into the living room and saw their grandmother coming down the hallway. The commotion in Karen's apartment tripled. "We were next door at Brenda's baking chocolate chip cookies. Mom said you were coming!"

Lillian made another round of introductions, and soon Bret felt a headache coming on. He excused himself and went to the bathroom to find a bottle of aspirin. He popped two and then stuck another two in his pocket for later. Instead of returning to the chaos down the hall, he decided to bide his time and burn at least five minutes off the clock.

While waiting, he took a minute to study his reflection in the mirror. Carefully avoiding the eyes of the man looking back at him, he turned to the side to see if the horrid sweater he was wearing made him look younger or older. It was obviously working a number for Bradley out there.

Bret huffed and let out a sound of disgust. If anything, the sweater made him look fat. While he was examining himself, something else caught his eye. He leaned over and squinted. Sure enough, he had a gray hair. Quickly he yanked it out and searched for others. There weren't any. *Good. I just turned thirty-two. I'm not supposed to have gray hairs. Bradley doesn't have any, and he's forty-two,* he silently told himself. *So…why is he dating a woman twenty years his senior?*

Bret sat down on the side of the tub and started to massage his temples. Some questions were better off not asked. Three minutes left, and his headache hadn't let up in the least. He'd always considered himself a people person. Brad might be young and have strange interests, but he didn't sense any real danger in his attachment to

Lillian—who was always fussing over something. For the first time ever, he wondered what Karen's father had been like and if she favored him in any way. Unfortunately he'd never know.

A chorus of voices echoed down the hall, complete with someone's shrill laughter. They were extremely loud, and after Karen's mom left, Chris was supposed to come by. Chris was scheduled to leave for Asheville in the morning, and Karen had promised to cook him a going-away meal. For the sake of convenience, and because Amanda was a no-show this afternoon, they decided to host it here at Karen's apartment.

"God, let it snow," Bret mumbled, then altered his request. "Send Lillian, Brad, and Marge home, and *then* let it snow."

He stood and made his way back into the living room just in time to see a weather advisory flash across the TV. It was a warning for snow and ice, and they had bumped the expected time into the early afternoon hours.

Bret could almost see the beads of sweat breaking out on Brad's forehead. "Welp, kiddos, that does it! Me and your grandma will have to come back and visit another time."

Brad moved toward the kitchen to retrieve their coats. "I have a feeling this one could be a five loafer," he said as he helped Lillian into a thick peacoat.

"Don't be silly," Lillian scolded. "Every time it gets below thirty degrees, Bradley is stocking my pantry with milk and bread! He's always afraid I'll starve to death if the power goes out."

"What happened to old man Hubert and his cow, Betsy?" Karen wanted to know. "With him living next door, you never had to worry about going without."

"Oh, honey. Didn't I tell you?" Lillian's face grew serious. "Betsy died a couple of months ago. It was just as well. Hubert and Susie are getting on up in age. They can't take care of the farm and the animals like they used to."

Karen simply blinked at her mother's words. "You mean Betsy is… gone? But…but…"

 Forgiveness for Yesterday

"Sweetheart, cows don't live forever, you know." Lillian leaned forward and hugged her daughter for consolation. The words were whispered, but Bret heard them nonetheless, "And neither will I. Might as well have a little fun while I can."

Sometimes it was easy to forget Karen had lived a very different life before he'd met her. She had suffered many losses, but she also came from a place where "next door" meant the adjoining acreage. It was also a place where cows were pets and men drove restored clunkers, not because it was stylish or affordable, but because it was some sort of tribute to America. Whoever Betsy was, he was willing to bet that Karen had milked her at least once and that he was going to get an earful the moment her mother was out of hearing range.

Instead of asking after the beloved Betsy, Bret began to usher the group to the door when the sound of the doorbell chimed.

"Who could that be?" Karen asked, peeping through the window.

Bret moved through the crowded space, and on the other side of the open door, he found Chris, Shelby, and Kyle standing in what had turned into an icy downfall.

"Hey," Chris said, shivering in the cold, "I know it's early and all, but we were in the area and decided to come on by. It's starting to sleet."

Bret opened the door a little wider, making it obvious Chris was busting in on something. For once, he was going to be able to explain to Chris that his timing was bad, and that they should probably call off their little going-away party due to the weather. Bret opened his mouth, eager to give Chris the bad news.

"What's with the ugly sweater?" Chris laughed. "You haven't gone spineless *and* blind, have you?"

Bret's mouth fell open as Lillian and Brad stood gaping at him. The look on their faces was hard to read. Brad was wearing his coat, making Chris oblivious to his mistake.

Chris took Bret's silence as an invitation to pile into the living room with their other guests. "What?" Chris finally asked, looking around and not understanding the blank stares he was getting.

"Mom, Brad," Karen said, intervening, "this is Chris, Shelby, and Kyle Lanning. Chris is a friend of ours—a good, but sometimes etiquette-challenged friend of ours. Shelby and Kyle are his children. They're friends with Holly and Scott."

Karen turned to Chris. "Chris, this is my mom and...Brad."

Chris eagerly stuck out his hand to Brad. "Let me just say it's a pleasure, sir. Your daughter plays cards better than any of the guys I know. Says she has you to thank. I still can't believe the way she hustled me. All I can say is it's a good thing we never play for money, or I'd be broke."

There was silence. Chris continued to pump Brad's hand. Apparently Chris thought Karen said Dad, not Brad. "Say, you look young to have served in Nam? In fact, you don't look much older than Karen."

Bret cringed.

"I'm forty-four, and I have no idea what you're talking about," Brad said when he found his voice. He turned to Lillian after a moment. "You're husband served in Vietnam? That war ended...twenty-nine years ago. You told me he didn't enlist until you were twenty-five. If you're fifty-one, Vietnam would've been over before he served." Brad looked thoroughly confused.

Karen chose that moment to accidentally hit the button that opened Brad's wet and broken umbrella. Everyone shrieked when they were once again sprayed with water.

"Sorry," she apologized over the incessant chatter that followed. Karen passed off the offensive item, and Bret breathed a sigh of relief when Karen's mom and her date filed out the door.

He had no more shut the door when Karen set her sites on Chris. "Are you crazy! What were you thinking bringing up his age?"

"What's the big deal?" Chris asked, shedding his coat like a snake and flopping down on the couch. "Okay...so I thought you called him Dad. That would mean your mother's boyfriend is..." Chris stared at the ceiling as he did the math in his head. "Only...thirteen years older than you. It's more like he's your older brother!"

"Genius. Real genius!" Bret answered and rolled his eyes when Karen put her hands on her hips.

"My father died to cancer ten years ago when he was in his fifties. My mother is lying about her age so she can date a younger man! And I can't believe you actually told on her *and* that I hustled you! She doesn't even know my father taught me to play poker! I'm sure he's rolling over in his grave as we speak!"

Chris paled understanding his error. "Yeah, well, that's what he gets for teaching you how to beat the pants off me in cards. Maybe next time you'll learn."

"Me!" Karen let out a wail of exasperation. "Oh forget it!" she said, collecting the girls to help her with supper.

Bret watched Chris pick up the TV remote. "What?" Chris asked again, still not reading Bret's look.

Bret raised a brow and pointed at his golden sweater. "Just so you know, Brad was wearing one just like it. Now I'll have to wear this thing again just to *prove* you're out of your mind. Geez! Talk about cramming your foot in your mouth! I think you managed to get your ankle in there too."

"Take it easy. So what if Karen's mom is stretching the truth a little?" Chris looked into the kitchen to make sure Karen wasn't listening. "I say, go, Mom! If things don't work out with him, maybe she can pass off my number. She's not bad looking."

Chris was joking. "I'm pretty sure you've burned that bridge." Bret leaned his head back on a pillow willing his nightmare to end. Karen was sure to be more than upset over her mom's little unveiling.

Two seconds later, Scott came back into the living room and sat down beside Bret. "Why would Grandma lie about how old she is? And I thought you liked her gift?"

Bret's eyes found Chris's again. *See!* He wanted to scream at Chris. His thoughtless actions and words affected everyone.

"Women do that sometimes. It's like a game they play. I do like the sweater, buddy. The sweater is a great gift…Chris was referring to the color. That's all." Bret looked to Chris for backup.

"Uh, yeah. Gold…mustard…baby poo—whatever it is you call that"—Chris motioned with his hands for emphasis—"doesn't do anything for me. I'm more of a blue fan myself."

"Brad's sweater was blue!" Scott piped.

"See! I'm sure I would've loved his."

Bret patted Scott's shoulder. "Maybe we should look for one for Chris. Kind of like a belated Christmas present. That way everybody can have one."

Scott nodded. "Good idea!" Quickly he ran off to show Kyle the magic set he'd gotten for Christmas, leaving Bret with a small sense of satisfaction. At least Chris would be getting his own ugly sweater to wear as punishment.

The satisfaction was short-lived as Chris kicked off his shoes and stretched out on the sofa. For some reason, the sight of his boss completely at home on his fiancée's couch topped off Bret's irritation.

Eventually Chris looked over and finally noticed Bret's continued state of displeasure, even if he did misinterpret the cause of it. "How was I supposed to know you two were wearing matching sweaters? He had his coat on. Come next week, no one will remember a thing. Are you watching this?" Chris motioned to the TV but didn't pause before changing the channel. Chris laughed as he did.

"You know, come to think of it, I bet the two of you looked like twins. Brad…Bret…you know what they say, like mother, like daughter. Maybe the four of you can do a double wedding."

Bret closed his eyes and prayed. *Okay, forget the snow, God. Just send Chris home so he can go to Asheville in the morning and start wrecking someone else's life for a change.*

It wasn't until late that evening when the sleet turned to snow and started to fall in earnest that Karen felt the pressure of Bret's burdens starting to pile up. She and Bret had just sent Chris and his kids on their way, their arms laden with leftovers, and Bret had hardly said two words since they'd arrived.

Tonight she'd pulled out all the stops. Fried chicken, country-styled steak, mashed potatoes, and at least three different kinds of casseroles topped every flat surface in her apartment.

Her mind drifted through the evening, but she couldn't find anything that would constitute Bret being so rude. "So do you want to go first or should I?" she asked as she collapsed on the couch beside him.

"What're you talking about?"

"Are you going to tell me what's got *you* so mad? Whatever it is, I don't think it has anything to do with my mother and her new boyfriend."

"I'm not mad," Bret said, pretending surprise. "What makes you think I'm mad? Wait, don't tell me. My lines are showing. If I'm not mistaken, you have a few worry lines of your own this evening."

They snuggled up, and Karen shifted her weight to get comfortable. "Who wouldn't be worried if they found out their mother was dating a man young enough to be their sibling? But there's something on your mind. What is it?"

He looked down into her face and kissed her. "You know you're getting really good at not letting me off the hook when I try to change the subject."

"Hmm, I think that means this dating stuff is working. Promise me something."

"What?" Bret asked, playing with a lock of her hair.

"That I won't end up like my mother. I get the feeling she's afraid of being alone with no one to take care of her. That *Bradley* is her way of reclaiming time that's been lost. I can't believe he's only forty-four. He's closer to my age than he is to hers."

"How old is she?"

"Sixty-two."

"Wow. She must take good care of herself. That's surprising with the way she worries."

"Yeah. Part of me is glad Chris spilled the beans. That's what she gets for lying."

Bret exhaled. "As much as it pains me to say this, if Brad cares anything for her, age won't make a difference. There were seven years between you and Eric. That's a big difference when you're eighteen. Not so much when you're in your forties."

"But their relationship is based on a lie. And we're not talking seven years, but almost twenty. There's a difference."

"You're parents really let you date someone who was that much older?"

"I know. Crazy, huh?"

"Definitely." Bret looked down at the ill-fated gold sweater. "What's this about her and her obsession with sweaters?"

"What?" Karen laughed. "You don't think she gave you and Brad some of Dad's old clothes?"

The idea took root, and they simply stared at each other as they realized how weird that would be. "Hey!" She laughed. "You volunteered to wear that thing so don't go blaming me! I hear recycling is in!"

Bret whipped the sweater off and tossed it on the floor. "I thought I smelt mothballs!"

Karen laughed in earnest. "Don't worry too much. She got rid of Dad's stuff long ago. She's just trying to find out what's in style these days. She has no idea not everything from the seventies made a comeback!"

Although Bret had removed the sweater, he was still wearing a white undershirt. It dramatically changed his look. Karen's laughter died down, and she pulled him close, liking the contrast of the white shirt against his dark features.

"Better. Much better," Karen said, running her fingers into his thick black hair and smiling. "At least you didn't get a green one."

"Great. I can't wait to see what I'll get for this year's Christmas. I'm predicting a pair of bell-bottoms or something made from polyester." They both shared one last chuckle. "I promise I won't let you end up like your mom if you'll promise me something in return."

"What's that?"

"Well, since I refuse to go bald, I want you to promise me that you'll still love me when I'm all gray—or that you'll at least help me dye my hair should it all change color."

"Deal."

Together they giggled at the thoughts of growing old together.

It didn't take long before their somber mood returned however.

"Not that the issue of Mom and Brad is anywhere near settled," Karen said, "tell me why you're still upset with Chris. After he finally got his foot out of his mouth, I thought he was kind of fun tonight. He did end up beating me in cards."

Bret tugged her close again and rested his head on her shoulder. "Come on! You let him win."

Karen grinned. "Okay, but it was just because I wanted to send him away on a happy note."

"Well, happy he was. I guess I'm still worried there's more going on with him than he's letting on. I saw the way he looked at you tonight when we all said our good-byes. It was like there was something he wanted to say to you but wouldn't with the rest of us around."

Karen sighed. "You know I didn't mean anything by cooking him that meal or the card game. I was only being nice. It'll probably be the last decent meal he gets for a long time."

"I know, but there's something I'm still missing. Even though he'd never admit it, I'm scared he's got a thing for you." Bret pulled away and sat up. With his head eye level, she studied him for a moment.

It was killing her to look into those trusting brown eyes of his and keep what Chris had done a secret, but she didn't feel right about betraying Chris either. He really didn't have a thing for her. Tonight Chris had been the same old Chris with a big dose of excitement. He'd been nothing but nice to her and had acted in such a way that let her know he understood the boundaries of their relationship. They were friends, and that was it.

The incident Bret was referring to was when Chris had expressed his thanks to her for the meal. "Thanks," Chris had said in leaving, "for everything. You have no idea what all this means to me. You're a good friend, and we both know I don't have many of those."

Karen had studied his face and noticed how he unashamedly met her eyes. After all, Bret was standing a whole arm's length away. His presence gave her the courage to speak what God had laid on her heart. "That's what *friends* are for. You're going through a lot of change right now, and I want you to know that I'll be here praying you through it. All of it. A day will come when you can look back and see God's hand was on you through the whole thing."

A tender look came across his eyes, and she knew he understood exactly what she was saying. That there was hope and healing, and she'd be praying he found it.

"Thanks, Karen," he said, pulling her into a hug. "You're the best."

And that was it. The memory made her understand the value of what hung in the balance, so she shared it with Bret. "He's searching, and it's our responsibility to show him where he can find what it is he's searching for—Jesus."

"Yeah, but you don't know Chris like I know Chris. He loves a challenge, and here you are, a woman who has been in his presence for what? Six months now and still managed not to fall head over heels for him? It's got to wound his pride."

"Pride?"

"Yes, his pride. Chris is always so proud. He's always bragging about how he's got it made, how much power he has at work and all the money he makes…his girlfriends, you name it. I'm tired of it. It almost makes me glad he's going away."

Karen lowered her chin as she concentrated on what she was hearing. Bret's claims were bogus. All men bragged on one thing or another, and any boasting Chris would've done shouldn't be taken all that seriously. Especially between friends as close as the two of them were.

It had taken her months to figure out Chris was an executive at Greeson Developing, much less the CEO. Even then she knew he was miserable in spite of the wealth his title had acquired for him. All this excess was in Bret's head, and it was causing him to act foolishly.

In light of her mother's insecurities and the lie it had produced, Karen could see her own secret wasn't doing anyone any good either. With Chris heading safely out of town in the morning, she decided it was best to tell Bret what had happened in Chris's kitchen as a way to put Bret's insecurities to rest once and for all.

Wrapping her arms around his neck, she kept her face at a distance so she could read his eyes. "I'm going to tell you something, and I don't want you to get mad."

"I don't like the sound of this."

She tugged on his neck. "Promise me."

 Forgiveness for Yesterday

There was a long silence, and eventually she had to ask again.

"Okay, I promise," Bret said, still reluctant.

"Awhile back, I was feeling some of the same things you are. Like I wasn't getting the full picture when it comes to Chris Lanning. That's why...well..." Karen paused searching her heart for the right words. She wanted to be truthful but not overly explanatory. "Let's just say I put Chris in his place. You can rest assured he knows where we stand. We're friends, that's all we'll ever be, and he's cool with that."

Bret's eyes narrowed in anger, and he jerked away from her. "I knew it! He made a move on you! When? What did he do? If he put his hands on you, I swear I'll kill him!" Bret darted off the couch and started to pace like a madman.

"Would you stop! This is exactly why I didn't say anything! And he didn't put his hands on me—at least not in the way you're thinking. It was just a look, but I knew what was going on in his mind, so I called him on it."

"Karen! I can't believe you didn't tell me this. Guys are competitive. Especially Chris. If he's thinking it, soon he'll be acting on it! Oh, he might tell you he's good with being your friend, but what kind of friend makes a move on his *best* friend's girl? There are no limits with this man!"

Karen's mouth fell open in disbelief. Had she not been completely convinced of Chris's remorse she would've backed down and considered Bret's point. But she was convinced—thoroughly to be exact. "Calm down. You're going to wake the kids. And you promised, remember? I told you, Chris knows where we stand, and even if he is lying and is simply biding his time, it doesn't change the way I feel about you."

This time Bret stopped midstride and knelt in front of the sofa where she was still sitting. "Karen," he said in a voice that was beyond tired, "Chris has this...this...I don't know...charm about him. Women fall prey to it all the time. It's like a drug. I'm worried because I don't know how far Chris is willing to go in an attempt to find what he thinks is happiness. Somehow destroying what I've got just because he can't have it doesn't seem so unrealistic anymore."

"Would you listen to yourself? Chris cannot destroy what we've got unless we let him. You not trusting me when I say that I handled it is one step in that direction!"

Karen didn't like the frown that appeared on his face at hearing her words. "Look at me," she said, turning his head to meet hers when he joined her on the sofa. "I love the fact that you are willing to fight for me, but would you quit comparing yourself to Chris? He's not half the man you are. *You're* the man I'm in love with, and I can't fathom why you think you would come up short in any aspect. Believe me when I say there's not a thing I'd change about you, except maybe the fact you have a tendency to think too much, but even that's not so bad half the time.

"I wouldn't even change the fact that you're a better friend than Chris deserves. Don't give up on him. Circumstances are putting some distance between us right now, and it would be so easy to cut some of the more personal ties. I think we all need the space, but let's face it. We're the only people Chris knows who'll point him to Christ. If we give up on him, he may never find what it is we both know he's searching for and is so close to finding."

Bret hung his head for a second before lifting it again. The worry was still there, but with it was a little more reason. "You're right. We need the space, but it still doesn't make whatever he did okay."

Karen sighed. "I promise you, Bret, if it were anything more than a look, I would probably think differently, but I don't. There's a lot hanging in the balance here. Chris's salvation could be at stake. I love you, but bear with me."

Bret silently nodded that he would. "I know what you're saying is true. But…this is hard. It's especially hard not knowing when it will no longer be an issue. Have you picked a date yet?"

The tension between them shifted. Now it was Karen who was put on the spot. "Not yet, but I've been thinking about it."

"Good. We've been engaged for a few weeks now, and everyone wants to know when the big day is set. Being godly doesn't come off as the thing to do in the locker room."

Forgiveness for Yesterday

Karen sensed there was more behind his words. "Did something happen?"

Bret shook his head. "Let's just say sexual purity loses its appeal on the general public. Especially when you've got an incredibly hot fiancée waiting in the wings and no one understands why."

"Waiting isn't easy for me either." Karen sighed. "This decision will be worth it. I promise."

"I know. If you would set a date, there would be an end in sight for at least one of my miseries. Everyone would know we're serious about each other."

Karen laughed at his ploy. "Chris already knows I'm serious about you. We're engaged! No one can miss a rock the size of this one!" She held her left hand up, but Bret didn't smile.

"So set a date."

"I will, but I need more time. The kids need more time. Not more time for me to figure out if this is the right decision, more time to adjust for what's coming. Everything has happened so fast. Us getting married will be a huge change for everyone, including you. I just want to make sure you've thought it through."

"Of course I've thought it through. I wouldn't have asked you to marry me if I hadn't."

Karen ran her fingers through his hair, thinking that if he knew half of what she felt for him, Chris stealing her heart wouldn't be much of a thought. "I'm so in love with you, Bret Sears. You're the man I dream of. You're the man I want. No one else is even in the game when it comes to competing for that."

For the first time all evening, she saw his smile reach his eyes. It didn't last long as he drew her into one of the more passionate kisses they allowed themselves when the kids weren't around. Minutes later when they were both breathless, she pulled back, realizing she wanted his kisses as much as she did the laughter.

She nuzzled Bret's neck thinking she really did have to set a date. It would give all of them a timetable to work with, and it would get Bret off her back.

Bret groaned when she put some distance between them.

"It's late, and the weather is bad."

"I know. Just let me hold you." He took two cleansing breaths. "Why don't you tell me about Betsy?"

8

Bret opened his closet door and thumbed through his shirts. The bad weather had cleared, and tonight he and Karen were attending a private charity dinner hosted by Richard Velmore and Edward Klein—their prospective clients who hadn't really signed a contract with Greeson like Chris had suggested. Plates were at five hundred dollars a pop, and Bret was going to see to it that Chris personally paid him back for the tickets since he was only going as a means to smooth over the rough edges Chris's absence had caused.

Bret sighed and settled on the French blue pencil stripe and paired it with a black silk tie. In order to keep the evening on a more carefree note, Darrell had suggested cocktails beforehand, but Bret had passed. He didn't drink, and Karen was already downstairs worrying a hole in his living room rug.

He straightened his tie and went down to join her. "Stop pacing. You look beautiful," he said, taking in her simply cut black dress. It was sleeveless and had a scoop neck she had accented with a long strand of cream-colored pearls. The look wasn't flashy or overdone but elegant and reserved. It was just right.

"Thanks. I just hope I don't say the wrong thing or spill something on myself. The last time we did this I had Chris at my beck and call."

Bret cleared his throat wishing she hadn't included a reference to the man who was costing the company a small fortune. "You'll be fine. Are you ready?"

"Almost." She turned to grab her purse and pulled out a lipstick. She applied it while looking in a handheld mirror. "I like that shirt. It makes you look professional—clean cut. It reminds me of my favorite crayon."

"Hmm."

Forgiveness for Yesterday

She put the lipstick back in her purse, and he reached for her wrist. He turned it over and planted a trail of kisses along it and the inside of her arm. "Want to color with me later?"

She gave him a coy look. "Only if you promise to color *inside* the lines."

Bret dropped her hand. It might be getting harder to "color inside the lines" with Karen, but he had no problem reading between them. Her little confession the other night had haunted his thoughts pretty much nonstop. What else wasn't she telling him? He'd give an easy thousand dollars to get Chris alone in a room somewhere and beat the truth out of him.

Bret smiled at the thought as he escorted Karen to the car. Before he knew it, he had consumed a plate full of lettuce and snails and was writing out an additional sum of money from his personal checking account. "Nothing has stirred my heart more," he said to Richard Velmore that evening. "I had no idea that so many kids living in the Triad area are illiterate." He placed the check in Richard's pocket, making sure the man knew who the donation had come from. Mr. Velmore smiled, and Bret took a moment to examine the man's eyes. When he did, he felt a strange sensation creep up his spine.

"Please tell Chris that I hate he missed this evening." The man stared at Bret, willing him to give an explanation as to Chris's whereabouts. Bret could feel himself starting to sweat despite the cold warning that continued to linger on his back. "It's unlike someone who's so…*social* to miss a party."

"Yes, well, you know how it is. Business before pleasure." From that moment on, Bret felt trouble brewing. He tried to shake the feeling, but it wouldn't leave.

On Wednesday, he came home and hit the button to open his garage door, glad to have another long day with the stresses of work behind him. With Chris off playing Mr. Construction Worker, he'd already clocked forty hours, and the next two days looked to be just as bad.

Bret put the car in park and started to collect his things. Normally on Wednesdays, he would swing by Karen's apartment for a quick supper, and then they would head off to church for the midweek Bible study. But tonight he just didn't feel like it.

He entered the kitchen, set his briefcase down, and went to the drawer for a bottle of aspirin. His head was killing him. He didn't know if it was the long hours he was putting in or stress, but something was constantly eating at him. Tonight, he just wanted to be left alone in peace and quiet.

He downed a glass of water along with two pills and started for the stairs to take a long, hot shower. Before he made it off the landing, he saw headlights outside in the driveway.

"Who can that be?" he murmured in complaint. He wasn't expecting anyone, but sure enough, a knock sounded on his front door.

"Amanda," he said, opening it to find the short bubbly brunette he would recognize anywhere. "What are you doing here?"

She shifted her weight, and for the first time, Bret realized she wasn't smiling. "Can I come in?" she finally asked.

Bret opened the door, giving up on his hope for a night where he had nothing to do but crash. Whatever was on Amanda's mind strong enough to bring her by his place had to be big. Not to mention he hadn't seen nor heard from her in several weeks.

He followed her through the kitchen and into the living room where he offered her a seat on the couch. She took it but didn't come out and voice the reason for her visit.

"What's going on?" he asked, trying to speed up the process. She tugged a pillow from the corner of the sofa and hugged it to her middle. She looked up at him without saying a word, but her hands were shaking.

"Amanda, are you okay? It's not like you to beat around the bush with something. Just come right out and say whatever it is you came to say."

"I know," she said as her eyes started to pool. "It's just that…this is bad. *Really* bad." She took a deep breath and studied the floor. "I'm pregnant."

Forgiveness for Yesterday

Seeing the way her bottom lip trembled and hearing the tremor in her voice, Bret let the impact of her words sink in. "You're pregnant with Chris's baby." It was a statement, not a question.

Her head nodded, and the tears started to come in earnest. He took the seat beside her to ease some of the shock her news brought. "Amanda, I…I'm…oh, man," he said, running his hands down his face, willing the throbbing in his temples to stop. "How did this happen? I thought you guys were being careful. Does he know?"

"Of course not! Why do you think I've been so distant until he got out of town? If he finds out, he'll kill me. What am I going to do?" she cried.

Gently he took her into his arms and cradled her while an ocean of tears gushed forth. Minutes passed, and soon his shirt was completely soaked. "Amanda, it's going to be okay," he said while squeezing her shoulders. "We'll go to Chris and explain things. It won't be as bad as you think. Just wait and see. I promise, I've got your back. Together we'll make him understand."

Immediately she pulled back, her tears of despair replaced with fear. "No! Chris cannot find out about this. He hates me! The last time we were together, he…he…he practically called me a whore. He threatened me…over nothing. There's no way I can tell him I quit taking the pill so I could get pregnant."

Bret's mind started to race. "You did what! Why?"

She buried her face in her hands. "I know! It was stupid, but I couldn't think of another way to make him stay. I thought if we had a baby together, he would finally come to his senses and admit he loved me. I thought it'd make him see that we could be happy together."

Bret stared at her as if she were crazy. *That has to be dumbest thing I've ever heard*, he thought. "I…I can't believe this."

"Oh believe it. I took three tests, and they all said the same thing. I'm pregnant!"

Bret watched the way she leaned over her knees and held her head in her hands. "I think I'm going to be sick," she said.

By the time he could return with a trash can and a wet cloth for her head, she was stretched out on the couch. "What am I going to do?"

she continued to moan. "Maybe I should just go get an abortion and forget this ever happened."

"Amanda, that is *not* the answer." His mind raced with what to say as to why. "Chris is not who you think he is."

"What?" Amanda snapped and sat up. "Is this where you tell me he's the CEO of Greeson Developing, not just some glorified construction worker? I know Bret, okay? Thanks to your company's little New Year's Eve party I read all about him in the papers. I know how he inherited his father's company and is worth millions. The man spent a few hundred bucks on me the entire time we were dating. I was nothing more than a cheap thrill for him! All the more reason I hate him!"

"Amanda, I'm sorry. Really, I am, but Chris is complicated. He cared about you, maybe not in the way you wanted, but I know he did. That's why I still believe there's enough left of his character that he'll step up and do the right thing."

She let go of an evil-sounding laugh while drying her tears with her sleeve. "What's the right thing, Bret? Surely you don't think he'll marry me."

Bret shrugged his shoulders. He really didn't know what Chris would do once his anger subsided. "You've got to tell him. He deserves to know."

"This is my decision to make, not yours. There is no way Chris Lanning will have anything good to say to me once he finds out how I manipulated him, how I lied to him. You don't understand. I mean it when I say he hates me, and you're crazy if you think I'd stoop to taking even one red cent he has to offer! But that still doesn't mean I can afford to raise a baby on my own. My rent and car payment are all I can manage on my income. I can't do diapers and formula and all that...that baby stuff. I work in a dentist's office!"

She stood up and started to bite on her fingernail. "If you loan me the money for an abortion, I swear I'll pay you back, and Chris will never have to know." Her eyes met his. "This will be our little secret, and I can assure you, I've learned from my mistakes. This will never happen again. Yes," she said more to herself than to him, "it just might work."

"Would you listen to yourself? This *did* happen, and it's not going to go away just because you want it to! There is a life at stake." Bret could hear the anger in his voice but knew it would only drive her away.

"Listen," he said, standing and pulling her to himself. He made sure to keep his words measured and calm. "I won't tell Chris, just please, don't do anything rash. I'll do everything I can to help you through this, as will Karen, but I can't stand by and give my approval on something I believe with all my heart is wrong. There are alternatives. You could put the baby up for adoption."

Standing there next to her, he could almost feel her desperation. Her bottom lip trembled again, and he held her tighter.

"Bret," she breathed into his chest. "You are so good. Why can't I fall for a guy like you?"

He held her a little longer before setting her back and looking into her eyes. "I am not good, Amanda. None of us are. Chris has made some really bad choices, and I know you don't believe me, but I know if you told him, he would say the same thing I'm telling you. He would tell you not to end a life. This is his child, his flesh and blood. Please don't take it."

She studied him a moment, and he prayed she could see his advice was completely heartfelt and right. He really did have the confidence that Chris would step up and do the right thing. He might not marry her, but at the very least he would see that neither she nor the baby went without.

She stepped away from him as her eyes fell to the floor. "Promise me, Bret. Promise me you won't say a word."

"Amanda, that's not fair."

"Yes, it is." She nodded. " Knowing Chris won't find out the truth is the only way I could ever find the courage to do what you're saying is the right thing. You owe me this much for hiding all the things you knew about him from the start."

Bret weighed her words carefully. He couldn't say that he trusted her, but what choice did he have? It really was her decision to make.

"Okay, then. I won't tell him, but that's only on the promise that you won't do anything impulsive. That you'll come to me first and that we'll talk it through."

Her shoulders slouched forward, but she gave her word. "Agreed," she said, slipping her arms around his middle. "Thanks for listening. I always knew you were a keeper."

Bret walked her to the door, and just before she slipped outside, something nagged at his brain. "When are you going to tell Karen?"

Amanda turned. "I don't know. I have the feeling she'll broadcast this to everyone, including Chris, regardless of what it will cost me. I knew you'd be more...sensible. I was hoping maybe you could tell her..."

"Oh, no." Bret shook his head. "This needs to come from you."

Amanda looked troubled but agreed.

Bret added, "I have to admit I'm a little surprised you would come to me. I mean Chris and I are coworkers and friends. And I've been loyal to keep his secrets from you."

Amanda crossed her arms. "Who better to know how manipulative and cruel Chris really is?" Her expression softened. "I know you would've told me exactly who he was months ago had your job not been the price for such a confession. I can get past you keeping his secrets—but now it's time for you to keep one of mine. That will be what settles the score between us."

Bret nodded, feeling an obligation to her out of guilt for the role he'd played in Chris's deception. "I won't say anything to Chris, but please say something to Karen. Soon. I can't keep this from her for long."

Bret waited until she backed her car down the drive before he cut out the porch light and headed toward the stairs. This time he took them feeling a weight that was twice what it had been thirty minutes ago. Amanda's choices were completely irresponsible, and now she was going to have to pay for them.

He paused when he reached the top step and placed his fingers on the switch to cut out the lights below. *What a mess!* Even if he and Karen decided to become intimate before marriage, he would still have enough sense to take care of his share of the responsibilities in the matter. *Leave it to Chris. At least I've got enough sense not to get myself into some of the situations he has.*

Goose bumps rose on his arm when immediately he felt something of a warning settle over him. *Be careful if you think you stand. It's pride that goes before destruction, a haughty spirit before a fall.*

Bret rubbed his arm and turned to look down the flight of stairs he'd just climbed. The warning was from the Bible, but he wasn't proud. He'd just stood in front of Amanda and told her that he wasn't good as in by nature. No one was. And even if he were, pride wasn't always a bad thing. It all depended on the context in which it was felt. Chris was the one who would never admit to having made a mistake. Bret's mistake had been letting Chris string Amanda along.

For a second, Bret stood there wondering how Chris would try to weasel out of this. Bret flipped the switch on the wall, surrounding himself in darkness.

Telling Chris was probably the morally sound thing to do. If it were him, he'd certainly want to know.

Still, even if he were to say something about Amanda's situation, he had no idea how he would go about choosing the words that would portray the depth and sorrow that their selfishness was about to unleash on an innocent life. He was glad his promise to Amanda would keep him from having to try. And keeping his promise to Amanda was important to him. He could only pray she had the right kind of pride in her to do the same.

9

"October sounds good. What do you think?" Karen asked the question to Bret as they sat in her apartment the following Saturday afternoon studying the calendar and how the weekends fell.

"October sounds like forever and a day away. How 'bout March?"

"That's next month!"

Bret laughed. "So?"

Karen reached for the pillow behind her back and threw it at him.

"What?" he laughed again. "You've been putting off setting the date for what? Four weeks now? Decide already!"

Karen reached for the calendar he reextended to her. Bret wasn't listening to her concerns. She was going to have to go about this a different way. "Planning a wedding is going to take more than just a few weeks. If we get married right away, I'm scared you'll feel cheated."

"Cheated? Of what?"

"The perfect wedding. I don't want to just throw something together."

"How hard can it be? We pick a date, you buy a dress and then we ask some of our friends and family to attend the ceremony."

This time she laughed out loud. "True, but you're forgetting a few things." She raised her fingers to count them off. "The location, the flowers, the cake, the rehearsal, the reception, and the stress that will compound with every decision. That's not even considering where we're going to live once it's all over."

"So hire a wedding planner."

Karen considered the idea. "Don't you think that's a little impersonal? And expensive?"

"Not if you get the right person. How do you feel about eloping?"

Forgiveness for Yesterday

She paused to think about that option as well. Surely that wasn't what Bret really wanted. Being the family man he was, Karen imagined that secretly he'd dreamed of having a big wedding where his entire family could play a part. That and if she agreed to elope, he'd insist they do it next weekend. Then she'd be left without excuse.

"What do you want?" she finally asked, trying not to give her anxiety away.

On that he smiled and slipped her feet into his lap. "I want a wedding that we'll both look back on and remember as one of the happiest days of our lives. I want it to be beautiful, sentimental, and something people will talk about for weeks afterward, but that doesn't mean I want to wait till the turn of the next century to see it happen."

"Hmm," she said, watching him reach for a clipboard of paper, pen poised to write down her decision. He was set on wrestling an answer out of her. A mischievous grin played on her lips. "Go ahead and put me down as the bride. That much I'm sure of."

She laughed when he actually wrote down the word bride followed by her name just so he could check something off. From there, he threw the clipboard on the floor and moved his fingers against the bottom of her feet mercilessly.

A chorus of laughter rang up through her protest. The sound brought Holly and Scott out of their rooms in her defense. With reinforcements on her side, she was able to gain enough ground so that she could at least dig her fingers into his ribs one good time. Bret hollered at the attack and tossed Scott and Holly onto the sofa before reaching for Karen's middle.

Round and round they went until Karen was sure something was going to get broken. "Uncle!" she cried as Bret finally relented on the group.

"What're you two doing?" Holly wanted to know, her face now red from effort.

"We're planning a wedding." Karen giggled. "Got any ideas?"

Scott piped up with his. "Yeah! How about a wrestling theme? I saw that on TV once. The couple got married on a roped off platform and everything!" The image brought another round of laughs.

"Oh sure! That's every girl's dream!" Holly moaned.

Bret laughed and collected the loose paper now littering the floor. "Sounds like they were cutting to the chase if you ask me."

Karen was the only one who got his joke so she tossed another pillow at his head.

"Don't start," she warned when he threw it back at her.

"We really do need to decide on something, especially if you want to do it before fall."

They all grew quiet, and then Holly's face lit up. "What about that house we went to last year with Chris and Amanda? That would be a cool place for a wedding if it was redecorated and all."

"Sweetheart, that old house won't be ready for a wedding any time soon. Last I heard, Chris had it all torn apart." Karen looked at Bret who confirmed.

"The Heritage House is definitely out. I talked to Chris yesterday. He said they haven't even started on the demolition process. It will be months and months before it's ready to host anything, let alone our wedding." Karen and Bret could both see disappointment cover Holly's face.

"It was a good idea though. Keep thinking," Karen suggested.

"It was a good idea," Bret said, holding up his finger. "There's a place not too far from there. It's a town called Lake Lure. It's small and quaint but beautiful. My parents used to vacation there when we were kids. Most of the town borders along the lake, and it's close to Chimney Rock. I'm sure Asheville is within an hour's drive or so. There should be tons of little churches or chapels tucked away in the hills. It would be perfect."

Karen watched as he sprung into action by taking a seat at her computer. He typed something in and then called them over to see. Bret scrolled down through some links and settled on one with photos. The images she saw reminded her of things she witnessed last fall when she had gone with Bret and Chris to Asheville to scout out the project Chris was now working on. The idea of getting married somewhere so close and similar to where their relationship had started was romantic.

Forgiveness for Yesterday

Bret pulled up several pictures of tiny chapels, but nothing struck her. "I don't know," she said. "Those are all pretty, but they're all so small. It's a shame we can't just get married outside."

Bret changed the words in the search bar, and a beautiful outdoor gazebo came up.

"Wow, that's nice," Holly said, taking in a white gazebo sitting in a park that was surrounded by the lake. "You could have a fairy tale wedding there, Mom."

Karen watched Holly's eyes glaze over. "You could have this big fluffy dress covered in sequins, and I could wear something in fuschia. We'd do our hair in curls, with tiny seed pearls laced into it. You could walk down a path covered with rose petals—right up to the gazebo. Oh, Mom! Do it! Say yes! *Please!*" Holly pleaded.

Aside from the big fluffy dress, Karen found she liked the idea. The location was small enough to remain private, yet large enough to accommodate the number of guests they would want to invite. It was all conveniently located next to several cozy inns and attractions, giving everyone something to do the day before and after.

Falling in love with the idea, Karen made a decision. "Call and see if it's available for the end of October. The leaves will be gorgeous that time of year."

"True," Bret agreed, "but the kids will be back in school by then. If we get married in…say…June, then we'll have the whole summer to move in and get settled."

Karen gawked at him. "That's not even four months away. I don't know…"

"Why not, Mom?" Holly asked. "June is the perfect time for a wedding. The flowers will be in bloom, the weather will be warm. You could do one of those sleeveless gowns and get married at sunset!"

"I bet one of those hotels has a pool! Can we? Can we do it in June?" Scott was now totally on board with the idea.

Bret smiled in earnest, seeing the kids were with him on this one. "Come on, baby," he coached. "Part of marriage is compromise, isn't it? Italy will be unbelievable in the summer."

"Italy!" Holly squealed. "We're going to Italy!"

"Not you and Scott," Bret clarified. "Just your mom and me." He turned to Karen, his hopes shining in his eyes. "Please?"

"Italy? For the honeymoon? You're kidding, right?"

Bret shook his head. "I was going to make it a surprise, but...yeah. We're going to Italy."

Karen knew the decision was made. "Yes!" she finally shouted through an enormous smile.

The kids high-fived, and Bret kissed her full on the lips despite their presence.

Karen watched them laugh and carry on as they made plans to cover the time between now and then. They were so excited about everything the future held. *Yes,* she thought quietly to herself, *we're really getting married...in June.*

Forgiveness for Yesterday

10

The next day, Karen pulled her car into the drive at Amanda's house, still struggling with the fact that she had committed herself to a June wedding. No one seemed to grasp what that entailed. Hiring someone to coordinate her wedding was one thing, but the reality of it all was another matter entirely.

Usually close girlfriends lived for this sort of thing, but Amanda had made herself scarce since she and Bret had gotten more serious. Karen remembered the day she'd gone to Amanda's to share the news of Bret's proposal.

"He proposed!" she'd cried as Amanda jerked her hand over to get a closer look at her new diamond.

"Are you kidding me?" she said, holding up Karen's finger to examine the solitaire in the light. "This has got to be at least two carats!"

"Two and a quarter," Karen proudly admitted. There was more twisting and turning while Amanda performed what could only be considered a thorough inspection.

"I can't believe this. The color. The clarity. It's amazing. I bet he dropped ten grand on this thing! And you've only known him three months! Unbelievable."

Karen hadn't considered the cost, but she'd suddenly felt a little guilty for showing it off and gently pulled her hand away. "He gave it to me in the park. There was this bouquet of roses there on the bench, and this time they were all red instead of pink and red mixed. He finally told me what the colors meant. Each week when one more rose in the dozen turned red, it was his way of saying that he was falling in love with me."

Amanda still looked confused.

"Pink roses are for someone you like, but red roses…red roses are for the one you *love*. All this time Bret was slowly telling me that he loved me."

"Wow…" Amanda's expression of surprise and subtle envy turned sad. "That's probably the most romantic thing I've ever heard. You're so lucky to have a man like Bret fall for you," she said. Karen had the sense Amanda was left wishing someone, *anyone*, would say those words to her.

"Forget about him," she said to Amanda. "It's been almost two months since you and Chris broke up. The right man for you is out there. You just haven't found him yet."

The rest of their day was supposed to be spent mooning over bridal magazines, but it turned into an afternoon of carefully avoiding the subject of Bret *or* Chris. The two of them hadn't talked about it since, but Karen was sorely disappointed that Amanda hadn't shared her joy. Amanda was the closest friend she had, and she longed for her to be happy and celebrate with her.

Karen honked the horn and continued to wait for Amanda to make an appearance. Today they'd agreed to take Holly and one of her friends out for burgers and a movie.

"Where is she?" Karen said to no one in particular.

"Want me to go to the door?" Holly asked.

"No. I'll go."

Karen was about to pound on Amanda's back door when Amanda opened it. "Sorry. I overslept and got behind." She pulled her hair back into a sloppy pony tail and grabbed her purse. She was wearing an oversized sweatshirt and knit pants.

What's the deal with the baggy clothes lately? Karen mused. *She usually likes to show off her curves.*

Amanda looked from Karen to the waiting girls in the car and gave Karen a watery smile. "Look, I've been thinking. I know things have been strained between us for a few weeks now, and it's because of my reaction to your engagement. I'm sorry about that. I am happy for you and Bret…it's just…well…you deserve to be happy, and I'm a lousy friend for not showing it. It was selfish of me not to. I want us to be true friends again."

Karen felt some of the weight pressing on her lift. "I know these last few months have been hard, but things will turn around. I'm sure of it."

They shared a hug, and together they walked down the pathway to Karen's Camry. Amanda smiled and greeted the girls in the backseat in an upbeat voice. "What are we seeing today?"

Holly answered her. "We don't know, but I'm hoping there's something with Freddy Prinze Jr. in it. He is *so* cute."

"He is, isn't he?" Amanda agreed. "Did you see Johnny Depp in *Pirates of the Caribbean: The Curse of the Black Pearl* last summer? He's hot too! I can't wait for the sequel."

Karen laughed in disbelief as she backed down the drive. "You think Captain Jack Sparrow is cute?"

Amanda smiled. "Okay, so the man could stand a bath, or two, but somewhere deep down, every girl likes a bad boy, and he's public enemy number one."

Karen tried to imagine Bret wearing a black trench coat, knee-high boots, and pirating a ship. The smile on her lips spread. "Maybe so, but Mr. Sparrow could also use a haircut and a little less jewelry… and a lot less eyeliner if you ask me."

Amanda giggled. "Party pooper," she teased like one of the preteens in the backseat.

"Mom, you're so out of touch. He's an actor. He has to wear that stuff. It's not like he walks around in real life wearing all that garb! Aren't you the one who's always telling me it's what's on the inside that counts?"

Karen bristled at having her own words thrown back in her face. Holly didn't have a clue, and she was being very disrespectful. She ignored the comment. "So where are we eating?"

"Anywhere. I am starved," Amanda volunteered as she reached into her purse and popped a mini Snicker's bar in her mouth. "What?" She garbled over the mouth of caramel and nuts. "I have to keep my blood sugar up or I'll faint."

"Since when do you have problems with your blood sugar?"

"Comes and goes." Amanda shrugged.

Karen whipped the car into the first burger joint she saw. By the time they were standing in line to order, Holly was at it again. This time she was trying to put Amanda in the middle of another disagreement. "When I turn eighteen, can I get a tattoo?"

Karen looked at Holly like she'd lost her mind. "Of course not."

"Why not? Amanda has one."

"Well…"

"What's wrong with a tattoo?"

Karen looked at Amanda in exasperation. She didn't want to fight this fight. Not here, not now. "Holly…can we just drop it?"

Amanda took charge. "It's okay. I'll handle this," she whispered to Karen.

Amanda turned to Holly who was suddenly all ears. "Holly deary," Amanda said, drooping a lazy arm around Holly's shoulders. "I am a grown woman, and I'm free to do as I please. However, I did not get this way without making a few rash judgments and mistakes that I wish I could take back. My tattoo is not one of them."

Karen rolled her eyes. "I can see you're really helping me here," she muttered under her breath.

"That's not to say I don't have half a dozen friends who feel differently," Amanda continued. "This one girl I know, she went to get her boyfriend's name tattooed on her shoulder. He was Hispanic, and the artist misspelled his name. Now this poor woman has something that translates 'cottage cheese' permanently marked on her body!"

Holly and her friend gasped in horror. "No way!"

Amanda nodded in assurance. "Yep. That's why you should think twice about getting anybody's name tattooed on yourself or anything else for that matter. Something like that stays with you *forever*."

Holly and her friend walked away to secure a booth rethinking the whole tattoo idea while Amanda turned back to Karen. "Satisfied?"

Karen smiled. "Very. Was all that true?"

"Every word—except the tattoo wasn't on her shoulder. It was her..." Amanda wiggled her eyebrows and glanced at her backside. "Can you imagine?"

Karen busted out laughing. "Only you would know someone with the words 'cottage cheese' stamped on their bottom! There wasn't a birthday...or should I say expiration date tattooed under it, was there?" This time they both doubled over.

After burgers and fries, they still had thirty minutes to kill, so Karen drove them to a shopping center near the theater. Holly was completely lost in her friend while Amanda and Karen were content to window shop.

"Thanks for helping me out back there with Holly. It's like she's trying to discover new ways she can manipulate me—like putting me in awkward situations where I'll be forced to agree with her." Karen looked back at the whispering girls. "I'm sure that's what she's doing now. Coming up with some new way to corner me."

"It's okay," Amanda said. "I was exactly the same way with my mother. It helps her establish her boundaries when she challenges authority and they respond. One day when Holly's a grown woman, who's free to do as she pleases, I think you'll be very proud of her." Amanda snickered. "Tattoos and all."

Karen quirked a smile at her. "Please!"

They continued to walk until they passed by a window displaying a mannequin wearing a beautiful flowing sundress. "Oh, this is so you," Karen told her. "Go in and try it on."

Amanda shook her head, but Karen forced her into the store and pulled Amanda's size off the rack. She selected one in aqua, then paused to consider the canary yellow. "Both of these would look great on you," Karen breathed. "You can wear anything."

She studied the items and then handed Amanda the yellow dress, wondering how the color would look in a bridesmaid gown. "Not just anyone can do yellow, but I think you can pull it off. You've got the right skin tones."

"You think?" Amanda said, taking the garment and admiring herself in a nearby mirror.

"Definitely. Everything looks good on you. I wish I had your shape."
Karen looked back at the dress rack. "With Bret's love for carbs, and
us eating out nearly every evening, I've gained at least seven pounds
since Thanksgiving. I've got to get back to the gym."

"Me too," Amanda murmured before disappearing into the
dressing room that was nestled in the corner of the shop. Karen
browsed, enjoying the new spring fashions that seemed to be displayed
extra early this year. The colors were a breath of fresh air, contrasting
with the drab colors of winter she was used to wearing. Now if only
the weather would cooperate. Ideas for her wedding consumed her
thoughts, and she was suddenly glad she and Bret had chosen to have
a summer wedding.

When Amanda emerged, Karen came over to admire the dress.
"This looks great. I *love* the yellow. It's almost like you're glowing.
Wonder how a bridesmaid gown would look in this color? We set the
date for June."

She watched Amanda's chin start to quiver, and immediately, she
slammed the dressing room door in Karen's face.

For a moment, Karen was speechless. "Amanda, I'm sorry. I promised
myself I wouldn't mention the wedding. It just slipped out."

Soft snubs echoed up from the opposite side of the door, a sure
sign Amanda was crying over something more than a slip of her
tongue. "Amanda? What's wrong? We don't have to do yellow. I can
choose something else. It was only an idea. You *are* going to be in the
wedding, aren't you?"

"Oh it's no use. I can't hide it anymore. Everyone knows!"

"Knows what?" There was more crying but no answer. Karen
looked up to see Holly and her friend at the front of the store trying
on sunglasses and hats. "Amanda, let me in!"

She heard metal slip through the latch, and she tucked herself inside
the tiny cubby and bolted the door back. "Amanda, what's wrong?
Why are you crying? And what's this got to do with my wedding?"

Tears streamed down Amanda's face. "This has *nothing* to do with
your wedding! I'm pregnant! Oh, what am I going to do?"

Karen felt like someone punched her in the gut. Talk about being out of the loop. "You're *pregnant*?" Her eyes drifted down Amanda's figure and rested on her abdomen in disbelief.

Amanda huffed at her doubt and pulled the cotton fabric of the dress taunt over her hips and stomach. "I'm starting to show!"

Karen's hands covered her mouth. She had put on a few pounds, but there was barely any evidence of what Amanda was proclaiming. "Are you sure?"

Amanda simply stared at her, and Karen realized how stupid she sounded. "Of course you're sure. How far along are you?"

Amanda shrugged. "I don't know. Ten weeks, give or take."

"Why didn't you say something? Does Chris know?"

"Of course he doesn't know!" Amanda hissed.

"Then you've got to tell him."

"No! This is exactly why I didn't tell you sooner. I knew you'd freak out."

"I'm not…freaking out…this is just…a surprise. Give me a second. This is a lot to take in."

"Yeah, well you've got about two minutes before Holly and her friend start to look for us."

Karen stood there debating what to do. The course of action Amanda needed to take was suddenly clear. She just didn't know how to convince her of it. "I still think you need to tell Chris. Together the two of you—"

"No! There is no way I'm telling Chris anything. After what he's done to me, he doesn't deserve to know. If he knew, he would kill me. You said yourself this is a lot to take in. After you've had time to think about this, I'm sure you'll see where I'm coming from." Amanda started jerking her clothes up out of the floor as another wave of tears unleashed. "He absolutely cannot know!"

"Okay, okay. You're right," Karen said as she drew her into a tight hug. "We'll take time and think about what to do. First, we'll get you to a doctor."

Amanda breathed a sigh in her ear. "I'm sorry I didn't tell you sooner, but I don't need you to give me some sort of lecture. Bret's already given me one. I just need some time to think about my options. With Chris in the way, I'll just get confused."

Karen felt like Amanda had punched her yet again. She drew back to study Amanda's eyes. "Bret knows about this?"

Amanda suddenly looked like a frightened animal that had been backed into a corner. Her mouth came open, but nothing came out.

As if on cue, there was a tap on the door. "Mom? The movie starts in ten minutes. We need to get going if we're going to get good seats."

"Be right out," Karen chirped with a happiness she didn't feel. "We are not done with this discussion," she warned Amanda, then left so she could get dressed.

When Amanda came out, she shoved the dress back on the rack. Karen caught her arm and felt truly sorry for her initial reaction. It hurt that Amanda had chosen to tell Bret first, and worse, that he'd kept this from her. But she couldn't bail on her friend. Not when she knew what lay ahead. "Amanda, I'm sorry. I had no idea. I'm just a little shocked." A little wasn't true, but Karen didn't make the correction. "We'll work through this together."

A single tear slipped down Amanda's cheek as Karen pulled her into another hug. "I love you, and whatever happens, you know Bret and I will help you through this." More tears slipped down Amanda's pretty face, and Karen wiped them away.

"Shush. Don't cry," Karen said. "Somehow...someway...God is going to work everything out. Just you wait and see."

11

Monday afternoon Bret sat at his desk and tapped a pen to his calendar. He'd just hung up the phone with Lake Lure Town Hall. Morse Park was unavailable the first weekend in June but May 29 was open. Surely Karen wouldn't mind moving the date up one week? Not when it would work out perfectly with Memorial Day being the following Monday. Bret remembered her surprised when he'd mentioned Italy for their honeymoon. He'd really gone out on a limb with that one.

Later when the kids weren't around, she'd questioned him about it a second time. "Italy? Are you sure? It's so far away, and so expensive."

"Quit worrying about it. This is a once in a lifetime kind of trip."

He refused to be put off by her reluctance mostly because he'd already paid a deposit. All he had to do was give the travel agent the dates.

He circled May 29 on his calendar in red and then marked through the weeks before and after it. This is it! My wedding day!" He wanted nothing more than to make Karen his wife. If he had it his way, they would walk down the aisle after church next Sunday.

Thinking of her, he picked up the phone and punched in her number. The call immediately went to voice mail, just like it had the other four times he had tried to call this morning. Come to think of it, they'd only spoken briefly the night before.

"Hey, sweetheart," he said, deciding to give it another shot. "It's me again. I guess you're tied up in some kind of meeting at work. Call me. I've got great news about the park."

He hung up with a vague feeling that something was wrong. Whatever it was, he was sure it wasn't anything major. Karen was the perfect woman for him. There were times when he felt like she knew exactly what it was he needed to hear and then went to the trouble of saying it.

The day wore on, and by five o'clock, Bret still hadn't heard from her. He tore out of the office intent on driving straight to her place. He opened his car door and was startled to hear Karen say his name. Her Camry was parked beside him.

"Karen! What on earth? I've been trying to call you all day."

She stared up at him from the open window, and she looked angry. "Get in. We need to talk."

Suddenly it dawned on him what this was about. She knew about Amanda. The two of them had gone to the movies yesterday, and Amanda must have told her.

Bret loosened his tie and threw it in the backseat of his car along with his briefcase. He expected Karen to be upset, but he could already tell she was going to be very childish about the way she handled her disappointment.

He strode around her car and got in on the passenger side. The inside was hot despite the cool temperatures outside. "What's wrong?" he asked, trying to play it safe.

"When were you going to tell me Amanda was pregnant? I can't believe you would keep this a secret from me!"

"Me? You're the one keeping secrets with *Chris*."

Karen gasped in horror. Bret really had no idea where the comment had come from, but it was too late. The words were said.

"I'm not keeping secrets. It was one look. *One look!*" she reiterated. "I didn't mention it because I knew you would overreact, just like you're doing now."

"*I'm* overreacting? You're the one who won't take my calls! Why should telling you Amanda is pregnant be my responsibility? She's your friend too! If she wanted your help, she would've come to you first."

Bret regretted those words too. They came out harsher than he intended. Whatever Karen was going to say, she bit her lip to keep it from happening. Instead she let go of an exasperated sigh and turned to face the window.

Forgiveness for Yesterday

"I'm sorry. I didn't mean it that way—"

"I've never seen her so desperate, Bret. She feels completely alone in this. I've tried to convince her to talk to Chris, but she won't hear of it. She says the only way she can even consider putting the baby up for adoption is with him being completely out of the picture."

Bret took the statement to mean Amanda's thinking had cleared and her first ideas of having an abortion were no longer being considered. He was glad she'd listened to reason.

"Chris should know."

"I felt the same way at first…but now I'm not so sure," he told Karen. "Chris should know, but now is not the time. There's still too much unsettled emotion between the two of them, and it's likely to keep her from making a rational decision. As long as Amanda knows she has our support, I'm hoping she will feel safe enough to think through her actions and decide what's best for everyone."

"What *is* best for everyone?" Karen questioned.

Bret wished he had an answer. Karen was always so steadfast and uncompromising. He should probably be more like her, but this was a very complicated situation. For some reason, there didn't seem to be a black and white, a definite side he should stand on. All he knew was that Amanda should carry to term and not telling Chris about the baby was the best way he knew how to convince her to stand by that decision. The rest would come in time.

"All I know is that this isn't going to work itself out overnight. Amanda has personal issues and Chris has even bigger ones. It's not like a baby is going to magically fix all their problems. My guess is when Amanda shows up with a kid who looks just like him, he'll be forced to deal with some things. All we can do until then is be there for her."

Karen took a deep breath and leaned back in her seat. "What if she gives the baby up and never tells him? God forbid, what if she has an abortion, and Chris never finds out? It breaks my heart to think we're the only ones standing between him knowing he has a son or daughter."

"Karen," Bret said, trying to be as gentle and logical as he knew how to be, "I really don't think abortion is something Amanda is considering. Maybe at first, but now that she knows she has us for support...threatening to tell Chris could open up that line of thinking for her.

"Regardless, we are not the ones responsible for making this decision. Like it or not, Amanda is the only one who has the power to make that choice. She chose to sleep with him, and now she has to face the consequences. If she chooses to keep the baby and involve Chris, we both know it will become a source for manipulation between the two of them. Face it. This child is not going to have an easy life. There will be no romantic wedding for Chris and Amanda and no ideal family for their child to grow up in—at least not with the two of them as parents.

"Whatever the solution, my promise not to tell Chris is so that she'll come to some sort of rational decision on her own."

"Are you sure? Chris would never let her give up their child or abort it."

"Trust me, a baby is more news than Chris can deal with right now."

"Why? What's going on?"

Bret let his gaze fall on something outside the car. The last thing he wanted to tell Karen about was his day and the disturbing meeting Darrell had called not even an hour ago. Chris had been gone for two weeks, and so far, he'd spent everything they allotted for his living expenses and then some.

"Chris spent ten grand off the bat, making renovations to some old cabin on the property just so he can have a place to stay. Nothing he's done has added any value to the estate!" Darrell had complained in an outrage. "At this rate, that old house is going to cost us ten times what it's worth!" He then assigned it as Bret's responsibility to find out where and how they could make up for the lost funds.

"Let's just say this project of his is off to a rocky start, and no one's happy about it."

"You've seen his plans, right? He can make it work."

In no way did Bret want to belittle Karen, but she simply didn't understand the business. "The more money Greeson pumps into this dead-end project, the more unsettled our board of directors is getting. Chris's total lack of interest in securing new, profitable business that could take Greeson to the next level is sending a very loud message to everyone in the industry." *An evidence that can be easily seen in the falling price of my stock*, Bret thought. "It's a sad realization that both my job and retirement rest in the hands of a man who seems bent on destruction. I guess I should've told you, but the last thing I want to do is announce to anyone that Chris has a baby on the way with a woman who can give his already questionable image a really nasty spin. It would only further escalate the problems the company is already seeing because of him."

Even though his confession was selfish, he could immediately see the fight leave Karen. "I'm sorry. I didn't know. I still don't understand why Amanda didn't trust me with this first. I hated finding out that you kept something from me. Especially something this big. I was starting to feel like we weren't on the same team anymore."

Bret gave her a weary smile. Despite their disagreement, he was still head over heels for her. "We will always be on the same team. I only found out myself just last week."

"Really?"

"Honest." Bret leaned in close. "Now is the time to wait. When the time comes to tell Chris about the baby, the three of us can do it together. That will be the best way. I'm sure of it."

Karen touched her forehead to his. "Thank you. Promise me you won't keep something like this from me again."

A gentle kiss passed between them. "Promise."

12

A brief break in the cold weather graced the Carolinas, and that meant clear blue skies and warm sunshine despite the early March date on the calendar. It was also the last weekend Chris planned to be in for several months. Because the weather was warm, and at Karen's insistence, Bret called and invited Chris, Shelby, and Kyle to meet up with him, Karen, and the kids at the park.

As soon as Chris and his kids strolled up, Karen noticed the change. Even though Chris had been back to the office a couple of times since leaving, this was the first time she had seen him since his going-away meal back in January.

Today, standing out in the bright sunshine, there was no denying a change. Chris had easily dropped ten to fifteen pounds and was in desperate need of a shave and a haircut.

"Mom, he could pass for Jack Sparrow's brother," Holly whispered in bewilderment.

Karen allowed herself an amused chuckle, but she also told herself not to stare.

"Hey, stranger," she said as she snatched a basketball away from Chris and tried to make a layup. Instead of the ball going in the hoop, it bounced off the backboard and nearly whacked her in the head. Luckily she ducked just in time.

A deep sound rumbled from Chris's chest, and he drew her into a friendly headlock. "I see you're still as clumsy as ever." He took the ball and gave her a personal escort to the nearby bleachers. "Stay," he instructed her like a puppy.

Karen bit her tongue. The incident was embarrassing, but Chris did have a point. She wasn't cut out for sports, and they all knew it.

Forgiveness for Yesterday

Instead of nursing her bruised feelings, she did what she was told and cheered for Scott. With some direction from Chris, he was able to make two shots in a row.

"Way to go, honey!" she encouraged her son.

"Mom, Shelby, and I are heading over to the swings," Holly said.

"Okay. Stay in sight."

Scott put up another shot, and it bounced off the rim. "It's okay, buddy," Bret said. "Here, try again."

The girls took off, and Scott positioned himself as Bret instructed. His arms looked pale and skinny after a winter spent in long sleeves. Karen really should have insisted he wear a coat. Karen held her breath willing the ball to go in. When it did, she clapped. "Awesome, baby. Keep it up, and you'll be next year's star player!"

"At least he's not got his mother's talent," Chris kidded, putting up a shot that was nothing but net. "Must take after his dad. Speaking of dads, how is *Brad*?"

Karen stuck out her tongue at him, then forced a smile. "You'll be happy to know that after many grueling conversations with my mother, he's no longer a significant part of the picture."

"That's too bad. An older brother figure in your life would be good for you."

Karen shook her head. "I think that's what I've got you for."

The boys played a game of H-O-R-S-E, and eventually they got tired of chasing the ball down. Scott and Kyle wandered down to the edge of the pond to look at the fish. Karen watched them for a while, deciding that Scott was really starting to shoot up in height. His brownish blond hair was darkening, and it set off his soft brown eyes. He was starting to look more and more like Eric instead of just acting like him. She wondered if one day someone would mistake him as Bret's biological son. The similarities were certainly there.

She turned her attention to the game that had started between Chris and Bret. Somehow being alone on the court had turned things serious. Listening to their manly antics and competitive spirit brought her a few good but stifled laughs. Names like "Mamma's Boy" and "Jolly Green Giant" rolled from their mouths. She knew they were just kidding, but if she told another woman she was a "Prissy Sissy," she'd get her eyes clawed out.

She decided not to debate on the differences between the male and female. The list was too long and the day was too pretty. Karen tipped her head back enjoying the rays the sun put across her face. There hadn't been much snow during the winter months—just enough ice to make everything wet and sloppy when it melted away by midafternoon.

She passed another look to the boys back at the water's edge. As if feeling her gaze, Scott stood and faced her. "Don't worry, Mom," he called, "we won't get too close." There was a look on his childlike face that said he was serious. Was she really that predictable? So much so her kids knew what she was going to say before she said it?

Turning back to the game, she decided that might not be such a bad thing. Karen sat for a while, admiring the way Bret moved around the court with ease. Their lives had been under constant change for the last six months. It was hard to imagine that in three more months they would be married. *God, are we ready for this?* The woman with "A Date to Remember" sure didn't think so. They had everything from food, flowers, and music to select, and Karen was at a loss on how to decide on any of it.

And then there was the honeymoon. On top of all the logistics of planning a wedding out of town, she just didn't see the sense in flying out of the country the day after it was over. Once the thrill of the idea wore off, Karen found she wanted something much more practical.

"We should stay at the lake where we can relax and enjoy ourselves," she'd eventually told Bret and then pleaded her case from the financial perspective. "Think of all the money we'll save on plane tickets if we sightsee and tour around the mountains instead." It had taken awhile, but after a few days, he'd reluctantly given in.

"Swear to me that we will go for our one year anniversary."

"Agreed," Karen had said, feeling a little guilty for disappointing him but was glad to see how he responded to her needs.

She studied Bret a little harder, wondering about the ways he handled pressure. Every day his job was becoming more demanding, so much so that he'd almost given up his volunteer position at church.

There were a number of other things on his plate, and with their marriage, that number would double. He assured her that he was fine with the way their relationship had progressed so quickly, but she wasn't sure he realized what he'd be getting in the mix. Two kids and a spouse were a lot to answer for. Not all men who had been bachelors as long as Bret had would handle that big of a change seamlessly.

"I know exactly what being married to you is going to be like," he said one evening, "wonderful." Still, Karen was smart enough to know that wonderful took work, lots and lots of continuous work actually. He'd gone on to assure her that together their faith would endure anything and that starting out with a family would only be an added blessing.

Chris jumped up and blocked Bret's shot before bringing an elbow down across Bret's shoulder. Karen sucked in her breath and saw Bret wince in pain. He shook it off and kept playing. *In thirty years, will he still call me wonderful?* She let go of a sigh, hoping it would be true.

Her thoughts shifted, and she focused in on Chris. She had been praying for him constantly, and if his physical appearance were any indication, her prayers were not being answered.

With Chris distracted by the game, she let her eyes roam over him, taking in the details that made her want to stare in surprise earlier. Even though Chris had lost some weight, she couldn't help but to notice how his T-shirt was stretched tight along his shoulders and arms. Chris had always been well built and athletic, she couldn't deny that, but now there was a ruggedness to him that practically exuded danger. Amanda's words rang in her ears. *"Everyone likes a bad boy,"* she'd insisted.

Karen felt heat rush into her cheeks. Chris definitely fit that description, but she couldn't help but to wonder what bad boy things would cause the dark circles under his eyes and the constant tick in his jaw. It didn't take a rocket scientist to see that Chris could knock back a beer or two, or six. For the first time, Karen wondered if he had moved on to something more. To hear Bret talk, Chris was having the time of his life blowing through his company's money, but for someone high on life, Chris sure looked like death. That could mean a number of things.

Karen dismissed her thoughts, fearful of the strange connection she felt to him. If he were using, it would definitely complicate things regarding Amanda and the baby, as well as the issues Bret confided in her that were going on at Greeson.

Right now Karen had enough to deal with seeing that Amanda got proper prenatal care. "I'm not an invalid," Amanda had said when Karen tried to make good on her word by making her a doctor's appointment at the best clinic in town.

Karen had been hurt by the rejection but was relieved to know that Amanda had kept the appointment and was now on a handful of vitamins and entering into her fourteenth week of pregnancy. She had even promised to be her bridesmaid regardless of the fact that come the end of May she would be over six months pregnant.

More taunts from the court caused Karen to look up. Bret was getting stomped. Rather than sit around watching Chris mop the court with her Prince Charming, she stood to move down to the water with the boys so Bret could save face. She heard one of them call out the score being 7–2 and decided to take a long walk instead.

The ball slammed into the concrete as Chris railroaded past Bret and went in for another layup. "Nine to four," Bret heard him chant. His shoulder was still pounding from Chris's earlier assault.

Bret noticed the changes in Chris long before they got on the court, but now that they'd been playing hard for more than twenty minutes, he was keenly aware of each one of them. Most of their games at the gym weren't this intense. Neither did he remember Chris being so fast or having this kind of endurance.

Making his way back under the basket, Bret was able to block Chris's next shot and steal the ball away from him. He dribbled out to attempt a long shot, but Chris was all over him.

Not able to get by, he opted for talking it out, "Man, you're killing me out here! If that's not a foul, I don't know what is."

Chris didn't take the bait. In fact, he didn't say anything. Again, Bret tried to get by and took an elbow in the ribs. Bret clutched his side and tried not to swear out loud. "What do you think this is, basketball or boxing?"

Chris stole the ball, and his shot was flawless. "Working sixteen hour days tends to separate the men from the boys, huh? That makes it 10–4." He smirked and went to grab the rebound. "How's it feel to get spanked in front of your girlfriend?"

The reference to Karen sent adrenaline pumping through Bret's veins. He wasn't going down without a fight. Not in front of Karen. He turned all of his attention to the game and gave his best effort. He scored another two points but was only able to block one of Chris's shots. As he went in for his next basket, Chris snatched the ball and elbowed him hard in the side and didn't stop as he went in for a layup.

"I believe that's the game," Chris said as he grabbed the ball and wiped his forehead with the back of his hand. "Want to go again?" he challenged Bret, who was still lying on the ground.

Bret refused the hand he offered and stood on his own. He didn't reply but put his head between his legs and gasped for air. He discretely scanned the area for Karen and was glad that she had stepped away while Chris finished him off. Whatever was eating at Chris, it was obvious he was being used as an outlet. He had been cocky and arrogant all through the game. Some of it was to be expected, but this was unprecedented. Some of those blows were on purpose.

"Man, what's wrong with you? You're acting like a jerk!"

"That's just your wounded pride talking. Don't be such a sore loser!"

Bret wiped his hands on his shirttail. The comment made him mad. "Sixteen hour days? Doing what? You've hardly got started on that place."

"How would you know? You and Darrell are so busy breathing down my neck about how much it's costing, I'm surprised you've had time to think of anything else." Chris put up another shot. Again, it was nothing but net.

"We are not breathing down your neck. You're the one who saw fit to sink a boat load of money in a property that's falling apart faster than you can rebuild it! I still can't understand why you would take junk off a guy like Clay. He's nothing more than a kid!" When Chris didn't retaliate, Bret kept on. "Why can't you just admit it?"

Chris stopped dribbling the ball and came over to stand in front of him. All the thrill of his win was gone, and it told Bret he hit his mark.

"Admit what?"

"That you're running. You're still running from Laurie Callahan and every decision you've made since then."

"I am not!"

"Yes, you are. Look at yourself. You're a total mess."

"Gee, thanks." Chris's sarcasm couldn't be missed.

"I'm serious," Bret said, trying to keep the conversation on track. "You look like crap. Are you using?"

This time Chris laughed. "You think I can manage to show up to work each day at 5 a.m. and control the bunch of babies you've got me working with while I'm on dope?"

When Bret didn't answer, Chris grew amused.

"I'd like to see you out there swinging a hammer for a living. You wouldn't make it one day!"

"Maybe. Maybe not. Not that I think you'd do so hot back at the office these days. Yesterday we got a letter from Velmore and Klein's lawyer. Seems they're weaseling out of their contract."

Bret enjoyed the way the news brought Chris to a standstill.

"They can't do that! They know we'll sue."

"Oh, yeah? They're claiming false pretense. Seems they were none too pleased when they found out you'd skipped town to work on a pile of junk out in the middle of nowhere instead of building their multimillion-dollar shopping center on prime real estate! You were part of the deal. Wake up! Our stock is dropping like flies!"

"Why is it my fault that Darrell promised them the moon and then expected me to deliver? He knew I was committed elsewhere. And the Heritage House is not some pile of junk…it's the ticket out of here."

Bret threw up his hands in exasperation. "That's where you're wrong. It's *your* ticket out of here. What I don't get is why you think you *need* a ticket out of anywhere. You have everything you could possibly want—power, position—but you won't stand up and take ownership! Why?"

"Because I'm miserable, that's why!" Chris snapped. "I have everything I *should* want except *her*!"

"So this is about Laurie! Did it ever occur to you that your problems are starting to take the rest of us down with you? Bad stuff happens. People leave. Get over it already! And while you're at it, you can keep your hands *off* my fiancée!"

Chris looked like he'd been slapped. "I've never put my hands on Karen."

"Yeah, well we both know it isn't because you don't want to!"

Chris flexed his jaw and looked away for a moment. "That is low. That is *very* low. But let me ask you something since you seem to think you know everything." He took another step closer and got in Bret's face. "If all this is about Laurie, then why can't I get her out of my head! If I'm running so hard then why am I not getting anywhere? You seem to think you have all the answers, Bret, so how do I simply, 'get over it'? And another thing, if I'm the one who has everything, you should be quick to remember that *I'm your boss!* Maybe you should start showing me some *respect*."

On the last word, Chris took two hands and shoved him hard in the chest. It wasn't enough to knock him down, but he had to take a step backward in order to keep his balance.

Before Bret could unleash the blow he wanted to deliver to Chris's jaw, Chris jerked away and grabbed the ball and his jacket from the ground. Heading toward the truck, he yelled at Shelby and Kyle. "Come on! We're leaving!"

Bret stood there trying to process what had happened as he unclenched his fist. "Coward!" he mumbled. Whatever it was that was tearing Chris apart from the inside out wasn't getting any better with time. In fact, it was getting worse.

He looked up to see Chris's back retreating across the park with Kyle and Shelby running along behind him trying to catch up. It was obvious how Chris's inability to cope had ruined Amanda's life, but he couldn't help to wonder what price Shelby and Kyle were paying.

Disgusted with the whole situation and the fact that he still wanted to chase Chris down and beat some sense into him, he wiped his brow and he uttered a curse word. He should be embarrassed for the way he'd lost his temper, but right now, he was too mad to feel anything but anger. In the past he would've prayed, but him and God weren't exactly on speaking terms these days.

"Bret?"

"What!" Bret snapped in reflex. It was Karen. "I'm sorry. It's just… now is not a good time."

Seeing he needed his space, Karen took a seat on the bottom of the bleachers and waited. Tense seconds passed, and he joined her. "I'm sorry. This has nothing to do with you," he said.

"I know. Let me guess. It has to do with Laurie."

This time Bret was the one who did a double take. "You know about Laurie?" For a split-second he was angry with her. He thought he knew all her secrets. "Amanda must have told you."

"Actually, Chris mentioned her once. No one knows what it's like to be dealt the unsuspecting blow of loss more than I do and the disappointment that follows. The last thing you want is the world to cater you a pity party. All you want to do is move on but some days you just don't know how."

Karen continued, "I didn't ask you about her because I didn't want to put you in the position where you had to choose where your loyalties would fall—to Chris or to me."

Karen moved closer and reached for his hand. "I can tell Chris's heart is broken, and he doesn't know how to handle it. He really needs a friend right now. What I don't understand is what kind of woman walks out on everything? And two weeks before her wedding? You knew Laurie too, right?"

Bret was silent for several seconds not having an answer as to why Laurie had done what she had. "Yes, but that doesn't mean I understand her. Chris has never been a saint, but he wasn't always the player you know him to be either. Just as Amanda draws out the worst in him, Laurie drew out the best. In some weird way, I think you

Forgiveness for Yesterday

remind him of her. You're the first woman he's met in a long time with enough backbone in her to stand up to him."

Karen smiled. "Laurie was like that?"

"Yes. Don't get me wrong. Laurie was a little on the quiet and shy side, or at least she was like that until you got to know her, but with Chris, it was like she drew a line in the sand and then dared him to cross it. In a world where he was handed everything, that was a first for him. It made Chris a better man—for a while at least." Bret sighed and leaned back on his elbows, wishing the change had been more than temporal.

"That's funny. I imagine Laurie to be a lot like Shelby. She's so energetic and talkative."

"Shelby tries very hard. The way Chris is running his life into the ground now is probably some kind of psychological fallout from Laurie leaving or from the way he was raised. Abandonment resonates strongly with Chris."

"I know Chris was adopted, but how was he brought up?"

"Chris lost his biological mom to the streets before he was five. He never knew his dad. He ended up spending a few years in foster care before Robert and Victoria Lanning took him in. They gave him everything he ever wanted, but you've heard the stories of kids who've been adopted. I don't think he ever felt wanted for all the right reasons—like he was where he belonged. I'm not sure he was ever able to erase those three years when he belonged to no one.

"When his parents died unexpectedly in a car wreck and he inherited Greeson, Chris immediately had a world full of people who wanted nothing more than to please him. Sometimes it's hard for him to tell what's genuine and what's an act. He needs what people call tough love. That's the reason he's so reserved when it comes to things of a personal nature."

Karen shook her head. "That is so sad. But it makes so much sense."

"It is sad, but Chris is so used to having someone come in and clean up his mess that he assumed raising Shelby and Kyle would be an easy thing to do, but it's not. He needs to wake up and realize he's the one responsible for dealing with his mistakes."

"What mistakes?"

"There are several." Bret paused in order to find honest words. It would be so easy for him to paint Chris in a bad light. "I'd say his first one was his motive for adopting Laurie's kids. It isn't as noble as it appears."

"Meaning?"

"He knew becoming their legal guardian would give him control. He made it all happen really fast just so he'd have some sort of power over Laurie in case she did change her mind. That's why I know he'll do the same thing again with Amanda and their child. Ugh!" Bret said in disgust at the realization. "Why can't anyone see what he's doing? A baby with Amanda will be one more hand for him to play. Nothing good will come of it!"

Karen was quiet for a few moments. "I don't know. I see something genuine in Chris when he's with Shelby and Kyle. I'm still praying that this will work out. That God will show Chris a greater love. Maybe a baby is part of that."

"That's just it. I feel bad because as much as I want to write Chris off, I know I can't. I really do care about him. He's like a brother to me, but there's a lot more at stake here than a couple of mixed up emotions. Chris is doing everything he can to get his mind off dealing with his problems, and he's dragging his job into it. You know that affects me. These days *I'm* the one who's cleaning up after him." Bret shook his head, more troubled than ever. "Honestly, Karen, I'm not sure how much longer I can handle this."

"What're you saying?"

Bret kicked himself mentally. He had said too much. Karen would worry. "Nothing."

"Do you really expect me to believe that?"

Bret felt his shoulders slump. "Things with this pet project of his have gone from bad to worse. Darrell is threatening to get the board of directors to act if Chris doesn't get his head in the game—and soon. I can't say that I blame him. If it comes to that, I'm going to have to choose the right side to be on. Unfortunately, I can't say that it'll be Chris's."

"Chris is the CEO. Can Darrell really take the company away from him?"

"If he can prove Chris's actions are a threat to the company and our stockholders' investments, he most certainly can. It won't happen without a nasty fight, but it's already in the works. I can feel it. Darrell and Chris are close enough that for a long time Darrell has chosen to look the other way, but he's starting to lose his patience."

"What about that big deal that was supposed to go through with that investing firm? Velmore and something?"

"I tell you, Karen, investors can be just as slippery as lawyers. They're not my favorite people. That's a bad feeling to have when they're the ones who make up the majority of your clients." Bret let go of another breath of frustration after raking his fingers through his hair. "What am I going to do? I feel so trapped."

Karen was silent for a long time, and Bret knew this time he really had said too much. "I'm sorry. I shouldn't throw all of this to you at once. It's not as bad as it sounds…I just—"

"Chris has a way of making things look just like he wants them to. He's really good at it. He's an excellent manipulator, and from what you're telling me, I know you aren't the only one he's manipulating. Sooner or later this is all going to come crashing in on him. I'm sorry, though. I know that account was going to be a big break for you guys. You shouldn't feel bad for telling me."

"Well if Chris doesn't get his act together, we could all be looking for a break somewhere else. I'm being honest when I say I've never seen him this low. There's no telling how far he'll take this."

"At least we can pray." She laced their fingers together and lifted up words that Bret knew were straight from her heart—her good and pure heart. "Lord, help Chris. He is so lost, and he's searching so hard. Make it obvious to him. Make it obvious that you and your forgiveness are what he's searching for. That he can't let go of his past and have hope for the future without first finding you. Heal his heart and restore his hope. In Jesus's name, amen."

When they lifted their heads, Bret felt stronger just for having Karen near him. They would get through this together. After all, they were a team.

"I love you, do you know that?" he asked, leaning over to give her a kiss.

She smiled for a moment before he saw a teasing glint in her eye. "I love you too, but man"—she pinched her nose closed—"I sure am glad this isn't a side of you I see often!"

"Are you saying I smell?"

"Profusely."

He grabbed her and rubbed the side of his wet face along hers for good measure. "Stop it! That's so disgusting!" She laughed, wiping away the sticky moisture. It was the sound he needed to send his troubles scurrying to the shadows.

They stood and grabbed their things and went off to find the kids. Hand in hand they made their way back to the car. At least Bret could be thankful for how this storm was bringing him and Karen closer together.

❧

Chris stared straight ahead, wishing the traffic light would hurry up. The quicker he got home, the better.

"What's wrong, Dad?" Kyle asked from the backseat.

"Nothing," he snapped, shooting his son a look that said to drop it.

Both Kyle and Shelby remained silent till Chris pulled up around the back of their house. On second thought, home wasn't where he wanted to be either. Chris waited till the kids got out and told them he'd be back in a few hours. He backed down the driveway and spun out of view.

Velmore and Klein were backing out? No wonder Bret was so agitated.

Anger flooded his system causing him to drive faster than was safe through what was a restricted area. He told himself to slow down, that it was all a matter of control, and control he could do—on the road, and in the office. Instantly a calm came over him. All he had to do was meet with Edward and Richard in person, make a few promises, and then feel his way through the situation from there.

Chris followed the streets into town, and the next thing he knew he was only a few blocks over from Amanda's. *What would it hurt*, he questioned himself. She was the only one who had ever been able to bring him any kind of happiness in the past. And she was a good listener. She was probably willing to spare him a few moments because even to him, their last parting seemed overly dramatic. The least he could do was offer an apology and redeem himself in her eyes.

He turned down Mottford and then onto Chestnut where he parked beside a car he didn't recognize. Her yellow Xterra was in the drive, so he started rehearsing his lines. He was smoothing out the words for the second time when he gently knocked on the back door. It was when she opened it that her eyes widened in surprise, and fear filled her face. The reaction made him feel terrible.

"Amanda. Hey. I was in the neighborhood and I…" His eyes shifted down in shame, and he immediately realized she'd gained some weight. But that wasn't all. He didn't know how he knew, but he did. Suddenly everything he'd been planning to say in apology escaped him.

"You're pregnant," he said in a quiet whisper of question as some sort of trance fell over him. Once again his eyes met hers, and he could see the fear in her double.

"Ch-Chris," she stammered and backed away as he jerked the screen door from her hand to get a better view of her abdomen.

"You're pregnant!" he said again in confirmation, all the tender tones from his voice gone. "You lying little…were you not going to tell me?"

Any answer she would've given was cut off as the door jerked open behind her and a lanky figure suddenly appeared by her side. "Is there a problem out here?"

It was some guy he didn't know, and judging by the arm he protectively placed on Amanda's shoulder, Chris knew he was probably in the dark on more than just Amanda's pregnancy.

"Luke, this is Chris," she answered the man. "Chris is an old friend who was just dropping by. Chris, this is Luke…my…my fiancée."

Chris eyed the man, but neither of them exchanged a greeting. They both knew Chris was more than an old friend, and it made the circumstances awkward at best. To erase all doubt, Luke leaned in and affectionately kissed Amanda's cheek and then gave Chris the once over.

"Make it quick," he said to Chris. "We were just leaving."

Luke slipped back into the house, and once again Chris lifted his eyes to Amanda's. He was more than embarrassed over his assumption, but he did want a little clarification. "So...you are...you know?"

Amanda narrowed her eyes before looking down. "Yes. Luke and I..."

"Sorry, I thought...never mind. I didn't know there was someone else. I was coming by to apologize, but obviously it doesn't matter, so I'll go." Chris turned to leave.

"Wait." A frustrated sigh left her as she stepped out onto the porch beside him. "What're you really doing here?"

"I told you. I wanted to say that I was sorry."

With her arms folded across her chest and the stubborn set of her jaw, he knew she didn't believe him. So be it. Now that she had someone else, it wasn't like he was going to stand there and grovel. She was pregnant with another man's baby for crying out loud. On second thought, maybe he didn't owe her anything.

Chris turned and went back down the steps toward his truck.

"Chris...wait! It...it means a lot to me that you'd stop by."

He stopped short and looked back at her standing there in the dropping temperatures. Out in the open, he could see that she wasn't very far along. It was a wonder he suspected her pregnancy at all. Knowing that she had forgotten him so quickly left him feeling cheap.

"How far along are you?"

"Chris..."

"How far along are you!"

She looked him in the eye. "I'm ten weeks."

"And when's the wedding?"

Forgiveness for Yesterday

"What is this? An interrogation?" When he didn't move, she answered, "Two weeks from today. We're going to the court house and then away for the weekend."

Chris counted the months in his head. He and Amanda had broken up right around Thanksgiving, and that was at least three months ago. She was telling the truth. At least she had finally come to terms with what it was she really wanted even if it wasn't convenient for him at the moment. He should at least be civil.

"Congratulations. I shouldn't have come by unannounced. It won't happen again."

He got in his truck and watched the way she went back inside without so much as a second glance. Only a few months ago he had been sure she was in love with him. Man, was he off base. It was strange how neither Bret nor Karen had mentioned this to him.

Poor guy. Chris chuckled to himself. Amanda was one of the most manipulative females he had ever met. It should've made him feel good to know she was now someone else's problem, but for some reason, it left him sad—disappointed even.

A few short weeks to forget me. What does Lanky Luke have that I don't?

If Amanda even felt one hint of what he once did for Laurie, there was no way she would already be engaged to marry someone else. The idea was insane. Then again, maybe they had gotten engaged because of the baby. Like that would fix anything.

"Women!" he said out loud to the empty truck cab. Their idea of love was one he would never understand.

Once he was home, he crashed in his recliner, questioning how he was going to mend the situation with Bret. Who wouldn't be edgy and accusing when their boss was having what appeared to be a mental breakdown?

Chris clicked on the TV but couldn't get into anything that was on. His mind wouldn't let him. Chris hit the power button on the remote, thinking he was a pathetic excuse of a man. It was almost like he was miserable because he wanted to be. *Why do I want either of them back? Laurie or Amanda?* Maybe whom he really wanted was Karen. Bret would have a coronary if that were true.

He was able to settle himself with the thought that if his love life were to settle tomorrow, every other area would still be a mess. He would still have the Heritage Project to deal with, a botched business deal to fix, and he would still have two kids he had no idea how to raise, not to mention a list of broken friendships that was nearly a mile long. Maybe blaming his problems on the women in his life was the easier way out.

Because it *was* so much easier to blame the things that were deep inside of him on one particular person or event rather than stand up and take responsibility for it.

The truth was, Chris didn't know where his deep disgruntlement was coming from or how much of it there was. All he knew was that his troubles were festering like sores and spreading as if they were an infectious disease. The fact that he felt powerless to stop it probably meant he should start seeing a shrink.

His head started to pound at the thought. Even Bret thought he was on drugs. Not that the idea hadn't crossed his mind, because it had. The only thing stopping him was knowing he'd lose it all a whole lot faster. Once again, it was all about control.

He tried to muster up the energy to look on the bright side, but a groan escaped him when another sharp pain pierced his skull. At least his absence put some distance between the bad example he was setting and his kids who were always watching. Maybe when he quit coming back home every weekend, things would improve. He was just tired, and Kyle interrupted his thoughts.

"Dad?" Chris's eyes flew open, and he saw Kyle sit down on the sofa already wearing his pajamas.

"What is it?" he said, closing his eyes again.

"Are you and Bret still friends?"

Who knows? "Yeah. We just had a fight. We'll work it out."

"Good," Kyle returned but continued to stare at him from the sofa. "Can we go to his church tomorrow?"

"Not you too!" Chris was certain his head would split open at the mention of religion. Keeping his eyes closed, he answered as he rested his head on the cushion of the recliner. "No, not tomorrow," he said, thinking that the true answer was probably not ever.

"Okay." A few moments passed, and then Kyle tried a second time. "Dad?"

"What is it, Kyle?" Chris's voice was strained, and his patience was already worn completely thin.

"I heard you say this is your last weekend home. Does that mean I'll never see you again?"

A knife sliced through what remained of Chris's conscience. Slowly he sat up and looked over to his son. Seeing the worry in Kyle's young face, all his self-pity faded away and he extended his hand. "C'mere."

Kyle was getting big, but Chris wrestled him close anyway. "Why would you think you'd never see me again?"

"Because that's what happened with Mom. She said she was going to work one morning, and then she never came home. Sometimes I worry that you'll never come home too. You wouldn't do that, would you? You know, leave forever and not tell us?"

Meeting Kyle's eyes, he found them filled with insecurities and doubts a ten-year-old should never have. Kyle had eyes that once looked like his.

"Look at me," he said to Kyle. "I am coming back. Right now I have to be away because of work, but it's not forever. We'll see each other at Bret and Karen's wedding in May, and then we'll spend the rest of the weekend together—just the three of us. I promise."

"I guess...do you miss us when you're gone?"

Under the depths of all his brokenness, Chris knew the answer. "Of course I miss you. I miss you because I love you. Nothing will ever change that."

"I love you too," Kyle said and leaned over for a hug. "Are you sure you have to leave?"

Chris sighed. "I'm sure." Chris patted Kyle's back for reassurance. "But tomorrow is one more day we have together. Let's enjoy it. Now run off to bed."

Kyle rose, and Chris watched him shut the door to his room.

He did love Shelby and Kyle, but it was going to take more than loving them to put him in the running for father of the year.

Chris recalled the only father he'd ever known, and what Robert Lanning would say about the state of Chris's life right now. He would be disappointed to say the least. Chris stood and went to the kitchen. Over the refrigerator, he found a fifth of liquor and then retreated to his own room for the night.

13

Chris's weekend was one of the worst he could recall. He'd spent most of the day on Sunday sleeping off the effects of how he spent Saturday night. The horrid experience still wasn't enough to keep him from repeating the mistake within a twenty-four-hour time span. Now that it was Monday morning, there was no guessing as to why he felt so bad.

He had somehow managed to sober up, and since Shelby was at home faking the stomach bug so she could miss a day of school, he decided to put forth the effort and make an appearance at the office before heading back toward Asheville.

He told Shelby good-bye and piled in his truck and made his way across town. Traffic was heavy, but his plans were to be quick. The construction crew back on the jobsite was scheduled to start tearing out damaged parts of the subflooring, and he needed to be there to supervise. Chris parked in his spot and made his way upstairs. He barely got his office door open due to the mess.

"What the—?" He swore at Adam who was nowhere to be found. He didn't have time to track down the phone number he'd come after without some help. Yanking open a stuck file drawer, Chris thumbed through a dozen file folders, then slammed the cabinet shut. The sound seemed to echo in his pounding brain.

He tried another cabinet, selected a folder, then dumped its contents on the desk and started sifting. So far he had completely renovated the cabin where he was living. Indoor plumbing wasn't something he felt he could go without. Friday his crew had started on the house, ripping out ceiling tiles, spotty dry wall work, and everything else that wasn't nailed down. This morning he was looking for the name of an electrician who owed him a favor. There was no sense mentioning the electrical hazard he had unearthed Friday afternoon to either Bret or Darrell if he didn't have to.

"Aha," he said, tucking the paper with the number he needed into his pocket. "Preston owes me." Chris left the open folder and his mess but made a mental note to check up on Adam sometime after lunch.

It had become Chris's personal goal to have the house completed by summer's end. It would probably kill him to do it, but that way he would be back in Darrell's and Bret's good graces before something really bad happened.

When he reached the stairs, he looked back and saw the hall that led to the accounting department where Bret's office was located. Guilt pricked his conscience. Sometime on Sunday, Bret had decided to be the bigger man and called with an apology.

"Look, man, about yesterday…" Bret had said. "You're right. I have been in your business, and I'm sorry. It won't happen again. I'll even make it up to you. You can whoop my tail on the court again before you head back out." There was a soft chuckle, and then with a deep breath, he added, "I can't say that I have any answers, but I'm here if you want someone to listen. Catch ya' later."

Whether or not the words were said in earnest or were from a man grasping at straws to make sure he still had a job, Chris didn't care. He'd choose to take the olive branch Bret was being kind enough to offer. Chris changed his direction. He needed to let Bret know he was sorry too and that things between them were good—or as good as they could get at this point.

Chris silently worked his way through a maze of cubicles and tapped on Bret's door. "Morning," Bret said, casting the missing Adam a look that said they'd continue whatever they were doing later."

Chris eyed Adam as he passed by. "My office is a wreck. See that it's clean before I get back."

"Yes, sir, Mr. Lanning. Chris. Sir." The man took off in a trot.

"Have a seat." Bret's hand offered the vacant chair.

"No thanks. I was just on my way out. Thought I'd stop by a second." Silence fell between them, and Chris felt awkward. He'd come here to apologize, second time in two days. This had to be a record. "I got your message yesterday, and I want you to know I would never fire you over what was said. We were both mad so…let's just forget it." There. He said it.

Bret frowned. "I didn't leave the message because I thought you were going to fire me. I left it because I'm worried about you."

Chris raised an eyebrow. "I know, and although I appreciate your concern, I've got this. I just hate that I was such a"—he paused to think of a description for himself that didn't include a curse word—"jerk about it."

"I was a jerk too. I shouldn't have overstepped my bounds like that. It's just that there's a lot of pressure around here with you out in the field." Their eyes met, and Bret shrugged.

It went against everything in him to say it, but Chris forced the words out anyway. "If there's anything I can do to help ease things between you and Darrell, let me know."

"I appreciate that. You're still going to be in the wedding, right?"

"May 29. Wouldn't miss it."

"Good…'cause you know, the day wouldn't be the same without you."

Chris nodded, and the conversation reached a lull. Chris took the opportunity to leave. The best way he knew to make up for the trouble he was causing Bret was to come out on top with the Heritage Project. If he could do that, it would go a long way in redeeming himself in the eyes of everyone.

Chris pulled his truck onto the interstate and soon managed to put a hundred or so miles behind him. Thick gray clouds lined the sky as he drove west, making the air seem colder than ever. For some reason, Old Man Winter would not let go this year.

Chris rolled his neck and shoulders, trying to stay awake. It would be late when he got back to the jobsite, and with this weather, all the workers would've called it an early day.

Chris ran some of the project details through his mind to keep himself occupied. It wasn't until he was about twenty miles out that he glanced up in the rearview mirror to see blue lights flashing.

Great, he muttered. He slowed down and gave his signal to pull off onto the shoulder. Having been through this numerous times before, Chris reached over into the glove box, found his registration, and pulled his license from his wallet. He had the documents waiting when a rookie wearing a gray suit walked up and motioned for him to roll down his window.

"License and…" The young man's words trailed off. The man took the documents and walked back to his vehicle. He was gone for what seemed like forever, and Chris knew why. He was getting a ticket for speeding.

Chris continued to sit in the truck, letting his mood sour over the situation. Eventually the officer tapped on his window again, and Chris rolled it down.

"Mr. Lanning, I'm giving you a ticket for doing seventy-five in a sixty-five zone." Chris blinked in disbelief. Surely he'd heard the man wrong. "Excuse me, did you say I was going seventy-five? In a sixty-five?"

"Yes, sir, I did."

"But it's only ten miles over? You've got to be kidding!"

"Do I look like I'm kidding? It seems speeding is nothing new to you, sir. The law shows no favoritism. One more time, and the great state of North Carolina will be removing your license and therefore your driving privileges! Is that understood?"

"But…"

The office leaned in to make his point. His breath fogged the top half of the lowered window. "You are going to slow it down or end up walking. Is that clear?"

"Yes," Chris said through clenched teeth as he reminded himself not to say anything he couldn't take back.

The officer handed him a pink slip and his documents back. "Have a good day," the man said through a taunting smile.

Chris rolled the window back up. He cranked his truck and cautiously pulled back onto the interstate with the officer falling in directly behind him. He was careful to keep it right on the speed limit for the next five miles. Eventually the patrol car switched lanes and pulled into the median to monitor oncoming traffic.

"What a jerk!" he said, seeing the man was gone. The ticket was a farce. It'd be thrown out of court leaving him with nothing but a hassle. It was a sure sign this week was starting off just as badly as the last one had ended.

His stomach rumbled reminding him of the hour. There was an exit up ahead that boasted an array of food. The time he spent on the side of the road put it just past five, and that meant the town of Black Mountain would soon be filling up with five o'clock traffic.

Chris sped up to beat the crowd. He made his selection and whipped it into the drive-thru of a Kentucky Fried Chicken. A woman wearing too much makeup held out her hand. "That'll be eighteen dollars and seventy-two cents."

"For chicken?" Chris clarified.

"No, for steak." Nevertheless the woman checked his order. "I've got one combo of fried chicken with two biscuits, an extra mashed potato and gravy, slaw and macaroni and cheese with one gallon of sweet tea," the woman said.

Chris handed her a twenty and decided he was in the wrong business. "Keep the change!" he said when she handed him the greasy bag of overpriced food.

From there he pulled out into traffic and fell into the far left lane where he waited in line to make the left turn that would put him back on the interstate.

When the light turned green, there were at least seven to ten cars in front of him. They all made it under the light with the last one slipping through on red. There was no way he could make it. Chris slammed on the brakes at the last second to keep from getting caught out in the middle of the intersection. The car behind him laid down on the horn just about the time his supper slid into the floorboard. "Aah…"

Chris looked at the huge mess and then in his rearview mirror at the man blowing his horn. He was in a flashy red sports car raising his arms and yelling something in Chris's direction. Chris jerked opened the sliding back glass of his truck and hollered profanity at the guy. It was impossible for the man to hear him, but he seemed to back off.

"What was I supposed to do? Run a red light? What's with people? And look at my truck!"

He tried to clean up what he could reach, but while he was fishing around in the floor, his hand touched something that hadn't been in the bag. Wrapping his fingers around its hard surface, he heard the same familiar horn coming from behind. Quickly he glanced up to see that the light had changed. "I'm going already!"

As soon as he eased off the brake, the guy behind him decided he was too slow. The little red convertible jerked to the left and through the intersection ahead of him. A split second later, Chris heard the shuttering sound of a transfer truck's brakes as it slid into the intersection and connected with the car.

In slow motion, Chris watched the massive truck push over the top of the red convertible, crushing it beyond recognition before it came to a screeching halt within feet of wiping out a gas station on the opposite side of the street.

The hairs on his arms stood on end. There was no doubt in his mind that the man in the car was dead. Slow silent seconds passed, and people started climbing out of their cars. Chris watched as one man ran over to help the trucker down from the rig, and another stood in the street warning the oncoming vehicles.

"Hey, man. Are you all right?"

Chris heard the words but was too dumbfounded for them to register. "That...that...was supposed to be me. My light was green," he finally managed to say without looking at the man outside his window.

"You don't look so good," the voice told him. "Hang on, buddy. They're sending the paramedics."

The man ran off, but his words snapped Chris from the trance. Looking down in his hand to see what it was that had saved his life, Chris found he was holding a red book. He flipped it over and ran his fingers across the gold lettering of the title. The words "Holy Bible" jumped off the cover, and cold chills pricked his skin.

It was the Bible he'd taken from a church several months ago. He had ended up there when he'd gone for a drive through the country one day in order to clear his head. He hadn't realized he'd walked out with it in his hand until he had gotten back to his truck where he tossed it on the dash.

Chris opened the cover. *Center Cross Community Church* was printed on the inside.

Incredible.

One of the kids must have stuck it under the seat because he had completely forgotten about it. Realizing the unlikelihood of God's Word literally saving his life caused all the walls he'd built up in his mind to come crumbling down. Sitting there in the middle of the intersection, he realized God was more real to him than the clothes on his back.

Why? Why would you spare me?

Chris opened his door and climbed out of the truck. Halfway across the street he recognized the same patrolman who had given him the ticket.

"Hey, buddy," the man said, "I'm going to have to ask you to step back to your vehicle. We're trying to clear the street."

At first Chris didn't answer. Instead he spun around in a full circle watching the action unfold around him. "It was supposed to be me."

The officer stared at him as he slipped into his reflective vest and raised his arms to signal the cars that were still sitting at the light.

"Sir, I'm going to have to ask you to step back to your pickup so we can work the accident."

"You don't understand," Chris explained, almost pleading with the man. "He was behind me. I looked down, and the light turned green. He got impatient and took off around my truck. It was supposed to be me!"

The officer held up a hand to stop the cars that were trickling by. Before he turned in the other direction, that same hand slipped up onto Chris's shoulder in compassion.

"I understand. I haven't worked this job long, but long enough to know it's not your day. It was someone else's. Be thankful you got a second chance. Not everyone does."

Chris nodded hearing the man, and a look of acknowledgment passed between them. "Now if you don't mind," the officer said, "we need to get traffic moving so we can clear this road for a wrecker."

The guy directed him back to his truck as the wail of a siren filled the air. Chris noted it wasn't the sound of an ambulance that made the noise—there was no need for that. It was the sound of a fire truck instead.

He looked over to what was once a shiny, expensive sports car. A white sheet was being draped over its front window and hood.

In a daze, Chris pulled open the door of his truck and looked back at the scene as if seeing it through someone else's eyes. *It's not your day. It was someone else's. Be thankful you got a second chance. Not everyone does*, the words replayed.

Sitting there in his truck he had no idea why God would choose to spare a wretch like him. The very God whose name he'd slandered only seconds before in a curse to the man who now lay dead in the center of the street was the same God who saw fit to give him another day of life.

"But why?" Chris asked.

Again, something he couldn't explain stirred his soul. For the first time in his life, something happened. He believed.

14

Chris lived through the days that followed the accident in a daze. His mind was too busy taking in the facts. Phillip Danbury, fifty-one, from the town of Black Mountain, had been the man driving the red car. He left behind a wife, a daughter, and a life full of successes. He was a doctor who had been on his way to his daughter's piano recital and had gotten stuck in traffic.

Although the newspaper mentioned the highlights of the man's life, there was no mention of Chris or how his life was the one that was spared all because he hadn't been paying attention.

Mr. Danbury's funeral was scheduled for Thursday afternoon, and out of sympathy for the man's family, Chris went. A cold rain penetrated the soggy earth as he stood by the man's casket, not breathing a word to anyone but to God alone. The question he kept asking was, "Why?"

Somehow it didn't seem right that he, the one with more troubles than he could count, was given another day of life to squander however he saw fit, while Mr. Danbury's family was grieving in a way he was all too familiar with. Chris didn't need to shake Mrs. Danbury's hand or see the tears on their daughter's face to feel their pain. He knew it, and he knew it well. He knew it because he had lived it.

During the moments after the wreck, he had sat in his truck more sure than anything that God existed—that he was real and had an active part in the lives of his creation. But if that were so, then why hadn't the same God who'd spared his miserable life spared the good life of Mr. Danbury or the lives of his own parents? Wasn't there a way where everyone could have a happy ending?

Despite the fact that Mr. Danbury's last words were spewed in anger at a man who hadn't made it through the traffic cycle, everyone who knew him said he was a Christian. Chris believed them. *Don't Christians deserve a second chance?* If not them, then certainly not me. Chris believed, but he didn't understand.

Questions continued to assail him as he pulled onto Willow Ridge, the road the Heritage House was located on. Mudholes lined the old dirt road, making the trip fitting for his mood. The clock on his dash told him it was after six. The workers had left for the day, and there was another cold front moving in.

Rather than see what his crew had accomplished, or demolished better yet, Chris sloshed through the yard and went inside his warm cabin in search of food and a change of clothes.

He shut the door and was met with a silence that under different circumstances would have been peaceful. Outside of the hum of the refrigerator, nothing could be heard. It was every bit of depressing.

Chris flipped the light switch, hung up his heavy coat, and considered his options. Drinking himself into a drunken stupor was out of the question, not if he was going to get anything done by the end of the day. Still, he wasn't ready to go down to the house and find something to do.

He moved to cut on the TV, then realized he didn't have one. Instead, he remembered finding an old radio in the house last week. He'd brought it out to the cabin thinking the old antique might be worth something. After scratching around in the closet, he dug it out and cut it on.

A sad laugh left him as he rolled the old-fashioned dial. It was easy to get cut off from what was going on in the world living and working in the middle of the woods. Ironically enough, the only thing he wanted to get cut off from was the reality of his life. No location on earth seemed to be able to do that.

A heavy metal song cut through the silence. Chris kept turning the dial. He was looking for a distraction, not a headache. The rest of the stations were static except for a man giving a news report. "There

153   Forgiveness for Yesterday

we go," he said as he turned down the volume just low enough to keep him company.

In the fridge, he found a half gallon of outdated milk, three slices of bologna, and a carton of sour cream. He searched out some bread and made bologna sandwiches. He finished them off quickly and then cleared away his trash. As he moved by the sink, he noticed the red Bible from Monday was lying on the counter.

Chris picked it up and set down heavily at his small kitchen table. He studied the Bible for a minute, still marveling over the coincidence of finding it the way he had. He pushed it aside and reached for a stack of letters he'd found in the attic of the old house. His eyes skimmed the envelopes, wondering what was inside. He would have to tell Karen that he'd found another stash from their century-old lovebirds: William and Ella Something.

Chris put the letters back on the table beside the other treasures he'd unearthed. A gold chain with a cross on it, a set of skeleton keys, and an old accounting ledger completed his stash. He pushed the items to the corner of the table and reached for the red Bible again.

What would it hurt? He didn't have anything better to do. Maybe it would give him some of the answers he was looking for.

The spine cracked when he opened the book, and he wondered where to start. Tentatively he flipped through the chapters. The names printed on the books in the back were familiar to him even now. *Matthew, Mark, Luke...* There was lots of print in red. If he remembered correctly, those indicated words spoken by Christ. He supposed if he wanted to find out more about who Jesus was, it would be best to start with words the man had said directly.

Chris turned to the book of John and read through the first two chapters. He kept reading until he came across the third chapter, the sixteenth verse. He paused because he knew he'd read that verse before. Out loud he read it again.

"For God so loved the world that he gave his one and only Son, that whoever believes in him shall not perish but have eternal life." He read the next verse, "For God did not send his Son into the world to condemn the world, but to save the world through him."

Chris studied the words for a moment and then picked up the necklace with the cross to mark his place. *If I believe, what do I believe?* He knew he believed in God and that Jesus Christ claimed to be his one and only son. He also knew that Jesus had died on the cross taking the world's punishment for sin.

A short laugh escaped him. It took more than believing to make a person a Christian. That much he knew, but he sure could use saving right now—Laurie, Darrell, his kids, Bret, this project. His life was one big mess, and he had no idea about how to turn it around himself even though it was of dire importance that he did.

But something told him this verse went deeper than that, deeper than the afterlife he'd heard the preacher at Mr. Danbury's funeral speak of. Could it be the *life* the verse referred to was something to be experienced while still here on earth? Something that carried on from here and into life after death?

Chris thought of the life Bret and Karen lived. *Can Jesus really do that? Could there really be that much truth to the things of Christianity? That much hope to be had?*

With a deep breath, Chris opened the Bible back up. This time he flipped through the first half. The pages fell open to where a small card was placed between the pages. It marked a book titled Psalms. There were a few notes on the card, most written in a feminine script. Chris laid the card on the table and started to read.

Psalm 40 headed the chapter and then under it in italics the words read, *For the director of music, Of David, A Psalm.* He took it to mean that David had written the fortieth psalm.

Once again, he cleared his mind, trying to focus on what the scriptures had to say. It didn't take much effort because the first few verses jumped off the page.

> I waited patiently for the Lord; he turned to me and heard my cry. He lifted me out of the slimy pit, out of the mud and mire; he set my feet on a rock and gave me a firm place to stand.

Chris read the words again. A slimy pit was exactly how he would describe his spiritual and emotional whereabouts. *Out of the mud and mire* the verse read.

Chris continued through the rest of the chapter, and when he neared the end, another set of verses caught his undivided attention. He actually sat straight up in his chair. Verse 12 started,

> For troubles without number surround me; my sins have overtaken me, and I cannot see. They are more than the hairs of my head, and my heart fails within me.

Unable to breathe normally, Chris felt his eyes dart back to the first of the passage. Despite the severity of this David guy's situation, the Lord had rescued him. His fingers tightened on the book like it was a lifeline. Was it possible that he and David had a few things in common? The verses didn't mention what kind of sins David had committed, but that they'd overtaken him. Chris could relate. Sin was what he was good at. The words penned in front of him could've easily been things he would write about himself.

Suddenly Chris knew exactly what had taken over and made such a mess of his life: sin. He was sexually immoral, a liar, a thief, he was jealous, and probably a host of other things the Bible and his conscience had warned him about through the years. If he felt bad for committing wrongs against people who cared nothing for him, how much more terrible should he feel for committing wrongs against a just and righteous God who loves him enough to send his only Son to die for him?

Chris finished off the chapter and then sat paralyzed with fear. He knew he needed to cry out to God to save him from a lot more than just his problems, but how? How, unworthy as he was, did he come before a God who was holy? He simply sat there, the words before him, replaying over and over in his mind almost teasing him. Just like God had spared the wrong man in the accident, it had to be a mistake. The just and righteous God of the Bible couldn't love a man who had sunk as low as he had.

The voice in his head grew louder. It called up the memory of Kyle's young face and the fear and insecurity that were haunting him. One image followed another, and before Chris knew it, all his sins played out before him. It left him wishing he'd never met Laurie Callahan so that he would've never been introduced to her God—a God who would forever remain just beyond his reach. Only something divine could constitute this burning hole in his chest, not a mere woman.

End it, a voice seemed to whisper in his ear. Chris's eyes moved purposefully across the room and rested on the nightstand by the bed where he kept a gun in case of emergencies. His throat tightened, imagining what the cold metal would feel like in his palm. He would've never imagined using it to do the unspeakable the day he placed it there, but that had been weeks ago. Things had steadily been going downhill since he'd left home, and they weren't going to change. He was kidding himself to think otherwise.

The hairs on his arms rose as he considered what to do. He sat there mindlessly listening to all the reasons why he should. *You're a liar, a manipulator…a drunk…*

Minutes passed, and slowly Chris realized he was staring out into space. He shook his head. Things were bad, but knowing what he did about the Bible, Chris knew he'd go straight to hell the moment he pulled the trigger. He pushed the idea aside solely because of what it'd do to Shelby and Kyle. He might be a miserable excuse of a father, but he had promised them. He'd promised that he would never leave them willfully.

Chris put the Bible back on the table and walked over to the door. He needed to get out to the estate house and clear his head. As he reached for his coat, he remembered the radio was still on. As old as it was, he was sure it was a fire hazard. When he stepped back to cut it off, the song that came on gripped his heart.

It started with a nice melody, but it was the lyrics that surprised him. They were about God and described him as a healer of hurts. They gave the impression that God was kind, tender, and merciful like a father who wanted to ease any doubts. The words tore at Chris.

More verses about bringing all you had before God for the taking followed. There may have been more to the song, but Chris didn't hear it.

Suddenly he couldn't stand the thoughts of living the rest of his life knowing God was real but never attainable by the likes of him. It was too much to bear. He didn't know how to bridge the insurmountable gap between who he was and where this real but mysterious God stood. He wanted that help David had written of, but it dangled just out of reach.

With a desperation and anger he didn't know he possessed, he took his arm and swung out across the surface of the counter, sending the radio and everything beside it crashing into the wall where it fell to the floor. A scream of frustration escaped from his lips, and he tore at his hair.

The silence that followed felt twice as thick as it had before. Once again Chris lifted his eyes to the drawer that was now just feet away. It beckoned him to come closer. So what if he broke a promise? What was one more promise when he'd already broken hundreds? All he had to do was take a step.

He took it, still not knowing if he could carry out the act. That was when he heard it. Out of the cold, unfeeling silence that surrounded him, he heard the word *whoever*.

Chris stopped. The word was so clear he questioned whether or not it had been audible. Glancing around the room, Chris knew it must have been his imagination. He was alone, only more words followed. "Not to condemn, but to save."

Hearing the words he'd just read repeated back to him aloud, he knew the voice belonged to God. The quiet that had enveloped the room again ended as his knees gave way, and he collapsed on the bed.

Cold chills ran up his arms, and a queasy feeling started in his gut. For a second, he thought he was going to be sick. All the thoughts and emotions that had been eating at him for the past couple of years worked their way to the surface. As he buried his face in his hands, a ragged sob tore from his throat, and he cried with all that was in him.

One by one, every block he'd carefully placed around his cold and hurting heart in order to survive began to fall. Tears streamed down his face as he thought about his parents, his disappointments, the example he'd lived before his children, of all the women he'd used and slept with, and how his sins had turned him into a man he hated. After all the things he'd explored in the name of redemption, could the answer really be so simple? He thought about his quest for fulfillment and how it had escalated all because one woman rejected the love he'd offered.

The pain he felt in his heart was suffocating. As much as it hurt him to be rejected by Laurie, Chris realized his sins were a rejection of God's love to him—a love that was divine and perfect even when he didn't understand it.

Sitting there on the bed, Chris knew he'd hit rock bottom—that there was no way out but up. He wasn't sure how long he sat there before he realized what he needed to do. Suddenly the way out was clear. Yes, he was a wretch, but the answers he wanted didn't lie in taking his life. They lay in giving it up.

His eyes were no longer blind; the words he saw as condemnation moments ago now offered a life-saving hope, a hope that he could have if he were willing to accept the gift Jesus Christ had died to give him. It was the gift of forgiveness. Jesus was the bridge between him and the holy and righteous God he'd discovered.

Hanging his head in shame, Chris fell on his knees in the floor and prayed, humbling himself before the God of all Creation. There, prostrate and broken, he cried out in repentance a simple prayer, "I'm sorry! Please forgive me!"

Incredible release overwhelmed him. It was so real it was almost intoxicating. Sitting there in the silent stillness as he marveled at the difference, Chris felt the plea of his heart start to change. Outside the forgiveness he'd just found, he wanted something like nothing he had ever wanted before.

"Change me, Jesus. Not just a part of me, change all of me. I can't settle for half-hearted faith. I want what you promised. I want that life you promised. Not just the eternal life mentioned in John, but the kind of life that changes a man while he's here on earth—I want that. You said *whoever*, and there has never been a *whoever* who wants it more than me."

The next morning, sunlight flickered through the window of Chris's cabin and over onto his face. He slowly came to and realized he was on the floor. His mind began to clear as images from the previous night surfaced from his memory.

He remembered reading from the Bible and hearing a song on the radio before losing the last bit of control he had. He remembered hearing a voice and then praying with everything in his being, first for forgiveness and then for life. He remembered pouring out his heart before the Lord and, after becoming emotionally spent, rolling over and going to sleep.

Sitting up beside the bed, Chris had no idea what time it was. Judging by the sun filtering in through his windows, he guessed it was late into the morning hours. He rubbed his eyes, realizing there was a brightness about the room that was hard to describe. The intensity of it almost made him want to shut his eyes and go back to sleep.

The sound of a Skilsaw filled the air, and it told him he wasn't dreaming. He pushed up on the mattress beside him, and his gaze lingered on the nightstand. He slipped open the drawer. Sure enough, resting in its place was the nine millimeter right where he'd placed it. Quickly he closed the drawer and rubbed a hand down his face.

"Thank you, Jesus," he said out loud.

God had been there when he had nowhere else to go. Chris stood and stepped over the items littering the kitchen floor and made for the bathroom. After brushing his teeth, and splashing some water on his face, he looked up at the reflection in the mirror. His eyes were red and swollen from the tears he'd shed. The sight left no doubt the memories he recalled this morning weren't imagined. They were real.

The only thing he still couldn't figure out was the weird light filling the cabin. It seemed to be coming from outside. As he lifted up the blind on the bathroom window, Chris's breath caught in his throat. He pulled the cord tight until the entire window was exposed.

Outside there was a thick blanket of freshly fallen snow covering the ground. The sun was shining down, causing a sparkling illumination on everything it touched. It was the most beautiful thing he'd ever seen. The mudholes and piles of lumber marking the renovation were covered. Even the dingy white paint on the house had a fresh coat of white. The snow had made everything fresh, clean, and beautiful. His hands went to his chest where they pressed against his heart. The scene outside his window was exactly what he felt like inside. He was different, clean, and renewed somehow.

Chris smiled. He still didn't have all the answers he wanted, and his life was still a mess, but there was more evidence that whatever had occurred last night really happened. He went back to the kitchen and searched out the red Bible that was lying on his kitchen table. The pages fell open to where the gold necklace was still marking John 3:16.

Chris skimmed through the words, letting his eyes search out the one word: *whoever*. A tentative smile started to grow. He knew why his heart wasn't so heavy anymore. This morning he was different because he was no longer a man condemned. He was forgiven.

Part Two

Therefore, as God's chosen people, holy and dearly loved, clothe yourselves with compassion, kindness, humility, gentleness and patience. Bear with each other and forgive whatever grievances you may have against one another. Forgive as the Lord forgave you. And over all these virtues put on love, which binds them all together in perfect unity.

—Colossians 3:12–14 (NIV)

15

The sunlight filtering down in Ashville, North Carolina, was the same sunlight that filtered through the blinds of Amanda's bedroom many miles away.

She rolled over in her bed and reached for a tissue, oblivious to the snowy scene outside her window. Five days had passed since Chris had come by on Saturday, but it was on Tuesday that her life had been forever changed. Amanda peeked through her curtains and saw that the snow and sleet had stopped falling. It looked to be an inch or so deep.

Whereas some people might consider the freshly fallen glaze a beautiful sight to behold, she only saw the weight of the ice hanging on everything, and it mirrored the weight inside her soul.

"Abortion." Amanda let the word hang in the air over her head, thickening the shame that seemed to color her existence. All week she hadn't dressed in more than flannel pajama pants and a cotton T-shirt—much less done anything as adventurous as fix up. The reality caused her tears to come in earnest.

It wasn't like she had planned to commit such a terrible act—even during the split second when she'd been sure Karen or Bret had told Chris about her pregnancy then sent him to her back doorstep as a means to prove it. Thankfully that misconception had cleared up at Chris's apparent surprise before she'd blurted out the truth.

After that dramatic encounter on Saturday, followed by a fainting spell at work on Monday, the doctor confirmed gestational diabetes. That is why her blood sugar had been all over the place. The doctor also told her that her blood pressure was abnormally high, and these diagnoses this early in her pregnancy were not a good sign. From that point on, something forceful had driven her decisions. She'd asked her

Forgiveness for Yesterday

brother, Luke, to stay in town a few more days and drive her to and from the abortion clinic who'd rushed her through on account of the coming weather. The decision had been her way of taking control, and she did it in the name of protecting her health.

Amanda groaned at her obvious failure. "Why do I still love him? It's not fair!" Now she had nothing left of Chris whatsoever, and she still felt terrible. She tossed her tissue in the floor and reached for another.

She lay there trying not to envision what people would say if they knew what she had done. Somehow she knew she couldn't explain things away with the smooth and easy talk the nurse had used to convince her abortion was her way out of the situation. The feeling in the pit of her stomach told her the truth: she had chosen poorly. Now on top of her anger and resentment, she had an increased sense of grief and guilt to deal with.

She drew another tissue and reached for the phone. She should at least call someone. Maybe the shame that seemed to cripple her appearance wouldn't be as obvious without a visual. Amanda picked off the number for her mom. As it rang, she remembered their last conversation. It was when she had told her mother that she and Chris had broken up. Amanda had been clever enough to gear the conversation so that it looked like the breakup was her idea.

"Amanda, honey," her mother had said after hearing her tale, "I keep hoping you'll settle down. You're not getting any younger. All your friends are married, and most of them have kids. From what you said about Chris, he sounded wonderful. Can't you two find a way to make it work?" The words felt like a slap in the face. She hadn't told her mother the truth, but still. She might as well have come out and said she was nothing without a man.

Amanda quickly punched the off button before anyone picked up. She couldn't deal with another rejection. Not today. Next she tapped in Bret's number. It wasn't like she expected him to understand her actions, but that night in his apartment he'd been more than willing to offer her a compassionate shoulder to cry on. Maybe he'd be willing to do it again.

"Pick up," she commanded the ringing tone in her ear. Much more of this and she was going to eat her way through another pint of Ben and Jerry's.

After five rings, it clicked over to voice mail. "You've reached Bret Sears with Greeson Developing. I'm sorry I am unable to take your call at this time. Please leave—" Amanda hung up without hearing the rest. Where was everyone when she needed them?

Her fingers paused over the keypad as she tried to decide whom to try next. When Karen's name came to mind, slowly her shame turned to complete and utter dread. She had never planned for Karen to find out about the pregnancy like she had, and she wouldn't have except for fate making her present during the fallout of a major hormonal surge that day in the dressing room.

The scene played in her mind of how devastated Karen had looked. Amanda bit her lip as her emotions shifted. *If Karen knew what it is I've done and how miserable I feel about it, would she still feel the same way?*

Indecision weighed on her and she tapped her fingers on the phone. Right now she just wanted someone to tell her that they loved her. Karen would do that, wouldn't she? The deciding factor was that she didn't think she could spend another moment in this room without someone to talk to. She punched in Karen's cell number. "Amanda," she answered, "what's up? Have you seen the snow?"

Amanda could hear the kids in the background. Obviously school was closed, and Karen hadn't been able to make it into work. "Uh… yeah. Do you think you can maybe swing by this afternoon when the roads clear up? There's something I want to tell you." Silence stretched out between them, and Amanda could feel her heart hanging in the balance.

"Are you okay?"

"Yeah. I just…I really need someone to talk to."

There was a long pause. "Yeah. Sure. Bret is coming over after lunch to sled with the kids. I'll try to make it by around two or so."

"Thanks."

Forgiveness for Yesterday

Amanda continued to wallow on the bed, rehearsing persuasive lines and excuses in her head. The next thing she knew Karen was hovering over her with a sack of food in her hand.

"Amanda, wake up."

"Huh?" Amanda asked, wiping her eyes. "What are you doing here? How did you get in?"

"I let myself in with the hide-a-key."

"Oh." Amanda scrambled around in the covers, remembering why she'd invited Karen over. "Sorry, I must have dozed off."

Karen pulled a bowl of soup from the bag and offered it to her. "You sounded horrible on the phone. Why didn't you tell me you were sick?"

Karen helped prop her up in bed and then offered her a steaming bowl of chicken noodle. Amanda eagerly took a few sips and then set the bowl on the nightstand. "Thanks. I can't remember the last thing I had to eat."

Concern laced Karen's eyes, and it traveled into her tone. "Amanda, you have to eat. The baby needs the nutrition and…"

Amanda's eyes started to fill. "Oh, Karen. The most horrible thing has happened." Her shoulders shuttered with the weight of her burden, and Karen sat down on the bed.

"What's wrong?"

When Amanda continued to cry, Karen's voice became soft and compassionate like Amanda had hoped. "You said you had something to tell me. What is it?"

At this moment, Amanda couldn't handle hearing the disappointment Karen was sure to express if she knew the truth. No amount of persuasion could alter her actions as being wrong. Dead wrong.

"The baby….I…" Amanda shook her head in total dismay. "I… it's gone."

A soft gasp came up from Karen, and immediately Amanda knew she thought the causes were natural.

"Oh, honey. I am so, so sorry. What happened? Why didn't you call?" Karen wanted to know all the details as she smothered her in a hug. Guilt rushed in closer than Karen's embrace, but Amanda couldn't find it in her heart to correct her assumption.

Amanda just shook her head. "It happened earlier this week. I didn't call because I feel so guilty. I didn't deserve to be a mother. The way I got pregnant...I had no idea how I was going to support myself and a baby or what I was going to do when Chris put two and two together."

"Sh," Karen breathed, taking her back into her arms. "Don't worry about Chris. He's the least of your problems right now."

"No," Amanda panted between dry heaves and the constricting sensation in her chest. "He....he...he came by the house late Saturday evening. He took one look at me and knew. I don't know how, but he did. At first I was sure you and Bret had told him, but then he seemed embarrassed, like he wasn't sure of himself, so I went with it. I told him it wasn't his."

Karen pulled back in confusion and concern. "And he believed you?"

"Only because Luke, my brother, was here. Chris doesn't know him so together we played it off like Luke was my fiancée, and the baby was his."

"Wow. What did he say?"

"I don't know." She sighed. "He called me a few names but then apologized for stopping by unannounced. I've never been so scared in all my life. He asked me how far along I was, and I lied. I told him I was only ten weeks. He left without saying much after that, but you know how guys are. They don't put too much thought into that kind of thing. Guys are too stupid to see the obvious."

"Yeah, but Chris isn't an idiot. He knows how you felt about him. You really expect him to believe you're already pregnant and engaged to marry someone else?"

Amanda raised a brow. "Only because he wants to believe it. Trust me, the truth is not something he wants to face in this situation. Nevertheless, if he thought for one second I was keeping something like true paternity from him, he would've beat the truth out of me right there on the back porch, Luke present or not."

"Has Chris ever hit you?"

Amanda debated on telling another lie, but they were compounding, and she wasn't sure she could keep up. "No, but I know that he would have. You've seen for yourself how he is. One minute he's your best friend and the next minute he's biting your head off. "

Amanda dried her eyes and cleared her throat seeing how Karen wasn't convinced. "You believe me, don't you?"

"Of course. Chris and Bret got into it Saturday at the park. I knew he was roaring mad when he left, but I don't understand why he would come by here."

"You are so naïve! He came by, apologized even, probably hoping I'd take him back for a quick romp in the sack. When he saw I was pregnant, everything changed. Him coming by isn't because he's suddenly developed a conscience and cares about my feelings. I'm sure finding out I was pregnant threw a real crimp into his plans!"

Amanda sighed, totally spent. "I know this sounds terrible, but part of me is relieved that I'm not carrying his baby anymore. I didn't want to look into my child's face every day and resent it because it was his. At the same time, it was the only thing of him I had left. And now it's gone…"

Speaking the words caused a dam of hurt and sadness to break. Her emotions jerked back to those of guilt and shame for feeling what she just confessed. Amanda cried until she couldn't see straight. Soon Karen was crying too, and together they finished off the box of tissues. "Why couldn't Chris just love *me* instead of whoever this Laurie woman is? Is that too much to ask? Do you know he wasn't even married to Shelby and Kyle's mom? I mean I can't even compete with a woman who was selfish enough to walk away from her own kids!"

Karen wiped at her face and pulled back. There were deep questions and surprise in her eyes. "What is it?" Amanda asked on a snub, glad to see she'd finally put a dent in Karen's idea of Chris.

"I know you were furious back at the first of the year when you found out Chris wasn't just some random employee at Greeson Developing—that he actually owned the company. When did you find out he and Laurie were never married, and why didn't you tell me?"

Amanda turned away. "It was back in the fall. Shelby told me one night when we were laying in bed talking. She said Chris adopted her and Kyle when their mother left. I confronted him over it, and that's why we got in such a big fight on the way home."

"But if you knew he was still caught up on her, why did you keep seeing him?"

"I don't know. I shouldn't have. It's just that…I thought I could change him. I thought I could make him forget her. I knew if I told you, you'd talk me out of seeing him. Do you know how humiliating it is to date a guy for months and then find out he's been lying the whole time? I felt like an idiot for not putting it together sooner!"

"But you knew he has commitment issues. Were the two of you not being careful with your birth control?"

"Yes…but…but…I thought if Chris could find room in his heart to adopt two kids that aren't even his, that he could find room in his heart for me too. Why am I so unlovable?"

"You're not unlovable. Even your name means worthy of love. I love you," Karen soothed. "Bret loves you too, and deep down, in some weird and twisted way, I think Chris wanted to love you. He just didn't know how. He's really struggling with some spiritual things. I don't know why he's acting like he is, but I do know this is not who he wants to be."

Amanda punched a fist into her pillows. "Would you quit defending him! I always fall for the wrong guy. Chris doesn't know a thing about love! That should've been a sign from day one. I'm so stupid. The way he was always talking down to me and expecting me to drop whatever it was I was doing and come running—it was like he wanted to see just how far he could take it. He has got to be the most egotistical male I know! I hate him!"

Amanda threw the empty box of Kleenex at the wall to make her point.

"Amanda….stop."

"Stop what? You're taking his side!"

Karen's mouth fell open. "I'm not taking sides! It's just hard for me to imagine Chris so…completely cold and unfeeling. I know there's a side to him that is tender, compassionate even. I know because I see it when he's with his kids."

"Karen, wake up! They're Laurie's kids! I used to think those same feelings would rub off on me, but I was wrong. Now I have no trouble seeing how shallow and insensitive he can be. Life is always about him!"

"Listen," Karen whispered, "you know Bret and I will help you get through this. Whatever it is that's going on with Chris, you have my word that if he ever tries to hurt you or take advantage of you again, we will both do everything in our power to stand in the way. Understand?"

Once again the tears started to flow, and Karen cradled her in a hug.

"I don't deserve you," Amanda breathed into Karen's shoulder, knowing the words were completely true. She didn't deserve friends who were loyal, ones who were kind and loving when she was someone who couldn't even be honest. Her conscience grew so heavy she squeezed out the next words to keep from passing out. "You and Bret are the best friends I have. If it weren't for you, I don't know what I'd do. Please don't give up on me."

16

Weeks passed, and the weather slowly started to clear. Karen lifted her hand to knock on Bret's front door. She and Holly were scheduled to meet the wedding planner at the flower shop to pick out flowers for the bridal bouquets, and Bret had agreed to entertain Scott until they got back.

Karen knocked on the door again and then checked her watch. He said he'd be here. She dug through her purse to look for the key he'd given her. She put it in the slot and opened the door.

"Bret?" she called into the quiet house. She heard the faint sound of running water upstairs and figured he was still in the shower.

Scott came up behind her and slipped in the door. "Is he here?"

"Yeah. I think he's in the shower. He'll be down in a minute."

Scott moved through the kitchen and flopped down on the sofa where Holly joined him. "Hey, can I walk down to the playground?" There was a small recreation area in Bret's housing complex.

"I don't know. This is a busy street. Only if Holly goes with you."

Scott turned pleading eyes on his sister who crossed her arms. "What are you going to give me if I say yes?"

Scott went over to the living room closet and got out Bret's basketball. "Why do I have to give you anything?" He dribbled the ball on the living room floor, and Karen's head turned at the sound. "Not in the house. You'll mess up the hardwoods."

Just as she said it, the ball bounced onto the glass coffee table. Karen held her breath praying it wouldn't break.

"Sorry," Scott said, grabbing the ball before it knocked something over. Last week he'd ruined a report Bret was working on when he spilt a glass of water while teasing his sister. "You know how Bret feels about you two horsing around in the house. Last week you two—"

"Oh, come on before she starts fussing at us," Holly said, cutting her off and pulling Scott by the arm.

"Be back in thirty minutes. We need to stop by the store while we're out."

"Yes, ma'am."

Karen heard the water shut off upstairs and then footsteps moving around on the ceiling. It was probably a good idea if she called up and told Bret they were there.

She moved to the corner of the kitchen and called up the stairs. "Hey, honey. We're here."

"Okay. Be down in a minute."

When she was about to walk away, a stack of magazines on the bottom step caught her eye. On the top she saw the one she'd been reading last weekend. There was an article about raising teenage girls in it, and she never got around to finishing it.

Karen picked up the stack and placed it on the bar before flipping to the inside cover. She found the article but only got two paragraphs into it before she heard Bret's feet on the stairs.

"Hey, how was your morning?" he asked, walking over to give her a kiss before moving to the refrigerator. He was wearing shorts but had yet to put on a shirt. Karen tried not to gawk, but the sight of his toned body made her stomach do a flip-flop.

"Nice, very nice." She smiled. "Are you still up for watching Scott while Holly and I meet with the wedding planner and florist?"

"Yeah, sure. You'll be back by lunch, right?"

"I hope so. I thought I might go by the store and then check on Amanda if I have time."

Bret pulled several things out of the refrigerator and tossed them into the blender. "How is she?"

"Okay, I guess. You know it's kind of funny. She's really opened up to me these last two weeks. I'm hoping that losing the baby has opened her eyes to some things."

"Like what?"

"Well, for starters, I'm hoping this whole situation has showed her there are consequences to her actions and that they don't necessarily affect only her. I'm also hoping this will make her think twice the next time she wants to get involved with a guy like the ones she's been known to date."

"Good point. Do you still think she should tell Chris about the baby being his?"

Karen tapped her fingers on the countertop, thinking through the question. "I do, but not right now. Right now she's grieving, and I think having the space to do that is important. With Chris part of the picture, she tends to get sidetracked by other emotions. At this point I'm not sure if she loves him or hates him. I don't think she knows either, but he's still all she talks about. I actually think it's a good thing he's tied up with this project of his. Maybe time will lessen the blow for Chris of how nature handled things between the two of them."

Bret eyed her for a moment, then reached for an insulated cup. "Nature?"

"What I mean is God saw fit to take a life. As hard as that is to accept, it was his solution—the one we couldn't see. I guess you could say I'm a little disappointed. I was really hoping God would get a hold of Chris, and he would swoop in and be her knight in shining armor."

"That's what I love about you. You always want a happy ending."

"I do, and I guess it could still happen. God can still change Chris's heart. They could still have a baby and live happily ever after."

"Whoa there! Don't you think that's putting the cart before the horse?"

Karen smiled. "Okay, maybe just a little since seeing it was probably Chris's last visit that caused her to become so upset that she lost their child..."

"Last I checked Amanda still needed some work herself. She was the one who quit taking her birth control as a way to force Chris into having permanent ties with her that he never wanted to begin with. She says he's the liar and manipulator, but in my opinion, she could give him a run for his money."

"You mean…she got pregnant on purpose?"

"Yes. At least that's what she told me."

Karen was shocked. "She implied to me that it was an accident. Why would she tell you something different?"

"I don't know. Maybe she feels like you'll judge her for the truth."

"And you're not?" Karen was starting to get worked up. "I'm sorry," she said. "It's obvious they're both lost and searching. It is hard not to judge her sometimes. That's why I have to remind myself that lots of people make mistakes. Some are just bigger than others."

Bret studied her. "Mistakes? A mistake is forgetting to pay the power bill. These were wrong and calculated decisions." He hit the button on the blender to put Karen's argument on hold.

When the noise stopped, Bret poured a thick brown liquid into his cup. His eyes met hers just as he was about to lift it to his mouth.

"Are you really going to drink that? It looks like dirt."

"It's a protein shake. I have one every morning after I go to the gym."

"That's disgusting. I hope you don't plan on kissing me after you drink that junk."

"Kissing?" He smiled. "Are you saying I should get that out of the way first?"

Karen laughed when he lowered the drink and pulled her into his arms. He kissed her once and then twice. Bret still hadn't bothered to put a shirt on so she moved her hands over his arms and chest, admiring his body. Where she had grown lax in her workout routine, Bret had gotten much more dedicated to his.

"Hmm," she sighed. "You've really been hitting the gym lately."

He chuckled under her admiration as she ran her fingertips over his biceps. "Like the results?"

"Hmm, hmm," she purred as her fingers slipped down to his abs.

"Where are the kids?"

Her eyes lifted to his. "Down at the playground. They just left."

He kissed her again, only this time it was more involved. Karen ran her hands into his hair, and a few seconds later he was lifting her shirt. At first he seemed content to brush his thumbs along her stomach, but slowly they inched their way up. "Bret, what are you doing? We said we'd wait."

"I am waiting. I'm just…sampling."

Again, his hands moved, and Karen stepped away. In one swift move he reached out and tickled her. "Stop." She giggled when he caught her again. "The kids could come in any minute."

"You said they just left!"

"They did, but they could come back."

"And you call me the worrier."

Karen studied his face, and suddenly he was serious. "Come on," he pleaded. "The wedding is two months away. What's it going to hurt?" He moved to kiss her again, and this time she let him. It was easy to get caught up in the passion. Before she knew it they were stumbling into the living room.

It wasn't until they fell backward onto the sofa and Bret tried to pull her shirt off that she knew they were crossing a line.

"What's wrong now?" he grumbled when she pulled away for a second time.

Karen struggled to sit up. "I don't want our first time to be on the couch in your living room while the kids are down the street. I want it to be romantic and special."

"Karen, whenever or wherever we're together for the first time, it'll be special. And who said we're going all the way? We can always stop."

All she had to do was raise an eyebrow, and a breath of frustration left him. "Fine. Have it your way, like always. Why is it so easy for you to turn me down?"

"Easy? Who says it's easy?"

"I'm not joking. You never seem to have a problem drawing the line and not crossing it. Me, on the other hand, I struggle with it every second you're in the room!"

Karen buried her face in her hands. This was a battle they'd been fighting for some time now. Maybe she should just give in. They would be married in a matter of weeks anyhow. "This is hard on me too, trust me. I know what it's like to be with someone, and I can't wait to be with you, but that doesn't make it right. I can see why you'd be curious…anxious even, but—"

"Wait," Bret said, slow and measured. "You don't think our wedding night will be my first time, do you?"

Her mouth opened, but nothing came out. This wasn't how she envisioned this conversation going. "I...was hoping?"

Bret gently took her hands and stared into her eyes. "Karen, I'm thirty-two. I've never been wild and crazy, but I'm a very different man than I used to be. I've been with a woman."

Heat filled her face, and she looked away. She was disappointed to say the least. *Did I really expect him to still be pure?* "Was it the girl at the party?" she asked aloud.

"What party?"

"The New Year's Eve party. You know, the girl in the red dress? The one you used to date?"

Bret's eyebrows rose in surprise. "Chelsey? You think I would sleep with Chelsey?"

Karen rolled her eyes. She'd seen for herself what a knockout Chelsey was, and she and Bret had dated for at least a few months. "What guy wouldn't want to sleep with her? She's gorgeous and doesn't mind flaunting it. You must have at least thought about it."

Bret suddenly looked uncomfortable. "Chelsey did not dress like that when I went out with her. Even if she did, you can rest assured I did *not* sleep with her. Believe it or not, I've never been that desperate. It was another girl from a long time ago. We dated during my sophomore year of college, and it was before I got serious about my faith."

Karen's disappointment must have showed.

"We were together a year, but it only happened a few times," he assured her.

"What was her name?"

"I don't know."

Karen crossed her arms and tilted her head to the side. "You went out for a year, and you don't remember her name?"

Bret sighed. "Katie Mandrel. There, are you happy? I remember her name."

"Were there others?"

"No."

Karen studied him. Having no other woman before her was preferable, but what Bret was confessing happened a long time ago. She was disappointed she wouldn't be his first and only, but she wasn't going to fault him for having made a bad decision. A smile spread on her lips. "So you're thirty-two and haven't been with anyone in…twelve years or so?" It wasn't really a question, just a statement made for clarification.

"When you say it like that…" Bret stood and walked back into the kitchen.

Karen winched at how she'd inadvertently landed a blow to his ego. "Oh, come here!" she said following him. "Can't I be happy there's only been *one* other?" She walked up behind him and wrapped her arms around his middle. "It means a lot to me that you've kept yourself for me."

Bret turned to face her. "Really? 'Cause there were at least a thousand times when I could've changed my mind."

"I know. That's exactly why I don't want to see us blow it right here before our wedding."

Karen searched his eyes. Something was still unsettled. She didn't mean to let it, but a smile slipped onto her lips at how hard he was taking this.

"Oh, forget it." Bret turned around and started to chug his shake.

"Don't be mad at me. I know that it's different for guys. In a few weeks we can have all the sex we want—guilt-free."

He didn't make a sound other than to sit the cup down on the counter. Eventually he turned in her direction again. "Is that a promise?"

She smiled at him. "I promise. Come May 29, I promise to give you something to smile about day and night for the rest of your life."

"Hmm…" Bret sighed. "I'm thinking I should get that in writing. Better yet, I think you should work that into your vows!"

She laughed out loud at his sarcasm. "I don't think so. This is between you and me and no one else."

"Oh, c'mon," he teased. "Can't I tell one other person? Something I'll smile about day and night would be so much to brag about."

"You're terrible!"

Forgiveness for Yesterday

He gave her a quick kiss on the forehead before turning to the sink and rinsing out his cup. "At least I'm not a tease."

Thirty minutes later, Karen and Holly left while Bret and Scott went to shoot hoops at the Y. Karen climbed in the car, still a little surprised at Bret's revelation. *Katie Mandrel. I wonder what she was like.* Bret would never sleep with someone he didn't care about deeply or even love. *I wonder why it ended…and why he pretended like he didn't remember her.*

There were many dangers when diving into relationships of the past, and it was a past that was more than ten years for Bret. Just because she was a little jealous of the mysterious Katie, there was no sense holding something against Bret that had happened before he'd made a commitment to the Lord or to her. The idea felt childish.

Thinking of the childish, she wondered if she should drive by and check on Amanda first. *Should I confront her about what Bret said? Did she really get pregnant on purpose?* she wondered. Just as sex threatened to complicate her and Bret's current relationship, it had severely complicated Amanda's entire life. "Sex can mess up everything."

"What?"

Karen turned at least three shades of red, realizing she had said the words out loud. "Uh…sorry, sweetie, I was just thinking out loud."

Holly looked at her like she was crazy. She probably didn't even know what sex was.

"I…uh…people can really get themselves into complicated situations." *Kind of like the one I'm in now.*

"How so?"

Karen felt her stomach drop through the floorboard. She was going to have to explain. Holly didn't know about Amanda's pregnancy because Karen hadn't explained more than what was absolutely necessary. After all, the baby Amanda and Chris had conceived would sort of be Shelby's stepsibling and that was a secret Karen didn't trust Holly to keep.

"Sometimes—in complicated situations—there doesn't seem to be a clear, easy answer for the problem. There's this friend of mine…she's got herself in some trouble with this guy she likes, only he doesn't feel the same way about her."

"Are you still *not* talking about you and Bret or are you *not* talking about Amanda and Chris?"

Karen stopped breathing. If Holly asked her straight up about Amanda being pregnant, she couldn't lie. *God, what a mess! Help me through this.* "I'm talking about Amanda and Chris."

"What happened to them? Why did they break up?"

"I don't know. Chris isn't ready for commitment. Amanda was. When he said he didn't want to be with her anymore, she took it pretty hard."

"She was in love with him, wasn't she?"

Karen sighed. "Head over heels."

"I still don't get it? Why would Chris break up with Amanda? She's beautiful, stylish…and she used to be so much fun to be around. What more could a guy want?"

"I don't know. Some guys fear being in a serious relationship. They don't like being accountable or responsible to someone else."

"Do you think that's why Bret was single for so long? Did he fear commitment?"

Karen laughed. "I don't think so. Bret has something people call an obsessive-compulsive disorder. He's worked really hard to get where he is in his career. I think he was too busy with college and climbing the corporate ladder to focus on being serious with someone."

"Well, I wish things would change for Chris. I liked him and Amanda being together. He's got to be the coolest dad ever—except for his temper. Did you know he lets Shelby wear makeup?"

"No way. Really?"

"Yep. Any chance I could start wearing it?"

"Sorry."

"Figures," Holly mumbled. "Can you imagine? With a little work Chris and Amanda would make the best parents ever. It really stinks that guys can be so slow."

"Tell me about it. I hope you'll let this be a lesson before you get serious about boys and that you'll take into consideration what God says about guarding your heart."

Things grew quiet, and then Holly asked another question. "What would you do if Bret did something really bad and broke your heart? Do you think you could forgive him?"

Karen thought about it for a minute. "Well…I…I'm sure I could. Depending on what it was, it might take some time, but I love him, and I'm committed to him. So yes. I think I could. That's what love is about."

Holly smiled, and Karen was surprised at how good the answer sounded even to her own ears. "So what kind of flowers do you have in mind? I hear daisies are the symbol of May."

"Roses. You definitely should go with roses. After all those red ones Bret sent you last fall, how can you not?"

"That was romantic. I got a bouquet every week until he proposed." This time both girls sighed.

"I guess we'll have to see what the professionals say."

"What was your first wedding like?" Holly asked.

"Simple. Your dad and I were young. He was fresh out of college, and I had just finished high school. We were broke. I wore my mother's dress because by then Daddy had already started taking treatments. There was hardly anything extra once the medical bills started rolling in."

"He died of colon cancer, right?"

Karen nodded. "When you were just a baby. I guess that's what's been fun about planning this wedding. In many ways I'm planning the ceremony I've always dreamed about."

"Then you should spare no expense!"

"Easy for you to say! I'm the one who has to pay for it."

"That's what you've got Bret for. He earns a lot of money, doesn't he?"

"Twice what I do, but he also works really hard. I guess that's something we're going to have to discuss in detail before we get married: finances."

They made it to the florist where Karen took Holly's advice. They chose to have fresh cut bouquets of yellow roses. Yellow for its meaning of promise of a new beginning. They were to be tied with a white satin ribbon.

"I'm so excited!" Karen squealed in anticipation of her wedding day as they climbed back in the car and headed to the store to pick up some groceries.

On the way back to Bret's, they swung by Amanda's, but she didn't come to the door. It was just as well. Karen wasn't sure how she was going to handle her newfound knowledge.

Holly helped tote in the grocery bags and placed them on the counter once they got back to Bret's. "Care if I go watch TV for a while?"

"Sure," Karen said. "See what's on Lifetime. Maybe we can catch an afternoon chick flick."

Holly went into the living room and turned on the TV. Karen could hear her flipping through the channels. "It's *Pirates of the Caribbean!*"

Karen grimaced. *Why is that on Lifetime?* It was one of Holly's favorite movies. "I'll pass."

"Suit yourself."

Karen went about putting away the milk, orange juice, and cereal. She glanced around Bret's kitchen, and although the place was immaculate, it lacked a woman's touch. Brown curtains on a brown wall accented by abstract art didn't exactly spell out home sweet home. That and there weren't any knickknacks or personal items sitting around.

She wiped down the counter, glad that Bret had agreed to move in with her. Although his apartment complex was more upscale than hers, there was a waiting list for units that offered three bedrooms. Karen's lease wasn't up until August, and although it was small, it would have to do for now. Hopefully by the end of summer they could find something permanent.

Rather than join Holly, Karen decided to make lunch. She found whole wheat bread in the cabinet and a butter knife in the drawer by the fridge. In no time she had two roasted turkey sandwiches, three ham and cheddar, and one bologna with mustard. She placed them on

Forgiveness for Yesterday

a platter and put them in the fridge so they could eat as soon as the boys got home.

At quarter past one, there was no sign of Bret or Scott. Karen settled onto a barstool at the end of the kitchen island and found the magazine she'd started on that morning. Picking it up, she began to read. When she got to the bottom of the page, she read the name of the author and noted his fancy degree.

In her opinion, the guy was way off base. Giving your teenager the freedom they desired would not keep them out of trouble or establish the trust he said was vital. Holly was too young to know what she needed, much less was she able to weigh through all the consequences of her actions. That was something even the grown ups in her life were struggling with at the moment.

Karen tossed the magazine into the trash and sifted through the others. When she got to the bottom one, her heart stopped cold in her chest. She lifted it from the pile and looked toward the living room to make sure Holly was still glued to the TV. Even still, her face felt warm as her eyes took in the cover.

It displayed a model wearing, well, nothing. Out of curiosity, Karen flipped it open and felt bile rise in her throat at the contents of the pages. *What...in...the...world? Bret...does...he read...this stuff?*

"Mom?"

Karen threw the magazine down like it was on fire. "What is it, honey?"

"Can I have something to drink?"

"Sure. Stay right there. I'll bring it to you."

"But Bret said to never bring food in here."

"It's okay. We can make an exception."

Karen shoved the magazine in a drawer, made the soda, and took it to her daughter who was still on the couch. "Use a coaster."

"Yes, ma'am," Holly saluted, looking surprised she could have soda in the living room.

When Karen was out of sight, she yanked the offensive literature from its hiding place and locked herself in the downstairs bathroom with it. "Okay, this can't be what it seems," she told herself. After two deep breaths, she opened the pages.

Once she got past the initial shock of what she was seeing, she found the articles weren't of much interest. But the photos—the photos were explicit.

Please God, let this be a mistake! A few moments later, Karen heard the back door open, and then Scott's voice mingled in with Bret's. *Keep calm, think rationally.* That was hard to do when she wanted to open the door, throw the vile magazine in Bret's face, and demand an answer. Questions about Katie and all the things she didn't know about Bret swirled around in her head like vultures threatening to consume her.

Knowing the man who owned this magazine was the very man her son idolized threatened to push any rational thoughts from her mind. *What if Scott had found this thing?*

Karen felt sick. She raised the lid on the toilet just to be safe. She didn't want to explain to Bret why she had ruined his bathroom rug. A few more moments and the nausea passed, but her train of thought didn't change. How well did she know Bret? Everyone had their secrets, but if Bret had a problem with pornography, she wanted to know before they said their vows, not after.

Suddenly Karen was hit with a wave of anger. No more than a few hours ago she'd been rolling around on his living room couch flirting with the temptation of not waiting for her wedding night! Karen placed her hands to her face as a cold sweat left her dizzy.

No, God, no! I'm so sorry about this morning. I should've never let things go that far. Tell me he's got some excuse or reason I'm not seeing. Anything!

Quietly among her panic, the Lord spoke to her. *Be still and know that I am God.* Be still? Who could be still at a time like this! "Calm down, Karen," she chided herself. This could just be one magazine. It's not saying he's addicted. Lots of men look. It's completely normal." *What am I saying?*

Her eyes moved to the corner where a basket held some magazines. She could hear the pounding in her heart, not sure if she was ready for the answer she was about to discover. Quickly she grabbed the stack. *Business World*, an old copy of *USA Today*, a Christian men's magazine—there was nothing more alluring than a copy of *Sports Illustrated*, and it wasn't even the swimsuit edition.

"Oh thank God!"

"Karen, are you in there?"

Her heart skipped another beat hearing Bret's voice on the other side of the bathroom door. He knocked again when she didn't answer.

"I'll be right out."

"Um…okay. Hey, did you tell Holly she could have a drink in the living room?"

"Yes."

"Oh. Uh…well…okay. Is it all right if we go ahead and eat?"

"Sure," she said as she worked frantically to reorganize the magazines strewn in the floor with the exception of one. Karen shoved *it* under the stack of linens in the back of the closet. Whatever Bret had to say in his defense, now was not the time to address the issue. They needed privacy.

Until then, all she had to do was pretend she hadn't seen what she had and that she didn't know what she did. She splashed some water on her face and took a deep breath. *Her* pretending, however, wasn't what she was worried about. It was Bret's.

⤎⚬⤏

Later that evening, Bret walked Scott and Holly out to the car. Karen had managed to survive the day, but she was ready to go home.

"See you two in the morning," Karen heard him say to the kids as he shut the car door.

"Can we go to the Pizza Palace for lunch?" Scott asked from the backseat.

Bret leaned down at the passenger side window and looked in at Holly. "It's your sister's turn to pick."

"I say let's do Chinese. Last time you made a noodle come out your nose."

"I did not! It only looked like that, but I agree. Chinese it is!"

Scott started to whine, and Bret cut him off. "I don't want to hear it. We've had a great day. Don't go home fighting with your sister because it *is* her turn to choose."

Karen watched the way Scott immediately changed his attitude. Bret's word was the final say. Holly and Scott respected that.

Please God. Give me the words.

Bret waved good-bye, but instead of getting in the car with the kids, Karen reached for his hand. "Care if we step back inside for a minute?" She was probably too tired to do this now, but the worry was gnawing at her. She had learned from earlier arguments with him that it was best not to let her feelings fester.

A puzzled look crossed Bret's face, but then he smiled. "Sure."

They stepped back into the kitchen where she crossed her arms and waited.

"What is it?" Bret asked in earnest, seeing this wasn't going to turn into the make out session he probably expected.

Silently Karen went into the bathroom and returned to the kitchen with the magazine in her hand. Tossing it in front of him on the counter, she felt panic close in over her when his face went red.

"It's not what you think," he said, moving closer. She jerked away making it clear she wasn't pretending any longer.

"You'd better have a good explanation for this…this trash that I found laying around your kitchen this afternoon! What would you have done if Scott had been the one to pick this up?"

"Calm down."

"Don't tell me to calm down! To think, just this morning I was considering giving in. It's been on my mind every minute since then that I wouldn't be your first, and now this! What's happened to you? Do I even know you at all?"

"Karen! Get a hold of yourself. It's not mine! It's…it's Chris's! He must've left it here when he was in last."

"What?"

Bret let out a sound that couldn't quite pass as a laugh. "It's old!" he reasoned further.

"You mean…this isn't yours?"

Bret shook his head.

"Oh, God!" Her hands came to her face in shame. "Bret, I'm so sorry. I thought…all day I tried to think of a reason as to why this would be here, and I simply couldn't find one. I couldn't come up with an excuse." She pressed a shaking hand to her forehead. "I'm so embarrassed."

"Come here." He wiped away her tears and kissed the top of her head when he pulled her into an embrace. "It's okay. Finding it here, I can understand why you thought what you did."

Karen pulled away and pressed her hands to her still burning cheeks. Although relief flooded through her system, she couldn't deny what a jolt the day had given her nerves. She looked up into Bret's eyes—eyes she knew would never lie to her. "I am really sorry. It's just that when I found this, well…all day I've been asking myself how well I know Amanda, and then there's the drama with Chris…looking is the same as cheating. After your confession this morning, for a second there, I wasn't even sure I knew you."

He pulled her close and stroked her back. "Nothing has changed. I'm still the Bret you have always known me to be. I do *not* have a problem with pornography, and I would most certainly not cheat on you. I love you. Trust me on that. Here," he said, taking the magazine, "we'll throw it away right now." He popped the lid on his chrome trash can and pitched it in. "Gone."

"Thank you. Thank you for understanding."

Karen stood there a few more minutes, enjoying how her world had just righted itself. "I guess I better go since the kids are already in the car. I'll see you in the morning at church."

"Sure."

Bret smiled at her as she walked back outside. Karen climbed behind the wheel. Suddenly seeing Holly's face, she remembered her daughter's comment from earlier in the day. "If Bret did something to break your heart, could you forgive him?" Karen's answer had been said mostly because it sounded good, not because it was what she actually felt in her heart. After today's scare, she knew if the magazine had been his, it would be a lot harder for her to get past.

Thank you, God, that this was all a misunderstanding. And if Bret ever does do something that breaks my heart, I pray that I'll remember it was I who first broke yours.

17

Bret turned his car off I-40 just like his GPS told him to. According to the address Chris had given him, he was supposed to continue traveling northwest by taking a right at the bottom of the ramp.

He made the turn and then settled in for what would be another fifteen minutes of countryside. When Darrell suggested he make this trip, it hadn't taken much persuasion to get him to leave town. When life should be falling into place, it felt like it was falling apart. And it was all because Karen had found that magazine.

Bret played the memories from Saturday night through his mind. She'd taken the whole issue to another level and blown it entirely out of proportion. That was why he'd done what he had. He lied.

The magazine she had been so irate over was his. How else would he know it was an old issue? He kept the current issues upstairs in his nightstand drawer.

The same familiar verse he'd been hearing from Matthew came to mind. "But I tell you that anyone who looks at a woman lustfully has already committed adultery with her in his heart."

But God, you said those words in a time when there wasn't a half-naked woman featured on nearly every street corner. Back then it was easier not to look. It helps me handle the pressure of…well, of everything. But lying… Lying was wrong no matter when it was done. Bret took a breath, trying to soothe his conscience. If Karen hadn't been so over the top, he would've told her the truth. But now? Now there was no going back.

The lie he told placed him under a conviction during the following morning's church service that almost killed him. He prayed a very repentant prayer, came home, and tossed out anything that may ever cause him to have to lie to Karen again. He promised himself and God that if the situation presented itself again, he would be nothing but honest.

Bret tapped his hand on the steering wheel. As much as he wanted to believe that, he knew it would come with great sacrifice. If one of the kids found something like that lying around, honesty wasn't going to cut it. *The women in those magazines aren't even real!* Porn was just a way for him to deal with temptation that seemed to come in waves. Most days he was fine. He hadn't actually given in and sought it out in weeks. But how did he explain that to Karen? He couldn't. She would simply never understand. He'd already admitted his jealousies over Chris and confessed his lackluster track record with women. Any more and Karen would start seeing him as the loser his high school classmates and his ex had always told him he was.

Bret couldn't let that happen. Not when Karen deserved a man whom she saw as loyal, honest, and strong in his faith. That was the kind of man she deserved, and that was the man she was getting. He was going to be that man.

All it was going to take was a tighter reign on his emotions. In a few weeks, they would be married, and he wouldn't have to deal with the issue anymore. Karen had promised. If he went back and told the truth now, she would think he was some kind of weirdo on top of being a liar when he really wasn't. *God help me here. This is not who I am.*

There was none of the peaceful reassurance he had come to expect. *I'm sorry I lied to her, Lord. I want to do the right thing, but there's so much pressure.* Bret's prayers were cut short when an automated voice told him to make a left turn.

Bret slowed the car and made the turn while scanning the roadside for the restaurant where he and Chris were supposed to meet. A sign came up on his right, marking the diner. "Curly Shirley's?" "You've got to be kidding," he said in disbelief as he saw what used to look like Chris's truck parked in the gravel lot out front. Bret gave his turn signal.

Another wave of anxiety twisted his stomach, and Bret put the car in park and reached into the dash for a pack of antacids. If the rest of the week played out like the first half had, he may end up eating the entire carton.

Chris threw up a hand, and Bret waved back. Even from a distance, Bret sensed something was different and not just the mud caked down the side of Chris's once spotless four-wheel drive.

It had been almost four weeks since they'd gotten anything more than a phone call from Chris. Something was up, and Bret had been strongly instructed to find out what along with some kind of evidence that would *prove* Chris incapable in order to tip the board in favor of initiating a forceful take over.

Seeing Chris's smiling face, Bret once again felt torn inside with the choice that was facing him. *This is it, Lord. It's what I've worked so hard for. It's right in front of me. The job...the girl...please don't let me lose it.*

Chris was excited to see the familiar black sedan pull in the parking lot of the diner. He remembered the day he'd stood in Bret's office, fumbling for words to give in an apology. So much had changed.

Chris smiled over the memory of when he'd given his heart to the Lord. He stepped outside that morning into the beautiful white snow that had fallen during night, sure it would be the first day of a new and different life. And it was. Unfortunately the moment he put his foot to the perfection covering the ground, the world and its problems had been waiting on him.

The crew he was working with was suddenly the most foul mouthed, crude bunch of guys Chris had ever met. It didn't help that they were constantly goofing off, messing something up or getting in fights. There were times he felt like he had signed on to run a day care instead of a group of professionally trained men.

The only way he found to rise above his surroundings was to immerse himself in the Bible. He couldn't count the days he'd put in fifteen hours on the jobsite and then stayed up another two hours soaking in the passages from John and Matthew, Mark and Luke. He didn't understand everything he was reading, but parts of it he did.

Looking back, he felt foolish for dismissing God as a myth, something that others could claim to believe in just because. Now it was plain for him to see. Not only was God real, he was passionate, self-sacrificing, and completely loving of those he came to serve.

"Hey, long time, no see," Chris said when Bret stepped from the car. He pulled Bret into a handshake and placed an arm over his shoulder. "I can't believe it's been nearly a month! How've you been?"

"Good. You?"

"Fantastic! There's nothing like this mountain air." Chris stopped and smiled, taking in a deep breath that smelled faintly of barbeque. He was hoping for a chance to tell Bret all about what had happened and how he wasn't perfect but was a changed man. "Hope you're hungry. This place has the best country cookin' in town." Chris chuckled seeing the way Bret eyed the building with caution.

"Curly Shirley's? You can't be serious."

Chris smiled. "The sanitation grade is more than passing."

"And what happened to your truck?"

"Work—that's what happened." Chris led the way to a booth by the window, and Bret took the seat facing the counter. It was just after six, and the place was filling up. They reached for menus, but Chris already knew what he wanted.

"So what's going on back at home?" he asked when Bret made his decision.

"Not much. Karen's good. The kids are great."

Chris felt the strain. "What do you say we get business out of the way first so you can call Darrell and give him his update? Then we can enjoy the rest of our visit without the pretense."

Bret actually tried to look surprised.

"Listen," Chris said. "I know you didn't drive all the way out here for leisure. Not when you've got a bride-to-be waiting at home. This is Darrell's little way of having you check up on me, see what's going on, and make sure I'm behaving myself. I get that. I know it puts you in the middle, but I honestly have nothing to hide. Actually I think you'll be impressed with the progress we've made."

"Well…I…"

Forgiveness for Yesterday

The waitress came by and interrupted what Bret was about to say.

"What'll it be, suga'?" She was someone new, and although she was young and pretty, she was all country, and she was giving Chris the appraisal most women did. In the past he would've flirted with her just to mess with her head.

"I'll have the blue plate special with sweet tea," he said.

The woman jotted on her pad and smacked her gum. "You get two vegetables with that. We've got pintos, fried squash, mashed taters, okry…"

Bret's eyebrows rose. "Did you say taters and…okry? What's that?"

The young woman rolled her eyes. "Taters are those white things that grow in the ground, and okry is that green pod-lookin' stuff."

"You mean potatoes and okra?"

"That's what I said. Taters and okry." She turned back to Chris and smiled. "You decide yet, baby doll?"

Chris swallowed his laughter at the way Bret and the woman were discussing his order. Only Bret would argue a local over dialect. He thought about asking if they had kraut just to see Bret's full range of facial expressions. "I'll go with the pintos and the fried squash." He nodded at Bret insinuating it was his turn to order.

Bret eyed him and then the woman. "I'll have a Coke." When he didn't say anything more, Chris looked at the waitress's name tag. "Tell you what, Crystal, why don't you bring my friend here a plate of the chopped barbeque. Load it up real high 'cause he's from out of town. Oh, and bring out some of that hot sauce. It's best when it's spicy."

One look back at Bret, and this time, Chris had to laugh. He was starting to pale. "Uh, actually," Bret said, "I think I'll have the homemade chicken salad on whole wheat. Throw in a side of the"— Bret flipped the menu back open —"fruit cocktail, if you don't mind… please?"

The woman scrawled the request, and Chris chuckled. "You were saying?"

"In English or Hillbilly?" Bret shook his head in disbelief. "Yes. Darrell sent me out here to see what it is you're doing. He also wanted me to give you a message. As you know, the VK lawyers worked their magic, and we won't be seeing a dime. Rumor has it they signed with Tighton Construction last week. Twenty million dollars in the deal with the promise to build seven more structures within the next three years. I hear they've made an offer on land in Alamance County, near Burlington."

Chris gave a low whistle as he processed the information. "Twenty million dollars is a lot of money. That combined with a three-year contract? I don't know what to say."

"You can start by saying Greeson took a huge loss on your behalf."

Chris nodded. "They did. I wonder why they're looking at land near Burlington. Anything that's available is what? Thirty miles or more from Greensboro? And it's a much smaller city."

"Beats me, but something's caught their eye."

Whatever the reason, the knowledge was sobering. "I hate to hear that. I know you all had hopes that this would be our big break. How's Darrell taking it?"

"Fair." Bret paused as if he were debating what to say and then looked him in the eye. "Chris…the board's not happy. It's been weeks. You haven't called, you haven't come back into town to follow up. What's going on out here? Half of the people in the office think you're out here in rehab."

Chris laughed loosely. "I told you. I'm working my tail off. Come by the house first thing tomorrow morning, and I'll let you swing your own hammer. You'll see. The good news is I think I've already found someone who might be interested in buying—a man by the name of Wayne Penry. He came out last week asking all kinds of questions."

Chris pulled the card Mr. Penry had given him from his wallet and handed it to Bret. "Says he manages resort property along the coast. He's looking for something in the western part of the state."

"Think he'd be willing to give us a fair price?"

This time Chris's smile bloomed big. "We both know there isn't a man alive who'd give us what we need to come out on top in this thing. This is not nor will it ever be the investment I thought it would. I've messed up. I know I should just cut my ties and count my losses, but I can't."

Forgiveness for Yesterday

"Why?" Bret paused. "This could really come down to you losing your father's company."

Chris grew thoughtful. "I don't know. I can't explain it. There are just some things that are more important than the bottom line. The best I can do is see this through and then find a buyer."

The waitress brought their drinks and their food. Chris spread his napkin out and prepared for Bret to bless their meal. When Bret reached for his silverware instead, Chris looked down at his plate full of fried chicken, pintos, and squash. He silently thanked the Lord for the blessing of a good meal, Bret's friendship, and the fact that he'd been given a second chance at more than one thing in life.

He lifted his knife and fork and noticed Bret was completely oblivious to the fact that he had just stopped and prayed. It was just as well. Chris was looking for a way to tell Bret about the changes that were going on, but it wasn't a conversation he wanted to have in a crowded diner. It would have to wait until tomorrow.

Chris pushed the disappointment aside. That was why he hadn't called, not because he had something to hide. Some things you had to see to believe.

18

The next morning, Chris pulled on a clean T-shirt and stepped outside onto the porch of his cabin. He raised his arms over his head and stretched his muscles. He would never forget waking up those first weeks after starting back at manual labor. Muscles he didn't know he had ached for what seemed like forever.

The sun was coming up, and it promised to be a beautiful day. A guy from the county was coming by first thing to inspect the newly poured foundation for the stables, and Bret was due to arrive shortly thereafter.

After spending time with Bret during their supper at the diner yesterday, Chris knew exactly what he wanted to say when he got Bret alone. He wanted to thank him. Not just anyone would've put up with his junk for as long as Bret had. "Thank God for faithfulness," Chris said to the morning.

The sounds of men working filled the air, and soon Chris became lost in the activity. It wasn't until around nine that a man wearing a hard hat and carrying a clipboard waltzed onto the site. "Hey, how're you doing?" Chris greeted, shaking the man's hand. For obvious reasons, having an inspector around made him nervous.

"Name's Henry. I'm here to take a look at the building foundation." Chris led the way around the back of the house and up the through the yard to the edge of the woods where they were putting the stables. The man looked over the trench filled with concrete and the cinderblocks that sat in it, making marks on his clipboard as he went.

A little while later Chris finally let go of the breath he'd been holding.

"Looks good," the man said. "Here's my card. Give me a call when you're ready for me to come back out and take a look at the framing."

Forgiveness for Yesterday

They were almost back to the man's truck when he passed by the side of the estate house.

"Uh-oh." The man grunted and stepped closer to the house. "That isn't good," he said, opening a wooden box that ran along the outside of the structure. "Who'd you hire to do this?"

The nervous feeling Chris had earlier was back. When electricity had been added to the house during the forties, they had chosen to run most of the wiring in boxes along the outside of the house. Compared to modern standards, it was a major fire hazard. Chris had questioned this himself, but his friend, Preston, who was an electrical engineer, assured him he wouldn't have any trouble with it. Because of that, rewiring the house was a corner Chris felt he could cut.

"No one. It was like that when we got here. It's covered under the grandfather clause."

The man scratched his balding head and studied the fuse box. "Maybe so, but I don't know that I wouldn't make some changes. I know I'm not authorized to come out here and inspect this, but I spent twenty years working as an electrician. This thing is ready to blow. It's bad enough the wiring runs on the outside of the house, but these connections are all wrong. You've got knockouts missing in the bottom of the box…a big rainstorm, and you could see some fireworks."

Chris could feel his blood pressure rising. Redoing the electrical could mean big bucks.

The man must've sensed his dilemma. "I'm sorry," he finally said, "I know with this already in existence we can't require you to fix it, but an old place like this…it'd be a shame to see it burn down, especially after all the work you're doing to improve it. Ideally, a house this old should've had all its wiring stripped out and redone years ago. But this here"—the man tapped the electrical box beside him—"is the heart. You've got to have it right or otherwise you're going to run into all kinds of headaches in the future." He motioned inside the house. "You got plaster walls in there?"

Chris nodded.

"I was afraid of that. Mind if I take a look around inside? Off the record, of course."

Chris debated whether or not if he should throw a match to the house himself and save the man his trouble. Starting over with the electrical work would be a nightmare. He'd cut all the corners he felt like he could. Unfortunately it didn't look like this would be one of them. "Help yourself," he finally said, trying to sound stern but not out right threatening, "but *off* the record, of course."

By midmorning, the man handed him a list of suggested repairs. There were bare wires in the attic, an outlet with a short in it on the back porch, and of course the faulty fuse box mounted on the side of the house that was a disaster waiting to happen.

"It's not as bad as I thought it'd be. I'd still try to replace the wiring since I'm sure you'll be updating the appliances and heating and air system. Back in the old days, they didn't have microwaves and dishwashers and such. That old fuse box will never be able to push that many amps. "

Chris thanked the man and filed the paper aside to deal with later. No sooner did he climb on the bobcat did Bret pull down the drive. "Perfect timing!" Chris grumbled. He jumped off the heavy equipment and went down to meet him.

"What took so long? We start work at sunup."

Bret shoved his hands in his pockets and looked across the property. "Wow! You *have* been busy."

Chris spun around and tried to see things through Bret's eyes. There were several signs of the demolition process lying around the yard. "It's a mess, but a new coat of paint makes a world of difference. C'mon."

Chris led the way through the main house pointing out all the positives. "Tongue and groove joints, four by six beams…they don't make them like this anymore. She's solid." He slapped an exposed beam to emphasize his point. "And here, take a look at this." Chris bent low showing off a fireplace mantel that had been stripped down to the original wood. "I'm making a guess, but I think it dates back to the mid eighteen hundreds. Look at the detail work. Every bit of this was done by hand."

"It's gorgeous." Bret lifted a hand and ran it down the piece. "Your guys do nice work."

Chris finished showing him the rest of the house, along with the barn and what they had started on the stables. An hour later, he ended the tour when they stepped back into the kitchen of Chris's cabin for a drink. It was the moment Chris had been waiting for.

"What'll it be? Water? Soda?"

Bret ducked his head inside, and Chris wondered if he was spying to see if there was something questionable to choose from that Chris hadn't offered.

"Water's good." Bret nodded, seeing Chris's fridge was clear from alcohol.

Chris grabbed a soda and a bottle of water and motioned to the two chairs at the table. "So what do you think?"

"I'd say you're more than halfway." Bret took a long sip of his water, and Chris knew this was his chance.

"There's something else I was hoping to tell you. In case you haven't noticed, the house isn't the only thing that's undergone a change. A few weeks ago…" Chris paused knowing his next words were going to be a real surprise. Bret sat up straighter, and Chris knew it was because he was anticipating something bad.

"I gave my heart to the Lord."

A blank expression played out on his friend's face, but it soon turned to question. "Really?"

"Yeah, surprising, I know. But it's true. It happened a few nights after my last visit home. There was an accident on my way back in that evening. I was sitting at a red light, and the man behind me pulled around and ran it. Right there in front of me, I witnessed a transfer truck smash into his car." Chris felt his eyes glaze over, seeing the incident as if he were living it all over again. "Seeing him die right there in the street got me thinking. It seemed like such a shame to keep wasting my life, not when God had made it clear to me that he had spared it for a reason. I picked up the Bible and started reading. Haven't been the same since."

"That's incredible. Really?"

Chris watched the way Bret continued to stare at him with questions in his eyes. Was it really that hard to believe he had turned around? Chris looked down at the table and dug at a chip in its veneer with his fingernail. There were still parts of that night he wasn't ready to tell anyone. Not even to Bret. "I guess I had to hit rock bottom, and I finally did. That was where Jesus found me." He sniffed, not wanting to tear up and make the moment more awkward than it was.

"So thank you," he continued on a fresh breath. "Thanks for standing by me, for being a faithful friend and an example when I was nothing but a jerk. I'm sorry for everything I put you through. Not just anyone would've put up with me, and I'll be forever grateful you did."

Bret stammered a minute obviously not knowing what to say. "No problem, I mean that's what friends are for. Wow." He laughed. "Forgive me. I knew something was different, but this is very unexpected. I'm glad you said something."

Chris chuckled. "Me too. I still don't have all the answers I'd like, but you're right. I'm different. I can't explain it, but I can feel it. It's like I can see for the first time. And being here...working on this house somehow helps me realize that God's working on me too."

"Amazing. So...what about Laurie? How are you feeling about all that?"

"It hurts, and I'm still disappointed, not only in what happened between us but also in her. It's funny though. Now that I have faith of my own, I feel like I've finally got back part of what I lost." Chris marveled at the irony of what he was saying. "For the first time, I'm actually starting to wonder if hope was the bulk of what I was really missing instead of her. Hope that was there all along, only I couldn't see it."

The phone in Chris's makeshift office started to ring. "It's probably Darrell calling to see what I've done with you. I'll call him back later."

Bret nodded. "I hope the two of you work things out."

"Me too, but for now as long as he doesn't show up and start telling me how to do my job, I think I'll be all right. Hang in there. I don't plan on letting him take my company without a fight, and as long as I'm in charge, you'll always have a job."

Forgiveness for Yesterday

Bret smiled. "Darrell tell you how to run a bulldozer?"

Chris took a swallow of the soda in his hand. "Bobcat," he corrected.

"Whatever. He would be completely lost. Work hard and work fast, and I'll be praying God does the same." Bret stood to leave.

"Hey, what's this?" he asked, holding up the gold necklace that was lying on the table. It was the one Chris often used as a book mark.

"It's a necklace I found last fall when we were up here fishing. Kyle managed to snag it on his fish hook in that old pond. I rediscovered it when I was cleaning out the house."

"Looks old, unusual."

"I'm sure it is. There's an initial on the back of the cross, an E."

"Hmm…" Bret placed the jewelry in a neat pile and offered Chris his hand.

Chris ignored it and took Bret into a full embrace instead. "I mean it," he said, hugging him for all he was worth. "Thanks again for all you've done. You're like a brother to me. I love you."

Bret slapped him on the back. "I….I love you too," he said, looking more surprised than ever. Chris walked him to his car and then headed back inside. He started to make some lunch when his phone rang again.

"Yeah," Chris said, snatching it from his desk in the corner.

"Chris. Hey. It's Karen. How are you?"

"Karen! I was just talking to Bret. Are you looking for him?"

"Yeah. Have you seen him this morning? I tried his cell, but there wasn't an answer."

"He just left but the reception around here is terrible. I would try again in about twenty minutes. He should be back to the highway by then. Everything okay?"

There was silence on the other end of the line, and Chris waited.

"It's nothing really." She laughed, but he could tell it was forced. "It's been two days, and he hasn't called. Like you said, maybe it's the reception. How's the project coming?"

Chris took the change of subject in stride. The last thing he wanted to do was get involved in a lover's spat. "It can be a huge headache at times, but I think we've turned a corner. In a few more weeks, you won't recognize the place."

"I can't wait to see it! We plan on driving out one day while we're in Lake Lure for the wedding."

Chris stretched out the phone cord and took a seat at the table again. It was good to have someone to talk to. "Speaking of a honeymoon, I found another packet of letters from our Ella Jackson."

"Oh? Tell me! What did they say?" Chris laughed at her sudden enthusiasm. Ella and William Jackson were a couple that had lived in the old farmhouse on the property back during the first part of the century.

Last fall when he'd been snooping around, he'd found a packet of love letters they'd exchanged during the First World War. Karen had been enthralled by their romance.

"I don't know what they say. It's not like I would ever read them."

"You're not fooling me, Christopher Lanning! I saw the look on your face standing in that kitchen last fall reading about a woman's undying love for her man. You were all into that!"

Just as Karen said the words, someone banged on the door and then stuck his head in without waiting for the okay. "Boss, we've got a problem out here!"

Chris turned around and fought the urge to roll his eyes. It was Gary who was always a little dramatic. "Be right there." When Gary continued to bounce in place, Chris snapped, "I said I'll be right there!" He waited until Gary went outside and shut the door before he got back to Karen. "I'll admit. Their letters were intriguing, but so what?"

"Uh-huh."

Chris chuckled. She wasn't buying. "Listen, I'm going to have to run. Bret should be halfway back to the interstate by now. I'm sure if you try again, you can catch him."

"Thanks, I'll do that. By the way, from now on, try to keep better track of your *junk*. I can't believe guys actually look at that trash. I've got kids to watch out for."

He had no idea what *junk* Karen was talking about. The persistent banging was back, and he didn't have time to ask. "Uh…sure thing. Take care," he said, hanging up the phone, his attention now on Gary.

"What is it?" he asked in impatience as he jerked open the door.

"The dam over at the pond is leaking. Jonathan said he thinks it's gonna go."

Chris felt his pulse kick up a notch. "What're you guys doing at the pond!" He ran out the front door and jumped in his truck with Gary climbing in the cab as he yanked it into drive.

"Some of the guys have been going out there during their lunch breaks. Only today they started horsin' around, and the next thing we knew the rocks started to slip. We had a really wet winter. One thing led to another and…"

Chris pressed the gas pedal further into the floorboard. Just last week some of his crew had thought it'd be funny to lock one of the new guys up in the Port-a-John. The thing ended up tipping over and caused all kinds of stink. Literally.

Chris made it down the driveway, turned left, and then jerked the wheel hard to take his truck off road across an open field to see what new trouble these idiots had gotten into. At the edge of the woods, he slammed the truck into park when he saw a small river pouring out of what used to be a full pond. Water gushed down the embankment cutting a path through the woods and onto the adjacent landowner's property. "This is bad," he said to no one in particular. There was nothing he could do but watch it drain.

Hands on his hips and his jaw set, Chris moved to the top of the hill to where a group of guys stood gawking at what was left of the crumbled dam. There was good reason for the fear he saw in their eyes as they stood there looking lost, not knowing what to do. "Which one of you…" *Watch your tongue*, something whispered inside his head, "overgrown…*babies* is responsible for this!"

None of the guys answered, so he got closer and louder. "I said, which one of you…*idiots* did this!"

Even from a distance he could hear Jonathan gulp. Chris walked over and fought the urge with everything he had in him not to yank the kid up by his collar.

"I didn't mean to, Mr. Lanning. It just sort of...happened."

Chris bit his lip so he wouldn't curse out loud. Before Jonathan could give him any details, Chris caught sight of three figures he didn't recognize coming up the hill from behind the pond. Although they varied in size, they all had the same face. Something told him he was getting ready to meet the neighbors.

When the three men were within speaking distance, the shortest one with dark hair spoke up first. "What in tarnation is going on out here? I've got a pasture full of horses down there standing knee-deep in water!"

The older man nudged the shorter one and told him to mind his manners. In an effort to get things on the right foot, Chris decided to take charge. "You must be the guys who work Willow Ridge Ranch. I'm Chris Lanning, owner of Greeson Developing." He extended his hand to the three, but only two of them took it. The short one snorted and turned away to spit on the ground.

"Please excuse our brother. His name is Garrett. I'm Tyler, and this here is our little brother, Ian." Tyler motioned to a man who had to be at least six foot, three. With the way Garrett was acting, he would've assumed he was the baby.

"We're the Steinman brothers." There was a long pause. "It seems you've had an accident."

"Accident!" Garrett said, mocking Tyler's words. "I'll say!"

Chris watched the way the men read each other, exchanging conversation without words. It was obvious Tyler and Ian were used to this kind of behavior from Garrett and could interpret each other easily.

Garrett walked around looking the group of construction workers over like he was some sort of investigator at a crime scene. He passed by Chris once more before announcing his verdict. "Don't ya'll dummies know better than to be playin' around a dam that's at least, shoot, I don't know, seventy, eighty years old?" He moved closer, his next comment just for Chris. "And by the way, we don't *work* Willow Ridge, we *own* it. That's *my* pasture down there you just put under water!"

Chris nodded. "Uh...yeah...I'm sorry about that...I—"

"Sorry? Sorry don't do me a bit of good. Best thing you can do is get back in your fancy truck and head back to the city where you belong. The last thing we need is a bunch of city slickers out here pretending to be cowboys."

Chris felt his body lunge forward to tackle Garrett, but Gary jumped on his right arm just in time. "Shut up, Garrett," the older brother named Tyler said, intervening. "It's obvious the man is telling the truth. It was an accident. You know, kind of like the time you decided to take a leak on that electric fence? Didn't go so well, now did it?"

Garrett's face flamed red when everyone snickered. "You shut up about that! It ain't like I knew it was on!"

Chris let the humor be a balm for his anger. Garrett was looking for a fight, and the worst thing he could do was give him one. He took a deep breath, prayed a word or two, and opened his mouth, not sure where the words he said came from. "I'm sorry about your horses. It seems some of my men forgot where they were supposed to be during their break. You can rest easy that they'll be taking care of any damages." He shot Jonathan a look that said they would be discussing how later. "Till then, my guys have work to do."

Tyler and Ian got the message and started back down the hill. Just as Chris was about to get in his truck, Gary opened his mouth.

"What's that?" he said, raising an outstretched arm and pointing across the emptying pond crater. The rushing water had washed away part of the embankment. "It looks like a...a hand."

Chris felt the color drain from his face. They all ran to the edge and peered down into the hole. Gary was right. Halfway across the length of what used to be a mucky pond bottom was something that undoubtedly resembled the skeleton of a human hand.

They continued to watch the waterline recede. Eventually it washed away enough dirt to reveal an entire human skeleton. Seeing it in its entirety, Garrett let into a blue streak of colorful curse words. Most of them contained adjectives describing rich people who didn't know how to leave well enough alone. "No wonder they say this place is haunted! It's got dead bodies popping up out of the ground."

The next thing Chris knew, one of them pushed the other, and then it was on. Gary, Jonathan, half of his crew, and the three Steinman brothers were rolling around in the grass, fists flying. Chris joined them in an effort to break it up but slipped down the embankment and into the mud instead.

Four hours later, and after two interviews—one with the police and the other with a reporter—Chris retreated back home on foot. He was sporting a black eye, was covered in dried pond goop, and was feeling every bit of the truth in Garrett's words. The whole Heritage property was cursed!

The good news was he wouldn't have to depend on Bret to relay to Darrell some hidden secret about what was really going on out at the Heritage property. Darrell could find out everything he needed to know just by watching the six o'clock news.

19

Bret adjusted the rearview mirror and exhaled impatiently. It was Friday morning, and he was sitting in his car outside of Karen's apartment waiting for her to make an appearance. He had gotten back into town yesterday afternoon, and although he and Karen had talked on the phone, this was going to be the first time he had seen her since he'd gone to Asheville to visit Chris.

He checked his reflection in the mirror again, wishing he had stopped for a haircut. Finally he saw Karen open the door and make her way down the steps. She was wearing a pair of white shorts and a soft lilac top. Her hair was pulled back in a clip. She was the very essence of spring.

She opened the door, and her presence filled his senses. He'd really missed her.

"Hi," she said, leaning in for a kiss. "Thank you for taking the day off. I missed you. A few days, and it feels like forever."

"Me too." He leaned in for a second kiss.

When he pulled away, her face was glowing. "Are you sure you're up for this? I've just about shopped Holly out, and there are still some things I need for the wedding."

"Sure," Bret smiled, meaning it. He would do anything to make up for putting distance between them by avoiding her calls and for the lie he'd told. At least the few days apart had given him time to think and deal with his guilt.

Bret pushed the week's memories aside, not wanting them to ruin their day. He had good news to share with Karen. He pulled the car onto Battleground Avenue and headed south before making his way over to Friendly Center. "I have some exciting news," he said, looking over at Karen who was sifting through the contents of her purse.

"Yeah? What?"

"I didn't mention this over the phone last night because I wanted to see your reaction and get your take on it."

"Okay..."

Bret parked the car, then turned to get a full view of her. "While I was in Asheville, Chris told me he finally made a decision for Christ." Karen's mouth fell open in surprise. Two seconds later, his ears started to ring because of the scream she let out. "Oh, Bret! This is wonderful! What happened? When? Tell me everything!"

He went on to relay everything that Chris had told him. "He told me he hit rock bottom and that Jesus was there waiting. I'm telling you, there was this...glow about him I've never seen before."

"Oh my gosh! I'm so happy for him. Thank you, Lord." She continued to go on and on and then realized she was rejoicing alone. "Aren't you happy about this?"

"Yes," Bret laughed, watching her. "I've just had a little more time to get used to the idea, but I also realize Chris still has a lot of demons to battle. I hate to sound pessimistic, but I'm curious to see how things play out."

"Chris Lanning does not play games when it comes to something like this. He's one of those who'll be all or nothing."

This time Bret laughed even harder. Karen had no idea.

"I'm serious," Karen continued. "Chris would never say something heartfelt like this just to reestablish good rapport with you or to buy himself some time with Darrell. If Chris says he's come to Christ, then he's come to Christ. End of story. Quit being so suspicious."

Bret studied her dazzling smile. "Okay," he said. "I am happy for him. Shall we shop?"

"Yes, we shall." Karen took his hand, and Bret ended up having more fun than he intended. His arms were laden with packages when he passed by a display window that captured his attention. "Here," he said, pulling Karen to a halt. She was looking for something to wear to the wedding rehearsal, and he had found just the thing.

"I don't know." Her eyes moved to the fancy sign over the door, and she worried a fingernail. "I'm sure it's expensive."

Forgiveness for Yesterday

"Go on," he said as he nudged her inside. "It's perfect." He waited just outside the dressing room while she tried it on. When she stepped out, his smile stretched wide. "See, I told you. It's perfect."

Karen twirled in front of the mirror, examining the cut of the suit. It was solid white with three quarter sleeves on the fitted jacket and a cinched waist in the skirt; the look was very feminine and flattering. He noticed how her smile faded as she stepped over and lowered her voice. "Bret, this suit is over three hundred dollars. It's beautiful, but that's way too much. I can find something much cheaper. Let's go over to that little boutique on—"

"Nonsense. This is the one. Go take it off, and I'll have the clerk ring it up."

She studied him a minute, obviously wanting to make sure he meant what he was saying. "I can pay you back," she finally said, somewhat embarrassed. "You've already bought so much."

"Karen, that's ridiculous. In a few weeks, I'll be managing both our accounts. Something like this suit you'll keep for years and wear a dozen different places. It's worth the money. Besides, I want my wife to be well dressed."

She resigned to his reasoning, kissed him on the cheek, and retreated to the dressing room.

While Karen was changing out of the suit, he added a few other things he thought she could wear to mix the outfit up just to prove his point. The suit was a purchase worth making.

"Thank you," she said as they left the shop and put the bags in his car. "You didn't have to do that."

"I know, but I love doting on you. I figure it'll take at least ten years before you bankrupt me," he said in a teasing tone.

Karen rolled her eyes and punched him in the ribs.

"Hey, let's get a milk shake," he said, changing the subject and dragging her into the ice cream shop where they started a conversation that left them laughing over every other word.

They ordered one vanilla and one chocolate and took their treats outside and started back down the sidewalk to enjoy the sunshine. They were almost back to the car when Karen voiced what was on her mind. "I wasn't expecting today to be so much fun. Not after such a long week."

Bret could hear the question in her voice. There was a bench nearby, and he led her to it. "I'm sorry for not returning your calls when I was out of town. The reception out there was terrible, but still, I could've called."

"Why didn't you?"

"For weeks now you've been warning me about all the changes we're getting ready to go through. It was nice to take a few days so that I could think and pray about the kind of husband I want to be to you. Seeing the change in Chris has really encouraged me. I've made some decisions, and well...I'm going to live every day of my life trying to be the man you deserve."

"Bret...that is so sweet. I did some thinking of my own while you were gone."

"You did?"

"Last weekend when I found that magazine, it made me realize that we have desires and hormones, and all these great things that make us tick as men and women. God made us that way, but we live in sex-crazed society. When we see someone who's attractive or something that's arousing *without* seeking it out, I don't think it's wrong to be stimulated by that. It's when we lust after something that it becomes a problem."

"I see. But doesn't the stimulation that's there naturally sometimes make it harder not to lust for more?"

Karen looked down at her hands. "That's just it. I'm afraid that's what I've done with you. I know you were joking when you called me a tease, but honestly, there have been times when I have done nothing to help you when it comes to pulling back on the reigns. You shouldn't carry that weight alone. Sure I can say no when it comes down to the moment of decision, but last Saturday morning when I knew you were struggling, I allowed myself to do some things that I knew would be hard for you to stop. We haven't talked much this week, but I really felt guilty about it."

"It's okay. I mean nothing happened."

Forgiveness for Yesterday

"Something did happen! These last few weeks we've allowed ourselves more privileges than what our hearts should've been okay with. I'm not a fool, Bret. Even though that magazine wasn't yours, I know you understand the kind of things that were in it. With the culture we live in, what grown man wouldn't? It makes me wonder what expectations you have for our wedding night. I don't look like those women—it's been a long time for me."

"Karen, you're beautiful. Those women…the ones in those magazines, they aren't real. You are. Whatever flaws you could possibly have, I promise to love every one of them."

Her relief was visible. "Thank you." She nodded. "I really appreciate the reassurance." Bret ached that he had ever given her cause to doubt, but not near as much as he hated the fact he had given her cause to feel guilty. He truly wished he were a man who had been able to keep their premarital relationship within what God said were the appropriate bounds. For the first time since Saturday, he considered if some of the guilt he had felt this week was for the very same reasons Karen had felt it: for the place he had let their physical relationship stray.

Bret searched his heart and found it was still mysteriously divided on the matter. He wanted to be with her—more than anything—but there would be no beauty in loving Karen physically at this point, at least no beauty that guilt couldn't taint.

"I know we've bent the rules, and I'm sorry for that. It burdens me to know I've done things that led to making you feel guilty. I wish I had the strength to say my mind is completely chaste when it comes to you, but we both know it isn't. My actions show as much." He leaned back on the bench, wishing this were the conversation they'd had a week ago. "I love you, Karen, but not being able to be with you yet is my greatest temptation."

"I appreciate your honesty, and I'm glad you agree. We have bent the rules. For a while there, I think we were both starting to question whose rules it was we were bending. I don't want to do that anymore. I want us to make a fresh start and honor God like we originally intended. It all makes me understand how Chris and Amanda got themselves into the mess they did. That's why I think we need to find someone who can hold us accountable."

"Accountable? Like who?"

"I don't know. It needs to be someone with the same values and beliefs we have as well as someone we can shoot it straight with. It should also be someone who'll ask us right out if we're keeping our minds and our hands where they belong and encourage us to do the right thing. It's humbling, but there's something to be said for knowing you have to answer for your actions. Every time I look at the kids, I think about it."

Bret wasn't sure about the comparison she made of them to Chris and Amanda, but he appreciated the rational way in which Karen was approaching this. At least she wasn't screaming or probing into days long gone. "I really wish we'd talked about this sooner. It would've been a huge help."

"You mean you'll do it? You'll find an accountability partner?"

"The wedding is only weeks away." Bret laughed. "I think I can make it."

"Temptations won't stop just because we're getting married, Bret. Satan knows our weaknesses and never fails to exploit them." She paused, and Bret could tell she was going to stand her ground. "Putting this into practice now is the perfect time to ensure its practicality and importance for the rest of our lives."

For some reason, the idea of someone keeping tabs on his sex life didn't settle well. Nevertheless, if it meant making her happy, he would give her his word. "Okay, but once we're married can't we just hold each other accountable?"

"Maybe on some things, but not when it comes to sexual temptations. We're too emotionally involved. Haven't you been listening? We would be tempted to lie to each other." Her innocent smile said she had no idea how squarely her words struck home with him.

Bret let out a nervous laugh. "Good point. We'll find someone to hold each of us accountable. Someone we trust and someone who believes like we do."

Karen smiled and rested her head on his shoulder. "Thank you." A quiet contentment filled the space between them.

"Do you remember when I told you about how God used the dark hours in my life to teach me to trust that he had something better in store than the feelings of loss and disappointment? How he did the same thing with David of the Bible?"

"I think so."

Karen went on. "David had the promise of being Israel's king, and even though he could've forced God's anointed blessing, he didn't. He waited on God's timing, and he honored God's commands. I know it's been hard, but I also know God will honor our decision and our sacrifice to wait."

"You're right." He smiled. "He will." Suddenly it was obvious why God had given him Karen. She was always encouraging him, lifting him up and pointing him back to his faith.

"So does this mean you've got everything you need for the wedding?"

"Almost."

"What could possibly be left? My car is running over."

"Well," she said, batting her lashes at him in an almost comical manner. "This really generous and gorgeous guy I know just bought me the most beautiful suit in the whole world, only he doesn't realize I have no shoes to go with it."

"Oh, he doesn't, does he? Well, I can remedy that. C'mon."

He helped her off the bench and watched in amazement as Karen went into a store and tried on the ugliest shoes he had ever seen. They were made of something that was supposed to resemble leather and were a ghastly shade of green. "Karen...I..."

"What?" she asked, completely serious. "They're on sale for $6.99. Think of the savings, and after all the money you spent on the suit, they're a completely practical choice."

"Practical, now there's a word. You're starting to remind me of your mother."

One giggle leaked out, and he caught onto her game. Without making a sign whatsoever, he changed his mind. "On second thought, I think you're right," he said, standing to admire the shoes. "Those really are you, only I'm thinking you should see if they have them in red because you're such a clown."

She gasped before reaching for one of her socks and throwing it at his head, only she missed and sent it sailing over the top of the aisle instead. Her eyes widened in surprise, and together they fell into a fit of laughter that ended with him chasing down her sock and placing it back on her foot as if it were a glass slipper. "I love being in love with you, Karen McMasters-soon-to-be-Sears." He chuckled. "Even if you have the saddest taste in shoes I've ever seen." He wrapped her up in his arms and placed a single kiss on her forehead.

"Aw, that is so sweet. It's nice to know you love clowns that much. I'm sure there isn't a thing in the world you wouldn't give me including a polka-dot tie and an orange fuzzy wig."

Bret snickered and buried his face in her hair. "You, my dear, are charging those shoes to your own credit card."

20

As the days continued to pass, the change Chris had been so eager and proud to tell Bret about was put to the test. The incident at the pond and the fact that it was covered by the news stations tuned the area residents into what Greeson Developing was doing to one of their most beloved historical markers.

The news that a multimillion-dollar company was sinking money—"faster than manure dries in July heat" according to Garrett Steinman—had a way of trafficking every historically concerned and nosy citizen within Buncombe County right to Chris's backdoor step. Unfortunately, when the Environmental Protection Agency got involved, Chris lost it.

Chris groaned remembering how he so easily quoted one of Garrett's lines to the agent who handed him a new list of restrictions yesterday. "Don't you people know how to leave things well enough alone?" he said as he threw what was none other than a grown-up temper tantrum.

After that he was also handed a fine to add to his growing stack of bills. The only good news of late was that because of whatever Bret had returned and said to Darrell, Darrell had eased off with some of the pressure. Chris knew this grace period wouldn't last forever, but for now, he felt like he had some time.

The thoughts of actually getting out of bed and facing the challenges that awaited him on the jobsite were daunting enough to keep him anchored in his sheets. He reached for his Bible and thumbed through the pages.

So far he'd read through most of the New Testament and had just started on the Psalms. He was still amazed that the same passages he had once viewed as condemnation now brought life when viewed through the cross. He did some more reading and then looked in the back of the Bible through the reference materials to see what he could find out about this man named David to whom he could so closely relate.

An hour later, Chris humbly slipped from the bed and got down on his knees. *Forgive me, Father. I know I don't always get it right, especially when it comes to my temper…and my mouth. I thought I'd struggle with laying down the alcohol, but somehow you've taken the desire entirely. It's my words that leave me feeling terrible. Please send someone to help me. Someone who'll be a positive influence to counteract what I'm surrounded by, day in and day out, on this job. Give me the words to tell Shelby and Kyle how much I love them and about what I've found in you. Don't let this all backfire in my face…*

After several minutes, his prayers came to a close, and for a moment, he sat in the quiet stillness of the room. *I am with you, my son. Always.*

Chris clung to the simple reassurance and regarded it with reverence. He got up and dressed, and by the time he made it out to the house, Sam, an older man who had years of experience as a skilled craftsman, was already working on one of the bedroom fireplace mantels.

Chris fell into work beside him, remembering the Lord's reassurance. When Sam started to sing along with the country song on the radio, Chris spoke up. "I hope you're not planning to join a band."

"That bad?" Sam laughed. "I'm not much of a country music fan, but it helps pass the time."

Chris nodded toward the radio sitting in the floor. "Feel free to change it if you want."

Sam looked at him. "You sure?"

"Anything but rap."

The man walked over and fumbled with the knobs for a minute. Soon gospel music filled the morning air. Chris's hands stopped moving. The Lord seemed to say, *Here is your help.*

He turned back to Sam who was patiently sanding the wood in front of him, while humming the lyrics to "The Old Rugged Cross".

Chris continued to watch him in his peripheral vision. He toyed with an idea for several minutes before giving in to it. "You go to church?" he finally asked the older man.

"I sure do—First Church of Clear Valley. It's a few miles south of here. You?"

"No." Chris chuckled. "Sunday mornings I'm here, like always."

Sam kept working. "You're the boss man. Why don't you call in sick one Sunday and go with me?"

Chris smiled. "I'm not sure if church is really what God intends for me, but thanks anyhow."

"Sounds like you've had a bad experience. If you're willing to give it a second shot, I bet my Millie would fix us up a nice pot roast after the service. She's the best cook around these parts. You can't beat her chicken pie and homemade apple dumplings."

Chris's mouth watered at the thought of a home-cooked meal. "Are you a believer?" he asked Sam, casting a glance over his shoulder to see the man's reaction to such a personal question.

"A believer in what?"

"Well…in Jesus."

Sam turned around and smiled. "The Bible says that even the demons believe…and tremble. If you're trying to ask if I'm a Christian, yes, I am. Back in 1972, the foulest mouthed sailor the US Navy had ever seen came stumbling into the closing of an old tent revival while on leave. The preacher man up front said a lot of stuff I couldn't understand that night, except for one thing."

Sam looked off in the distance, recalling the memory. "He was talking about mercy and grace. He said, 'Mercy is not getting what you deserve and grace is getting what you don't deserve.' He explained the gift of mercy like a child who had gotten caught doing something wrong and his daddy not punishing him for it. He illustrated grace by saying the father went on to buy the child a new toy instead. In a way, that's what God did for us. He didn't give us what we deserved for our sin, which was death, but he also gave us what we didn't deserve, himself. Those words changed my life. I knew the mercy and grace that preacher said I could find in Jesus was what I needed. I had certainly tried everything else."

Sam picked up his sandpaper with a fresh glimmer in his eye. "What about you? Are you a believer? Or something more?"

"I believe. I mean, yes, I'm a…Christian." Chris didn't mean to stumble over the words. He had just never made that statement before. "It's just that…well…this is all very new for me. Do you really believe God can change a man's heart? Just like that?" Chris snapped his fingers to show the instantaneous kind of change he was talking about.

"The heart, absolutely. His habits…" Sam shrugged. "That usually takes a little longer. I mean it when I say I was rough around the edges."

Suddenly Chris was very interested. "How did you change? I mean, I understand the heart change, but how did you—"

"Crucify the flesh?"

"Yeah."

"It wasn't easy. I'll give you that much. You can get involved with church and do all kinds of good things, but none of it means a hill of beans unless it comes from the heart. For it to come from the heart, you have to have a relationship with the Lord, and to have a relationship, you have to communicate."

"Communicate?"

"Yes. You have to read God's Word, study it. See what he has to say. Then you have to not only pray, but you have to listen and then do what he says."

Chris took a moment to evaluate himself. "I'm doing all those things already. Or at least I'm trying. But like you said, a lot of it I don't understand. I want to do right, but I still keep messing up."

Sam actually laughed. When he turned around, however, there was no mockery in his eyes, just love. "And you will keep messing up—none of us are perfect. Prayer, studying the Bible…those things feed the Holy Spirit that is now within you. You and I were once used to doing our own thing, and that was feeding the flesh. It'll take some time, but the most important part of messing up is repenting. Without repentance there can be no forgiveness. By repentance, I mean true sorrow and a desire to change. You want to know how I knew I truly was a changed man? How I knew the Lord had really worked a number on me?"

Chris nodded, curious.

"The day after I gave my heart to Jesus, I opened my mouth, and the words that had so easily come out before felt like acid on my tongue. I fell to my knees in repentance, but for years every time I mashed my finger on something, that same sin was right back." Sam gave a thoughtful look and grinned.

"As time wore on, I guess you could say those instances became less and less. It's kind of like me over here sanding on this old mantel. Years of paint, dirt, and decay have settled over what was once a beautiful piece of art. The original craftsman never intended for it to look like this. A hundred years of use and abuse really adds up.

"Now I'm just a man working a trade, but in a way, God looks at me the same way I look at this wood. He sees all my sins and imperfections, but he doesn't throw me into the fire. He doesn't only see what I am, he sees what I can be. That's why he picks up his sandpaper, and he starts sanding. He starts whittlin' away all that junk that keeps me from being my best—almost like he's restoring me to what he intended for me to be all along, only he gives me new things too, things like faith and hope." Sam shook his head in amazement. "I wish I could say I always do the right thing, but I don't. It's more of a life-long process. O' Lord, that we might live up to what we've already attained! But whatever you do, never forget mercy and grace."

Chris smiled. There was light in the old man's eyes that he admired.

"Tell you what. If you don't think you're ready for an actual church service, our pastor just started a Bible study that's meeting in a coffee shop downtown. I think they meet on Thursday evenings. It's nothing formal, just a group of men getting together and discussing the Bible from what I hear. Why don't you give Pastor Mark a call and check it out? I know he'd be glad to have you."

Chris took the card Sam handed him with the pastor's name and number on it. Later that evening he pulled it out, debating on whether or not to take Sam's advice. A small group meeting in a downtown coffee shop sounded more his style than an actual church service. Still, he wasn't sure getting involved with a group of people who could very well turn out to be a bunch of hypocrites was the answer.

He punched in the numbers on the card, asking himself what was the worst thing that could happen. This time around, he had faith of his own. He wasn't dependent on someone else's. Two rings later, a warm, rich voice filled his ear. "Pastor Mark here."

Suddenly at a loss for words, Chris paused a second too long.

"Hello?" the voice asked again.

"H…hi," Chris stammered. *This is ridiculous. I'm a grown man, the owner of a multimillion-dollar company. I shouldn't be stammering like a teenage girl.*

"Um…my name is Chris Lanning. I think Sam Parsons is a member of your congregation. Anyway, he gave me your card. Said that you and some guys were meeting for a Bible study on Thursday nights. He thought it sounded like something I might be interested in. He asked me to give you a call."

"Sure thing. Sam's a good friend. You said your name was Chris?"

"Yes, sir. Chris Lanning."

"Great. A few guys and myself have been meeting at the Coffee Café on Thursday evenings at seven. It's real informal—most of the guys come straight from work. Right now we're studying in the book of Philippians. You're more than welcome to join us if you'd like."

The man seemed nice enough and didn't ask any probing questions about who he was or what his life story included. Chris agreed to come and got directions to where the café was located.

When he hung up, some of his anxiety over stepping out of his comfort zone faded. If he got involved with something that would have a positive influence on his life, it was bound to help him with areas where he struggled.

In the end, it would probably lead to him sharing about his past and opening up about some of his heartaches, but if facing rejection and disappointment was what it took to fan the flame of hope that had ignited in him, it was well worth the risk.

21

It was the Saturday before their wedding when Karen sat at Bret's kitchen table going over last-minute wedding plans while Bret packed up his belongings into brown cardboard boxes.

She closed her notebook, not believing that in a matter of days she would be the new Mrs. Bret Sears. "Need some help?" she asked Bret who was taping up a box.

"I've got it. I packed up most of everything last week and put it in storage. This is the last of it," he said, writing the contents on the side in block print. "I hope it doesn't take too long for us to find a place. I want us to have something that represents us."

Karen smiled. "My apartment doesn't do that?"

"No. To me, it represents you and the kids and *you* starting over. I want us to have a place that's all ours." He put the tape away and made some sort of note on the clipboard system he had created in order to follow what had been packed and where it was stored. Karen didn't dare question him about it. It all seemed a little tedious to her.

"What about you? How are things coming on your end?"

"Okay, I guess. I'm so glad we decided to hire a professional wedding planner. Trudy has done so much of the work. It's been fun to sit back and just say yes or no. This is turning out to be the wedding of my dreams."

"Your first wedding wasn't?"

"Eric and I were broke. Dad was taking treatments." Karen shrugged. "Mom couldn't afford anything like what I've put together this time."

Bret smiled, but Karen saw the crease in his forehead light up like a neon sign. "You did keep it in budget, didn't you?"

"Hmm….mostly. There were a few extras that I sprang for, but I made sure I cleared all the big stuff with you before I gave the okay. What about you? Have you written your vows yet?"

"Yep. You?"

"No…but I'm working on them. I did buy the unity candle we're lighting during the ceremony. It's tall and white and has the verse from Mark 6:9 on it. It's the one that talks about two becoming one. It's really pretty."

"What about the dress?"

"The dress is a secret. Holly would kill me if I gave you even one little hint."

"That great, huh?"

"Exquisite," Karen teased. "Did you book the hotel rooms for the wedding party?"

"We have ten rooms at Lake Lure Inn. I also booked the cabin where we'll be spending our honeymoon."

" A cabin, huh? Do I need to bring anything special?"

"Not a thing."

She cut her eyes at him. Where she had been secretive about the dress, he had been secretive about the honeymoon. All she knew was that they were staying in Lake Lure. "Is it nice?"

"It's not Italy, but it'll do."

Karen ignored the sadness in his voice. "Please," she pleaded. "Just give me one little clue!" She tilted her head to the side and poked out her bottom lip. It was the look that drove Bret crazy.

"Pitiful," he said before caving. "All I'll say is there's a hot tub, an on-call masseuse *and*"—he paused for emphasis—"it's located on a very secluded section of the lake with a private boat slip."

"Really!" she squealed. "I can't wait to see it and the Heritage House. Have you talked to Chris lately to see how things are coming?"

"More than once. He knows we're driving out middle of the week and has promised no catastrophes or dead bodies while we're there."

Karen had watched the news clip. Unbelievable. "Does he know Amanda is a bridesmaid?"

"I forgot to mention it, but I'm sure he'll handle it. He's even started going to Bible study. Our conversations have taken on a whole new nature."

"Does this mean your earlier reservations are gone?"

"They are. Chris has pulled a lot of stunts in the past, but this time I think it's the real deal. What about Amanda? Any progress with her?"

"I don't really know. I dropped by her house one day this week and discovered she's remodeling the bathroom." Karen remembered the visit and how she had tugged on an old T-shirt and helped her paint. They had cranked up the radio and sung along to some of their eighties favorites, but it wasn't the same.

"It wouldn't surprise me if she's going through a depression. The signs are all there, the withdrawal, the seclusion." Karen let go of a sad sigh. "I think remodeling the bathroom is a way she's able to keep herself distracted. I did the same thing after losing Eric." Her voice softened, still somewhat in question over hers and Bret's decision to stay out of things between Chris and Amanda. "Do you still think we're doing the right thing by not telling Chris about the baby? It's kind of strange he never asked you about her supposed fiancée, don't you think?"

Bret set down the milk carton he'd taken from the fridge. "Chris has moved on, and I think we should too. It's not our place to tell him Amanda was carrying his child. Besides, what would telling him change? It's not like he'll have the opportunity to meet his son or daughter. That and he and Amanda tend to bring out the worst in each other. Chris finding out about Amanda's lies now would give them both a reason to create a really big stink at our wedding. Are you the one who keeps putting the milk in the door of the fridge?"

"Yeah. Why?"

"Well…nothing. It's just not the coldest place. I like to keep it in the back. That way I know it's good till the sell-by date."

Karen simply looked at him. "Okay…I'll start putting it in the back." When he went to the cabinet in search of a glass, she got back on topic. "I still think Chris has a right to know. After all, we are talking about his flesh and blood here. It could mean closure for the two of them."

"Chris already has closure. Let's wait a little while and see how they handle being together next weekend. Maybe Amanda will see how much Chris has changed since giving his heart to the Lord, and that will prompt her to move on as well. I do imagine just being around her is going to tempt him in more ways than one. "

Karen's mind started to work. "What if you're right? What if the two of them start talking? Now that Chris is a Christian, they could finally work things out. They might have a shot."

"Didn't we have this same conversation a few weeks back?" Bret said, reaching for her hands and hushing her chatter. "It is *not* a good idea for the two of them to get back together."

"No…maybe. With God, all things are possible."

"Yes, but Chris is still Chris and Amanda is still Amanda. If they get back together, it could ruin everything Chris is trying so hard to change about his life. From what I gather, Amanda is still…confused. You just said you think she's depressed. Now is a really bad time for Chris to be her rebound. Chris might seem totally different, but he's still human. He could end up hurting her again."

"If Chris gave his heart to the Lord, he's not the one who's making the changes. God is, and he can sustain them." Karen thought about it a little longer. She didn't want to see anything come along that would hamper Chris's faith or distract Amanda's heart. Not at this point. "I agree that we'll give it some time, but I'm not totally ruling this out."

Karen decided to change the subject so they wouldn't argue. "If we go out to the Heritage House, you won't end up working will you?"

Bret raised a brow, his look amused. "Trust me, the only thing I'll be working on is keeping my hands off my new bride while we're in public."

She giggled at him. The last few weeks had been extremely challenging, but she could honestly say both their hearts and consciences were clear. He lifted his hands to her face and gently stroked his thumb across her cheek. "Something tells me regardless of how spectacular everything turns out to be, you're going to be the most beautiful part of the wedding."

Karen could feel her eyes shining with the love she felt in her heart. She leaned in to close the distance between them, relishing the fact she only had to wait seven more days before they could be together in every possible way.

Just as their lips touched, the front door flew open, and Holly came in followed by Scott. "Touch me one more time, you little punk, and you're going to get it!"

Immediately Karen turned to see Holly punch Scott in the shoulder. The action caused him to drop his basketball and sent it crashing onto the kitchen table, knocking over the glass of milk Bret had just poured.

"Cut it out you two!" Bret hollered.

Holly and Scott froze hearing him raise his voice at them.

The quiet that engulfed the kitchen was tense. Karen reached for a paper towel to clean up the mess while Bret composed himself. "I'm sorry. I shouldn't have yelled, but your mother and I have told you time and time again there are to be no basketballs in the house!"

"He started it!" Holly seethed through clenched teeth.

"Did not!" Scott retaliated.

"Enough!" Bret yelled again. "Scott, take the ball back outside, and you," he said to Holly, "go put on your swimsuit. We're leaving in ten minutes."

Karen watched the way Holly stormed off to the back of the apartment. She knew Holly's dismay had nothing to do with getting in trouble. All of Bret's extended family had flown in early for the wedding, and they were meeting up at Bret's parents' house for a barbeque.

Instantly, the conversation she had shared with her daughter only days ago came to mind. They were in the dressing room trying on bathing suits—something she had refused to do with Bret on their shopping excursion—when Holly confessed her anxiety.

"Mom," Holly said that afternoon as Karen asked her opinion on a brown and pink tankini, "have you always been so...blessed?"

She would've thought Holly was speaking of something else had she not been staring at her chest.

"You think I'm blessed?" Karen had all but laughed.

"Yes! Look at me. I'm as flat as a pancake."

"Holly, you're eleven. I'm thirty-two. You're supposed to be as flat as a pancake."

"Mom," she moaned, "half the girls in my class are already a B cup. Shelby is a C!"

Karen blinked her eyes in disbelief. Her mind raced as she carefully chose her words, trying to steer away from the flowering terminology her own mother had used in similar moments. Luckily, she ended up including only one reference to plant life.

"Girls your age…they mature at different rates. I was a complete string bean until I was sixteen."

"Sixteen!" Holly gasped in terror before standing and pushing out her chest in front of the mirror. "What are implants?"

"Implants?"

"Yeah, Shelby said Amanda has implants. What did she mean by that?"

"Uh, well…implants are…well…you know, when they put something in there to…make them bigger." Karen looked back at her reflection, studying it more intently. "Amanda really has implants? I didn't know that."

Karen let the memory fade, amused at how she and Holly both started positioning themselves strangely in front of the mirror at that point.

Putting on a swimsuit in front of all Bret's nieces and nephews was sure to be the reason behind Holly's sulking as well as why Holly had invited Sarah, a friend from church, to tag along to the cookout instead of Shelby.

Ten minutes later when Holly had yet to make an appearance, Karen went to check on her. "Holly?" she said, tapping on the bathroom door. "Can I come in?"

The door unlocked, and Karen poked her head in. Holly was sitting on the counter wrapped in a pool towel, tears streaming down her face.

"Oh, honey, I'm sure it's not that bad. Stand up. Let me see."

Reluctantly her daughter stood up and dropped the towel. Holly was definitely on the slim side, but the suit they had found was very stylish and age appropriate. Karen examined her daughter and tried not to smile. "I think you look great. Keep in mind, though, when toilet paper gets wet, it tends to clump. It would be terrible to lose those and clog the pool filter."

Holly yanked the stuffing out of the bathing suit top, her face full of despair. "What am I going to do?" she wailed.

This time Karen smiled. "I promise one day you're going to wake up and be a full grown woman with all its privileges and curves. Till then, let's not rush it. Every female has her insecurities, including me. You don't have to get in the water if you don't want to."

Holly wiped at her eyes. "Good, because I'm not going to." She pulled on an oversized T-shirt on top of the suit and reached for her jean shorts. "What are insecurities?"

Karen thought on what to say and opted for total transparency. "An insecurity is something that makes you feel vulnerable... exposed or lacking in some way. Just like you wish you looked more like Shelby, I wish I were shaped more like Amanda. She's so petite. She can wear anything—not to mention the obvious reasons we've already discussed."

"You mean the implants? I don't understand. Just go get some."

"I could but...God made me the way I am for a reason." Karen thought about the women in that horrible magazine and Bret's promise to love each of her imperfections, just as they were. "But beauty isn't always about looks. There's this old saying, 'Beauty is in the eye of the beholder'. Simply put, it means determining whether or not something is beautiful often has to do with who it is that's doing the looking. As for me, when I look at you, all I can see is that you're beautiful. I think that because I love you."

Holly gave her a watery smile, and Karen stepped to the hall to give her daughter some privacy. "Mom," she said, opening the door and sticking her head out once Karen was down the hall. "I think you're beautiful too."

22

Bret opened the fridge and pulled out the potato salad Karen had made. They were going to be late for the barbeque if this crew didn't get it together.

"Hey," he said to Karen as she came back into the kitchen. "Are you crying? What did she say now?" He set the bowl down. "I'm going to go and have a talk with her."

Karen wiped at her tears and stopped him. "It's nothing. She's just growing up so fast. Let it be."

"If you ask me, I think it's a little immature for her to still be fighting with her brother so much. Do they ever get along?"

"On occasion."

"Being?"

"Christmas morning, birthdays…Leap Day."

Bret could see she was being serious. About that time, Holly walked in. "Cheer up," he said. "In thirty minutes I'll be throwing you into the deep end of the pool in front of all your new cousins, clothes and all."

Holly's eyes grew wide in fear and surprise as she looked at her mom. "You told him? How could you?"

"No!" Karen protested. "I haven't said a word."

"Said a word about what?" Bret wanted to know.

"I can't believe this!" Holly stormed out to the car. "You told!"

Karen looked at Bret. "Thanks."

"What did I do?"

Karen grabbed the potato salad, along with a gallon of tea and went outside.

"Women! They're crazy."

He yelled for Scott who instantly appeared by his side—no tears, no waiting, no anger, no shoes either, but all smiles.

"Hey, buddy. Grab your shoes, and let's go!"

After ten minutes of searching for Scott's flip-flops, they all got in the car with Bret having the mind-set of a race car driver.

"Don't forget. We're picking up Sarah," Karen said as he gave his signal to take the ramp for the interstate.

"Sarah as in Sarah from youth group? We're going to be late!"

Karen shook her head and gave him the address.

"Whatever."

Mindlessly he drove across town and finally into one of the worst-looking trailer parks he'd ever seen. It wasn't hard to notice the attention they were getting because every player on the basketball court stopped to watch as they rode by.

"Are you sure she lives here?" Bret uttered, casting Karen a sideways glance and checking the GPS. "Yes, at least this is the address her mom gave me. We're looking for 904."

Bret drove past one dilapidated trailer after another. *816...897...604.* Bret slowed. The nine had fallen off at the top and become a six. "This is it." He pulled the car in the drive of a green and white trailer with no underpinning and a fan in every window. They all silently waited for Sarah to make an appearance.

"Should I honk the horn?" Bret offered when she didn't show. "It's not like we're getting out."

"Please *don't* honk the horn," Holly pleaded from the backseat. "She'll be here in a minute."

Eventually Sarah and a woman wearing cutoffs and a faded tank top came to the porch. Sarah smiled and waved at Holly. She hoisted her bag higher on her shoulder as she bounded down the steps and toward the vehicle.

Bret watched Sarah's mother eye the car as she took a long draw from the cigarette in her hand. Karen rolled down her window. "Ms. Bailey, you did say it was okay if we steal Sarah this afternoon, didn't you?"

Bret flinched at her choice of words. *Great, Karen, why don't you go on and ask if we can shoot her up here when we're through.*

"Sure," the woman frowned. "What time do you think you'll have her back?"

A low-riding truck passed behind them playing loud thumping music. Karen looked at him for the answer. "Are you really going to make me come back here after dark? We could get shot!"

"Sh," Karen hissed, darting her eyes over the back of the seat toward Sarah who had climbed in between Holly and Scott.

"Fine. Tell her sometime before dark. Tell her we'll call in case we chicken out."

Karen rolled her eyes and turned back to Sarah's mom. "We'll have her back no later than eight, but you have my number if you need us."

Once again Ms. Bailey's eyes trailed the length of the car. Tossing the used cigarette on the ground, she put it out with her flip-flop and bent low so she could speak directly to Bret.

"My shift at the diner starts around seven, but I won't be back till twelve. Sarah can let herself in."

Bret backed down the drive and drove faster than was safe on the way out of the trailer park. He didn't feel any better about Holly and Sarah's new friendship until he was on the outskirts of Kernersville near his parents' home that was nestled safely in its gated community.

They arrived, and the kids piled out of the car, but Karen continued to sit.

"What's wrong?" he asked, thinking she would have more to say about Sarah's situation and his bizarre behavior.

"I'm nervous."

"So am I. We'll call sometime this evening and—"

"No, not about taking Sarah home. About meeting your family. I know I've met your parents several times, but this is different. Your entire family will be here, and it's right before the wedding. What if they decide they don't like me?"

"Relax. They've been dying to meet you. What's not to like?"

"Really?"

 Forgiveness for Yesterday

"Sure. This has been a long time coming. Even my little brother is married with kids."

Karen continued to chew on her fingernail until he slipped her hand in his.

"You'll do great. I promise."

They ended up having a wonderful time. Karen fit right in with his sister, and at one point, they were doubled over in laughter sharing old stories about growing up. He was sure by evening's end they would be swapping recipes and promising to e-mail with ideas for Christmas.

By seven o'clock, Bret was ready to call it a night. He collected Karen and the kids, and together they said their good-byes. Thankfully, Karen decided to call Sarah's mom to see if she could stay the night so they didn't have to drive her home.

"See? I told you it would go fine," he said as he pulled up to the curb outside her apartment.

"I had a good time. Your family is great." The kids got out, and Karen waited. "You're kind of quiet. I saw you talking with your brother. Is everything okay?"

"We're good. Just a little history I don't care to share. What about you? Did you and Holly make amends? I noticed she didn't get in the pool."

Karen smiled but remained quiet.

"I have a confession to make," Bret finally spoke. "A lot of times I'm totally lost when it comes to you two. One minute you're all weepy over each other, the next, one of you is storming off, and now you're smiling but won't speak. How am I supposed to know what's a mood swing and what's the real deal?"

"You really don't know women, do you?"

"I'm clueless."

Karen giggled. "Let's just say Holly's feeling a little insecure these days. It'll pass."

"I saw one of my nephews flirting with her. I almost said something, but then figured it would embarrass her. How's that for reading the female perspective?"

"Better." She giggled. "But I'm glad you didn't say anything. She would've been mortified."

"Good. I figure I can give it a few years and then smack her first date around to make up for it."

"That's so sweet of you to take up for her."

"Of course I'll take up for Holly. She's going to be my stepdaughter. As much as I'm not looking forward to meeting the guys that'll want to date her, I know it's coming. As a matter of fact, if they know what is best for them, they're not looking forward to meeting me either."

Karen laughed. "She's going to *love* having you for a stepdad. You know, I wonder what you're going to look like when you go gray. At this rate, it could happen prematurely."

Bret chose not to think about how right she could possibly be. Instead he smiled. "That's what I'm here for. To be loved! Now get busy." He leaned over to kiss her good night, and shortly thereafter, Karen pulled away.

"Six days, twenty-two hours, and ten minutes," he said, checking the clock on the dash. Karen only laughed as she shut the door and moved to the stairs. "Good night!"

23

The day Bret and Karen were married was one of the craziest days there had ever been. Forgotten shoes, a photographer who couldn't find the park on time, and Karen's mom bringing some guy named Bradley to the ceremony unannounced left Karen on the verge of a nervous breakdown.

"It'll be okay. It's not like I'm getting any younger. A year from now, you won't even remember he was here," Lillian counseled Karen while Amanda stood nearby with a paper lunch sack in hand lest Karen start to hyperventilate.

Amanda verbally agreed with Lillian's words even if she didn't understand nor believe a single one Karen's mom was saying. *Anyone who gets married out of town is crazy!* She silently mused as she checked her reflection in the tall mirror in their makeshift dressing room. The only good thing about this wedding was the fact she wasn't six months pregnant. She would look like a giant Butterball turkey in the hideous yellow gown Karen had picked out.

That evening, however, when the sun was dipping low on the horizon, spraying a romantic glow over Hickory Nut Gorge and into Morse Park, Amanda changed her mind. The scene unfolding in front of her was one of the most beautiful settings she had ever seen.

Slowly she turned her eyes toward the back of the crowd where Karen started to make her way down the aisle between the white chairs that had been spread across a lush green lawn. Even from several feet away she could hear Bret's breath catch in his throat. She was an absolute vision.

A long satiny gown flowed around her feet. It was sleeveless with tiny sparkling rhinestones sewn in a swirling pattern along one side of the waist and hip. Her hair was swept back from her face, a few stray curls spilling down one side. Every eye was on her, and her eyes were on Bret's.

"More than exquisite," she heard Bret whisper when they joined hands.

Amanda turned trying to remember what to do. She hadn't been able to get off work and drive in a day early so she could attend the rehearsal. Karen had simply told her to watch for Holly's cues. And she wouldn't be here at all if Karen hadn't nearly twisted her arm off with guilt. Karen didn't usually resort to such tactics, but clearly she'd made an exception.

Amanda listened as the minister read from a Bible and then asked Karen and Bret to exchange vows. Bret's eyes filled when he spoke words that would remain forever in Amanda's mind.

"Karen," Bret said, taking her hands and staring into her eyes as though they were completely alone, "the day the Lord brought you into my life is the day he showed me what love was. Not only did he lift me out of the loneliness I was willing to settle for, he gave me a woman who has a heart that resembles his.

"You are always strengthening me, lifting me up, and teaching me about promise. I want our lives together to remind everyone of the beauty of his grace and the miracle of hope. As your husband, I promise I will honor you, love you, and provide for you each and every day the Lord gives us together as man and wife."

A smile crossed Karen's lips, and a tear trickled down her cheek. She spoke her promises to Bret before they exchanged rings, and Karen's cousin, who was also a bridesmaid, stepped to the side and played a song on the violin while they lit a candle in symbol of their unity.

Moments later the minister said a closing prayer and turned the happy couple toward the crowd. "Ladies and gentlemen, by the power vested in me, first by God and then by the state of North Carolina, it is with great honor and privilege I introduce to you for the first time Mr. and Mrs. Bret Sears." The minister turned to Bret. "You may kiss your bride."

All of their family and friends clapped as Bret leaned in and gently kissed Karen, not once but twice. They started back down the aisle almost as if they were skipping. Amanda watched them go, lost in a daze. *Out of the loneliness he was willing to settle for...*

The music switched, and Amanda watched Karen's cousin put down her instrument and then take her seat. It was an easy mistake, but tragic nonetheless. Her absence left Amanda to return down the aisle on Chris's arm instead of with Bret's brother.

She met Chris's eyes as he stood making the same realization she had. He was the first one to step forward, and after clearing his throat, he positioned his arm for her to take it. The action was the offering of a truce.

Bittersweet was the moment when once again their bodies connected. For a moment, Amanda was sure her left arm would burn clean off her body as she relished the feel of him pressed to her side. She could feel the thick muscles beneath the sleeve of his tuxedo working under her hand as the smell of his cologne drifted over her senses. The whole episode left her with an overwhelming sense of longing. This should've been her wedding, and Chris should've been her groom.

When they made it to the edge of the grass where the other members of the wedding party were gathering, he let her go. "Amanda, I—"

"Pictures everyone! I need you all to follow me so we can get pictures before the sun is completely gone."

The photographer rallied them together and took one picture after another while Amanda painted on a plastic smile, pretending Karen's happiness was her own. It wasn't until much later when people were filing under the lofty gazebo to enjoy the reception that Amanda finally found herself alone.

She smoothed a hand down her yellow dress as she watched Karen and Bret take to the dance floor and start to sway.

"Amanda..." a voice spoke from behind.

She turned to see Chris standing beside her. He was offering her a glass of punch.

"Thank you," she said as she took it. Their fingers brushed, and together they stood watching the happy couple move effortlessly to Steven Curtis Chapman's song "I Will Be Here". For a time, she and Chris were both lost in thought.

"It's good to see them happy," Chris said, finally breaking the silence. "This has been a long time coming for Bret. Karen is a very special lady."

"I know what you mean. They're two of a kind. They make a great couple." Chris looked at her, and she wondered what he was thinking. Before she could stop them, the words were out. "So were we."

"Amanda—"

"I'm sorry." Again she paused, seeing something tender in his expression. "I shouldn't have said that. It's just hard not to dream with all the wedding fanfare."

He let go of a long sigh and took her empty glass to set it on the table behind them. "There were times when we were happy, but something tells me what those two have will endure the good *and* the bad." He looked at her, and concern lined his face. "What happened to Luke? And the baby?"

"I…" Her eyes fell to her feet. The lie was getting easier to tell, but this wasn't just anyone she was telling it to. She debated on telling Chris the truth and would have were it not a sure way to ruin a lovely day. "I lost it back in March. Things with Luke and I…fell apart after that."

For a while he was quiet, and she wondered if he believed her.

"I'm sorry," he finally said. "I didn't know."

When she didn't raise her head, he hooked a finger under her chin and tipped her head so he could stare into her eyes. "I know that must have been hard to bear. Are you all right?"

"I will be. These last few months have been…brutal."

"They've been hard for me as well."

For a second, she didn't know what to say. Did that mean what she hoped it did? Was life without her really that difficult for him? If so, maybe they still had a shot. "What do you say after the reception we grab a drink? You know, for old time's sake?"

Even in the dim light, she could see how his shoulders instantly tensed, and he drew to his full height.

"I don't think that's a good idea."

Obviously. His quick answer hurt more than it should have, and it was evident in her tone. "It's not like I'm suggesting we run off and elope," she hissed. "It's just a couple of cocktails, not a wedding announcement!"

"I know, but you and I both know we can't do drinks. There's too much history between us."

"I know why you came by that day back in the spring. You missed me. You practically said so yourself. You missed the way we were when we were together—the way I could take your mind off…things."

She slipped in closer, putting a hand to his chest when he didn't deny it. With her heart in her eyes, she looked up and decided to go totally out on a limb and confess the reason for the bulk of her misery. "I miss you too. I want to hate you, but the truth is, I can't. I'm in love with you, and not just for the obvious reasons."

"Amanda, please…don't do this," he said, gently removing her hands and backing away.

Amanda held her breath because his rejection made it hard to breathe.

Chris's eyes made a quick sweep of the crowd. "Things in my life are different now. I'm not like I used to be. I know you don't understand, but you'll have to take my word for it. I've changed."

"So have I. Didn't you hear me? I'm finished playing games. I love you. If you would just let yourself—"

"I can't. Falling into bed with you isn't something I can do in good conscience anymore." Chris looked around again, surveying the crowd. It wasn't hard to see how self-conscious and nervous he was suddenly acting.

"Who said anything about falling into bed? I'm telling you how I really feel." Suddenly she put two and two together. "You're seeing someone."

"No."

"Then…what is it? Why do you keep looking around?" Her hands went out to his, and he quickly removed them from her touch. "You're acting like a frightened animal." She studied his erratic behavior, but she didn't understand it. She was tired of his games.

"What's wrong with you?"

"I'm not…interested in…women—"

"You mean you're gay!" Amanda gasped louder than she should've. The comment stopped all of Chris's movement cold. His eyes bulged out at her.

"No!" he insisted through clenched teeth before grabbing her arm and dragging her behind a row of bushes. She could tell by the ticking in his jaw that she'd pushed some kind of invisible button.

He leaned in close, his voice thick and strained as it brushed her face. "How can you think that after all the times we were together?"

"Actually, I can't say I know anyone who's more into women than you. So what on earth is wrong? Why are you running from me like you're scared? You're sweating!"

"You don't understand. I told you, I've changed. I can't sleep with you because I *don't* love you."

She flinched as the words ripped out what was left of her heart. Her features contorted, and she forced herself not to cry. "Is that *all* I'll ever be to you?"

"I'm sorry. That came out too harsh. What I meant to say was—"

"Save it!" Amanda stood there looking at him and easily recognized what she saw in those vibrant pools of blue—complete and utter disdain. How could she forget? Chris didn't want anyone to think he was capable of loving the likes of her.

Hurt turned to anger, and it overrode her good judgment. Hot tears streamed down her face, and she was seething with rage. "You can go on keeping yourself shut off forever as a way to keep from getting hurt, and I may be less than perfect, but let's face it. At the end of the day, we're both alone. I've seen enough of you to know the truth. There's more than meets the eye. At least I'm courageous enough to tell you I want it. You on the other hand, won't admit to anyone including yourself that you could ever love a woman like me.

Forgiveness for Yesterday

If that's true, then tell me, why did you keep coming back? Time after time, when you could've had anyone, you always chose *me*!"

She finished her speech by raising her hand and striking his left cheek. For a second she wasn't sure which one of them was more surprised by the action, him or her. Fear didn't have time to register because he quickly caught her wrist and jerked her to him in a surprisingly intense kiss.

When they broke apart, they were both breathless. It was Amanda who chose to speak. "You can *pretend* to find me physically repulsive, just like you can pretend *not* to love me. At least now we both know the truth. You're lying. You should at least be honest about that."

He didn't have anything to say because the look on his face said it all. She had totally blown his cover. She turned on her heel and sauntered off, willing to bet her last dollar that come midnight, Chris Lanning would be knocking on her room door asking, no, begging her for a lot more than drinks. When he did, this time she would be the one to turn him down.

Bret and Karen's wedding day wound down as each and every precious moment turned into a cherished memory. The flowers, the cake, the dancing—it was all perfect. Karen stroked a hairbrush through her hair remembering another wedding day that occurred many years ago.

What would Eric say if he were here? She didn't have to wonder for very long because she knew. He would be happy for her.

As fantastic and thrilling as the day had been, Bret had made it clear it was the wedding night that mattered so much to him. "Oh, Karen. You're not eighteen anymore." She put the brush down and gazed at her reflection in the full-length mirror in front of her. She felt like the most cherished woman on the face of the earth when she came down the aisle and witnessed Bret's reaction at seeing her. "More than exquisite," he'd said. The memory gave her goose bumps.

Hopefully, those would be words he would repeat as she stood in front of him tonight, totally vulnerable and totally his. She had chosen a candlelight white, floor-length satin gown with thin delicate straps in which to present herself.

She slipped on the matching robe and made her way through the log cabin to the back porch where he was waiting. It was pitch-black out save for tiny lights along the water that glimmered like stars.

Karen slipped out the door, interrupting the concert of crickets with the squeak of its hinges. Hearing it, Bret looked up. As he did their eyes locked. Karen held a single candle and she placed it on the table in front of him. The golden glow it cast over her allowed him to drink in her beauty.

"Karen…I…you're…." She smiled seeing he was at a loss for words. He reached for her hand, and she took a seat beside him.

"What's this?" she asked when he handed her a small velvet box.

"Just something to remember today by."

"As if I could forget! It was beautiful, wasn't it?" There was a dreamy quality to her voice as she remembered their special day.

"Not nearly as beautiful as you, Mrs. Sears," he said, pulling back her robe at the neck and kissing a bare shoulder. His fingers drifted to the golden necklace she was wearing. It was special to her, and she rarely took it off. She looked at Bret, noticing how his eyes were thoughtful.

"You once told me the necklace you wear is something Eric gave you—an anniversary present, I think. I could've bought something to replace it, but I didn't. I still want you to wear the chain he gave you, only with this. Go on, open it."

She lifted the lid on the velvet box. Inside there was a pendant designed with two diamonds.

"It's called a Lifetime Pendant. I want you to know that I will never try to replace him, Karen. I only want to add to the joys in life he brought you."

Karen pressed her fingers to her mouth, fighting back tears. Bret took the box from her hands and removed the pendant. "The reason it's called a Lifetime Pendant is because the design allows you to add diamonds that signify life's special events as they happen. There are already two diamonds on it because I feel like we've passed two milestones.

"The first diamond in the pendant is for the journey life gave us that led us to this day. I know yours has not been an easy path, but it has made you into the woman I love, and for that, I'm grateful. You're always loving me and pointing me back to God when I seem to lose my way. Waiting for you has been the hardest thing I've ever done. I thought I was a patient man, but I guess patience all depends on how bad you want what it is you're waiting for. Just so you know, you were worth the wait.

"The second diamond is for the journey you and I are starting this day as husband and wife. I know it won't always be easy, but love is a decision, and it's one that I've made wholeheartedly. From this day forward, I will honor you as my wife, my lover, and my friend."

Karen fingered the gold pendant while Bret's words penetrated her heart. He was such a special man. Never would he want her to forget or try to replace Eric. Rather he pointed out how her loss had shaped her faith and trust in the Lord and how it was something he loved about her. Neither was he disillusioned that all their days together would be spent in marital bliss, but he was committed to working through the tough times and standing by their decision—a decision to love.

Sitting there with him, she was overcome by the love and respect she felt. She turned to allow him to unfasten the necklace around her neck and slip the pendant on. When he was finished, she looked into his face with eyes that stared straight into his soul.

"I love you, Bret Sears, more than you'll ever know. You're a good man—a thoughtful and considerate man—and now that I'm you're wife, I'm grateful there will be no more guilt between us. Now I can fully express the love I have for you, and it will be right, not only in our eyes but in the eyes of God as well."

Setting the box to the side, she stood and took his hand, leading him off to do just that.

24

Amanda admitted it. She loved him. It was late as Chris rolled over, willing himself to forget her words and the kiss he'd initiated. *God, am I really in love with her? Am I that blind? I was only trying to right a wrong.*

Somehow righting a wrong left him wide awake in the middle of the night. The temptation had started when she'd offered to grab a drink and escalated to frightening when she'd pressed her incredible body up against him.

Chris felt the heat inside him rise as a host of their sensual memories played before his eyes. He looked at the door knowing Amanda's room wasn't far away. Instead he rose to take a cold shower.

Thankfully he had chosen to stay in Chimney Rock, a tourist town just a mile or so from the hotel in Lake Lure where the others in the wedding party were staying. In this case, however, a hundred miles would be too close. *Impossible*, he thought.

Chris dried off and returned to his bed knowing it was very well possible indeed. What had driven him to kiss her? How could she still rouse such a reaction from him? Sadly, she'd left him so high strung he figured it was either kiss her or smack her back. He didn't want to be that man.

All that talk of love was probably due to the desperate place Amanda found herself in after having lost her baby and her fiancée. Knowing that it was her own confused and unstable emotions calling the shots, Chris managed to drift off quoting the few verses of scripture he knew, over and over in his mind.

In the morning, he woke early and slipped out of his room and down the stairs to grab a cup of coffee. Chris scanned the street, deciding on a restaurant called Laura's House—seems it was fitting.

Forgiveness for Yesterday

It was a tall two-story restaurant with a front wall made of glass that overlooked the town. If it had been a shack on a hill, he would've chosen it simply for its name.

Just as he pulled open the door, a tall and smiling figure standing in the corner caught his eye.

"Man, am I glad to see you!" he said to Bret as he slipped an arm over his shoulder. "Where's Karen?"

"She's on her way. We were starving."

Chris shook his head. Bret was beaming, nor could he miss the discreet wink Bret passed his way.

"Pace yourself, Romeo. This marriage stuff is for life."

"I know. What are you doing here?"

"Coffee," Chris answered, not wanting to spill his problems to Bret while he still had that morning afterglow. "Couldn't sleep."

"Has this got anything to do with Amanda? I saw you two *talking* at the reception. Things looked…intense."

Chris wondered what part of intense Bret had witnessed. There was a coffee cart nearby, so Chris poured himself a cup. "Sorry about that. I hope we didn't make a scene."

"No, I think I was the only one who saw. That woman's got enough nerve to sink a ship." Bret shifted his weight and put his hands in his pockets. "So…if you couldn't sleep, was it because you were alone?"

"Of course. Jumping back into bed with her isn't something I can do without wreaking havoc in both our lives."

Bret looked at him almost as if he were dumbfounded. "You really turned her down?"

"The woman's crazy. She told me what happened with the baby and how emotional she was because of it. She's going through a tough time right now, and I hate it for her, but she doesn't need me clouding her thoughts. I've changed, but I'm still not ready to fall in love, and I don't think I'll ever be ready for more kids."

Chris took a sip of the steaming liquid in his hand. "What?" he asked, seeing the confusion on Bret's face.

"Nothing. I just didn't expect to see you take that news so well."

Both men looked up to see Karen approaching.

"Good morning. What are you two over here whispering about?" she asked, slipping her arm into her husband's.

"We were just discussing how beautiful the blushing bride looks after her wedding night. By the way, you don't have a sister, do you?" Chris moved to add more cream and sugar to his cup.

"No, but I'd love to set you up with Bradley. Interested?"

Chris nearly spewed hot coffee on both of them. He continued to choke while Karen explained. "I ran into Amanda at the hotel this morning when I was checking on Holly and Scott. She keeps asking me if Bradley's secretly your new boyfriend. What's that all about?"

Bret let go of a deep chuckle.

"I'm going to kill her," Chris said, shaking his head before smiling at a giggling Karen who knew she'd gotten the best of him. "Thanks, but no thanks on the Bradley thing. And you can assure Ms. Amanda that I am *not* gay, just…reformed."

Karen quirked a smile at Bret and shrugged a shoulder. Then they rubbed noses.

"You two should get a table so you can quit dripping this sappy love mess all over the entryway. It's gonna ruin the carpet."

He heard Karen giggle again as he went to the counter and paid for his coffee. Outside he took a walk down the street, thinking of Bret and Karen and smiling over last night's misery. He was a lot of things, but being attracted to other men was not one of them. He swirled the coffee in his cup, thinking that if he ever got an opportunity to share his faith with Amanda, he should take it.

Immediately his eyes lifted to scan the faces on the street. If Bret and Karen were here, Amanda was sure to be lurking close by. Rather than risk another embarrassing encounter with her, he made a right under the sign for Fibber McGee's Bed-and-Breakfast and took the stairs to his room.

Chris slipped the key into the door recalling the look in Bret's eyes when Karen was close by—the look that said he had finally found everything he'd ever wanted. In the light of day, Chris realized Amanda had been right when she'd called him on some of his unspoken feelings for her. For a long time, it was easier to think he didn't care about her at all, but that wasn't true. He did. It just wasn't the kind of love that deep and meaningful relationships were built on.

Chris let go of a deep sigh as he turned the knob on the door in front of him and stepped into the air-conditioned space. Shelby and Kyle were still sound asleep on the sofa bed. He set his cup down on the small table in the corner and shut the door behind him.

He moved across the living room toward the balcony that overlooked the Broad River so as not to wake them. As he opened the sliding glass doors, the soft snores behind him changed slightly.

Turning back to look at their sleeping figures, he was filled with a sense of responsibility. Shelby was fast asleep, her dark auburn hair fanned across her pillow as dark lashes rested on her cheeks. Words from yesterday came back to him about honoring and cherishing those you loved. Chris wondered if he knew how.

Maybe he could get some input from the guys he was meeting with during his Thursday night Bible study. The group had turned out to be new believers like him—guys who sometimes had more questions than answers and most days didn't know where to start.

Chris had only been to two meetings but remembered how at the last one he'd lagged behind to ask the pastor a question he didn't want to ask in group. "I'm learning a lot," he'd told Pastor Mark, "but there is one thing that keeps tripping me up."

"What's that?"

Chris fumbled with his words, but he finally swallowed his pride and gave the pastor the highlights of the last two years. "If Laurie was a Christian, how could she walk out on her own kids and me without looking back? Won't she have to answer for that? It's the one thing that keeps flying back in my face, and I'm afraid it's tainted my view on people who profess to be Christians. I have a hard time trusting them."

"That is tricky." Pastor Mark had taken a minute to think it through and then said things that had kept him awake most of the night. "Only Laurie knows what her relationship to Jesus Christ is. You cannot judge that. Secondly, whatever she did or didn't do doesn't change who Jesus is."

"I'm not sure I follow."

"It's like this. A lot of times when people say they're Christians, other people interpret that to mean they think they should be perfect as Christ was perfect. Then when they don't live up to a certain standard the other person has set, they're labeled as a hypocrite. What they don't realize is that Christians are not perfect but forgiven."

Pastor Mark leaned forward again, and Chris found himself hanging on his every word. "I'm not saying what Laurie did is okay or that the hurt she's caused should be dismissed. But Jesus is who he says he is in his Word, not who people always make him out to be with their actions. He gives us a choice in what we do, and we don't always do the right things. That still doesn't change the deity of Christ and his ability to save. I know this is tough, but just as Jesus has forgiven you, you need to forgive Laurie."

Pastor Mark had then given him some scriptures to look up and pray over. Colossians 3:13 was one of them, and it backed up the pastor's claims. The verse said that because Christ had forgiven him, he should forgive Laurie. And Chris had committed more sins than he could count.

He remembered how the pastor had gone as far as to urge him to try to forget the things Laurie had done and explained that meant no longer dwelling on them or holding her actions against her. It was in the past. They could not be changed. These were words of truth he needed to heed, but right now the idea was too much for him to grasp.

As if sensing his stare, Shelby rolled over, and once again Chris was struck by how life had made him a single dad. It wasn't something he had set out to accomplish, but nonetheless it had happened. Chris thought of his new friend Sam and his words about how he would continue to sin as long as he was human. It didn't mean he was any less of a Christian, but a work in progress.

Chris lifted his face to the morning sun, and despite the warmth of its rays, a breeze of sadness nipped at his heart.

Lord, I need your help here. You've forgiven me for a long list of sins, and now you're asking me to forgive Laurie for hers. I want to, but I don't think I can do it on my own. Chris thought about his feelings for Laurie and how deep they ran. *I have a lot of anger and hate I need to deal with. Regardless of what I feel, I know you love us both...unconditionally.* His heart grew quiet. *Lord, if forgiving Laurie is your will for me, then help me do it. Show me the way. Show me how to get past this. Show me what it means to forget.*

Once again, Chris thought of Bret and Karen and how perfect they were together. He was used to being the one who got the girl, but this morning, he honestly couldn't say he'd ever had what Bret had found—a woman who loved him as much as he loved her.

He looked down to the river below, noticing how the water was constantly changing and parting over the obstacles in its path, yet nothing seemed to slow it down completely. *Love should be like that*, he mused. *Maybe some day.*

Sounds of Shelby moving around came to him, and he and looked back inside. She was sitting up, looking at him with bleary eyes, bedraggled hair, her knees drawn to her chest. She looked so young, so vulnerable. A smile lifted the corner of his mouth.

There might be some things that felt bigger than he could handle when it came to living out a life of faith, but wasn't that what faith was all about? Anything was possible with a God as big as his.

I mean it, Lord. If it means moving on, help me forgive her. Help me forgive Laurie so that I can start loving those around me the way they deserve to be loved.

25

Chris spent all of Sunday with Shelby and Kyle, and somehow having the entire day set aside just for them, he felt like he was meeting them for the first time. Shelby was quite the comedian, and Kyle was as smart as a whip.

They hiked in Chimney Rock Park and toured through the village. They even bought silly souvenirs from Bubba Leary's General Store. Several movies had been filmed in the area, and Shelby was completely taken with the knowledge. She went on and on about how dreamy the idea was, but Kyle was more impressed with the history and the adventure that was offered.

All three of them cherished every moment of their time together, and it showed Chris that no matter what he'd done, he still had a place in their hearts. When it was time for the kids to head home, Chris reminded them, "I know it's been hard with me being away, but I've given it a lot of thought. It's not fair of me to uproot your lives when I'm more than halfway finished with this project. I want you to stay with Marie at our house through the summer. By fall, I will move back home even if it means putting someone else on this project."

"But you'll miss the entire summer!" Kyle cried.

"I know. That's why I've worked it where I'll be able to come in for a couple of weekends. I'll miss you two, but I need to see this through. It's only five weeks until the Fourth of July." He turned to Shelby. "I'll be in Greensboro that whole week—so we can celebrate your birthday. It's not every day a girl turns twelve."

Shelby studied him, and somehow Chris sensed she was trying to determine whether or not he would make good on his word. "We can even do that water park you and Kyle have been hounding me about."

Forgiveness for Yesterday

"Really?"

The look on Kyle's face told him he didn't know what he'd just committed to, but it didn't matter. He was going.

"You promise to call?" Shelby asked.

"Every night. I want to hear all about cheerleading camp. I'm proud of you for making the squad. I know you worked hard for it."

"Thanks, Dad," she said, hugging his neck.

He put them in the car with Bret's parents for the trip home, and the first half of the week drug on mindlessly. By Wednesday, Chris dipped his paintbrush into a can of paint thinking he'd go crazy.

He slathered paint onto the front door of the Heritage House, but the sound of a car turning up the drive turned his attention. It was Bret and Karen. He'd almost forgot they were dropping by around lunch.

Putting the brush down and wiping his hands on a rag, he walked out to meet them. Bret and Karen were sitting in the circle drive with their mouths hanging slightly ajar. Chris saw the changes in the estate nearly ever day and had started to take them for granted. Every time someone else saw them, it reminded him of all that had transpired.

The house Bret had witnessed just a few months back no longer existed. In its place was a transforming two-story mansion boasting fresh white paint, a stately front porch, and bare but sweeping grounds.

When Karen stepped from the car stammering for words, he couldn't resist the feeling of pride that welled up in his chest.

"Chris! This is amazing," Karen said with wonder in her voice as she pushed past him like he was invisible. "Everything is so…different. This is going to look as if…it's brand-new." There was a long pause as she admired the undergoing changes. "And the barn, it's gorgeous. I'm glad you went with red. It really pops. This place looks like something out of a painting."

Bret joined her and gave his approving smile. "You've really covered a lot of ground since I was out here last."

The two followed Chris up the wide front steps. "We still have a ways to go, but it's coming along. Watch your step. The paint is wet, and there's stuff lying everywhere," he said as he opened the front door and led them into the foyer.

They moved to the parlor just to the right, and he couldn't help but notice how Karen and Bret stood in front of the fireplace and snickered. They whispered a few secretive words and fell into a giggling kiss. He could've sworn he heard one of them utter something about bats.

"You two have got it bad," Chris said, rolling his eyes. Obviously, he was on the outside of an inside joke. *Newlyweds.*

A loud crack followed by a crash sounded from somewhere in the back of the house, and Karen jumped. "What was that?"

"They're tearing out the kitchen cabinets. At least that's what they're supposed to be doing. Come on, I'll show you the upstairs." A reciprocating saw started somewhere in the kitchen, and Chris noticed the way Karen gripped the banister as if the whole place might crash in on her head.

"Relax." He laughed. "It's not like this place is going to cave in. Then again…"

Upstairs Chris showed them how he'd restructured all the rooms so that each suite had a private bath. Even without the final touches of color, new fixtures, and refinished flooring, the rooms had a feel of elegance about them. "You'd never guess this place has witnessed over 180 years of life."

"This is going to be gorgeous," Karen said as they were standing in the front bedroom that centered the upstairs of the house. "It's nothing like I remember. And the view—you can see for miles up here. It's almost like a sanctuary." She ran her hand over the extra wide windowsill, admiring the changes. "You do beautiful work. I had no idea you were this talented."

Chris felt heat rising in his cheeks. He wasn't used to such praise. "When you've got something to work with, it's all about bringing beauty that's already there to a state where it can be appreciated."

They marveled for a few moments longer; then, Bret whispered something to Karen, and she excused herself. "I've been wanting to tell you about some things going on back at the office," he told Chris once they were alone.

"When the media covered the incident at the pond, at first I thought Darrell was going to flip. Then we started getting all these

Forgiveness for Yesterday

phone calls. People were calling in to say how much they appreciated Greeson taking the initiative to invest in a place so many others had written off.

"Seems the people of Buncombe County are really impressed by your efforts to restore this old house back to its former glory and the fact that you're doing it without using a dime of state money. They're saying they wished more companies out there would do the same for other small communities. They see it as the big guy giving back to the people by making an investment that honors their history. It's really given Greeson a lot of positive attention in the papers back home. Darrell's been blown away by it."

Chris couldn't believe it. "Does that mean he's no longer pressuring the board?"

Bret nodded. "If you ask me, it's going about it the hard way, but at least something good is coming from this. For now."

They joined back up with Karen who was waiting outside. Chris went to follow up on some phone calls while Bret and Karen were content to explore on their own.

"Positive attention," he said in awe as he returned to the porch to finish his painting. This time, he dipped another paintbrush in white paint and touched it to a window frame. He had once told Bret there was something more important going on here than work. Chris now knew what he'd been getting at that day. The whole Heritage House project was about redemption. Not his redemption in Darrell's eyes and the eyes of Greeson's board members but about redemption in general—restoring that which was lost to that which was found.

Chris smiled to himself, and soon his mind became lost in ideas for the yard, the pond, and everything else. Thirty minutes later, he heard the sound of the front door open up behind him. "There you are," Karen said. "We've been looking all over. We brought lunch. Are you hungry?"

"Am I breathing?"

"Ha, ha," she said, waving a bucket of fried chicken in front of his face. Bret came around the front of the house and joined them. Together they found a shade tree, and Bret spread out a blanket. They enjoyed their lunch and finished it off by catching Chris up on what was new back home. At some point during the conversation, Karen's mouth fell open. "Is that *your* truck?" she asked in disbelief.

Chris turned to see what was left of his Chevy parked along the edge of the yard. "Unfortunately, yes. But that reminds me…"

Chris took off in a jog and returned with a thick stack of envelopes. "What's this?" Karen asked as he handed them to her.

"It's our Ella Jackson letters. I still haven't gotten to read them."

"Oh!" She squirmed, wiping her hands on a napkin. Karen settled up against Bret and pulled out the top letter. "Okay the date is May 2, 1917. Dear Charles," Karen started then stopped. "Wait a minute. The guy in the first letters was a William."

"So what?" Chris asked. "I thought there was another leg in here." He was searching the bucket for one last piece of chicken.

"What do you mean 'so what'? This letter is to someone else."

Chris found what he was looking for, and suddenly the details came rushing back to him. "You're right. They were William and Ella Faye Jackson, and they were married a few months before he was sent off to the Great War. She used to touch his picture that hung in the hallway because she missed him."

Bret looked at the two of them, surprised at how much they remembered. "And you people think I'm the romantic. At least I'm living in the twenty-first century."

Karen elbowed him and then continued to read. "Dear Charles, I can't tell you how much I appreciate you lending me a hand now that William is away." She gave an expression that said, "Point proven." "Will has only been gone for a little more than a month, and I find there are many things I can't do on my own. You've been so kind to keep my wood box full, and you made that repair to the roof. I'm sure I would've caught my death of cold had you not come to repair the leak.

I pray that Cathleen would forgive me for keeping you so long that afternoon. I know you are a busy man with your doctoring practice and five children to feed. It seems I enjoy your company just as much as I do your care. Sometimes I envy your wife for her responsibilities.

As for me, my days are empty, and my nights are long. It is fair to say that we are all making sacrifices."

"Hmm," Bret said. "That sounds kind of cozy. Wonder what they were doing besides repairing the roof on that long afternoon?"

This time Karen swatted his leg in rebuke and opened another letter. The second and third letters revealed that Ella became employed with the good doctor Charles Heritage as a way to fill her lonely days and make a meager income while her William was away at war. Nothing else implied more than friendship.

"See, they were friends. That's all," Karen said, folding the third letter and putting it back in its envelope.

Before she could start on the next one, Chris's curiosity got the best of him. "That's funny," he said, wiping his own hands. "If they were just friends, then how come I found these hiding in the attic under a loose floorboard?"

He took the stack and pulled out the letter on the bottom. His eyes scanned the page, and he found just what he suspected. The friendship of Charles and Ella Faye had become much more. "They were having an affair."

Bret sat up all of a sudden interested in what was going on. "Give me that," he said, taking the letter and letting his eyes roam the page. After only a few seconds, he gave his conclusion. "I'd kill her. She wasn't working for the doctor. She was sleeping with the doctor."

"Wait a minute. You mean to tell me the undying love of Ella Jackson grew cold after only a few months of William being away?"

"Dear Charles," Bret read, "I tell myself I never meant for this to happen, but if that is true, then why do I think of you nearly every waking moment of my day? Your arm brushes mine, and it ignites a fire in me that cannot be quenched. When we're together, the passion between us draws me like a moth to a flame. I feel helpless to escape and find myself relishing in what I once knew as sin, only I have no desire to repent."

Karen shook her head. "How sad. They were supposed to be together forever. How could she stop loving him?"

"According to this, she didn't. She's in love with both William and Charles." Bret's eyes moved further down the page. "Listen to this, 'While it is William's name I bear on my heart, it is yours I bear on my body and soul—as will our child.'

"While William was off getting shot up for his countrymen, she was pregnant with the doctor's baby!"

"No!" Karen gasped in horror. "This is like something from a terrible soap opera."

Bret tossed the letter on the blanket and lay back down, his hands behind his head. "Nothing says romance like adultery. I'd definitely kill her."

Chris listened to Bret's words, and they sent his mind racing. "The skeleton in the pond. They were supposed to run forensics to find out who it was. Do you think…if Ella was pregnant and William returned to find her with a baby…"

All three of them shuffled through the letters, looking for something that would provide a clue. Other than finding a faded photograph of a woman standing in front of a porch Chris would recognize anywhere, all three of them came up empty handed.

It wasn't until late that night that Chris realized he'd had the missing piece all along. He tore out of bed and flicked on the overhead light and reached for his Bible. There in between the pages of the Psalms was the gold necklace with the cross charm Kyle had found on the end of his fish hook last October. It was the same one the woman in the faded photograph was wearing. The one engraved with an E.

"It was her! It was Ella!" Chris said out loud, marveling at how the mystery had come together. The body they found in the pond was the infamous and adulterous Ella Faye Jackson.

26

Amanda pulled out a compact and stared at her reflection. She fished out a lip gloss and tried not to frown as she touched up her makeup. More than three weeks had passed since Karen and Bret's wedding, and usually the feelings of disappointment and loneliness that followed such an event were gone by now. But not this time.

Somehow watching Karen dance off to her happily ever after so quickly magnified the lack of that type of love and happiness in her own life. Amanda cringed thinking of the way she had thrown herself at Chris during the reception.

I am such a fool. Now he knows I'm weak and desperate! She tried to push the memory from her mind as not to let it ruin her lunch. She was meeting with Karen and was looking forward to hearing about something other than wedding plans and bridesmaids' dresses.

As soon as she stepped from the car and entered the restaurant, she saw Karen wave at her from across the room. They were meeting at Green Valley Grill, one of their favorite places.

"Hi," she said, taking in the smile that seemed to be permanently affixed to Karen's face. She was wearing a new white suit with a soft pink camisole underneath the jacket. It made her look young and fresh. "Sorry I'm late. My last appointment ran over. Nice suit."

"Bret picked it out. It's the one I wore to the rehearsal."

"Classy. But what should I expect? The man has a way with fashion."

Karen giggled. "I know. It's weird having a husband who can accessorize better than I can. Check out the shoes."

Karen pointed her toe to the side of the table so Amanda could see her strappy new pair of heels. "Ooh la la! Those are sexy."

"That's what he said. Wait until you see the workout stuff he bought me. Now I can sweat in style."

Amanda smiled but started looking through the menu. She could forget the suit and heels and even the workout clothes. Money was tight. She was lucky if she found someone who'd lavish the expense of a good meal on her.

They studied their menus for a few minutes, and Karen started with the small talk.

"So what's been going on? I've been so busy since we got back from the honeymoon I haven't had time to catch up."

Amanda shrugged and set the menu aside, having decided on a salad due to her lack of appetite and funds. "Just the usual. To work and back and then a movie or two on the weekend." Amanda hesitated. "I did meet someone."

Karen's smile grew broader, and for a moment, she looked surprised. "Tell me!"

"Well," Amanda said, glad to have something to share, "his name is Preston. He's super good-looking, tall, dark—the whole package of course—only none of the macho stuff. He's an electrical engineer. Says he designs circuit boards and wiring harnesses for large industrial equipment. Anyway, he asked me out last weekend, and we ended up seeing a show at the coliseum."

"Interesting. How did the two of you meet?"

"He said he got my number from a friend. We've only gone out once, but I could tell, he wants to see me again."

Karen didn't respond, and the waiter came to take their order. When he was finished with Karen, the gentleman turned to her.

"I'll have the house salad, please. Ranch dressing on the side."

"Of course. Would you like to add chicken or shrimp, ma'am?"

"Um…" Amanda chose to ignore the title and checked the menu to see how much extra it would cost. "No, thank you."

The man left, and when Karen remained quiet, Amanda sensed something was wrong. "What is it? I thought you'd be happy to hear I was moving on."

"I am but…are you sure this guy isn't like the others?"

"Of course I'm sure. So far he's been a total gentleman."

"Is he a Christian?"

Amanda fought the urge to roll her eyes. "I don't consider *myself* a Christian. And I don't attract guys like Bret if that's what you're wondering. Preston is a really nice guy, and I enjoy spending time with him. That's a place to start. Right? What about you? How's the married life? Is it everything you thought it'd be?"

When what should've been an immediate answer didn't come, Amanda knew she was onto something. "What are you not telling me?" she asked again, probing a little deeper.

"What are you talking about?"

"I asked you how the married life is and you ignored me."

Karen smiled. "Bret's...great. It's great."

Amanda lowered her chin and lifted her eyes in a calculating stare. "Life with Mr. Romantic is just great? Sounds likes there's trouble in paradise. Give!"

"Nothing..." Karen started fiddling with her napkin. "It's only been a few weeks. We're still...adjusting."

"To?"

"Living with each other."

"Hmm. I can't imagine living with someone as meticulous as Bret is would be easy. Do tell!"

Karen laughed at her enthusiasm. "With the excitement of getting married, I don't think either one of us thought about what it would be like to actually be living in the same space—especially not in an apartment the size of mine."

"Why *did* you guys move in there? Bret's place was so much nicer."

"True, but it only had two bedrooms. I can't ask Holly to room with Scott even if it's just for a few months while we search for something more permanent. She's at that age where I'm sure making any sacrifices in order to please me goes against some kind of unspoken preteen creed.

"My lease is up in August, so we hope to buy something soon. Bret's been single for a long time, and now he's got a whole house full of people to adjust to living with including Holly who spends at least forty-five minutes on her hair every morning while he's waiting for the shower. It's just taking a little getting used to for all of us."

"I can imagine." There was a long pause, and Amanda tapped her fingers on the table, hoping to hear more. "So you're not going to give me anything juicy, are you?"

Karen laughed again. "What is it you're hoping to hear?"

Amanda rolled her eyes in mock frustration. "Something to use against him! He's got to have some disgusting habit that I should know about! Doesn't he snore or leave his toenail clippings lying around? Anything that tells me your life isn't as perfect as it looks from the outside looking in."

Karen's hand slipped across the table to briefly touch hers, and suddenly she was wearing the look. Her here-is-my-opportunity look. "Amanda. Your prince will come, just wait. You've been through so much lately. Are you sure the answer you're looking for is finding what you think is the perfect man?"

Maybe. Sure wouldn't hurt. Maybe her prince was Preston. "Look at you. When you moved to Greensboro, it was all I could do to get you out on a Friday night. Now you're happily married, have a wardrobe I'd kill for, *and* within a few months time, you'll probably have a mansion to live out the rest of your life in too. How has this been bad?"

"Bret is an awesome guy—even if he is the only man I've ever met who actually folds the dirty laundry and has his own color coding system for canned goods—he is great. I'm very blessed, only it's not because Bret is successful and is in love with me. The faith we share binds us even closer than the love we have for each other. If you would listen to your heart, I think you'd find that *that* is what you're really longing for, not another man."

Amanda searched her eyes and wondered what Karen really meant by her words. "Speaking of men, did you ever find out what's gotten into Chris?"

"Yes, I did," Karen said just as the waiter brought their food. She waited until he left to continue. "Chris gave his heart to the Lord. He's a new believer."

Amanda sat in silence not believing the words that came out of Karen's mouth. *Chris Lanning found Jesus? Karen and Bret's Jesus?* "Are you serious? That's why he didn't show?"

"Of course I'm serious. What do you mean, 'That's why he didn't show'?"

"Oh, Karen," Amanda said, hanging her head in shame. "Nothing...I...when we talked at the reception he was acting all weird, but I never imagined..." She debated whether or not to go any further. "I didn't mean for it to happen..."

"What?" Karen asked impatiently.

"We got into this huge fight, I slapped him, and then...he kissed me."

"Chris kissed you? What? Why? What kind of kiss of was it?"

"It was intense." Amanda shrugged. "Kind of like an I-hate-you-but-love-you-at-the-same-time kind of kiss. I can't say that I'm all that surprised. I pretty much drove him to it."

Karen was stunned. "But...why? How...? I thought you hated him."

"I do...but one look at him, and I forget everything he's put me through. He was so kind and caring. I understood his kiss because I feel the same way about him. It's like trying to figure out Dr. Jekyll and Mr. Hyde." Amanda remembered the way he had swore that he didn't love her. "Are you sure Chris has found religion and not something like...AA?"

"Why is this so hard to believe? You said for yourself you could see how he's changed."

Amanda fumbled for words. "You weren't there. He wanted me, but for some reason, he wouldn't let himself give in. It doesn't take a rocket scientist to see that Chris is not exactly saint material. He's the kind of man who does what he wants, when he wants. He's never even been to church. Religion is just another excuse for his inability to commit to an actual relationship."

"This is not about going to church, and it's not about being a saint. Chris finally realized that he'd hit rock bottom. That he was lost and needed a Savior." Karen leaned forward in her chair. "I know you don't like to hear me go on and on about who Jesus is, and the last thing I want to do is preach at you, but he is a big part of who I am. You saw what he did for Chris. Nothing can explain those changes except for something supernatural. Now Chris is a believer who is trusting Jesus to call the shots, and he's not the same because of it. The fact that I'm still around shows I'm hoping that after all that's happened to you, you'll see the light as well."

Amanda balked at her cutting words. "Is that all I am to you? Some mission project?"

"I didn't mean it that way. That came out wrong," Karen reasoned.

Tears pooled in Amanda's eyes. Karen wanted her to believe, but Karen didn't know the truth. It was impossible for Jesus to accept her now after what she'd done.

Should I tell her? Should I tell her the whole horrible truth so that she'll drop this dreaded conversation, cut her ties, and quit wasting her time with me?

"Amanda, I'm sorry. Truly I am. I didn't mean it. I'm glad you finally told Chris about the baby being his. That took a lot of guts. Now maybe the two of you can put this behind you."

"Chris doesn't know the baby was his."

Karen looked confused. "But Bret said that he and Chris talked. That Chris said you told him."

"There must be some sort of misunderstanding. I assure you. I did not tell Chris the baby was his."

"So are you going to tell him?"

"No!"

"But I hate keeping this a secret."

"It is *not* your place to run my life! What's done is done. Let it be!"

Amanda looked down at the table between them. Suddenly she was no longer hungry. "You know what?" she said, grabbing her purse from the back of the chair. "Why don't you save yourself the trouble? Some people are simply irredeemable!"

27

The week of July Fourth brought Chris back home. He had plans to spend the entire week in Greensboro, and only two of those days would be spent in the office. That was where he sat catching up on paperwork when the phone on his desk started to ring.

The administrative assistant's extension popped up in the window, and Chris answered in a happy greeting.

"Mr. Lanning," she started and then hesitated a moment. Chris's smile widened. He could almost see her scratching her head at the change in him. *This is almost fun*, he thought.

"There's a lady on line 1 asking for a Christopher Lanning. She says her name is Lydia Hoffman. Do you know her?"

"I don't know." He didn't recognize the name, but he was in a good mood. "Put her through."

A few seconds passed and the phone rang again. "Greeson Developing, Chris speaking."

"Hello, Mr. Lanning," the lady greeted, "You don't know me. My name is Lydia Hoffman. I'm Laurie Callahan's mother."

The papers in his hands stilled. *Did she just say she was Laurie Callahan's mother? As in my Laurie Callahan?* Chris felt his heart rate double.

"I'm sorry, ma'am. Can you repeat that?"

"You do know Laurie, right? Laurie Callahan?"

Chris yanked the phone out of its cradle and nestled it against his ear. "I *knew* Laurie a few years back. Why do you ask?"

"Mr. Lanning, is there some way I can meet with you?"

Chris was silent except for the pounding of his pulse in his ears.

"It's important. I wouldn't ask if it weren't."

Chris debated on what to do. Laurie's mom could be calling for a number of reasons. She could want money, to claim her grandchildren, to tell him Laurie was in trouble...dead—anything. He rubbed his hand down his face and stifled a groan at what her contacting him could mean.

Chris swiveled in his chair, thinking he'd clear the day if it meant finding closure. Nevertheless, he didn't want to sound anxious. "I'm in the office tomorrow. How's ten o'clock?"

She confirmed the time was fine. "Okay, then. See you tomorrow morning."

Chris hung up the phone as a tidal wave of emotions washed over him. Surprise, nervousness, and then curiosity battled his nerves. It took a few minutes before he got the feelings under control.

Ms. Hoffman's request probably had something to do with Shelby and Kyle. She probably wanted to see them. If she did, he had bad news for her. It wasn't going to happen. Not when he was finally making progress in getting his household together. Up until today, he wasn't aware the woman was still alive. Laurie had never mentioned her.

God, will this ever be over? As soon as he felt like he was turning a corner where his past was concerned, something new would come up. *Give me the strength and wisdom to handle whatever it is Lydia could possibly want.*

Chris had to force the phone call and the meeting from his mind. Going to bed that night, however, he couldn't ignore the feeling that some of the missing pieces he'd searched for about Laurie's leaving were about to fall into place whether he was ready for them to or not.

It was nine o'clock the following morning when Lydia dressed in her best navy pantsuit and drove to the offices of Greeson Developing. She parked in the shadow of a sleek glass building and walked up a pathway surrounded by a thick manicured lawn.

It had been presumptuous of her to make the flight from New York two days ago, assuming this man named Chris Lanning would agree to see her at such a short notice—or at all for that matter. But

Forgiveness for Yesterday

he was her last hope, so she made the flight on chance that he would at least hear her out.

Lydia tipped her head back to look at the building's tall facade, wondering if her daughter had designed its elegant appeal and what affect she had on the heart of the man who owned it. *Laurie sure knows how to pick them.*

As she was told, at the desk Lydia asked for Chris Lanning. A young and attractive receptionist escorted her up a flight of stairs where she was seated in a contemporarily designed waiting area. Copies of *Architectural Digest* and *Business Weekly* lined the black coffee table in front of her, and a vase of what looked like sticks sat in the floor beside a black leather sofa. She reached for a magazine and then pressed her palms into her pant legs, focusing on remaining calm instead.

A tall, dark-haired man who couldn't possibly be anyone other than Chris Lanning himself started her way. He had the most beautiful eyes. They were the color of the Caribbean seas.

"Ms. Hoffman?"

"Lydia, please," she said, standing to offer her hand in greeting.

Like a professional, he took it. "Chris Lanning. Right this way."

She followed him down a short hallway and into an office where he closed the door. He motioned toward a seat across from him, and she took it.

"Thank you for seeing me, Mr. Lanning. I know this must be unexpected."

His blue eyes studied her for a moment but gave nothing away.

"Chris," he finally said as he took a seat behind the desk.

"Chris," she tried again, suddenly unsure of where to start. "I suppose you must be wondering why I asked to see you."

He nodded, so she continued. "I came here to ask you if you've heard from Laurie. I was hoping you knew of a way I could get in touch with her."

"I'm sorry, ma'am. I haven't spoken to your daughter in more than two years. Any words I would have to say to her would not be friendly."

Ms. Hoffman bit her lip and frowned. This was ridiculous. It had been two years. Surely this man had moved on. "Very well then," she said, gathering her purse. "Thank you for your time."

Chris's left brow rose in surprise. "You mean that's all you came here for?"

Lydia paused, her body hovering just above the chair. "Oh, Lydia. What does it matter?" she said to herself as she sat back down, physically and emotionally exhausted. She shook her head and looked Chris in the eye. "No, it's not. I came here on the off chance that you might still care—at least enough to hear me out."

When he didn't object, she continued, "It was two years ago, you say?"

"Yes," Chris clarified. "More like two and a half to be exact."

"I was afraid of that. Did she tell you she was leaving, or did she just disappear?"

Suddenly Chris looked uncomfortable. "She left without saying where she was going."

Lydia pursed her lips and shook her head. "Laurie could always be such a stubborn child! I'm also assuming she never spoke to you of me or her father."

"Never, and now that you mention it, very little of her past in any regard. What's this about?"

Lydia scooted forward in the seat, curious to see how this man would react to her suspicions. "I think I know why she left."

Chris eyed her closely. She took a deep breath and settled in to share what she thought Laurie should've shared from the start. "Seth—my ex-husband, Laurie's father—always wanted a child. The doctors said it would never happen, but when Laurie was born, Seth was beside himself with joy. He doted on her, spoiled her actually. Secretly I think he was hoping for a son, but there was nothing Laurie's little heart desired that her father didn't try to give to her.

"And then came Elizabeth, Laurie's little sister. Suddenly our world was filled with two of everything. We had two daughters who were as different as night and day when we weren't even expecting one."

Lydia knew she was rambling, but she didn't care. It had been so long since she'd been able to speak freely with anyone regarding her daughter, and this man looked very interested.

"In those days, we lived up North. Seth went to school to earn his CPA and worked nights washing dishes just to keep us out of foreclosure. He worked his way up and eventually found himself in the right place at the right time. He took a promising position—one that led him to earning senior partner at what would eventually become Hoffman and Associates, an accounting firm that caters to high-end clientele."

Lydia paused to smile at the memory. "Those were the days. By that time, Seth not only had the heart but also the means to give his family everything. When Laurie was sixteen, she knew she wanted to go into financial law. Her father couldn't have been more proud. Elizabeth, however, was more like me. She was more dramatic, and emotional. She had a love for the arts that could not be quenched. To Elizabeth's dismay, Seth saw her interests as a lack of ambition. He loved her, but he didn't understand her. In many ways his affections for Laurie portrayed themselves as favoritism. It was as if Laurie was the golden child and Elizabeth the prodigal.

"It was when Laurie was finishing up her degree at Princeton that she received an acceptance letter into law school. Her dreams were finally coming true—or so we thought. At the last minute, Laurie announced that she would not be returning to Princeton in the fall, but that she desired to pursue a career in architecture instead.

"Needless to say, her father was highly disappointed. Not just with Elizabeth, but now with Laurie as well. I can still remember that fight. Seth and Laurie were at each other's throats. It didn't take Seth and me long to regret our threats. When some words are spoken, they can never be taken back. We tried to make amends, but things were strained between us.

"Unfortunately, this all happened during one of Elizabeth's bouts with depression. She was younger and much less sure of herself than Laurie. I can only assume seeing the rift between her sister and us is what drove Elizabeth to the edge.

"Looking back, we should've known something was wrong. The pills...the late nights Elizabeth was known to keep. Laurie tried to talk with her. In fact, she went to visit with Elizabeth at college for a while, but that only seemed to make matters worse. When Laurie convinced Elizabeth to come home for fall break, it was obvious Elizabeth had put up a wall that even her sister couldn't breach. She had completely shut down.

"A few weeks later, Elizabeth drove her car off a bridge as a means to take her own life. Laurie was never the same after that."

Lydia wiped away a stray tear, still unsure of how things had come to that point. "She was devastated. For days, she locked herself in her room, only coming out to disappear into the night unexplained. She was moody and depressed. In a lot of ways, Laurie started acting like Elizabeth had just before her death. We felt like it was her way of grieving, so we let her be. But then everything suddenly changed.

"James Callahan came into the picture. James, or *Jim* as we called him, was an aspiring young lawyer who worked for one of Seth's clients. He took a liking to Laurie, and the two of them began to date.

"At first we couldn't believe how fast things turned around. Jim and Laurie almost immediately became inseparable. Laurie was no longer spending her evenings locked in her room, avoiding Seth and me. She was happy again. It was like having Jim around gave us one of our daughters back.

"It was no surprise when they eloped. At first we were hurt, but then we found out Laurie was pregnant. Although I don't know if marriage was the answer to Laurie's unplanned pregnancy, we weren't going to hold it against her or Jim. We wanted them in our lives. Even though Laurie wasn't able to finish her degree, Seth seemed to accept that. With Laurie's marriage, he had the son he'd always desired, and our first grandchild was on the way.

"Jim came to work with Hoffman and Associates, and everything was finally finding a new sense of normalcy in our lives. Then one day when Shelby was just a baby, Jim and Laurie up and moved away. Seth had been toying with the idea of expanding, but it seems Jim had other plans. He and Laurie moved to Atlanta, taking more than half of Seth's clients with him. For years, Seth struggled to get his business back on track.

"Still, Laurie was our only living daughter, so we reached out to her. For months there was no response until one day we received a letter. According to Laurie, Jim had become very possessive, threatening even, and he didn't want her to see us. Seth wanted to force our way into their lives, but I wouldn't let him. By this time, Laurie was pregnant again, and I was scared for her. Do you know it's been ten years since I've seen my granddaughter? And I don't even know my grandson's name!"

Lydia stifled a moan at the heartbreaking admission. "It was like the son we thought we had found in Jim came to steal what little we had left." She wrung her hands in expression of the agony Jim had caused.

"A few years passed, and Laurie called to say she and Jim were getting a divorce. I was hopeful that things would finally open back up between us, that she would move back home, and that we could meet our grandchildren, but then…then it came out that Seth had been having an affair. The news was…devastating. I couldn't handle my own situation, let alone take care of Laurie and two children."

Lydia stood and gracefully moved to the window. She laid her head against the glass, remembering just how painful the years she had just recounted had been. She heard Chris shifting in his chair and wondered if he felt out of place with such a private admission from someone he didn't even know.

"I'm sorry," he said. "I knew Laurie was married and divorced, but nothing about her father…or her sister. Laurie never spoke of anyone other than to insinuate things were strained, and it was best that she remained apart."

Lydia let out a bitter laugh and returned to her seat. "Those years cost us more than I'm letting on. While it was obvious Laurie didn't know how to reenter the chaos that had become our lives, she did occasionally write. More so as the years passed. That was how I found out about you.

"She wrote to me of a man she was working for as well as dating. She never gave me a name, so I did some research. I'm sorry to have learned about your parents. Death is a tragic thing.

"Laurie told me that she was in love with you and was planning to remarry. She said you were everything she had always wanted and never been able to have. The news was happy, and it gave me hope. If she was going to marry you that meant Jim Callahan was out of the picture. For her to remarry meant she was free of him."

Chris shook his head. "I don't understand. They were divorced. Of course she was free of him."

"Men like Jim Callahan don't just disappear because their ex wives want them to. He was a cruel, conniving man. He would never let Laurie truly go unless he was forced to. Learning about your engagement made me hopeful that something had finally forced his hand. I was hopeful that one day I'd get my daughter back completely—only both of us know it didn't happen.

"That November—the last time you spoke with her I assume—was about the same time I worked up the nerve to call her office. They said she had disappeared. That she left work one morning and never returned. I was certain she was dead. For over two years, I feared the worst until I saw this..."

Lydia opened her purse and pulled out a neatly folded newspaper article from one of the national papers. She passed it to him.

"This was published six weeks ago. I knew Seth was tied up in court with company affairs, but nothing like this." She watched Chris scan the headlines. Surely he would see what she was referring to.

"Chicago Man Found Guilty for Twelve-Year-Old Crimes," he said out loud before he began to read the article silently.

She gave him a few moments to gloss over the facts but stated the obvious. "Turns out Jim was never the man we thought him to be."

Lydia gently placed her hands on his desk, pleading for Chris to see what was right in front of him. "He was far worse. He was embezzling money from Hoffman and Associates as well as every other company he's ever worked for. I believe Laurie was the one who finally came forward with enough evidence to put him away."

Chris remained silent.

"Don't you see? She knew! It was why he took her away from us. Why he kept her away from us! All those years we lost were because of him!"

Lydia wanted to go on and on about how awful Jim Callahan was and all he'd stolen from her, but the man across from her wasn't sharing anything. In fact, he had an expression that was absolutely unreadable. Maybe he really didn't care after all.

She slumped back in the chair, seeing she was alone in the quest to find her daughter. She supposed she always would be.

Chris sat studying the woman in front of him. With her perfect posture and willowy frame, any evidence he needed to prove her claimed identity was obvious. She was Laurie's mother. Still, her story was almost unbelievable, borderline preposterous, but that didn't mean it couldn't have happened.

Chris continued to read the article, but he couldn't get past the name stated in the first line: Timothy James. The only legal dealings he'd had regarding Laurie's ex were during his adoption of Shelby and Kyle. James—or Jim Callahan—hadn't been a part of the kids' lives since his and Laurie's divorce. According to his attorney, Jim had severed all parental rights and willfully given Laurie full custody what was now six years prior.

The newspaper had a photo. It was hard to tell exactly what the man looked like from the grainy print and paper creases over his face, but Chris was sure he'd heard the name Timothy James before—and somewhere unconnected with Laurie.

Out of respect, he didn't voice his most honest thoughts. "That's a pretty amazing story. I can't say that I've heard any of this in the news, but then I can't say I've been up on current events."

Lydia sighed. "So you don't believe me either?"

"It's not that…if Laurie did play some part in convicting Jim, why would she wait twelve years to come forth with the evidence?"

"Because that's when she was about to marry you."

Chris shook his head. "I don't follow."

"You're a wealthy man, a very wealthy and *powerful* man. And Laurie was in love with you. I told you Jim would never let her go. What if he threatened her in some way? To me, her disappearance seems very timely. And she didn't just disappear, she vanished. Who can do that without the help of the authorities? Isn't it possible that she chose to make the ultimate sacrifice so she could finally sever Jim's power over her?"

Chris narrowed his eyes in consideration. "I searched for her. Thoroughly, I might add. Forgive me, but you're starting to sound like a woman who's on a manhunt for a guy who's already been found guilty beyond question. It looks like the courts have done their job."

Seeing his interpretation of her intentions, Lydia shook her head in frustration. "How can I possibly let this go when there's so much more to the story? I came here hoping you might know something. To hear that you still love her. It's been six weeks since the verdict, and Laurie hasn't appeared to make amends with me, nor her father. I was hoping she would at least return to make amends with you."

"With all due," Chris said on a sarcastic laugh, "I can't imagine Laurie showing back up after all this time. Unfortunately the man Laurie knew me to be wasn't a very forgiving one, especially not for an offense like this. If she wanted to get word to me, she would've done it sooner rather than later."

Chris shook his head at the absurdity of the thought. Nevertheless, he didn't see the need to be rude. "Rest assured if I *do* see or hear from her, I will most certainly pass it along that you're looking for her—after I get some answers of my own."

Lydia nodded and drew out a card with her contact information on it and passed it to him. "I want you to know that I truly believe Laurie loved you. I think there was a time when she blamed her father for Elizabeth's death, but now I don't wonder if she blames herself. I'm not sure she ever got over it."

Chris grew uncomfortable. "If Laurie loved me, she would've at least had the decency to tell me all this herself—from the start."

"I'm sorry my coming here has pained you. You were all she talked about in her letters."

Chris stared into the woman's eyes, so familiar, yet new. "You don't keep secrets from people you love."

Lydia shook her head, eyes filling. "No, but secrets are powerful things. They drive us to do the unimaginable if we let them. Jim was a persuasive man. Seth might have fallen for him, but I never did. I've come to learn that exposing secrets robs them of their power. Is it too far-fetched to consider that Laurie came to the same conclusion twelve years too late? There is more than one way to serve a sentence for our crimes. All I want to know is that my daughter and my grandchildren are safe."

Chris thought heavily on her words. "Can I keep this?" he asked, holding up the paper.

"Sure. There's more online if you care to look."

"I will."

Chris rose and moved to open the door. Lydia nodded with one last thought. Her head tipped up, and for an instant he could see the same flecks of hazel that still haunted his dreams. "I don't know when Laurie will return, or even if she will, but I hate to think of her out there alone…with no one. And my grandchildren…*please* let me know if you hear from her."

Guilt pricked Chris's conscience. It was easiest not to say anything about Shelby and Kyle because it would be one less worry for him in the long run. Their adoption records were sealed. If Lydia didn't know their whereabouts, she wouldn't ask to see them or try to find a place in their lives through him.

Chris looked down at the card in his hand in a daze. Lydia's name faded away, and in his mind, he asked a thousand questions. If by some chance he was able to answer even one for this grieving mother, he knew he should. "I will give this to Laurie, but regardless of what she does, if I hear from her, I will call."

On that promise, a teardrop fell, and Lydia discretely wiped it away. She was too choked up for words. The sight made him feel guilty for doubting her sincerity. Seeing her figure retreat without a good-bye, Chris knew he couldn't part like this.

"Lydia…wait…" The woman turned to face him, tears brimming in her eyes. If this were a hoax, she was the best actress ever. She looked so much like Laurie, and he was a complete sucker for tears. A hug was inappropriate, so he gave her something better.

"Your grandson—his name is Kyle. Kyle Benjamin. I imagine he's turned out to be a pretty good kid. Shelby too."

Lydia's smile was sad but genuine all the same. Silent tears slipped down her cheeks as she turned, and then, just like her daughter, she vanished from sight.

Chris thought about his visit with Laurie's mom the entire afternoon. He was just beginning to wrap his mind around the conclusion that her story was probably true, howbeit the saddest and most unfortunate thing he'd ever heard, he had no reason to doubt what Lydia had said. But true or not, it still didn't put Laurie back into his life, and it still left him waiting in limbo, not knowing if and when she would return and the repercussions it would cause if she did. All of it revealed there were serious gaps in Laurie's history he wanted to know about.

The verse from Colossians on forgiveness came to his mind and it loomed large. *I'm trying, Lord. Laurie should've at least trusted me enough to confide in me. We were getting married. We were starting a life together.*

It left an uneasy feeling in his gut to know that something this significant lurked unknown in her past and that he'd almost married her without having a clue. Lydia had implied that Laurie had felt threatened, but what about Shelby and Kyle? If Laurie had reason to fear, didn't that mean she had reason to fear for her children as well? Maybe that was why she'd kept their grandmother at a distance.

Chris felt his face pale thinking of what he'd do if something happened to Shelby or to Kyle. Fear was a terrible thing. He looked down at the newspaper clipping on his desk, suddenly wanting to be with his kids.

Forgiveness for Yesterday

It was long before five; nevertheless, he prepared to leave. He lifted up a prayer of thanks that his and Lydia's paths had crossed and that Jim Callahan had finally received justice, but he decided to leave his more worrisome thoughts behind. He had the rest of the week off, and he didn't want his conversation with Ms. Hoffman to put a damper on his time with Shelby and Kyle. A certain young lady he knew had a birthday coming up, and there was some shopping he needed to do.

28

Karen flipped the switch for the bathroom light and made her way to the living room of her apartment. Bret was standing in the middle of the room tinkering with the ceiling fan. It was Friday evening, and they had plans to go over to Chris's house for Shelby's birthday party. Holly and Scott were already in the car.

"What are you doing?" she asked, walking into the room.

He pulled the chain dangling from the fan. "I can't get this thing to cut on."

Karen flipped the switch on the wall. Nothing. "I don't know. It's always been kind of finicky."

"Hmph."

Bret was wearing a pair of pleated navy dress shorts, a freshly pressed button-down oxford shirt, and brown leather loafers. Before, she had always found his pulled-together look appealing, but today it came off as being a little stuffy.

She moved to grab her purse from the coffee table. When she did, he pulled her into his arms. "You look nice."

"Thanks."

He kissed her, but she felt reserved. "Last night was wonderful."

Karen smiled. "It was." He kissed her again, but something wasn't the same.

"Are you okay?" she asked after pulling back to stare into his eyes. There was something on his mind, she could tell.

"Of course. Why do you ask?"

"I don't know…I can't help feeling there's something you're not telling me."

Bret shrugged a shoulder. "It's nothing really. It's just that we've been married for six weeks, and somehow it feels…longer."

Karen frowned, unsure of how she was supposed to take that.

"What I meant is we're still living in this apartment. I thought we'd be ready to move by now."

"I thought we planned to stay here until my lease runs out at the end of August."

"I know…but…I think we should get serious about the house hunting. That's only two months away."

"Okay…call a realtor on Monday." Karen looked at him. The wrinkle between his brows was showing. "Are you sure this isn't about last week?"

There was a twitch in Bret's jaw. One day when she'd gotten home from the grocery store, she found the entire pantry reorganized alphabetically. He'd spent the whole afternoon working on it. When she asked him about it, he acted as though it was completely normal.

"What? I did it by color but then realized the labels will change as they update products. Alphabetized is the way to go." She had only stared, unsure of what to say and he'd taken offense.

"This is not about the kitchen cabinets or the fact that I'm the only one in this family who seems to know what it means to sort laundry. It's not even about the fact that we're spending the evening at Chris's with a bunch of kids we don't even know. I'm just anxious, I guess."

"Well, don't be. Wherever we live, we'll all be together, and that's what matters." She pecked a kiss on his cheek. "Let's go. I don't want to be late."

Silence followed them to the car, and Karen welcomed it. She gazed out the window thinking that in another month, it would be Holly who was turning twelve. *Where have the months gone?* She remembered her fight with Amanda that day in the restaurant. They hadn't spoken since. She felt terrible about it, but it wasn't her place to make another apology. Karen let go of a deep sigh. Things were so different a year ago.

She was still praying for Chris, hoping he wouldn't fall back into a lifestyle that so many new Christians had the tendency to do, and that Amanda would find those changes in him to be genuine and real. Karen wanted Amanda to be drawn to God because of Chris, and she wanted it to happen now.

God, you know how I feel about Chris. Please don't let him settle for mediocre faith—faith that is easy to slip into only on Sundays. I want him to be passionate about you. Passionate about you like Bret is passionate about you. And I want Amanda to believe!

She turned to the side to admire the man sitting beside her. They were sitting at a stoplight, and Bret was tapping his fingers on his knee, and it wasn't in time with the music on the radio. It was a sign his agitation had chosen to linger.

"What's wrong?" she asked again, seeing his expression was grim and closed off.

"Why do you keep asking that?"

Karen flinched.

"Sorry," he said. "The guy in front of us doesn't know how to drive. He's left his signal on for two miles, not to mention he's changed lanes at least ten times. Some people don't deserve to have a driver's license."

Karen turned to look back out the window. *God what's wrong with him?* There was no answer, but Karen already knew there wouldn't be. She was suffering with a little impatience herself.

They pulled into Chris's drive and were the first guests to arrive. The kids piled out of the back, and Karen went around to the trunk to start unloading. She'd told Chris she would help with the food since Marie wouldn't be able to come until later.

She started passing the grocery bags to Bret. "Oh, no," she said, realizing she had left one behind. "I didn't grab the one from the fridge. It had all the cold stuff in it. I can't make the dip without sour cream." Tentatively she turned back and looked at her husband. She just couldn't ask. "I'll run back and get it."

"No, no," Bret said, handing the bags to Holly. "I'll run down to the store and take care of it."

Karen made a face by biting her lip.

"Why will that not work?"

"I need the bag from the apartment. It had other stuff in it as well. Guests will be arriving by the time you get back, and you know I can't have a cheeseburger without that special cheese I can only get from a deli."

"Whatever," he sighed. "I'll be back." He kissed her on the cheek and climbed back in the car.

Karen waved good-bye, and she and Holly started hauling the groceries up to the porch. Shelby opened the door to let them in the house. Shelby was wearing a matching outfit of pink shorts and a glittery tank top. The outfit wasn't revealing, but Karen could see the reason for Holly's distress. Shelby was developing a lot faster than most girls her age.

"Happy Birthday!" she said, giving Shelby a hug.

"Thanks! I didn't think you guys would ever get here! Look what Dad bought me!" She pulled her hair back from her neck to show off new earrings. "They're diamonds! A quarter carat each! Can you believe it? I'll be the only girl in the seventh grade with her own diamonds!"

"Whoa," Holly cooed, admiring the jewelry.

Karen praised her as well. "Those are gorgeous, Shelby. Be sure to take special care of them."

"Oh, I will. Where's Bret?"

"He's coming. We forgot a bag back at the apartment. Where's your dad?"

"He's just getting out of the shower. He'll be out in a minute."

Shelby and Holly helped her set the bags of chips and cookies down in the kitchen and then tore off for Shelby's room upstairs while Scott went to search for Kyle.

Karen unloaded the groceries and tidied up a bit while she waited on Bret to return. When she passed by the dining room, she saw where the presents were supposed to go. She slipped Shelby's gift from her purse. It was the Backstreet Boys' latest album. Karen smiled as she placed the wrapped CD on the table beside a cluster of balloons that were tied to a centerpiece.

On the way back through the living room, her hand came up to admire the ornate work on banister of the stairs. Chris had a beautiful home. What were the chances she and Bret could find a place like this? Again, Bret's sour attitude came to mind regarding the matter of their living arrangements. She would suggest they buy land and build, but she wasn't sure Bret could deal with that kind of stress right now. It would present way too many things for them to have to agree on.

Karen went to the kitchen and started pulling down bowls and the other things she would need once Bret got back with the sour cream and trimmings. It wasn't long before she heard a door shut down the hall.

"Karen!" Chris said as he came into the kitchen barefooted, wearing a pair of cargo shorts and a T-shirt. He paused to give her shoulders a quick squeeze. "How long have you been here? And where's Bret? He doesn't expect me to grill all these burgers by myself, does he?"

Karen smiled seeing how he went straight for the refrigerator to reach for a soda. "No. We forgot the bag with the cold stuff in it. He ran back to get it."

"Did you get the good cheese from the deli?"

"Yes!"

"Awesome!"

Karen watched him wash his hands and dry them on a towel. He started spreading raw meat on a platter, preparing to go out to the grill.

"Can I help?"

"Nah. I've got it."

She watched him work, thinking that he looked more handsome than ever with a fresh shower and suntan while moving about the kitchen with an ease he would never admit to having.

"You love this, don't you?"

"What?"

"Cooking."

Chris smiled, and the dimple in his left cheek dug in hard. "Yeah, but don't tell anyone. It'll ruin my image."

"Too late. Most people already know you're the kind of man who helps little old ladies across the street and makes anonymous donations to charities. There's nothing wrong with that."

"Tell that to the boys on the construction site. They'll have a heyday with it."

Karen laughed but understood his point. In an effort to direct her thoughts away from Chris's good looks, she tried to make small talk. "So are you ready for this? Shelby is turning twelve. It's the last year before she becomes a teenager!"

He chuckled and reached into the cabinet by the stove and searched for the pepper. "There have been so many changes in my life during the last six months, I think the better question would be is *she* ready for this. I tell you Karen, I think I'm going to sit on that girl until she's at least twenty-five."

"Hmm, you know that's not a bad idea. Feel like sitting on Holly while you're at it? She already thinks you're the coolest dad ever."

"Thanks, but one girl is plenty. If it weren't for Marie, I don't know what I'd do. I guess I'd be on my knees twice as much as I am already."

"Things are that different, huh?"

"Yes! God is really working on me." Chris stopped what he was doing and looked at her. "Isn't it amazing though? I mean I truly feel like a new man. Life's not perfect, but all that baggage I was carrying around is somehow a whole lot lighter. I don't feel condemned anymore."

Karen smiled, noting that the joy in his eyes had never shone so brightly. He was practically glowing. "You are a new man, and you're most certainly not condemned. Ezekiel 36:26 tells us that God will give us a new heart and a new spirit. That he will remove our heart of stone and give us a heart of flesh."

"Thanks, but part of me feels like I owe you an apology."

"An apology? For what?"

He set the pepper shaker down. "For that day here in the kitchen when I asked you to….well…keep what I was about to do from Bret. I should've never put you in that position, and for that I'm sorry. I'm just glad you had the guts to put me in my place. I respect you for it."

Karen blushed at hearing such a thing. "It's okay. I mean it all worked out."

"It did, and I can't blame you for telling him. I just never would've guessed he could get past it. I know I couldn't have. You guys have been an incredible example of faith and forgiveness to me, and I have to tell you, it played a large part in my coming to Christ."

Karen nodded, appreciating his words but didn't know what to say.

Chris finished peppering the meat and started loading up things onto a tray. The fact that he would still feel the need to apologize to her after all these months said a lot. There was something undeniably special about Chris. It was like she almost couldn't help but to love him. He was fun, easy-going, and although he wanted you to think he was shallow and insensitive, he really wasn't. There was a lot more to him than met the eye, especially now that he was a believer.

Softly something whispered in her ear, and it caused Karen's heart to miss a beat. *You married the wrong man.*

Chris turned away, and Karen felt the blood drain from her face. *That's a lie. Things between Bret and I happened a little fast, but Bret's the man I'm supposed to be with…*

As much as she wanted to ignore such an idea, the image of Chris and her together made perfect sense. They had everything in common. They both had kids about the same age, they enjoyed being outdoors, they loved to cook, and now Chris believed. Had Amanda seen something she hadn't? Was that why she was so jealous every time Karen stood up for Chris?

The same little voice told her that Chris had no idea where to find canned peas in his pantry, and that if he did, they wouldn't be located between the peanut butter and the pickles. And what about all that flirting?

No. No! I am in love with Bret. We're adjusting, that's all.

If that were the case then why, she asked herself, hadn't she had any of the admiring thoughts that had just run through her mind when she stood watching her own husband in their living room a mere thirty minutes ago? Her desiring thoughts were for Chris.

Chris turned back to face her, and she felt her cheeks start to warm. She was embarrassed that somehow he could read her mind.

"Are you okay? You got quiet."

"What?" She shook her head like she didn't understand what he was talking about.

"I asked if you were okay. You look flush."

"I'm fine. I…just…can I have a glass of peas?"

"Peas?"

"Tea!" Karen fought the urge to bury her face in embarrassment. "What I meant was, can I have a glass of tea, please?"

He moved to pour her a glass, and when he handed it to her, confusion was written all over his face. She set the tea down without taking a sip. Dropping her head into her hands, she closed her eyes. The last thing she should do was spill her worries out to Chris, thus deepening her connections to him.

"The truth is, I don't know if everything is okay. Bret and I…a few weeks ago, things were fine, better than fine, but now it's almost like something's wrong, and I don't know what."

Chris's brow transformed into lines of concern, and he leaned forward on the counter. "You guys just got married. What could possibly be wrong?"

"I don't know. It's the same reason I called you back in May. It's like there's this wall up between the two of us—almost like there's something he's not telling me. It wasn't like that during the wedding, but now… I'm not so sure.

"He moved into my place, and I know it's crowded, that he was used to having his space, but when I ask him about it, he tells me it's nothing. For some reason, I'm starting to think my apartment is a real problem for him. "

"So look for some place new."

"We want to, but we've been so busy with the wedding and all. Our engagement was so short, we didn't have time to look beforehand and now…" Suddenly something dawned on her. "You don't think he regrets getting married, do you? His life was so…organized. He was happy. Now he just seems…irritated. What if it's me?"

"Karen, that is not it. Bret has always been…irritated."

"Then how come I don't remember him that way? I feel like he's either shutting me out or trying to make the move on me!" *Oh, no. Where did that come from? Did I really say that out loud?* There was a long pause of silence, and she noticed how Chris's brows had shot nearly to his hairline.

"I'm sorry." She blushed, seeing how she'd embarrassed them both. "I shouldn't have said that, but this really has me worried. Did you know he alphabetizes food?"

Chris let out a lazy chuckle. "No, but I can't say I'm surprised. Spending day in and day out with someone gives you a lot of insight into their personal quirks. I knew this was coming with whomever he married."

"Why didn't you say something?"

"Like what? 'Hey, by the way, did you know you're marrying an obsessive-compulsive freak?' It's twice as bad when he's stressed."

Karen was silent.

"Come on, you don't think it's a MBA in accounting that makes Bret so good at what he does, do you? It's all about the need for control. It's what makes him one of my best employees. But at the same time, Bret is hard on others. I think he's twice as hard on himself. You know that much is true."

"I understand what you're saying, but I can't help but to feel there's something bigger at the root of his recently disgruntled state."

Chris let go of a deep breath. "Why do women always do this?"

"Do what?"

"Take something that's nothing and make a big deal out of it? And you're always assuming that if something is broken that you're the cause of it—which is usually true," Chris teased her with a smile, "but every molehill doesn't need to become a mountain."

"What are you saying? That he's telling me the truth? That this sudden change in his personality is really nothing more than his way of handling stress? And that it probably has nothing to do with me?"

"I don't know. Bret has seemed…a little more neurotic lately, but I don't know that it's anything to worry about, and it's certainly not because he married you. You're by far the best thing that's ever happened to him, and he knows it. He's always been one to stress over work, and he's used to living on his own. Maybe it's a combination of things. Being a dad isn't the easiest job in the world either, and now he's got two kids to watch out for."

"I tried to tell him that, but he wouldn't listen."

"Well, there you go." Chris could still see she was worried. "Relax. He'll work through it. Give him some time."

She let go of a deep breath and smoothed her hair back from her face. "You're right. If he's just stressed out, does that mean things are no better between you and Darrell?"

"They're better—not ideal—but better. Even if they weren't—" Chris stopped midsentence and looked her square in the face. "Do you *really* love him?"

Karen looked up into the eyes of a friend, a dear friend, but what she saw looking back at her instantly reminded her of the reason why she hadn't fallen for Chris. It was because Bret had stolen her heart first. Stuffy shirts and organized vegetables, she was in love with him for all of his *wonderful* attributes, not his bad ones. The doubts that had been washing over her vanished.

"Yes." She nodded. "I love him with all my heart."

"Then accept him for who he is and love him in spite of who he isn't."

She nodded again. "Thanks. I will."

Karen wiped away the condensation on the tea glass and finally lifted it to her lips.

Chris took the opportunity to get even with her. "Oh, and about that other thing you mentioned—just so you know, guys *hate* hearing the word *no.*"

The liquid she just managed to get down, all but came back up and out her nose. "What?" she coughed in surprise.

Chris laughed seeing her reaction. "It burns twice as bad when it's coffee! You heard me. Don't turn him down."

"We're newlyweds!"

"I know, but there will come a day. You're female. After the initial thrill wears off, you all say no."

Having been married before, she knew what Chris was saying was true, but she and Bret were nowhere near that point. Their love life was very exciting. At least it was to her.

"Thanks…I think." She took another sip of her tea, reflecting on Chris's words. He was very insightful this afternoon, and it was a little surprising. "How do you know so much about marriage? I mean you pretty much define the word *bachelor*. No offense meant, of course."

Chris laughed. "None taken. Unlike a lot of people, I've seen both sides of the tracks. My real parents were never married, and a lot of my foster parents fought all the time. But my adoptive parents…they were very much in love with each other. I guess it comes from a lifetime of watching what works and what doesn't. It's why I couldn't settle for what I had with Amanda. No offense meant, of course."

"None taken." Karen tipped her head to the side, curious. Even if the day came when Chris and Amanda shared the same beliefs, their personalities were both so much alike that a marriage of balance between them would require constant work.

"Do you ever think the two of you might work things out?"

Chris shook his head. "That relationship was unhealthy at it's best. Amanda has issues, and me… I can't handle the temptations she brings. I need someone who's going to help keep me pointing in the right direction when it comes to things of the Bible and faith. I hate that I hurt her, but at the same time, I don't think either of us are what the other one needs."

There was a break in their conversation, and Karen could clearly see Chris's regret. If she were going to say anything about him being the father of Amanda's baby, now would be the time. She thought on Amanda's secret and how it was forcing her to choose loyalties.

Karen tried to form the words, but something wouldn't let her. It just didn't feel right. The news was Amanda's to share. What was it Chris had said about giving a person time? "I guess we can all learn from our mistakes." She laughed a little considering how things had changed. "I can't believe you just stood there and gave me what sounds like biblical advice on my marriage. You're a piece of work, you know that?"

"Funny"—he chuckled—"that used to be one of my best pickup lines. It was usually right after I said it that women started telling me *no!*"

Karen laughed. "Come on. Let's go outside before Bret walks in here and finds us together all red faced and embarrassed. I don't think I can explain it away twice."

Chris grabbed the tray, and together they moved outside to the grill.

There was one more thing on Karen's mind as she saw Bret turning up the drive. "Chris," she said, getting his attention, "when the right woman does come along, she's going to be getting a very special man."

He winked at her. "Thanks. For a while there, I think we were all starting to wonder."

29

Shelby's party lasted through the night. To make up for his absence in her life, Chris wanted this year's birthday to be special, so he'd told her she could have a sleepover. She had originally come to him with a list of friends she wanted to invite, and some of them had been boys.

"Shelby," he'd explained, "you know those boys can't stay the night."

"Well, duh! They can come for a little while, but the girls can make plans to stay over. Oh, please, Daddy, please! It'll be so much fun!" From there she'd poured on the charm and turned her adorable little face into a weapon that penetrated his strongest defense.

"Okay, but just this once and only because it's your last birthday party ever. Next year you'll be a teenager, and we're celebrating at the monastery."

The sarcasm was completely lost on her, but at this hour, Chris wasn't quite sure what a monastery was either. It was 2:00 a.m. on Saturday morning, and he was more concerned about how he'd fallen for such an age-old routine.

Incessant giggling drifted down the staircase and through the cracked door of his bedroom. "I'm definitely turning to mush," he said. Chris threw the covers back, pulled on some jeans, and walked to the bottom of the stairs. He didn't bother to put a shirt on and could only imagine Shelby's reaction to him coming upstairs without one. He'd have to get his point across from here.

"Girls! Light's out!" His voice boomed up the opening and down the hall toward Shelby's room. Everything got quiet, and a smug smile crept up his tired face. The scampering of feet sounded across the ceiling and was followed by silence.

"Good," he said to himself. They knew he meant business. He walked back to his room not denying how good it felt to be obeyed.

Forgiveness for Yesterday

Ten minutes later, another round of high-pitched laughter rang out. *God, please don't let me go up there and kill those girls. It will look so bad.* Chris tugged a pillow over his head, and the next thing he knew, his alarm clock was sounding that it was already past eight.

He reached over and almost hit the snooze before remembering that they had plans for the day. After Shelby's friends went home, he had promised to take Kyle and Shelby to the water park they both had been begging to go to since spring.

Oh, well, he thought. *I didn't plan on being up half the night.* Chris hit snooze, but his conscience woke him before the alarm sounded again. *Be a man of your word!* He groaned but obeyed, and by the end of the day, he was glad he did. He and the kids ended up having one of the best times he could remember.

There was none of the sudden outburst of emotions that drove him crazy from Shelby, and somehow Kyle didn't say one mean word to his sister. The day was a blessing, but by Sunday morning, a very tired Shelby sat drooping in front of her cereal bowl while Kyle was going on and on about everything they'd done and what he wanted to do again.

"Remember the slide with the seventy-foot drop straight down? I can't believe Dad got on that!" Kyle was beside himself with excitement over the memory. Chris couldn't believe he'd done it either, and for a few seconds there, he was wishing he hadn't, especially not after their earlier visit to the infamous Pizza Palace for lunch.

"And then there was that wave pool. How do they do that?" Not waiting for an answer, Kyle asked another question. It was the one Chris had been waiting for. "Can we go back at the end of the summer? Please, Dad, can we?"

Chris lowered his newspaper. "Let's all recover from yesterday first." He looked over at Shelby. "What's wrong with you this morning? You're awful quiet."

Shelby looked up from her full bowl of soggy cereal. "I'm fine, just tired."

Kyle chimed in with a reason for Shelby's mood. "Brittney called last night and told her she's fat. That's why she's been moping around all morning."

"Shut up! You need to mind your own business, Kyle!" Shelby wadded up a napkin and threw it at him.

"Hey!" Chris commanded. "Both of you stop it." He looked to Shelby for an explanation. "Is this the same Brittney who stayed over on Friday?"

"Yes," Shelby answered, shooting daggers at Kyle with her eyes.

Chris could see she was hurt and remembered how Brittney came off as being the leader of all Shelby's friends. He hadn't said anything, but during the party, he'd come in the house to find Brittney searching through Shelby's dresser drawers. "You are *not* fat, but I'd try to pick better friends if I were you. I get a bad feeling about that girl."

Shelby didn't say anything, but she did start to eat. A few minutes later, Chris folded down the paper and asked a question of his own. "Do you two want to go to church with Bret and Karen this morning?"

Kyle's and Shelby's eyes widened in surprise. Before he could say anything else, Kyle let out a big, "Yes!" and then dashed off to get dressed. Shelby was the one who continued to sit and stare at him like he'd grown a second head.

"Well?" Chris looked at her, waiting for an answer.

"Sounds good to me. Are *you* going?"

Taking the last sip of coffee, Chris tried to think of a way to explain what had taken place in his life on a twelve-year-old level. He hadn't meant to put it off this long, but for some reason, he just didn't know how to tell the kids about his salvation.

"I was planning on it. I'm sure you've noticed by now that something has changed in me. A few months ago I asked Jesus into my heart, and since then, God's been showing me things—things I want to change in my life, and going to church is one of them."

A smile lit up Shelby's face, but her eyes still held questions. "What kind of changes are you talking about?"

"Spending more time with you and Kyle for one. I realize I need to get more involved with the things you guys are doing."

Shelby swirled the spoon through her cereal, and he could see the wheels turning. Something was coming. "I've noticed you haven't brought home a new girlfriend in a long time. Is that one of the changes you want to make?"

Chris looked at her, and the life he'd lived in front of her and Kyle flashed before his eyes. It was nothing out of the ordinary for them to see him bring home a date one evening and then find her at the breakfast table the next morning wearing one of his shirts, nothing more.

"Shelby," he began, "I've not been the best dad to you and Kyle. I've certainly not set a good example for you with the way I've acted, and I'm sorry. You deserved better." He paused, taking in the tender expression that hung on her curious face.

"I want you to know something. I've been living my life completely for myself, never thinking twice about it until recently. God has showed me how selfish that was, and things are going to be different now. I can't do the things I did before and be okay with it."

"I've noticed you're not drinking beer anymore either. Is that part of the change?"

Chris chided himself for not realizing how sharp she was. "Yes, it is. Alcohol seems to go hand in hand with a lot of the behavior I want to change. If I don't drink, it's easier for me to stay on track and do the right things."

Shelby's eyes started to water, and somehow he could sense her tears were not happy ones. *Be patient with her.* "What's wrong? You're crying."

"I'm glad you've changed, but if you have Jesus, you don't need us anymore."

"Why would you think I don't need you just because I'm a Christian?"

"Because"—she sniffed—"Kyle and I were all you had after Mom left. Now you've found something that makes you happy, and that means you don't need us to do that."

"Shelby, I just said that I'm going to start spending more time with the two of you so that I can get more involved. Do you think I adopted you and Kyle because I needed someone to keep me happy?" When she nodded, Chris felt terrible. "I feel like you adopted us because you felt sorry for us. Is that true?"

"I…uh…. I did feel sorry for you, but that's not the reason. The situation with your mother…it's complicated. I'm not lying when I say I adopted you and Kyle because I wanted you. I still want you. I want you because I love you. You two mean the world to me even when you don't make me happy."

Chris leaned forward on his elbows and spoke from his heart. "Just because God is opening my eyes to all the things I've been doing wrong doesn't mean all my problems are going to vanish or that I'm going to be happy all the time. Christianity doesn't work like that. Nothing will change the fact that I'm your father and I love you— even on the days when I still get it wrong."

She nodded, and he hoped she understood what he was saying. She wiped away her tears, and the sniffling subsided. Every day she was a little more mature, and a little more emotional. That's why it didn't surprise him when she asked her next question.

"Do you still hate Mom?"

"Hate…is a strong word. I still don't know what made her leave, but I can't go on pushing people away because of it. It was destroying me. It was destroying us. I'm sorry for being incredibly self-centered in the way I handled her leaving. I made it all about me. I know that only added to the hurt you and Kyle were experiencing. Can you forgive me?"

Shelby studied him for a second and started to smile despite her damp cheeks and red eyes. To his relief, she got up from the table and kissed him on the cheek as she wrapped her arms around his neck in a tight hug.

"Of course. I love you," she said. "You're a good dad."

He took her into his embrace, touched by her compassion and more so by her endearments. "I love you too, and thanks. I needed to hear you say that. Now go get ready. We don't want to be late." He gently swatted her leg with the newspaper so she wouldn't see the way her words affected him. They were sweet, and it eased some of his anxiety over meeting her long-lost grandmother earlier in the week.

As Shelby walked away, Chris had one more question. "What was all that giggling about the other night?"

A giggle escaped her as she turned back to face him. "Dad!" she wailed and crossed her arms. "All my friends think you're cute. It's so…disgusting!"

Her confession caused him let go of his own giggle. He rolled his eyes and shook his head. "Girls!" He heard her feet move up the stairs and knew it was a good thing he didn't go upstairs the other night without his shirt on. The giggling would've gone on until dawn.

⁂

Shelby took the stairs two at a time. She slipped into her bedroom and shut the door. Her father's words were fresh on her mind, and the smile on her lips deepened. She hoped he didn't take long to tell Kyle about the changes he wanted to make. Kyle had been so worried back when Chris started leaving town and not coming back for weeks at a time. The worry only intensified the more Chris was away. She was sure Kyle would like the part about their dad getting more involved, but she didn't know what he would say about Chris becoming a Christian.

Sometimes Kyle went to church with her when she stayed over at Holly's, but he didn't seem as interested in religion as she was. He would often sit in the back of the class with some of the other boys and make jokes. It was nothing unusual for the teacher to call him out.

She let the concern for Kyle go and moved to search through her closet for something to wear. Kyle was Chris's biggest fan, and she was sure Chris giving his heart to the Lord would make Kyle stop and consider that there might be more to church than whether or not his friends would be there.

She pulled down a new shirt and skirt she'd gotten for her birthday and started to put it on. The skirt was a little tight, but then it was the one Brittney had bought her. Shelby checked the size. It was an extra small. *Figures.*

She held her breath and squeezed the button closed anyway. She fished out some white sandals to match and spotted the black velvet box her dad had given her for her birthday. It was sitting on her vanity. The earrings were the nicest things she'd ever owned. Just wearing them made her feel special. She swept her hair back into a loose ponytail, remembering her dad's words as he'd given them to her. "These are precious, Shelby, just like you are precious to me. Take good care of them."

Shelby flipped open the lid on the box, but the jewelry wasn't there. "What?" she asked the empty room. She distinctively remembered taking them off Friday night because she didn't want to wear them to the water park on Saturday.

Frantically she searched the vanity top, and then its drawer, but there was no sign of her diamond earrings. "Think, Shelby, think!" *I know I put them right back in their box when I went to bed Friday night.*

Something horrible started in her gut, and she thought she was going to be sick. "Dad is going to kill me!"

She continued her search until she heard Chris calling from downstairs. He was saying it was time to go. A tear threatened to spill from the corner of her eye. Things might be changing between her and her dad but she wasn't quite ready to test her father's words just yet.

Shelby tore the ponytail holder out of her hair and covered her ears with her long, thick locks. She couldn't tell Chris the truth. If she did, he would think the precious and special gift he'd given her meant nothing when it really meant the world to her. All she knew was the earrings had simply disappeared.

30

Come Monday morning, it was time for Chris to head back to work. He was leaving town for Chicago to special order some materials, and then he would finish up his work week at the Heritage House. It would be at least another five days before he could see the kids again.

He packed his briefcase and slipped the overpriced snapshot he purchased on impulse from the water park gift shop on Saturday in with his papers. Seeing Shelby's and Kyle's smiling faces, he shut the leather case, determined to get to the airport on time.

After church yesterday, he finally worked up the words to share with Kyle about his decision for Christ. Other than being pleased to hear he would be attending church with them when he was in, Kyle didn't have much to say. Shelby's response, however, continued to linger in his mind. Never had he imagined he would see her go up to the altar at the end of the sermon and pray to receive Christ for herself.

When they'd gotten home, she explained some of the questions that had been going on in her own heart. "I was holding back because I was scared you'd be mad at me because I wanted to be a Christian. It's why I kept asking you all those questions. I wanted you to decide what you believed." She meant nothing by the innocent words, but they had cut him to the bone.

At twelve years old, Shelby understood God's plan of salvation. What she didn't know was how to show it to him. Chris tried not to think of what would've happened if he had continued on in his anger and frustration against God and everyone else. He thanked God for opening his eyes sooner rather than later.

After his bag was checked, Chris quickly boarded the 9:00 a.m. flight that was scheduled to arrive at Chicago's O'Hare later that afternoon. Flying wasn't something he did often, and since this trip was off the record, he spent the extra money and flew first class.

Once the flight got underway, he checked through his notes and confirmed that his meeting with a sales representative from Architectural Design was set for the following day at three. His meeting there would last a little over an hour, but the meeting he had this evening with a man at a company called Enterprise Properties was the main reason for his trip.

Enterprise Properties was a mega corporation, and their CEO, Tucker Fennel, had called him persistently during the last several months wanting to talk about buying out Greeson. At first, Chris's answer had been no, but with the changes that had occurred over the last few weeks and months, Chris had started to reconsider.

From a business perspective, it sounded like the deal of a lifetime. Enterprise was offering to buy his controlling shares in the company in exchange for Chris's cooperative assistance and discrete exit from the business.

Chris tried to imagine what it would be like to no longer own the company his father and grandfather had built from the ground up. The job brought him a lot of headache, but the roots went deep. No one would come right out and say it, but he knew if he sold out to Tucker, it would mean the loss of jobs for some of those who'd spent years building the company up beside him. Guys like Darrell and possibly Bret.

Chris pondered the nagging at his soul. He didn't want his reason for selling to be about revenge for the way Darrell had gone behind his back and worked strategically to bring his leadership into question these last several months. He wanted it to be about doing what was best for everyone.

The Heritage House Project would wrap up in another month or two, and Chris dreaded the thoughts of returning to his desk. What would he do with himself if he no longer had an obligation at Greeson?

Forgiveness for Yesterday

He pushed the burden of making a final decision from his mind. There was plenty of time for that. Nothing would be decided until he had all the facts, had prayed about it, and received an answer from the Lord. *Show me, Lord. Show me what's best for everyone.*

He let go of a sad chuckle and realized that nearly every area of his life was on a roller coaster. He was falling in love with his children so fast he didn't know what to do, work had him second-guessing what he'd spent a lifetime trying to accomplish, and the conversation with Lydia Hoffman had been rolling around in his mind for a full week.

He had even gone as far as to pull out the note Laurie had written when she left. It had been scribbled down on the edge of a blueprint of a project they'd been working on together. Having only seen it yesterday, her words were easy to recall.

> I can't explain what's happened. Just know I never thought I would be writing this. I can't go on pretending anymore. I know you won't understand, and I wouldn't ask you to try. You deserve all the happiness life can give you. Forget me and move on.
>
> PS: Take care of the kids and tell them I love them—more than they know.

He studied the words in light of Lydia's story, and other than a nine-digit figure above the writing that he hadn't noticed before, nothing else had changed. The mystery had him stumped. He did end up calling a friend of his who worked for the Justice Department—someone who would know where to start.

So far he found out that the firm Laurie's dad, a Benjamin Seth Hoffman, owned and operated since the seventies had been plastered all over the news in recent weeks. Seth was infamous for taking on somewhat shady but high profile clients and more than likely had a few skeletons in his closet.

The money trail connected to Jim, however, was seemingly an unending ravel of surprises. "The biggest news is that one charge connected him with a known human trafficking ring," his friend had told him. "I can't get you the name of the witness, but they had enough evidence to put Jim Callahan away for life without parole." Chris didn't like the way his hunch told him the witness had been Laurie.

He was finally able to pinpoint where he recognized the name Timothy James from. He had once been a prospective client of Greeson—right about the time when Chris started dating Laurie.

Timothy, a supposed junior partner with Velmore and Klein Investing at the time, had been seeking out information on building an office complex. It never came to pass but Chris remembered the guy because he'd taken him out to dinner one evening, compliments of the company.

Heavy drinker and obnoxiously rude, he had asked a bunch of personal questions that had little to do with real estate development. Shortly thereafter, he seemed to drop off the map.

At that time, Chris had been disappointed that Velmore and Klein Investing had chosen to go another route, but now he made a whole new connection. Jim very well could have been playing him the fool while fishing for information as leverage to use against Laurie.

Jim's connection with Richard and Edward and their recent breach of contract with Greeson correlated nicely with Jim's trial and conviction. All of this meant Lydia was probably right. It was likely Jim had enough means and influence to threaten Laurie with something, and unfortunately, she'd taken the bait.

Chris supposed he would never know what Jim's intentions were toward Greeson, but nothing would change the fact that Laurie was out there somewhere, and she hadn't returned now that Jim had been sentenced.

And then there were the things Chris feared—like reporters who dug for details. Someone would eventually connect the dots regarding Laurie and Jim's children and Chris's adoption of them. Then he would have Lydia to deal with.

The thought of their lives getting wrapped up in media drama made his head spin. Praying for Laurie rather than stewing over her had a way of extinguishing the final flames of his resentment, but at this point, it wouldn't take much to rekindle his bitterness. Learning there was no way to heal the past except for by releasing it was a lesson he knew he could still easily squander.

Chris leaned back in his seat and closed his eyes. Words from a long-ago conversation with Pastor Mark rang out through his mind. He might be able to forgive Laurie, but he still didn't know how to forget her. The best he could do was pray that God would continue to work in him so that one day his heart would learn to love again—in spite of all she'd done.

31
Downtown Chicago

Collin Porter stepped to the edge of his office, feeling like he was going to be sick. He had grabbed a polish sausage complete with peppers and onions from a vendor on Roosevelt and Wabash during lunch, and it was quickly becoming one of his worst decisions ever.

"Hey, Jessica," he said, walking next door and waving a manila file folder. "I'm going to have to cut out of here early. Any chance you might be willing to take my three o'clock? Everything you need to know is right here."

"Sure." She reached out her hand for the file and dropped it in her in-box. She was surprised he would trust her. After all, she was the new girl. "Say, you don't look so well."

"Tell me about it. Steer clear of the polish vendor over by the Potbelly. See you tomorrow."

Jessica watched him disappear, glad for the warning. Polish sausages were an old-time favorite. She finished up what she was working on, and in an effort to fight off the midafternoon slump that came with missing another night's sleep, she made a trip down to the break room for a coffee. The next thing she knew, Kari was buzzing her on the intercom system.

"There's a Mr. Lanning from Greeson Developing here to see you."

Jessica smiled. Surely she was hearing things. She reached over and pressed the orange button to summon Kari.

"Excuse me," she asked. "Who did you say was here to see me?"

"There's a Chris Lanning from Greeson Developing here to see you. It's Collin's three o'clock. Remember, you said you'd take it?"

Jessica's mind started to race. Surely it wasn't the Chris Lanning she knew. It couldn't be.

Forgiveness for Yesterday

"Give me just a second," she squawked into the phone as she scrambled for the file folder Collin had given her a few hours ago.

She ripped it open and skimmed the pages inside. She stopped only on the words 1823, plantation house, Greek Revival, Asheville. Evidently Chris was working on some type of restoration project. *Since when does Greeson Developing take an interest in historical architecture?* There was even a figure jotted in the margin that probably represented the budget Chris was trying to work within.

God what are you doing? Why does the past always have a way of catching up with me when I'm least expecting it?

Out of habit, her hand went to her pocket. Not finding the silent alarm she was used to having, she told herself to breathe. *It's over. This is just a fluke. No one knows who you really are.* Automatically her hand went to the short black bob of a haircut witness protection had left her with. She slipped on a pair of reading glasses to better hide her eyes. There was no way out of this. She was going to have to see him.

After a deep breath, she paged Kari. "Send him in."

Jessica stood, realizing that out of all life's unfairness, this had to be the worst.

Chris took the hand a tall and slender woman extended to him. "Good morning, Mr. Lanning. It's nice to meet you. I'm Jessica Shelton, one of Architectural Design's sales consultants. Unfortunately Collin, the salesman you've been speaking with over the phone, is out of the office this afternoon sick. I'll be the one helping you with your order."

She instructed him to a chair across from her desk, and he took it. He looked up to find that she had buried her head in a file folder of what he assumed was full of information pertaining to him.

"Tell me about the Heritage Estate."

Chris settled into the chair, forever anxious to talk about all that had gone on with the project. Twenty minutes later, he had told Ms. Shelton about the history of the Heritage House, some of the problems they'd encountered along the way as well as his vision for the property once it was complete. "I tell you I'm so attached to this, it's really going to be hard to give it up."

"Why do you have to?"

Chris thought about the question. "Other responsibilities, I guess. My company doesn't usually take on something of this nature."

Jessica smiled, and although she didn't look at him directly, he could tell she was pretty. For the sake of conversation, he kept things going. "Once this is finished, I know the house will be a real credit to the area. I'd consider restoring another historical structure if it weren't for keeping local historians off my back." Chris chuckled. "At one point, I think I had every citizen in the county over the age of seventy calling to keep tabs."

"You know what they say. It's easier to ask for forgiveness than it is for permission."

Chris paused, hearing the familiar quote. Something uneasy stirred in his gut. "Uh...I think the actual quote goes something like, 'It's easier to ask forgiveness than it is to *get* permission.' It's not hard to ask for permission, but it's often hard to get it. There is a difference."

"Oh," she said, looking embarrassed at being corrected. "I'm sure you're right."

He nodded, unable to ignore the fact that something was definitely familiar about this situation. He was feeling something akin to déjà vu.

"How about a glass of water before we get started. I'm parched after all that talking."

The woman's eyes lifted to the table in the corner with the water pitcher sitting on it. "Oh...uh...sure."

Chris glanced at the awards on the wall while she stood to comply with his request.

"Jessica was it?"

"Yes, sir," she said as she offered him one of the two glasses she was holding. He didn't fail to notice how her hand trembled slightly when he took it.

"How long have you worked here?"

"Not long."

"Hmm. How did you end up here in the South Loop of the Windy City?"

The woman gave him a look that said he was getting too personal. "That's a long story, but it all boils down to work, and speaking of which, this type of project is exactly what has made Architectural Design a leader in our industry. I'm sure that we'll have what y'all are looking for."

Chris let go of his best smile. "Y'all? That southern accent must be part of the long story you're not interested in telling me."

A nervous laugh escaped her as she resumed her position behind the computer. "Where were we?"

Chris was no idiot. He knew how to read people, and this woman was not interested.

That's a shame. Although she was a little too slim and pale for his liking, she had a pretty smile. There was also some sort of sadness about her that he wanted to fix. He scolded himself for the thought. *You're going to be in town for one day! It's not like you're going to fall in love with her—even if she isn't wearing a ring. You're a new man. Act like it.*

Jessica pulled up a screen full of photos that were similar to the Heritage House in style and size.

"I'm looking for something to replace a damaged but very detailed ceiling medallion in the dining room. It wouldn't be such a big deal, but the design of the medallion is repeated in nearly every room of the house. The ones on the bedroom ceilings are plaster and in decent shape and can therefore be painted. The dining room, however, has an oak ceiling. I need something that can be stained."

Jessica nodded her understanding. "This is at a home in Georgia," she said, pointing to a house with a colossal dining area centered by a huge chandelier. "The owner commissioned us to design the crest hanging on the wall based on his family's Irish coat of arms. Wolves are thought to be merciless and the oaks in the background symbolize great age and strength. As you can see, there is a lot of detail to the design." Jessica pulled up more photos. "He chose to repeat the crest in the main entrance and again on the master suite wall."

"Impressive," Chris stated, noting the almost demonic look in the wolf's eyes. The detail was commendable, but overall, the piece was gaudy and overbearing. "I think it seems a little medieval...gothic. I want something that says class without the dominance."

He smiled at her. "The good news is if you can create that, then finding something to match what's already in the bedrooms should be a piece of cake. Here"—he paused to search through his briefcase—"I have a picture I can show you."

"Oh, I see," she said, studying the photo. "I'm sure we have something similar in stock."

From there, she pulled up one file after another, but Chris found something wrong with each product and suggestion. Every once in a while that same feeling would return. Like there was something that was drawing him to this woman. She was obviously doing everything she could to avoid eye contact with him, but he didn't understand why. He was purposefully difficult just to prolong their time together.

"Well," she huffed on an exasperated breath, "you are obviously a man who doesn't cut corners. I suggest you place a custom order or replace all the medallions in the house despite the expense. It'll take a few weeks more, but I'm sure you'll be pleased with the outcome."

Chris then argued over pricing and delivery dates. By the end of the ordeal, she was so nervous she all but knocked over her water.

"Are you always this nervous?"

"Are you always this hard to please?" she snapped back at him.

Chris's brows rose in surprise.

The woman in front of him composed herself. "I'm sorry. It's just that...well, with Collin sick...there must be something going around the office. Please...forgive me. We are more than grateful for your business."

She pulled up his account and started typing in his information. As she went down through the blanks, she filled out what she knew and asked him for what she didn't.

Chris saw the opportunity for finding out more about her was closing. If he didn't say something soon, he was going to lose his chance. Why it mattered, he didn't know.

Forgiveness for Yesterday

As if in slow motion, Chris watched as she lifted the water glass to her lips, took a sip, and placed it on a nearby coaster. She then reached up with her right hand, pulled out a lock of hair near her ear, and wrapped it around her finger as she studied the screen in front of her. He would recognize that gesture anywhere.

Instantly the faint familiarities he had been feeling grew until they became a full-fledged recognition. "Laurie," he said, watching the woman's head snap around and her brows draw together.

He sat there staring at her in disbelief.

"Ex…excuse me?" she finally asked in his silence.

Chris simply sat and stared at her, completely unable to speak. It was as if he had swallowed his tongue. Was he imagining things? She obviously had no clue what he was talking about.

"Um…I'm…sorry," he finally managed to say in order to buy himself time. "It's just that you remind me of someone I used to know. Someone I thought I knew quite well actually."

She nodded her understanding. "I get that all the time. Everyone has a twin. I think I have three or four." The comment was said with so much confidence he questioned whether or not he was right. Chris forced a laugh, then watched as relief streaked across her eyes—eyes the same fiery hazel as Shelby's.

She continued through the paperwork asking for exact dimensions and material preferences. He answered all her questions in an automatic response all the while forming a plan that was designed to make him sure of her true identity.

"I just remembered. I have some other photos of the property if you'd like to see them."

"Actually, it's getting late."

"Oh no. I insist." Chris opened his briefcase and gathered the rest of the snapshots he'd made of the house. Taking them, she said all the right things and marveled at all the right moments. "This is really nice. You say it's a few miles outside of Asheville?"

She flipped through one, two, then three more photos.

"About twenty minutes away. It's in a place called Clear Valley, just within the shadow of Black Mountain. I've relocated there until the project is complete." He decided to punch a button and see what happened. "My home is in Greensboro where I live with my two children, Shelby and Kyle." He said their names slower than normal, but her motions never faltered. "What I said earlier…about the accent…what I meant was it sounds like you might have spent some time in North Carolina yourself."

Another tight smile but no eye contact. "No."

She was lying. It took effort to keep his tone even and measured when he really felt like jumping over the desk and wrestling the truth from her. He had one more question in his arsenal, and he fired it. "Do you have children?"

She closed her eyes for a heartbeat. "No. I just recently married."

Another lie. She flipped through one more picture and then another. With only three photos left in the stack, Chris knew in that moment he was about to lay down his last hand. If it didn't work, he would have to risk a direct confrontation and chance that she would call security.

Jessica picked up the top photo, studied it, and as she was reaching for the next, she froze. The next picture in the pile was the one he'd been waiting for. Shelby and Kyle stared back at her, smiling from a day spent at the water park. For several moments, she sat there unmoving and silent, and he knew she'd locked eyes with the two children she just denied having.

Chris watched as her facial expressions displayed a range of emotions. She went from cold indifference, to surprise. The show ended with a deep frown of regret. Her eyes were brimming with tears.

"I knew it was you," he said, almost in disbelief.

Her eyes didn't lift but remained glued to the photo. A soft sob drifted up and hung between them. The tension was so thick Chris didn't know the words to breach it.

"How are they?" she finally asked.

He didn't hesitate with the answer. "They're fine. Friday, Shelby—"

"Turned twelve. I know. Next year she'll be a teenager." A sad laugh slipped out as her eyes finally met his as she removed her glasses.

What Chris saw unveiled in them stole his breath. There was a hurt so deep he questioned what had put it there.

"Why, Laurie?"

She shook her head at him, a tear spilling down her cheek. "Don't do this, Chris. Please." She looked back down at the photo when another sob tore from her throat. The sound of it broke his heart.

"Are they really okay?" she managed.

"I can't say I've been the dad they deserve, but they're fine. They miss you."

She reached for a tissue and started to dry her eyes. "How did you know it was me?"

He gave a sarcastic laugh. "My question is how did I *not* know. Somewhere along about the word *Georgia*, I got pretty sure. Why didn't you just tell me?"

Chris slipped forward in the chair trying to piece together this puzzle, too amazed and too shocked to say very much. All the conclusions he'd come to on the plane were suddenly being tested.

"I remember everything, Laurie. *Everything*," he said slower. "The sound of your voice when you sing along with the radio, that tiny strand of freckles across your nose that's only visible when you're not wearing makeup, the way it felt to wake every single morning and wonder if that would be the day you'd return or if I'd at least hear from you. I remember all of it. The only thing I can't figure out is why you didn't tell me."

"How much do you know?"

"Enough to say you should've trusted me with the truth."

Laurie simply shook her head. "Jim Callahan was my worst nightmare. He refused to go away. The only way I could stop him was to do what I should've done twelve years ago. You can't possibly understand the decision I was faced with."

"You're right. I don't." Chris marveled at the truth of his words. He was sitting across from the very woman whom he'd grieved years of his life away hating, and now that he finally had her within his reach, he didn't know what to say.

No doubt, part of him was still mad at her, but part of him wanted to pull her into his arms and try to recapture what they'd lost. She looked so fragile and tender—so broken. A hurricane of emotions was whirling around in his heart, and he had no idea what the outcome of the storm would be.

He suspected this unplanned meeting was God in the process of working out the miracle he'd been foolish enough to request. At the moment, Chris was unsure what actions would enable or hinder what the Lord wanted to do. Depending on her words, his emotions could easily swing either way.

"Chris, I…you have every right to be mad at me for not telling you the truth, but believe me, I did it for your own good."

Anger it was. "*My* good?" he hissed. "Pray tell, how was vanishing into thin air for *my* good! Or for the good of your children? The way I see it, you've been completely selfish!"

"You don't understand!"

"Then make me!" he said, raising his voice at her.

For the longest time, she didn't say anything. All she did was shake her head and cry. Chris took the time to get himself under control, but she was severely testing his patience. "Do you have any idea what your unexplained leaving did to me? What it did to your kids?"

Her continued silence sent him right back to the boiling point. He deserved some kind of acknowledgment from her. "Talk to me!" he yelled, trying not to curse.

"What do you want me to say?" she cried through angry tears.

Chris raked rigid fingers through his hair and tried to get a hold of himself. "I want you to say that you're sorry! That walking out on us was the worst mistake you've ever made. We were engaged for crying out loud! If you didn't trust me enough to tell me Jim was still a threat to you, you should have at least cared enough to say good-bye."

"I did more than care! I loved you!"

"Oh yeah, then how come all I got was some lousy note saying you had changed your mind? That I should forget you and move on?"

"You were supposed to read between the lines!"

"I did, and it nearly killed me!"

There was a buzzing noise. "Ms. Shelton, are you two all right in there?"

"Yes. We're fine," Laurie responded through the intercom before giving Chris a silent warning.

Chris took a breather. His emotions were getting the best of him. He looked around her office in disbelief. "It still doesn't look like you're coming back to me."

Laurie stood and slammed her fist down on the desk between them to punctuate her statement. "I needed you to think that I'd left... for a while. Not forever! That way you wouldn't poke around asking questions. So that no one would!"

Her face softened. "Do you think I'm some kind of expert on abandoning everyone I love? That I ever imagined being gone this long? Do you really think I intended to walk away and never see my kids grow up?"

"Of course that's what I thought because that's exactly what you told me! I had no reason to doubt anything you had ever said until your mother shows up telling me about parts of your life I had no idea existed!"

Suddenly she was surprised. "You spoke with my mother?"

"Yes. As odd as it sounds, last week she came to see me. It's how I know about...well, about everything."

Her hands went to her face. "Is she okay? Did Jim threaten her?"

"She's worried sick about you. She also told me her whole conspiracy theory. From the looks of it, she's right. You were really the one who provided the evidence that finally put Jim away?"

"In a round about way...yes."

"Then...then...what does that mean?"

"What it means is that I've spent the last two years in protective custody. That this"—she grabbed a lock of her hair—"is my new identity. That I'm lucky I didn't go to jail myself! I keep telling you that you don't understand because you don't.

"Jim Callahan is a terrible man. He's done terrible things. Things I didn't know about but could have prevented had I possessed the courage to speak up years sooner, but I didn't. Instead I was willing to keep quiet in exchange for what I thought was him letting me walk away. Here's what I learned: men like Jim do not *let* their victims walk away."

Something inside of Chris went cold. "Tell me what he did to you."

Laurie crossed her arms in defiance. "No."

"Okay…then tell me what happened that morning after we got off the phone."

"I got a call from him. He tried to force me to steal from you. He wanted me to bleed you dry. And he would have. When he threatened to make me a widow if I didn't cooperate, I'd finally had all I could take. I couldn't marry you knowing he'd always be one phone call away controlling me! That's why I had to do something about it."

Laurie collapsed in the chair, visibly shaken.

"Laurie…you could've just told me. We could've dealt with this together." There were a thousand other things Chris wanted to say, to ask—about Elizabeth, about how deep Laurie's scars really were, what Jim had done to her that she still hadn't shared. But now was not the time. Silence fell between them and for the first time ever things were awkward.

"So…what now?"

"Right now I'm staying close by so I can see what happens to my father. His hearing is scheduled for next month." She crossed her arms over her chest in defense again. "I'm sure our government would love to know you've just waltzed in here and in a matter of minutes blown what has taken thousands of man hours to cover up. I still can't believe this turned into the fiasco it did."

The last two years flashed before Chris's eyes. He had made his fair share of mistakes, too. "So you're not a knight in shining armor. As it turns out, neither am I."

"What's that supposed to mean?"

"Just that I've had to seek out some forgiveness of my own."

Questions peppered her eyes.

"The kids are fine. I'm doing my best to give them the life they deserve."

Chris stood and perched on the corner of her desk. His anger was spent, and the desire to touch her was overwhelming. He reached for her hand, and she let him take it. He looked into her eyes, and for a moment, they became totally lost. It was Laurie who looked away first.

"What kind of weird fate would bring our paths to cross again? And now of all times?" she asked.

Chris knew it was the answer to his prayers, but he chose to keep that to himself. "I really did come here to place an order for the project I'm on. Honest. The fact that whoever I was supposed to meet with isn't here and you are says there's someone bigger in charge. There is something greater behind this, Laurie. I know it. We owe it to that someone to try to figure it out."

Fear entered her eyes, and she tugged at her hand. It was her way of retreating back into what she was comfortable with. Suddenly she was the professional he'd met upon entering the room. He figured most of her fear came from the fact she wasn't willing to admit that maybe God still had something in store for them after the mess they'd been through. He wasn't even sure himself.

She dried her eyes with a tissue and finished up his paperwork like they were complete strangers. Chris played along hoping it'd give her the composure she needed to think rationally.

He played the part until she was ushering him to the door, but there was no way he was going to walk out without her knowing exactly how he felt.

She was within an arm's reach, and he didn't have to think about it; it came as natural as breathing. He reached up and cupped her cheek in the palm of his hand. Chris felt his heart squeeze at the bittersweet moment. "Don't make me leave like this."

Her eyes became downcast, and it relieved him to know she wasn't going to argue. Eventually she turned her head into his hand, and it offered him hope that maybe, just maybe, she was feeling a fraction of what he was at having been reunited. "Meet with me, Laurie. Just to talk. Nothing more. I promise I won't yell at you."

"What would it change, Chris?"

"I don't know. Nothing? Everything? You owe me more than some chance encounter and then sending me off pretending like it never happened."

She released a deep sigh and put her hand over his. "Where?"

He gave the name of his hotel. "Eight o'clock. We can order in if you'd like." He brushed his thumb over her cheek, fighting the urge to kiss her.

"I'll be there."

Chris smiled. The three words she spoke told him what he wanted to hear, but the unspoken ones, those told him she remembered everything about the way they used to be and that she missed it just as much as he did.

Forgiveness for Yesterday

32

At quarter past eight, Laurie made her way down the hall on the tenth floor of the Four Seasons hotel. The day was turning out to be the longest of her life. She questioned herself for the millionth time as to why she agreed to meet with Chris. The best she could come up with was that he was right. She owed him.

Chris should hate her after what she'd done, and maybe he did. If the situation weren't so tragic, she would've laughed at the fact that life had turned her into all the things she hated. Even without an actual sentencing on her behalf, in this situation the law had a peculiar way of being just. She had lost everything.

Her eyes scanned the length of the hall again. She lifted her hand to knock on the paneled door boasting the right numbers. Before she did, the door swung open and a broad figure knocked her into the wall on its way out. Fear gripped her, and she screamed.

"I'm sorry," Chris said, stopping in his tracks at the sound. He reached up to steady her, and she quieted. "Are you okay? I was coming to find you. You're late."

She was shaking. "Traffic was horrible."

Chris stepped back to the door and held it open as she slipped by him and into the room beyond. He had changed shirts, and the fresh smell of his shower lingered. She stepped inside, trying to calm her nerves and ignore the fact that their privacy wasn't an illusion. She wished she had agreed to a more public setting—anything less intimate than a bedroom.

She took a seat at the small table by the window, searching for the words to say.

"Should I call for room service?"

"No, thank you. I'm not hungry."

"Me either." Chris took a seat on the foot of the bed and faced her. "I know I asked you to come here so that we could talk, but I honestly don't know where to start. There's no reason for you to be scared."

She stood. "Maybe I should go."

All he had to do was look at her, and she sat back down. The seconds dragged out. "How long are you in town?"

"I leave tomorrow morning, first thing."

She nodded, her own lack of words now showing.

"Laurie," he tried again. "You believe me when I say that I didn't plan this...this meeting? It was out of my hands."

"I know. I believe you, and you are right. I owe you more than pretending. It's just...I freaked out. Your face was the last one I expected to see." She stood and started to pace back and forth in front of the television set. "I guess I should start at the beginning."

And so she did. She wasn't two sentences into what she thought were the pertinent details when he reached for her hands and pulled her to a stop.

"What?" she asked rather surprised. "I thought you wanted to hear everything that happened."

Chris studied her for a moment. "I do, but not tonight. Tonight is about us."

Laurie felt her face pale. Somehow the idea of "us" seemed more dangerous than a full confession. "Chris..."

"I know. This is probably a bad idea, but the more you talk about what you did and why you did it, the madder I get. I want to hear everything you have to say, but not tonight. Tonight I just want us to be together."

Laurie blinked at the idea.

"We can go somewhere if you'd like. I really just want to spend some time with you."

"I don't plan on staying long." She scooted around him and started examining the room furnishings before moving back to her seat at the table. "I've always heard this place was nice."

"Would you stop? Ask me about the kids. You must be dying to know how they are."

He can read my mind. It only took her a second to determine what she wanted to know. "With Shelby turning twelve, I'm sure she's giving you a real fit with the boy crazy stuff, huh?"

Chris laughed. "She is. Some days she changes so fast, I hardly recognize her. She's beautiful…she looks a lot like you. We've started going to church with Bret and his wife, Karen. We—"

"Bret's married? When did that happen?"

"End of May. This Sunday Shelby walked the aisle and made a decision for Christ."

"Really?" There was a long pause of silence, and she looked away. "That's…wonderful. What about Kyle? Is he still into sports?"

"Basketball mostly. The kid's a whiz at math. I'm sure he gets it from you. We live in the house you and I built. We have a dog, and Marie still takes care of things when I'm not around."

She smiled as she studied the peace behind his eyes. "It sounds like you all are happy."

"On the outside. The truth is we're coping. This summer has been really good for us. Speaking of family, your mother wanted me to give this to you." Chris stood and pulled out his wallet to hand her a business card. "It's her contact information. Like I told you earlier, she's very worried."

Laurie studied him, wondering how much her mother had said. The room around her faded away, and once again, she was that scared young girl, the one whom Jim had found and said all the right things to, the girl he had turned on and used to his advantage. "My mom… we haven't spoken in years. It was just easier that way. After Jim and I married, he became very possessive. When Shelby was born…he insisted we distance ourselves…" Laurie's voice trailed off. She would forever regret hurting her mother the way she had.

Chris nodded as though he understood though she knew he didn't.

"When Jim and I divorced, I wanted to contact her, but then Jim convinced some woman to come forth and claim to be my father's mistress. It ruined my parents' marriage, and ultimately, I felt responsible. I guess there was a part of me that knew Jim would always be keeping tabs, finding something to hold over my head. I didn't want her to be a part of that."

Chris studied her for a long, hard moment. "What did he threaten you with, Laurie? The day that he called there was something more, wasn't there?"

There it was. The question she had been dreading. "I told you. He wanted me to steal from you. He said that he would make me a widow if he had to in order to get to your money."

"Why? Is money that important?"

"To some people. When Jim and I split, I gave him all the evidence I had regarding his embezzlement. In exchange, he was to give me the divorce I wanted and disappear from my life. Jim's alimony is what bought me a new start. It's how I finished school, started a career, and raised two kids on my own. Jim always resented me for being able to live without him."

Chris sat there staring at her. "Why do I get the feeling you're not telling me everything?"

This time Laurie's eyes began to pool. When Chris knew everything, any chance of his still loving her would be gone. But wasn't that what she deserved?

When she finally found her tongue, she told him. "He...he didn't just threaten you that day. He threatened Shelby. He said he would tell her the truth about me...and who her father is if I didn't agree to his plans."

"But isn't Jim Shelby's father?"

Laurie took a deep breath. "No. Jim is Kyle's father, not Shelby's."

Chris took some time to digest the information, and Laurie's tears started to fall in earnest.

"Sh," Chris soothed as he stood and tried to draw her into his arms. "You can tell me anything," he pleaded.

Laurie refused the comfort of his embrace and squeezed her eyes against the pain of this long awaited moment. "Shelby's father was my sister Elizabeth's boyfriend!"

Chris felt the blow as she made the confession and collapsed into his arms. "Sh," he said again over her tears.

When things settled some, he spoke. "Tell me about him."

"He…he…was the guy she was dating right before she died. She was on meds…she'd just gotten this huge role in some off-Broadway production. When I went to see her, she begged me to party with her. Normally I wouldn't have, but my parents and I were fighting. I was sick of all the pressure. I was sick of being the good kid. We…we smoked something, and the next thing I knew I woke up in bed with some guy I'd only met one other time in my life—her boyfriend. I didn't mean for it to happen. I was going to tell her, but somehow she found out before I could say anything. She wouldn't even speak to me. Weeks passed, and one night she took a handful of pills then drove her car off a bridge. Oh, Chris, it's all my fault!"

The full admission took everything she had, and she exhaled deeply having let it go.

"I…I am so sorry," she heard him saying. " You had no way of knowing she would take her life."

Laurie pushed back and frantically wiped away her tears. "Don't say that! I knew something wasn't right, but instead of becoming her ally, I ended up betraying her in the worst way!" Another torrent of tears washed down her face.

It was easy to see Chris wanted to draw her back into his arms and say all the things she'd longed to hear those many years ago, but she wouldn't let him.

"You didn't mean for it to happen. Everyone makes mistakes."

"Not like this! I married Jim to cover up the pregnancy, but when he found out I lied to him, he was furious with me. I felt so guilty… and alone! And now I can't even say I'm sorry. Elizabeth will never be able to forgive me. She died hating me!"

Chris stood there, holding her and letting her cry until she was completely spent. When her crying jag ended, Chris tipped her chin up and stared into her eyes, looking way down into the hidden places of her heart—to the places where her hurts were the deepest. "Elizabeth may not be able to forgive you, but God can. All you have to do is ask."

Standing there looking up at him, she knew he said all the right things. But how did she explain? She and God hadn't spoken in years.

Her plans hadn't worked. Instead, she had turned into someone who had made it a habit to betray the ones she claimed to love the most. Out of all the people she'd let down, God was first on the list. She wasn't someone God wanted to forgive.

Chris gazed down at the woman who he had blamed for his every sorrow and pain for the longest time and understood a new depth of God's mercy. Seeing Laurie here, now, something in him let go.

"Laurie, when you left, I was devastated. We all were, but for some reason, I took it to another level. For a long time I used to think there was a fine line between love and hate, but seeing you today…now…I know which side of that line my feet are firmly planted on. I can't say that I'm not angry with you anymore but *wanting* to hate you fueled a fire in me I couldn't control. I would probably still be trying to had the Lord not gotten my attention and showed me what it was doing to both my heart and my life.

"Shelby isn't the only one who gave her heart to the Lord. I chose him too, and it's made all the difference. I know you believe in God, but I'm not so sure you understand the depths of Christ's mercy, nor his forgiveness, and how it enables you to forgive others…and yourself."

She let go of a hoarse laugh. "I don't deserve forgiveness!"

"No one does." Chris paused then continued, "If the roles were reversed and Elizabeth had done this to you and you knew that she was completely remorseful, could you forgive her?"

"Of course."

"Then assume she would do the same for you. Through Christ, nothing is unforgivable, Laurie. Nothing. Every time you hold this against yourself, you're taking what Christ did on the cross and making it into something else—something less."

Any further words of protest were cut off when Chris pulled her within inches of his face. "Even after all we've been through, there is still a part of me that loves you. I will always love you. Nothing you could ever do or say will change that." Slowly and hesitantly he lowered his mouth to hers. It resulted in a long and passionate kiss.

Somewhere in the fog of satisfied longing and return, Chris felt her surrender. Her fingers dug into his hair, and his thoughts became muddled as the taste, the feel, and the comfort of her crashed in all around him. Laurie believed him, and she clung to him like a lifeline.

Their embrace became more passionate as slow seconds ticked off. Seeing her completely lost and undone allowed him to justify his attempt to kiss away all her hurts.

And the way she responded, it ended the doubt he'd felt in his heart since the day she walked away. She loved him, and for the first time in a long time, he felt whole again.

Chris deepened the kiss, working his hands down her back as he allowed himself to remember everything about her. Time and distance might have kept them separated for years, but now they were together, and Chris felt vividly alive under her touch.

They continued to remember and relive each other's embrace, welcoming each step up a climb that was completely intoxicating. It wasn't long before Chris knew they were entering dangerous territory.

Being alone with the woman he loved, far away from home in a hotel room, he wanted nothing more than to turn their kisses into something more—a lot more. He knew his original intentions were honorable, but at that moment, he couldn't remember what they were. A few more seconds passed. He breathed her name and didn't recognize his own voice.

Suddenly a man he did recognize entered into his thoughts. It was David—the David of Psalm 40. In studying the Bible, he had also learned that David had written Psalm 51—a chapter of repentance for the sins he had committed with Bathsheba.

The word adultery entering his head seemed to unleash all kinds of warnings about the sexually immoral and just how dangerous of a position he had put them in. It was hard enough having Laurie turn her back on him once. He knew what it was to be abandoned. In this moment, she was weak and vulnerable. Taking things further would leave her confused and him without any guarantees.

Pulling back at the thought, Chris found what he needed to safely bring them back to reality. He ended the kiss, but rather than step apart and break his contact with her, he wrapped his arms tightly around her shoulders, and she buried her face in his chest.

Help us, Lord. Help us survive whatever it was I saw in her eyes. The pain of what she's kept hidden so long...

They stood there a long time, just being together.

Eventually Laurie broke the silence. "Chris, I don't know what to say."

"Say you'll come back with me. That we can start over."

"I can't. The trial may be over, but I'm here because this is where I feel safe."

"You're here because this is where it all started."

"How better to face what it is I've done?"

"How better to punish yourself *because* of what you've done?" Chris held her shoulders and looked in her eyes. "Listen to me. It's over. Your life is with us now...or at least it can be."

"I don't know. There are some things I need to think through."

"Such as?"

"I've carried this burden for more than a decade. I know I can't ask you to wait forever, but I need time. I need to make things right... with my parents."

"You need to make things right with Shelby and Kyle."

Laurie didn't say anything.

"That's what you're afraid of, isn't it? You're afraid they won't be able to accept you back into their lives after all that's happened?"

Tentatively she nodded. "A parent's love is different. Shelby and Kyle are young. They don't understand how complicated this is. And I pray they never will. How can I march back into their lives and ask them to pretend these last few years haven't happened? They deserve better."

"You can't ask them to pretend, but you can ask them to forgive. You can have a second chance." He tilted her head up when she looked down. "I don't expect them to understand all the reasons why you left, but I think your presence will eventually speak louder than their questions.

"They love you. *I* love you. You've faced your past. Now you should release it. You have to in order to have hope for the future. Don't let your shame and your fears rob you of what I know you could have if only you'd believe…"

"I want to believe but…"

"But what? It won't be easy? Of course it won't be, but you're a fighter, Laurie. This whole situation you're in proves that you're one of the most stubborn, strong-willed women on the face of the earth! You have a blinding passion for those children, and it might be stupid of me, but I love you all the more for it. Now it's time to have a little faith in them. You alone know the price you've paid for severing ties with your parents. If you stay away from Shelby and Kyle…you'd be doing the same thing to them. The only person you'll be protecting if you don't face your fears is yourself, and that would be completely selfish."

"That's not fair!" She seethed at him, looking mad enough to stomp her foot.

But Chris wasn't about to stop there. "Tell me you love me."

"What?" she whispered in disbelief.

"I can see it in your eyes. I can feel it in your kiss. Tell me you love me. That you never stopped loving me."

Her anger melted, and her expression became tender. She backed out of his arms, but Chris knew he was right.

She made it as far as the door before she finally spoke. "I do love you," she said. "I will always love you, but what if I'm not who you think I am? I've gone down so many roads to get here, I'm not sure I know how to get back to where it is you are. To the person you think I am…or was."

Chris felt pin pricks in the back of his eyes. "Yes, you do. Listen to your heart."

Slowly she shook her head no. "I can't."

The decision broke his heart. She may love him, but after all he had said and done, she still didn't trust him.

"Laurie…"

"Please, Chris. Don't make this harder than it has to be." She opened the door and stepped through it as fresh tears started to fall.

He followed her as she made her way out into the hall. It was killing him to see her go. "Laurie, please. If you can't trust in me, trust in the Lord."

"I can't, Chris. Not this time."

Chris hung his head. Her decision was made. He lifted his eyes one more time as they filled with unshed tears. "You said yourself that a parent's love is different. God is a parent, Laurie. Remember that. There is nothing he won't forgive, and there is nothing he won't enable his children to forgive as well."

He watched as she stepped into the elevator and then was gone.

Chris watched Laurie Callahan walk out of his life for a second time. This time there was no mysterious reasoning, yet no plausible excuse, just that she was gone. She had not been sentenced to the iron walls of a prison, but she had chosen the walls of fear, unforgiveness, guilt, and shame instead.

Chris went back into his hotel room and sat down on the bed. A weary hand came over his face. He wished it weren't true.

Can't she see how much I love her? If anyone knows about going down roads that take you far away from where you want to be and leaving you not knowing how to get back, it's me.

Simple but profound words came in the quietness that ensued. *Love is patient, my child. Be patient with others as I have been patient with you.*

Chris took the words to heart. If Laurie did return, it would take time for all of them to adjust. That didn't mean it was impossible.

He went about preparing to call it a night, a prayer echoing through his pain. He didn't know what God had in store, but he knew he was going to have to do the very thing he wished Laurie would do. He was going to have to trust.

He would have to trust in the Lord that his timing would be perfect and that God would somehow teach Laurie her own lessons on what it meant to forgive and to be forgiven.

33

Chris made it back from Chicago with a clearer perspective than he anticipated. Rather than reach for his tool belt first thing Thursday morning, he picked up his cell phone and made a call to Tucker Fennel at Enterprise Properties. Mr. Fennel was surprised to hear from him so soon, but Chris didn't see a need to delay.

"I appreciate your more than generous offer, but I'm going to choose to decline. Something happened while I was in Chicago and… well, let's just say I've come to realize there are some things that mean more to me than the bottom line."

The words still echoed in his head some three hours later when he was heading back from the local hardware store. He gave his signal and turned left onto Willow Ridge. About a quarter mile from the jobsite, Chris rolled down his window as he passed by the property adjacent to the Heritage estate.

The things he'd been referring to on the phone with Mr. Fennel were Shelby and Kyle. Bret. Karen. Even Darrell—family. He didn't look forward to returning to his desk, and the sea of paperwork that awaited him, but it was time. Sometimes life wasn't all about self.

Chris looked out across a field at the dilapidated farmhouse that stood in a nearby cropping of trees. What he saw made him bring the truck to a complete stop. Maybe there was a solution where everyone came out a winner. He put the truck in reverse and backed up until he sat directly in front of the old house with the plunging roofline and cracked, peeling paint; then he cut the engine. *Wonder who owes this place*, he thought.

A plan started to form in his mind, and a smile lit up his face. After sitting there for a full five minutes, smiling out the window like an idiot, but sensing God's approval, Chris cranked the truck and pulled it into drive. He had another phone call he needed to make.

34

Bret squinted his eyes at the numbers dancing on the screen in front of him. He pulled off his glasses and pressed his thumb and forefinger into his eye sockets. It was too early in the day to let a headache start.

He chanced a glance out the window only to find the late summer heat was scorching everything in sight. Karen and the kids had gone to church while he'd opted to stay behind to get caught up on some things around the house. Seeing how he'd missed a few Sundays already this month, he thought another one wouldn't hurt.

First, he'd worked on the leak under the kitchen sink like he'd promised Karen he would. Then he finished by rinsing all the dishes and loading them into the dishwasher. From there, he did some vacuuming and then pulled out a chair at the computer and set in to pay the bills and balance their checking account.

Now, after ten minutes or so, he was checking the last line for the fifteenth time. There was a charge showing up, and he couldn't find it in the checkbook register. He was going to have to ask Karen about it.

Pushing the paperwork aside, he sifted through yesterday's mail. He pulled out the bill for the cable and tore it open. It was for almost a hundred dollars. "What on earth?" Bret scanned the bill and the services they subscribed to. Down at the bottom, he saw the reason for such a tab. He'd forgotten about those late-night movies he'd purchased a few weekends back. "Geez! You really pay for convenience."

He stood waiting for the guilt he was used to experiencing to settle in on his shoulders like a wet towel. When it didn't, he left the computer to pour a tall glass of orange juice. In the last few weeks before he and Karen married, he'd done great at resisting the temptation to look. And even now it was only in moments of his greatest weakness that he slipped and ended up with something like the cable bill as evidence of his failures.

Rather than think about broken promises, Bret drained the glass of orange juice and downed two aspirin. Karen was a good woman. She loved him, and she worked hard at everything she touched. He knew their marriage was no exception, and the efforts she was putting forth hadn't gone unnoticed. While he was moody and disappointed over one thing or another she was always trying to make things better. That didn't mean he thought she would understand if he were to open up about some of his more private struggles and the way she constantly drove him crazy by asking if there was something wrong. If she knew what he was battling against, she would totally flip.

They were still looking at houses, but to assure her that his problems were nothing he couldn't handle, he'd agreed to sign another six month lease for the apartment they were in. In all honesty, it was a decision based on what was the best way for them to save money. The homes they were interested in were out of their price range, and with the engagement and wedding, and now Karen's car on the blink, the last year of his life had been very expensive.

He would do whatever it took to provide for his family, and if that meant spending another six months in this rat hole, he would do it. At least he'd found a solution to the car issue. Standing there in the kitchen, Bret smiled remembering how he'd passed by the lot and spotted it—a red Corvette. He had to admit, the car was a little on the sporty side, but he brought it home, anxious to see what Karen's reaction would be.

She had come running down the steps only to halt on the last one. "You said it was a convertible, but it only has two seats," she reasoned.

Bret had been expecting the comment. He slipped an arm around her shoulders, fully prepared to give the sales pitch of his life. "Here's what I'm thinking: I'll give you the BMW, and this will be our fun car." Both his hands went in the air to demonstrate. "Picture this: you and me, the top down, the wind blowing through our hair, the sun on our faces. We're cruising down some coastal highway, a million miles from everywhere."

When he'd finished, the look on her face had been one he'd never seen before. "It's not even new, and it has super low miles," he argued. "It goes from zero to sixty in less than five seconds! Five seconds," he repeated in sheer awe, hoping she would catch his excitement.

An eyebrow went up along with a red flag of warning. "Nice. But what do *I* think? I *think* you've lost your mind! That's what I think. We're two hundred miles from a coast of any kind! That means you, me, Holly, and Scott stuck in rush hour traffic in a car that only has two seats! Two seats!" she repeated, mocking his excitement rather than catching it. "I'm thinking minivan! If you were going to have some sort of midlife crisis, I wish you would've done it sooner rather than later!"

The memory faded, and Bret shook his head. He was *not* having a midlife crisis. Things just hadn't turned out like he'd planned. He loved Karen and the kids with all his heart, but he had gone from being a bachelor to a responsible husband and father of two overnight. He had known this was coming, but he had expected a little more cooperation.

"Minivan. Yeah, right!" He thought of Brad, Karen's mom's weird friend. "That Vet is a car worth naming!"

He polished off a second glass of juice, and the lock on the door turned. It was Karen and the kids.

"Hey, honey," he said, moving to take the bag she carried and kissed her cheek. Scott scooted in and set another bag down on the counter. "I see you stopped at the store."

Karen smiled. "I thought I could get a jumpstart on the week. What did you do while we were gone?"

"I vacuumed, fixed the sink, did the dishes. What's for lunch?"

"I just got home!" Karen started to unload the bags, and Holly came through the door carrying two more.

"Here," Holly said, chunking the bags down on the counter.

"Is that everything?" Karen asked.

"No, there's a few left, but since I carried these two up, I figured Scott could go down for the last round."

Karen gave her a pointed look. "You know he can't lug more than one full bag up here at a time. I want you to go back and help him."

"Me? Why me? I do everything around here!"

In order to flee the scene of a coming fight, Bret offered to go down to get the last of the groceries. Coming back up the steps, he kicked the door shut with his foot. Karen had started cooking.

He put away the canned goods and adjusted them on the shelf to make sure all the labels were facing out and washed his hands at the sink. "Need some help?" he asked, trying to speed things up. He was hungry.

"No, I've got it."

He went back over to the computer and remembered why he'd taken a break. "What is this charge here? It's for almost two hundred dollars at Walmart. It's not written in the register."

"Hmm," Karen sighed and bit her lower lip as she leaned over his shoulder. "Looks like where I bought groceries last week. I must have forgotten to write it down."

Bret felt the muscles in his neck tighten. "What do you mean you forgot? Karen it's two hundred dollars. You're the one who insisted we put everything into one account. How am I supposed to know how much is in there if you don't write stuff down? I can't do a budget knowing only half of what goes out."

"Well...I..."

"And you really spent two hundred dollars on food? What on earth did you buy? We ate out most of last week, and you had to go to the store again today."

"Bret, I'm sorry. I just forgot. Okay?"

"No, it's not okay! The same thing happened last month. If you want me to take care of the finances, you should at least help me out by staying organized. Groceries really cost that much?"

When she didn't answer, he got up and walked over to the stove where she was putting together some sort of instant casserole. It was the kind he hated. He lowered his voice but asked her again, "I said, 'What did you spend the money on?'"

She stopped stirring and looked up at him. "I didn't want to say anything, but Sarah's mom called. She said they didn't have any money for groceries and asked if we could help them out. I didn't feel comfortable giving her cash, so I bought some things and took them over."

Bret felt the blood drain from his face. "You mean to tell me you went over to Sarah's—alone? Karen!" he shrieked. "What were you thinking? That trailer park is like something out of Harlem!"

"They didn't have food! What was I supposed to do, let them go hungry?"

"It's not that I mind you helping them out. It's that you went over there by yourself! You could've been mugged or raped or even worse— killed. Why didn't you ask me to go with you?"

At that she actually laughed. "Yeah, right! You were more scared than I was."

The comment grated his ego down to a nub at the same time it sharpened his anger to a striking point. "You are not to go over there ever again. Do you understand me?"

Just about that time, the dishwasher kicked into another cycle, and Bret felt his socks become wet.

"Ugh!" he growled in frustration and threw a dish towel on the floor to mop up the water. He opened the door on the washer, and a blast of steam filled the already hot kitchen. Karen scrambled to help him clean up the mess.

"I thought you said you fixed this!"

"I did!" He peeled off his wet socks and started toward the hall closet to get his tools.

"Just call the maintenance man."

"For what, Karen? Everything in this stupid apartment is broken!"

He shoved the chair under the desk as he walked by. He wasn't gone a full minute before his conscience got the best of him. Just because she made him feel inadequate on top of everything else wasn't an excuse to yell at her. He walked back into the kitchen, tools forgotten, and tenderly put his hands on her shoulders.

"Listen, I'm sorry. All week I deal with people who are ungrateful and less than proficient. It usually ends up creating one big headache that I end up having to deal with. It's hard to come home and experience the same thing."

He expected her to wrap her arms around him and tell him she understood—that she really did appreciate his efforts and that she'd never go to Sarah's trailer park again. But she didn't.

"I hate to disappoint you, but have you ever stopped to think that you're not exactly *proficient* at some things yourself? I probably forgot to write down what I spent at the grocery store last week because I'm sure I was rushing to pick the kids up on time so I could come back here and cook *you* supper! All that was after I had put in a full day at the office. Why are you completely insensitive to what it is I have on my plate? You need to cut me and my *stupid* apartment some slack!"

He closed his eyes. He really didn't want to fight with her, but he was the man of the house and he would have the final say. "I said I was sorry. I know you work, cook, and take care of the kids. I just wish you'd see where I'm coming from. It worries me sick that you're out running around, endangering yourself while catering to the poor—or should I say the lazy?"

"Sarah's mom has a job."

"She works half a shift at some dive two days a week. You can't support a family on that. People know how to work the system, and they're good at it. But this isn't about them. It's about us. I forbid you to go over there again. Do you understand me?"

Karen laughed, and it wasn't because she was amused. "You forbid me? You *forbid* me? Let me tell you something," she said, shaking a spoon in his face. "Last time I checked, I have a mind of my own, and you will not *forbid* me to do anything!"

She threw the spoon down, splattering some type of thick brown liquid all over the wall. "And another thing…" She spun on her heel and opened the pantry doors beside him. She reached in and moved a few cans around and then knocked one over. "I can't stand knowing the alphabet soup is on the top shelf in the left hand corner of the cabinet each and every single time I come home!" She reached for her purse. "You can fix your own lunch! I'm going out!"

Bret watched her storm from the kitchen and heard her slam the door behind her. He stood there wondering if it were possible for his blood pressure to get any higher without him actually passing out.

He braced his hands on the counter, waiting for it to happen. When it didn't, he took a seat. *God, I love her. I swear I do, but some days she makes me so mad! Where does she get off talking to me like that? We were working at it. We were doing great…. Okay, Karen was working at it and was doing great but…*

There was no answer from God, and none of the peace he'd experienced in the past came rushing in to comfort him. His eyes drifted to the computer, and he knew what he could do to take his mind off of the things that were wrong with Karen. The women he looked at online never talked back. They were simple, uncomplicated, easy, and always available.

No. I can't. It will solve nothing. He walked over and shut the machine off. He hated feeling controlled by his emotions and dwarfed by his desires, and right now, anger was stealing the show.

35

It was during the first week of school when Shelby sat on the couch doing her homework. Her dad walked into the living room wearing his running shoes. "Thought I'd go for a run. Wanna come?"

Shelby chewed the end of her pencil. "Are you asking if I *want* to go, or are you saying that I *should* go?"

Chris bent to tie his shoelace. "I thought taking a run would be a way we could spend some time together. You know, do a little father-daughter bonding?"

He stood and started to stretch. She waited to see if there was a catch. After all, she was still a little surprised and unsure of her dad's reaction to the fiasco that happened with Brittney earlier in the week.

Shelby drew her legs up and let the scene from Wednesday play out in her mind again. She had been dumping her books in her locker between classes and was heading off to gym. With only ten minutes to make it from C hall to the locker room before the other girls got there and found her losing her lunch in the back stall, she had to get a move on.

Anxiety had rolled over her at the thought, but she couldn't stand being the butt of one more fat joke. She had taken off down the hall without looking first.

"Hey! Watch where you're going!" someone had said as she stepped into the flow of the crowd.

"Sorry." She turned around to see Grant Freeman, the eighth grade center, standing behind her and holding his toe. "Grant! I didn't see you. Are you okay?"

He tossed his blond hair out of his face and stuck his chin out. He was gorgeous, just like a movie star. *Great job, Shelby. Step all over the school's best athlete. Fat as you are, he won't be able to play tonight.*

Forgiveness for Yesterday

"I'm fine, but next time, look where you're going." He turned on a dime and dashed off to chase one of his buddies down the hall but not before flashing a quick smile back at her. She blinked her eyes in disbelief. Had she been one second slower, she would've missed it.

Her heart fluttered in her chest as she turned to head in the other direction only this time someone slammed into her, knocking her purse to the floor. "Oh, Shelby! I'm so sorry! It's crazy in here. I can't get used to this new class rotation. Here, let me help you."

Shelby tried not to panic as she fell to the floor to retrieve her belongings. "Howard," she said, watching him scurry around beside her, "you really don't have to do this."

"A pretty girl like you…you'd think I would've seen you coming. You're an angel."

Shelby rolled her eyes as she reached for her lip gloss before putting her purse back on her shoulder. She tugged on the strap only Howard wouldn't let go. "Howard, my purse!"

"Oh," he said, staring at her like she'd grown wings. "Sorry. I…I—"

"Aw, look what we have here! Two lovebirds." The sound of Brittney's voice cackled in her ears, and Shelby remembered how she'd been completely filled with dread.

Brittney had been relentless when she had gotten the news that Shelby made the cheerleading squad and she hadn't. "I see you're ready for the game tonight. Maybe some of the exercise you'll get will help you drop off the pounds. You know, I'm surprised they even make uniforms in your size!"

When Shelby didn't answer, Brittney turned to Howard. "What were you doing down on your knees, Howy? Asking her to marry you?"

The girls with Brittney laughed. Together the group of them looked down their noses in disgust and started to walk away.

"Did you see her hair?" Shelby overheard one of them ask as they started down the hall. "That style is so last season! I can't believe you used to hang out with her."

Tears had burned her eyes. She knew her hair wasn't the only thing Brittney and her friends thought was last season.

"Ah, don't let those girls get to you, Shelby. You're twice as pretty as they are."

"Forget it, Howard!"

Just as the girls were about to disappear around the corner, Brittney looked back and tossed her hair over her shoulder. That was when something sparkled as it caught the light. Shelby's breath caught in her throat. From twenty feet away, there was only one thing that would sparkle like that—her diamonds.

From that point, Shelby wasn't sure what happened. The next thing she knew was that her history teacher was pulling her off Brittney while at least twenty kids were egging her on. She had managed to get in one good punch before being hauled off to the principal's office where she was suspended for three days.

Even though she would probably be kicked off the cheerleading squad for such an outrageous act, seeing the look on Brittney's face had been worth every measure of discipline that had followed.

Shelby just knew that when her dad had to drive home in the middle of the week to straighten the mess out, he'd ground her forever, but he hadn't. Instead, he explained that he knew what it was like to feel like the whole world was against you, and while he didn't condone her actions, he commended her for standing up for herself. That and he managed to speak with Brittney's parents and get her jewelry back.

Shelby smiled at the memory and touched one of the earrings safely displayed on her ear. "Can I ask you something?" she said, seeing her dad was still standing there waiting on her decision.

"Sure."

"I know you don't like to talk about her, but I was wondering…do I look like Mom?"

Chris put his hands on his hips and cleared his throat. "Yeah. In some ways. What makes you ask that?"

Shelby shrugged a shoulder. "I don't know. I mean, I remember what she looked like and all, but did you think she was pretty?"

"Of course I did. Your mother is beautiful."

Shelby told herself to be content with his answer, but deep down, she wasn't. Rather than meet her father's eyes, she reached for the

Forgiveness for Yesterday

pillow next to her and hugged it to her waist. "After this week, I guess you realize that some of the girls at school make fun of me. They say I'm fat. Is that true?"

Chris raised a brow, but his eyes never faltered. "No, it's not. Does this have anything to do with that guy? Howard something?"

"Dad," she said, dragging his name across a moan. "His name is Howard Crestmire!" Shelby blew a wisp of bangs out of her face and rolled her eyes. "He's the biggest geek in school, and he has a crush on me. It's devastating."

"How so?"

"How so?" she cried. "He follows me around like a puppy! It's ruining my reputation. Right before that fight, Brittney and a bunch of her friends just so happened to walk down the hall when Howard was helping me pick up some things that had fallen out of my purse. They asked him if he was down on his knees proposing." Her hands went out to display her horror. "It was completely humiliating!"

"Shelby, guys like Howard grow up and run Fortune 500 companies. One day he'll probably be a millionaire."

Shelby tilted her head to the side in consideration. "Funny, because right now he's twelve, and he picks his nose. All the money in the world can't compensate for that!"

"Says who?"

"Dad!" She laughed seeing he was trying to get her to smile. "You're not helping!"

"I'm just joking. C'mere," he said, extending his arm and joining her on the sofa.

With one arm around her shoulders, he tucked her close and used a tone she hadn't heard in ages. "So the kid has issues. We all do. But you know what I think?"

"What?" she asked, eyeing him carefully.

"I think those girls are jealous. It seems that over the summer you...well...you grew up quite a bit. I'll bet that they're wishing they were as mature and as pretty as you are."

Shelby scoffed. "If I'm so pretty and mature, then why aren't the cute boys following me around and picking up the stuff I drop? It's only the rejects."

"Boys mature at a different rate than girls do. That and the cool ones are probably scared to death they'll embarrass themselves in front of their buddies. Guys like Howard have nothing to lose."

Shelby pondered the idea. Brittney had said something a time or two during the spring about how she'd kill to have her figure. It was right before she started telling her how fat she was. "You really think those girls are jealous?"

"Shelby, I know. Your mother is beautiful, just like you are beautiful, but beauty isn't the only thing that makes you special. You're smart, funny, and you can be passionate about what you believe in."

"Really?"

Chris smiled. "Really."

Shelby tipped her head back and rested it on Chris's arm. It felt so good to talk with him like this. "Remember the way Mom used to sing? She could just make up something on the spot, and it would sound as good as anything you'd hear on the radio."

"I do. She loved show tunes. She would always sing them just to drive me crazy." He laughed.

There was a long pause of silence, and Shelby could hear the ticking of the clock as happy memories of her mom danced before her eyes. "Do you think she remembers us? You know, like we're doing right now?"

Chris's chest rose, and then she heard him sigh. "I know she does. She always used to say that you and Kyle were her pride and joy."

Shelby smiled. "I remember. Even after the way she left, I still miss her sometimes. Is that okay?" Her voice was full of emotion.

"I think it's more than okay. I think it's healthy."

More silence ensued, and Shelby tucked a strand of hair behind her ear. There was still something that she wanted to know, and even though she'd been told before, she wanted to hear it again.

"Dad?"

"Hmm?"

"Why did they both leave? Was it because of something I did?"

She felt Chris sit up beside her and could tell without looking that he wanted her full attention. For a moment, she feared she'd pushed too far. The last time she asked that question had been in the days just after her mother disappeared. Of course, Chris had given her the answers he was supposed to at the time, but today she wondered if he finally knew the truth. The look in his eyes told her he was debating heavily on what to say.

Eventually he pulled her to him and cradled her head against his chest. His embrace was tender, yet secure. It was the embrace of a father. "No, Shelby. Neither your father nor your mother left because of you, because of Kyle, *or* because of me. Your mother…she needed to handle some things. Sometimes life is more complicated than we want it to be. Situations and mistakes—sometimes they're hard to deal with. We act, and then we can't take it back."

Shelby shook her head, spilling unshed tears on Chris's shirt. "I don't understand. What situations and mistakes? What was there to take back?"

"Oh, Shelby," Chris sighed. "I wish I could give you more than that. Just know that your mom loves you. She loves you and Kyle more than anything else in this world—and so do I."

Chris bowed his head and planted a kiss somewhere deep in her hair. She closed her eyes, feeling safe despite his mysterious answer. Chris might know more about her mother's leaving than he was willing to confess, but the thing that mattered most at this moment was what he was willing to share.

"I love you too," she said, wrapping an arm around his middle, "and I always will."

36

Bret lay in bed reading. He and Karen had made up from the terrible fight they'd had over her going to Sarah's and how he managed their canned goods, but he couldn't say that things were back to normal.

After spending another disappointing afternoon with a realtor, looking at houses they couldn't afford, Karen announced she'd finally gotten all the charges from their wedding and reception in on her credit card. When she gave him the total, he'd hit the roof. Another yelling match followed and resulted in her storming out.

Bret checked the digital clock on the nightstand. It was almost ten, and she hadn't come home yet. Thirty minutes later, he heard the apartment door open. Bret tried to concentrate on the book in his hands until she came into the bedroom to find him waiting up on her. "Where've you been?" he asked.

"Out."

"Karen—"

"The reason I snapped today is because I've not been completely honest with you," she said matter-of-factly.

"I know. I wish you would've told me you went that much over budget on the expenses. I could've been better prepared."

"That's not what I'm talking about." She fidgeted with her hands. "Bret, I know."

"You know what?"

"I know what you've been looking at online."

In an instant, Bret felt his world shift on its axis. His fear must've showed on his face.

"Don't try to deny it. I have proof. A few weeks ago I installed some monitoring software on our computer. Every time the computer

Forgiveness for Yesterday

is turned on, the program runs undetected in the background. When a pornographic site is pulled up, it sends me an e-mail, telling me what site and when it was accessed. I installed it to protect the kids, but when I started receiving notifications and checked the dates and times, I knew it was you."

"Karen…"

"Was that magazine I found in the spring yours?"

"Yes," he whispered.

Karen's face contorted in anger. "How could you do this to me? How could you lie to my face?"

"I don't know…you were hysterical, but I *don't* have a problem with pornography."

"Did you not hear me? I said *every* time a site is accessed, I'm notified. You *have* a problem with pornography!"

"And that gives you the right to spy on me?"

She went into the closet and came out with a suitcase.

"What're you doing?"

"I'm going to my mother's."

"It's late. The kids are asleep."

"I'm not taking the kids. They're staying here with you. I need time to think."

"Time to think? About what?" The idea of her running off and telling her mother everything made him angry. When she didn't acknowledge him, his temper boiled. "Fine! Run crying to your mom. See if I care!"

She packed her belongings and left without saying another word.

It was a few nights later when Bret concluded sleeping without Karen by his side was nearly impossible. He padded down the hall and into the kitchen.

White light from the refrigerator spilled across the floor, illuminating the darkness around him as he searched for something to eat. Milk, eggs, and a head of lettuce: not much for a midnight snack. Bret shut the door and opted for the cookies he found in the cabinet.

He took two and then purposefully left the bag on the kitchen counter as he remembered Karen's complaints about his neatness. He stopped and sprinkled some crumbs for effect. Even though it was dark and he couldn't see them, he still knew they were there.

"Ugh!" he said, raking them into his hand and dumping them into the sink. He just couldn't do it. Call it an obsessive-compulsive disorder or whatever, he couldn't leave the crumbs.

He tried lying on the couch, but after thirty minutes, he still wasn't sleepy. Eventually his mind wandered to the phone call he'd made to Karen earlier in the day. Lillian had told him Karen had gone for a walk and that she'd left her cell phone behind.

"I'm sorry, Bret. You just missed her. Is there something you'd like for me to tell her?"

Bret had struggled for the words. It amazed him how Karen and her mother could bicker for months, yet when something went wrong, Karen immediately returned to her side. By now, surely Lillian was privy to every one of his flaws. "No. It's nothing I'm sure you haven't already heard."

Lillian was so silent Bret thought she'd hung up. "Did the two of you have a fight?"

"Sort of," he said, surprised Lillian hadn't raked him over the coals with accusations. What was the use in having a mother-in-law if you didn't ask for advice regarding her daughter? "I want to tell her I'm sorry. Got any suggestions?"

"As a matter of fact, I do. When Eric died, for a while I thought I'd lost Karen too. She's just like me. She doesn't handle change well, and that one pretty much did her in. Karen has made some real progress in these last few years, but unfortunately, I can't say it's come without creating an independent streak at least a mile wide. Combine that with how stubborn she can be, and…well, you get my drift.

"For the last year, you guys have been going through one change right after another. No matter what Karen says, she's gotten used to not having someone else to answer to. Oh, I know she loves you and values your opinion, but I imagine that change alone has been hard for her to handle."

"What should I do?"

"I can't tell you what's going to work. Just know there's no room for pride in your relationship with the Lord or within your marriage. Saying you're sorry and then acting like it goes a long way."

Bret let the conversation with Lillian fade into the dark. He lay there trying to decide the best way to act on Lillian's advice and show he was sorry for lying to Karen and for getting caught looking at things he shouldn't have been. That still didn't mean he had a problem with pornography. As far as change, the open bag of cookies on the counter was proof of his willingness.

Speaking of which, Bret went back to the kitchen to grab two more cookies and spotted his laptop sitting on the table. Gifts had worked in the past. "What would Karen like?" A few seconds later, he was surfing the web, looking for that something extra special for when Karen returned home.

Bret browsed several sites, deciding now that they were married, lingerie would be appropriate. An intimate gift would show her she was the only woman he truly desired. He found lots of things he liked but nothing he thought Karen would actually wear. He studied the woman in one of the ads displayed in front of him. In a way she reminded him of Karen, only this woman was smiling. She actually looked happy.

What does it matter? I'm using my laptop from work. It's not like Karen will ever know.

He battled his conscience but only for a moment. Soon Bret was completely wrapped up in the images on the screen. He clicked a link and a video started to play.

"What in the world?" he whispered into the darkness as the hairs on his arm stood on end. The video wasn't of women. It was of young girls—girls about Holly's age and younger. He had stumbled onto a child pornography site. Bile rose in his throat, and he felt like he was going to be sick.

"Bret?"

Bret jumped up from the seat and let out a curse at hearing his name called in the dark. "Scott! You scared me!" Quickly he turned around and closed the laptop, praying Scott hadn't seen the video.

"What are you doing?"

"Uh...nothing. Just...I'm just working."

"Oh." Scott nodded. "Can I have a glass of milk? I couldn't sleep."

Bret's heart came back into his chest. "Sure." He went over to get down a glass while Scott crawled up into his chair.

"Can I ask you something?" Scott questioned.

"Sure."

"I've been thinking. None of the boys in my class call their dads by their first names. Since you and mom got married, I was hoping I could start calling you dad."

Bret set down the milk jug and walked over to stand beside Scott. He placed an arm around his shoulders and handed him the glass of milk. "I think that's a great idea."

"Good 'cause I don't remember much about my first dad. Mom says he loved us a whole bunch. She also said he was a good man and that he made her happy all the time."

"It's good to be happy."

"Are you happy?"

Bret chuckled. "Of course I'm happy. Why would you ask?"

Scott shrugged a shoulder. "I don't know. You and mom fight a lot. Is that why she went to Grandma's without us?"

Bret drew in a deep breath, not sure how to explain. "No. Your mom...just wanted some quiet time. And just because we've been fighting a lot doesn't mean we're not happy."

"It doesn't?"

"Of course not." Bret tried to explain further, but he was drawing blanks.

"It's okay," Scott assured him. "I think I know exactly what you mean. I love Holly. She's my sister. But that doesn't mean she can't irk a kid to death sometimes."

Bret smiled. He couldn't have said it better himself. Scott chugged the milk and handed him the empty glass. "Can we get a dog?"

"Not tonight, buddy. It's time for bed."

Bret walked him back to his room and pulled the covers up. "Go to sleep now, okay?"

"Okay. Dad?"

"What is it?"

There was a slow hesitation, and Scott cuddled a worn out teddy bear. "Why were you looking at those girls on the computer?"

Bret felt his stomach lurch. His mouth went dry, and suddenly, every excuse he could make wasn't a good one. "I didn't mean to be."

Scott frowned. "Kind of like an accident? Like when my basketball broke the glass in the coffee table last week?"

"Yes. Kind of like that."

"Oh." Scott nodded.

Bret tousled his hair and forced a smile. "Good night, buddy."

"Good night."

This time Bret made it as far as the door before Scott called out again. "Dad…"

"Yes, Scott."

"When I grow up, I want to be just like you. You're the bestest daddy ever. I love you."

Bret felt his knees threaten to give way. Tears formed in his eyes. He didn't deserve to be Scott's dad or his role model. He didn't deserve to be anyone's. He managed a smile for Scott's sake and braced his hand on the door for support as he choked out a few last words. "I love you too. Sleep tight."

The moment he closed Scott's door, the dam of denial his heart had been shrinking behind broke. *What am I doing? This isn't whom I want to be.* Tears filled his eyes as he sat down at the kitchen table and looked over at the laptop. Dress it up with words like insecurity or say it was a way for him to cope, but Karen was right. He had more than a problem with lust. He had a problem with a sin God hated.

Oh God, what's happened to me? What seemed like a flaw or struggle these last months was really an abomination before a holy and righteous God. He'd been a fool to convince himself otherwise. He might be able to keep it together for a few weeks at a time, but not when the temptation came on so strong that he felt like he had no choice but to act. Those were the times, like tonight, when he made any excuse he could to justify his actions. *I am such a fool. I should've listened. I should've found someone to hold me accountable.*

Bret knew it had been good advice, but he also knew why he hadn't heeded it. His pride wouldn't let him. He was the guy who everyone thought had it together. He was the leader, the role model, "the bestest daddy ever".

Suddenly, sitting there in the kitchen, Bret made a connection. The moment his sexual integrity had started to fade was the same moment his pride had become his idol. Like a cancer, it had seeped into every avenue of his being and started taking over, fueling the fires of selfishness until it eventually promoted itself above all else.

Pride was the reason his Christian image had become more of a burden than a blessing. Somewhere along the way it had become more important to him to be accepted in the eyes of his friends instead of Christ. Pride was what made him miserable when Karen had the backbone to stand by the decision to wait until they were married to become sexually involved when he had tried to change her mind.

It was the driving force that made him want to excel in his work, his career, and in his role as husband and father—good things—only more shame filled his soul. There was nothing prideful about what he'd been doing when Scott walked in, and he didn't need Karen to tell him that.

It took several minutes, but the Lord continued to unveil what had been previously hidden to his eyes. Chris, Amanda, and then Sarah's mom came to mind. The way he viewed them and the way their lives had turned out also found its root back to this particular evil. And as stupid as it seemed, pride was why he refused to buy a minivan.

Sitting there stripped to his soul, Bret knew it was pride that had fueled his words of denial when he'd lied to Karen about the magazine. The worst part of it all was that pride was a sin he cherished.

Rather than speaking to God, God spoke to him through a gentle whisper across his barrenness. *Darkness is as light. Repent and return to me, my son.*

Bret knew the simple words were a scripture reference, but he hadn't picked up his Bible in so long, he wasn't sure where the verse was from. Nevertheless, he got the message. He didn't have to tell God about the sin hidden in his heart. God already knew.

The God he'd been avoiding already knew all the secrets he was so reluctant to share. Instead of bowing his head, he fell face down on the cold kitchen floor.

"I'm sorry, God. I've been thinking I can do this on my own, but I can't. I need your help. I've been feeling like an old man because I'm so tired of trying and failing all the time." He rubbed his eyes with his fists when the faces of the girls he just saw came back to haunt him. Those girls were some man's daughter—a precious daughter like Holly. He crawled to the trash can where he threw back the lid and was sick.

If God didn't deliver him from this weakness, it could cost him everything. Heavy moments passed as his heart constricted in terror and shame over the power this sin had in his life. Scriptures from the Psalms came to him, and he prayed David's words as his own.

"Create in me a pure heart and a willing spirit to sustain me. Don't cast me from your presence. My spirit is broken and contrite. Heal me with your forgiveness. I'm begging you. I want to be a better man, but I can't. Not without you. The only good in me is you. Empty me of this terrible thing, my selfish pride. It's tainting everything—even the good things, *especially* the good things."

Bret didn't know how long he kneeled there confessing. His list of sins felt long, many of his grievances intertwined and connected in some way. Eventually the heavy spirit he had come to associate with his very being lifted from his shoulders. It was replaced with a freedom he couldn't explain.

Bret stood, his knees and his back hurting. It was almost dawn. Rather than open his laptop and chance seeing what he already knew was there, he left it to deal with in the full light of day. He was tired of allowing himself to get just close enough to something that was really sucking him in and destroying him in the process. His control was merely an illusion. He would no longer settle for the shadows, not when he knew what it was like to bask in the full light of his Savior's love when it was shining in all of its glorious strength.

37

Karen slowed her run to a jog as she made her way up the path that wound around to the back of the cemetery. Thick woods surrounded the lot, and the sun was peeking over the horizon. She topped the last hill, and a familiar headstone came into view. Her slow jog became a walk.

She hadn't taken the time to run in forever. The last time she was here was a few days before her wedding. She had come to say her final good-byes to Eric, fully intent on starting a new and wonderful chapter with Bret as his wife. What had happened?

Karen knelt on the ground in front of Eric's tombstone, wondering how she and Bret had gotten off to such a rocky start. Her hands went up to brush away some stray leaves from the base of Eric's marker. She still couldn't believe he was gone. He was buried six years ago to the day.

Her lungs burned from exertion, or was it from something more? This week her world had come crashing in on her. Not only had she confronted Bret about what she'd discovered but she'd gotten a call from Amanda early yesterday morning. They hadn't spoken since that day in the restaurant back in June. Karen was surprised she would call at all.

"Can we meet? Somewhere we can talk?" Amanda had asked. "I have something to say that I think you're going to want to hear."

Karen had agreed wanting to get some things off her own chest. She drove all the way from her mother's over to Amanda's, determined to clear the air between them. It was over a cup of tea that Amanda gave her an apology and some news Karen hadn't expected.

"I'm sorry for what I said when we were at the restaurant. I didn't mean it. The truth is you're the only real friend I've got. You actually care enough about me to be completely honest with me—even when it hurts. I feel like I owe you that same kind of honesty.

"The baby Chris and I had together…well I…" Tears had pooled in Amanda's eyes. "I didn't lose it naturally. I chose to have an abortion."

Karen had sat silent, letting the weight of Amanda's words fall on her soul. Tears pooled in her own eyes. There were a thousand questions she wanted to ask, but all that came out was, "Why?"

"I think we both know why. I…it seemed like the best choice at the time. As soon as it was over, I wished I hadn't. But I can't take it back. I'm sorry. I'm sorry I lied to you about it. For all the lies I've told you since then. I was too ashamed to tell you the truth. Can you ever forgive me?"

Although Karen's anger over Amanda's more subtle deceptions flickered in the back of her mind, it was obvious this was the big secret that had sat looming like an empty tomb in their friendship. Karen was mad, disappointed, and hurt. But Amanda was hurting much deeper than she ever would over this, and she had been waiting for a response.

"I…I don't know what to say," Karen stammered. "I wish you would've felt free to talk to me about it." The anguish on Amanda's face moved Karen to do what she knew she should. She lifted her arms and gathered Amanda into a hug. A multitude of emotions and questions battered Karen's mind, and they sat weeping for a long time.

Karen tipped her chin to let the morning sun burn off yesterday's memories, but the emotions and questions remained.

"God, my life was finally coming together, and now it's falling apart again. What went wrong? Why is everything such a mess?" *What could I have said to make Amanda change her mind? Why didn't she tell me sooner?* "None of this turned out like I thought it would."

For some reason Karen suspected a judgmental response was the reason behind everything from Amanda's carefully woven confessions to her out right lies about losing the baby. And what would she have said had she known the truth? Probably the things her friend had feared the most.

"God I've really stuck my head in the sand. I want to say I never saw it coming…but I can't. Part of me always wondered. It was just easier to convince myself it couldn't happen. I feel like I failed her. I feel like I failed *you*."

Karen wiped her eyes with a tissue she found in her pocket and reached over to pluck a wild rose from a nearby bush. It was yellow, and on seeing it, Karen remembered the roses from her wedding day and how the color represented the promise of a new beginning.

A deep sigh released into the morning quiet as she as she reached to place the yellow rose on Eric's grave. "Ouch," she complained when a thorn from its stem pricked her finger. Crimson sprang forth and began to stain the white tissue in her hand.

The flawless material soaked up the dark stain, and it reminded her that God's perfect love hadn't come without a price. The Holy Spirit whispered to her heart, *You can't save her—only my sacrifice can.* And it was the truth. It was the blood of God's perfect Son that was shed to make remission for sins. And not just Amanda's sins, but for Karen's sins as well.

But what about Bret? He lied to me! It hurts so much to know he looks at those disgusting women! He didn't even say he's sorry!

My grace is sufficient…

Karen marveled at the yellow rose and the white tissue still in her hand. The blood from her finger was lost in its folds. She became freshly aware of how God's forgiveness and grace allowed her to have the newest of beginnings in Christ no matter where she was in her walk of faith.

Amanda was not her project but her friend. Bret was her husband, the man she'd promised to love and to cherish at all costs. "Forgive me, Lord. It's by your sacrifice that even the worst of sinners can be redeemed." Tears filled her eyes. "Help me forgive Amanda because something tells me it's through my forgiveness that she will come to understand yours. Give me not only the words I should've said a long time ago, but give me the heart with which to say them and mean it. Help me leave the outcome to you.

"As for Bret, I ask that you give him a broken heart over his sin. Restore him to the man he was when we met. Heal the damage this has caused between us."

Karen continued to pray for both Amanda and for Bret and then stood and tucked the tissue in her pocket. She walked back to the path where she started the mile back to her mom's. Her pace picked up when she reached the main road. She'd been gone for two full days, and it was time for her to head home.

38

The weather started to cool off, and Chris decided to host a post Labor Day barbeque. He fired up his grill, glad that things were wrapping up on an old project and just getting started on a new one. He invited Bret and his family over to celebrate the news.

Caught up in watching Kyle and Shelby play in the yard, he didn't hear their car coming down the drive until it rounded the corner of the house.

"Nice ride," he complimented when they got out of a burgundy SUV.

Karen and Bret exchanged a cautious glance. "It's a compromise," Karen offered. "I didn't want the sports car he picked out, and he couldn't bear the thoughts of a minivan. So we settled."

"Not bad. It gets what? Twenty miles to the gallon?"

Bret stepped up onto the deck with his wife at his side. "Thirteen. The cool thing is it goes from zero to sixty in three minutes and twelve seconds. Three minutes and twelve seconds," he said with mock awe.

Karen punched him in the side, and Bret kissed her on the cheek. "I love you, you know that, right?"

"I know," she said. "One day when we're *both* old and gray, I'll be glad to buy you that *same* convertible."

"Really?"

"Yes. It should be much more practical *and* affordable in forty more years."

"Hmm, vintage!"

Chris breathed a sigh of relief seeing how they were nothing but smiles. He had been too caught up in everything that happened over the summer and with work to have kept tabs on Bret and Karen's marital issues. "Personally I think you should've made the plunge and bought the minivan. You two are too cute not to multiply."

This time Bret and Karen exchanged a wide-eyed expression.

"Not so fast. I bet you're glad to be home," Bret said, changing the subject.

"You have no idea. I've been living with a group of guys who think dining at the local Taco Bell is living it up. Peanut butter has become a staple."

"What happened to Curly Shirley's? I thought it was your favorite place for fine dining."

"Some of the boys couldn't agree on what to play on the juke box one evening. One thing led to another…" Chris rubbed his free hand down the back of his neck, recalling that day. "I got to meet Curly Shirley in person."

Bret chuckled. "Let me guess. She's a three-hundred-pound woman with bright curly red hair."

"Close," Chris replied, "except the *she* is a he."

"Please tell me you're joking. Curly Shirley is a man?"

"Yep. Short for Sherill Beckman. The place looks nice after the remodel, or at least that's what I hear. I've been banned from the premises."

Chris closed the lid on the grill and let the burgers cook. The four of them got comfortable in the plush chairs on Chris's back deck and watched the kids play fetch with the dog.

"Any luck on searching for a house?" Chris asked, bringing up what he wanted to discuss.

"No. It took a month to settle on a car. Everything we like in our price range is either in such bad shape it'd take a fortune to fix it or it's too far out of the city. We've been thinking about building, but we're not sure we want to tie up that much time, especially with the winter months coming."

"I've been there."

Karen joined in their conversation. "How's the Heritage Project wrapping up?"

"Great. We have an offer to purchase."

Chris tried not to laugh as surprise filled Bret's face. News like that should've crossed Bret's radar long before now.

"I thought the man you spoke with back in the spring changed his mind? Who's the offer from?" he asked.

"Me."

"You? But…it's already yours."

Chris finally laughed. "Technically…but I've decided that I want to sell out my controlling shares at Greeson. Come Monday, I will officially be making an offer to Darrell, and any of the other executives who are interested."

Bret's brows rose at hearing his words. "What? But…this is your dad's business. Are you sure?"

"I'm selling to friends," Chris smiled. "I know you guys will do each other right. Darrell has been wanting to loosen the reigns and take the company full speed for a long time now. I'm only holding him back. He'll take the company where my father wanted it to go, and it's not like I plan to become completely uninvolved. I'll stay on the board, but I want to have personal responsibility for the assets in Asheville."

Chris laughed. "It's not like I'll see a return on them otherwise. Who knows? I may drop in the office now and then just so I can keep tabs on the two of you." Chris winked at Karen.

"Why would you want that old place?" Bret still wanted to know.

Chris's smile grew shy. "You know that old house has grown on me. After all that time I've spent up there I feel like I'm a part of it now. The kids are actually looking forward to a move."

"But…" Karen looked lost.

"The girls will adjust…"

"Are you sure?" she questioned. "You've worked so hard to carry on what your father left to you. I hate to see you give up such a lucrative job."

"Come on. Both of you know it's never been about the money for me. I finally have an opportunity to do something I think I will love. God is showing me I can't keep running in two directions and trying to be someone I'm not. Trust me, I've prayed about this nonstop, and I feel God telling me to see this bed-and-breakfast thing through.

"And seeing how I know this really great couple who's looking for a place in this neck of the woods…I didn't think I'd have much trouble selling my old house. Interested?"

Chris smiled in earnest when Bret's and Karen's gaze locked.

It was Bret who started to stammer first. "I…we…would love to buy, but…the wedding…and the car. I'm not sure we can afford it right now."

"The guys in Asheville are putting the final touches on the estate as we speak. Unless something goes wrong, my lawyers have promised that within a few weeks, I'll be a free man to start building a new home on the east border of the Heritage property. That will leave me with one house too many." He went on to name the price he wanted for the house directly behind them. It was a price that was well below market.

"Absolutely not," Bret said. "We can't take advantage of you like that."

"I'll admit, it's an offer only available to good friends, but it's the least I can do after all you two have done for me."

Bret shook his head. "Still…we can't."

"What? You don't like it? It's not big enough? The way I was figuring, it would leave you some extra cash to buy into some really good stock that I have a feeling will skyrocket in about six months to a year from now."

Bret looked like he was going to cry. "You don't understand what this means to us. You planned this, didn't you?"

Chris didn't answer. "I love you guys. You're family." Chris got up to check on the meat lest Bret see his own tears. He flipped the burgers, then challenged his friend. "Think about it, but in the meantime, let's go and burn off some energy."

Chris bounded down the steps and grabbed his basketball. "Come on, Pretty Boy, let's see what cha' got!"

When his first shot was nothing but net, Bret still hadn't moved. Chris turned around to see why he hadn't replied to his taunt. Bret walked over and threw an arm over his shoulders. "Thank you," Bret said. "You're a better friend than I deserve."

Chris didn't say anything but only smiled. Bret was wrong. He was the undeserving one. It felt really good to give back to two people who'd given him so much.

With the meal over and Karen finishing up the dishes, Bret took the opportunity to slip his arms around her waist. "Okay if I go outside with Chris for a little while?"

"Sure. I'll be fine."

He kissed her on the back of the neck and studied her for a long moment. As long as he lived, he would never forget the nights she'd spent at her mom's and the day she'd come home. Before he could tell her about coming face-to-face with his sins and about how his pride had played into them, she told him about Amanda's confession.

"I should've been a better friend to her," Karen said.

It was at that point Bret also realized his pride had done nothing to help Karen be the friend Amanda deserved.

"We both could've done things differently," he said. It would've been easy to let that become the focus of their conversation, but he'd made himself push on.

"About what you said before you left…you were right. For months now I've been struggling with pornography. It started out with something simple, but then it grew. I thought it'd go away when we got married, but I was wrong. I've already called our pastor, and he's going to meet with me. I'm sorry for lying to you but more than that I'm sorry for letting this come between us."

Amazingly, that afternoon she had cried with him instead of at him. The forgiveness she was exhibiting to him on a daily basis came not because he was able to justify his actions but because he hadn't been able to. The idea was amazing, but then it was the same way Christ had handled his confession as well.

"I love you," he said, kissing her on the lips, glad that she'd agreed to marry him in the first place.

"I love you too. Go spend some time with Chris."

Forgiveness for Yesterday

Bret stepped out into the cool evening, glad that he and Karen were finally on the right foot. He handed Chris a glass of sweet tea as he settled into the lounger beside him.

"Thanks," Chris said, sitting the glass down.

Other than a deep sigh, they sat there enjoying the comfortable quiet like only good friends could. After several minutes of gazing up at the stars, Bret took a guess at what was on Chris's mind. "Still haven't heard from her?"

"No. Two months, and she hasn't called."

Weeks ago, Chris had filled him in on Laurie's mom visiting and then on running into her while he was in Chicago. He couldn't believe the odds of that happening, but it was like Chris said. Something bigger than the two of them was at work.

"Did you ever mention seeing either Lydia or Laurie to the kids?"

"No, not yet and I'm glad. I did call Laurie's mom, and we talked for a long time. Laurie told her Shelby and Kyle are with me. Lydia wants to meet them, but we both agree to give it some time. At least Laurie is talking with her mom again, and that makes me hopeful."

"The sad part is it will break Shelby's and Kyle's hearts all over again to know that their mom could return if she wanted to, but hasn't. What is taking her so long?"

Bret thought on it a minute or two and tried to see things from Laurie's point of view. "Maybe she still feels scared or guilty. Sometimes it's not the past we're afraid of, it's the future and facing the consequences of what we've done. The knowledge can be crippling."

"Maybe so. I can't believe I didn't recognize her right off, but she looked so different, so broken. I can't imagine all she's been through, and on top of that, it's like she's punishing herself. I know she's afraid of what the kids' reaction will be if she suddenly reappears. I've tried to tell her that they'll adjust, that they'll forgive her, but I know she doesn't believe me."

"Chris, are you sure? I mean Shelby and Kyle have had some really rocky years. Introducing their grandma and presenting the hope that their mom will return is a lot for them to deal with. Living with Holly has showed me that the preteen female is unstable at best. What if it doesn't go so well?"

Chris laughed. "I'm pretty sure it's the female part that has to do with being unstable, not being a preteen. Honestly, I have no idea how either one of them would react. All I know is that if we love each other, then we should be able to pull together and work through her returning. But there's nothing I can do. The ball is in Laurie's court. If she isn't willing to at least fight for what we had, then maybe she isn't whom I remember her to be after all."

"You once told me that I should do whatever it took to hang onto Karen. If it's God will for you and Laurie to be together, she will have to deny her heart to keep it from happening. That takes a lot of energy and effort. Sooner or later, you'll hear from her."

"I sure hope so."

"Will Marie be making the move with you to Asheville?"

"No. Right now she's in Disney World. I sent her and her whole family on vacation."

Bret looked over at him somewhat surprised. "That must have cost a fortune."

"Trust me"—Chris laughed—"she was well overdue for a raise. I'm really going to miss her."

"I wasn't going to say anything, but Karen's always dreamed of living here."

"Good, however there is one stipulation that I forgot to mention."

"What's that?"

"You have to help me move."

Bret looked at the large, sprawling house behind him. "I'd be doing myself a favor to purchase it fully furnished." Bret chuckled.

Chris started to laugh, and soon both of them were recalling priceless memories.

39

"I was right," Amanda said as she pulled up the drive of what was soon to be Karen's and Bret's new house. The summer heat was long gone, and now it was fall. Karen and Bret were helping Chris move out so they could make plans to move in.

"If only time could bring a change like this for me," she said.

Chris was in Asheville and seeing only Karen's and Bret's cars parked in the back, she figured it was safe to go to the door.

After taking a deep breath, she climbed from her Xterra. She was only halfway to the back door when she remembered a vow she'd made to herself after the last time she'd left this place. She swore to herself that she would never fall for another man who wasn't looking for forever. Aside from her lingering feelings over Chris, she had kept to her word.

Preston, the guy she had been so hopeful over, turned out to be nothing but a jerk. They had seen each other a few times during the summer, but when she refused to sleep with him, he finally admitted his relationship to Chris. They were friends.

"Why did you put out for him and not for me? Tell me, Amanda, did Rich Boy have to pay for it?" Preston had said before becoming almost violent with her in the car. Luckily, she managed to find another way home that night where she did some serious reconsidering as to what made men appealing to her.

It was those very thoughts that led her to giving a long, overdue apology and the truth to Karen. Amanda remembered that painful conversation and how they were still working to rebuild their friendship. That it was damaged at all was entirely her fault.

Amanda pushed the knowledge aside and stepped up to place her fist to the back door. *I'm not that girl anymore. I swore, never again.*

Since that afternoon when she'd told Karen the truth, she really was trying to get her life in order. Karen had given her some pamphlets from a local pregnancy care center where they offered a class on abortion recovery. She was scheduled to start the sessions next week.

Without the burden of secrecy between them, Amanda allowed her heart to open up to what Karen had to say about God's love for her and about his forgiveness. She still wasn't on board with all of it, but it no longer felt so offensive to her.

The back door cracked open at her touch, and she slipped her head in. "Karen?" There was no answer. She checked the kitchen but only found boxes. Amanda reached for the door, but the sound of feet on the stairs stopped her.

"Hey, I thought I heard someone. Are you looking for Karen?"

It was Chris. She really hadn't expected to find him here, and coming face-to-face with him left her searching for words. "I…uh, yes. Her car was out back, and the door was open." Amanda motioned with her hands toward the backyard feeling foolish for coming in his house uninvited. "Sorry, I shouldn't have come in," she said, turning to leave.

"Amanda…wait."

She paused at the sound of her name on his voice. A flood of memories came at hearing it, and slowly she turned back to face him. He was wearing jeans and a T-shirt with no shoes—the sight, a familiar one.

"What is it?" she asked, her voice small and lost in the big and empty room.

Somehow standing there in front of him, she felt completely transparent.

He descended the last few steps and set the box he was holding down on the floor. "Karen's not here but…I owe you an apology," he said. "A true apology."

She was speechless as she stood and watched the arrogant Chris she'd always known struggle to find the right words as he moved in place. "I wanted to tell you I was sorry that day I came by your house way back during the spring. I tried to say it again at the wedding, but then my emotions got the best of me, so…" Chris stopped diverting his eyes, and his gaze locked onto hers. "I'm sorry for taking advantage of you, for using you the way I did. I was nothing but a selfish jerk when you deserved someone who would have loved you and appreciated you for who you are. I couldn't give you that because at the time, I honestly didn't know what love was."

Before she could stop it, hope sprouted from somewhere deep inside her broken heart, but it was quickly washed away with regret. "You…you really came by that day…that day in March to tell me you were sorry?"

"Yes." Chris paused and shifted his weight. "I'll admit my motives weren't completely selfless. I was hoping you would take me back, but I really did come by to say that I was sorry because I was. I never meant to hurt you."

She swallowed the sob that threatened to tear from her throat. She remembered Chris's words from that evening—the apology he had so loosely been trying to make. If only she had told Chris the truth from the start. If only she had listened more closely. The pain she had been trying to bury came fully alive in her heart. Their baby had died in vain.

Chris must have sensed her anxiety. "Amanda, what's wrong?" he asked. "Is everything okay?"

Amanda felt like she was going to be sick. "I…it's just a little nausea. I haven't been feeling well." She breathed in through her nose and forced herself to speak. "And now? This apology is so that you can…"

"Now I'm completely on the up and up. God is really working on me. He's done so much already, but he's far from being finished. I have a lot of the answers I needed, but at the same time, I'm still asking a million questions." He took a step forward, his eyes never leaving hers. "Please don't take this the wrong way, but I'm far from being the man you deserve. You shouldn't have to settle."

Amanda looked down at the floor, not knowing what to do with such a humble admission. If anyone would be settling, it would be him.

Gathering her courage, she lifted her head once again and looked into Chris's face. For the first time ever, she could see his heart in his eyes. They were a vibrant blue, not the slated color they were when he was angry or confused. Seeing the change in him was real, she searched for the words to tell him of the child they had conceived and would never know. If they ever stood a chance together, it would only come after she found the nerve to confess the full and shameful truth about how she had manipulated him and then taken a life that wasn't hers to take.

"Chris...I..."

She looked down again, unable to meet the goodness staring back at her for very long. Karen might be able to forgive her deceptions, but regardless of what Chris had found, nothing could enable him to forgive the unforgivable. How could he forgive her when she couldn't even forgive herself? She liked this new Chris and wanted to remember him as such. The words simply wouldn't come.

Instead, she formed sentences that spoke of her truest regrets. "I knew what I was getting into with you. I can't say that it was smart for either one of us, but it was my choice to make, and I made it. I should've been honest when things started to change on my part, but I wasn't. Instead, I tried to make you love me, and that was wrong."

He nodded in agreement. "We're both responsible for our mistakes."

Gently a smile spread across her face, and Amanda let it grow. This time she held no hidden motives. "This whole God thing..." A blush crept up her cheeks, but she went on, "If anyone needs to give an apology, it's me for what I said at the wedding." Her hands briefly went to her face. "I'm so embarrassed. I knew you were different, but I never imagined it was because of your faith. I'm glad you finally got things worked out. Really."

"Thanks. I hope you will too."

He smiled, and her breath caught in her throat at the sight of it. Finally she saw the man she had always hoped he would become, only now that it had happened she also saw something more. Like Bret and Karen, Chris had something she still didn't understand.

For a moment, she wondered if the God Karen, Bret, and Chris had found was merciful enough to forgive her too. If so, then maybe he would give her a future better than she had ever dreamed. If she was seeking forgiveness for all her wrongs, God was probably the first person she needed to speak to.

"Take care of yourself, you hear?"

Turning back to face the door so Chris wouldn't see her cry, she replied, "I'm working on it."

40

November that same year

The weeks turned into months as Chris finished packing up his life and started a new one in Asheville. Because he never intended for Shelby and Kyle to essentially grow up in a hotel, together they drew up plans for the log cabin that was now being built where the old farmhouse up the road had once stood. He had wanted to save it, but even he knew when he was licked. Their new home wouldn't be ready for another month, so in the meantime, they were living at the Heritage House. The kids had high hopes to be in their new home by Christmas, but seeing how it was already the week before Thanksgiving, Chris doubted it would happen. New house or not, this year, Chris was very aware of all he had to be thankful for.

He pulled back the curtains on the parlor window and admired the season's first snow that covered the ground. After checking on Shelby and Kyle who had already gone to bed, he reached for his coat and slipped it on. The earth crunched under his boots as he stepped off the porch and headed out for a walk.

Turning down the long, curving drive, he turned west and walked along the dirt road. The sky was black as ink and dotted with a million stars that shone in full brightness. It was on nights like this that he wished he'd moved out here sooner. The part he loved most was that even the slightest sounds could be heard. Chris stopped in the snow so he could listen to the nothing. It was as if the whole earth lay silent and still, standing in awe of its Creator.

He breathed in the crisp mountain air and once again praised God for finally getting his attention. He could've missed much more than the beauty of a dark winter's night.

Forgiveness for Yesterday

There was still no word from Laurie, but then he was giving her time as God had instructed him. He knew he couldn't wait forever and had promised himself that if he hadn't heard from her by the New Year, that he would do his best to let her go.

Chris sucked in another deep breath and made a fresh resolution to give the entire situation to God. It was a resolve he had made time and time again, yet all he had to do was think of her, and worries clouded his mind like his warm, moist breath that curled up in smoky swirls into the cold night air in front of him. Her face, her touch, her voice—they were all seared into his memory. He missed her so much he questioned if the ache he felt was from the cold or from longing.

Standing there in the cold, aching anew, Chris realized something. Somewhere in all that had transpired, the very thing he couldn't fathom happening had somehow come to be when he wasn't looking. It still amazed him to know that even though he had judged God and Laurie both on partial information and circumstance, the Lord was faithful enough to pursue him until the truth sat staring back at him. God had called him to forgive as he had been forgiven, and God didn't have to give him any of the details surrounding Laurie's disappearance, but out of his tender mercies and grace, he had.

The one part Chris had never understood was how he was supposed to forget. Standing there in the cold, he thought that maybe forgetting was more of choosing not to remember instead. Chris smiled at the revelation. He had truly reached a point where the hurts of his past no longer dictated his actions in the present. There were parts of his conscience that would always remember Laurie, but the pain and anger that kept him in a spiral of destructive behavior no longer existed. And that made him a free man.

Sometime during his thoughts, Chris walked the length of the road and then turned around to head back home. He topped the hill and could see the large estate house sitting tall and proud on the horizon. It rose out of the darkness like a beacon of safety calling him home.

Chris stopped and marveled. The Heritage House would always have a special place in his heart because it was here that he found Jesus, and it was here that he had experienced another renovation project of sorts—not one that replaced things like faulty fuse boxes or plaster walls. It was here that he had experienced a deeply personal transformation of his heart—a truly magnificent redemption.

Whatever did or didn't happen in his life, he would always have his faith, and that made all the difference in the world. He smiled to himself as a peace filled his heart like he'd never known and then started his journey home.

Please visit www.traceymarley.tateauthor.com to connect with Tracey. Look for *Strength for Today*, book 3 in the Heritage House Series, to find out what happens in the lives of the characters as they embark on a new season of joy and trial as they discover what it means to draw strength from the Lord.